Also by Laura Griffin

UNTRACEABLE
WHISPER OF WARNING
THREAD OF FEAR
ONE WRONG STEP
ONE LAST BREATH

And look for
the next book in the Tracers series:

UNFORGIVABLE

Coming soon from Pocket Books

"An exciting police procedural starring a wonderful cop and an intriguing 'femme fatale.'"

—Genre Go Round Reviews

THREAD OF FEAR

"Suspense and romance—right down to the last page. What more could you ask for?"   —Publishers Weekly Online

"Catapults you from bone-chilling to heartwarming to too hot to handle. Laura Griffin's talent is fresh and daring."

—*The Winter Haven* (FL) *News Chief*

"A tantalizing suspense-filled thriller. Enjoy, but lock your doors."   —Romance Reviews Today

ONE WRONG STEP

"Griffin's characters are well developed, the narrative complex, and the dialogue skillfully written in this suspenseful romance."   —*Romantic Times*

"Griffin has more than proved that she is a force to be reckoned with in the world of romantic suspense novels. *One Wrong Step* is a sexy and thrilling novel that will keep readers turning the pages."   —Queue My Review

"*One Wrong Step* starts with a bang and never lets up on the pace. Laura Griffin is an exceptionally talented author who has a knack for keeping her readers on the edge of their seats. The twists and turns of the story leave the LeMans racetrack in the dust."

—*The Winter Haven* (FL) *News Chief*

LAURA GRIFFIN

Unspeakable

POCKET BOOKS

NEW YORK LONDON TORONTO SYDNEY

Pocket Books
A Division of Simon & Schuster, Inc.
1230 Avenue of the Americas
New York, NY 10020

This book is a work of fiction. Names, characters, places, and incidents either are products of the author's imagination or are used fictitiously. Any resemblance to actual events or locales or persons, living or dead, is entirely coincidental.

First Pocket Books paperback edition July 2010

POCKET BOOKS and colophon are registered trademarks of Simon & Schuster, Inc.

For information about special discounts for bulk purchases, please contact Simon & Schuster Special Sales at 1-866-506-1949 or business@simonandschuster.com.

The Simon & Schuster Speakers Bureau can bring authors to your live event. For more information or to book an event contact the Simon & Schuster Speakers Bureau at 1-866-248-3049 or visit our website at www.simonspeakers.com.

Interior designed by Julie Schroeder.
Cover design by Jae Song.
Photo of river by Marco van Wijnbergen-stock.xchng.

Manufactured in the United States of America

10 9 8 7 6 5 4 3 2 1

ISBN 978-1-4391-5295-9
ISBN 978-1-4391-6323-8 (ebook)

ACKNOWLEDGMENTS

My heartfelt thanks to the amazing folks at the FBI Academy, particularly Carolyn Brew, Ladislao Carballosa, and Ron Peterman. Also at the FBI, thank you to Erik Vasys and Leslie Hoppey, who shared so much knowledge and experience. Other law enforcement and forensic experts have patiently answered my many questions and deserve thanks: Mark Wright, Phyllis Middleton, Jen Nollkamper, Chris Herndon, D. P. Lyle, Greg Moffatt, and Katherine Ramsland. Any mistakes I've made here are all mine.

My sincere appreciation goes out to the dedicated team at Pocket, including Jae Song, Ayelet Gruenspecht, Danielle Poiesz, and especially Abby Zidle. And thank you to Kevan Lyon, a wonderful first reader and trusted friend.

PROLOGUE

Laguna Madre National Wildlife Refuge
N 26° 13.767 W 097° 19.935
1:03 P.M. CST

J amie Ingram had exactly twenty-seven minutes to score.

Challenging, but not impossible, provided she didn't get distracted. She loaded her supplies: binoculars, batteries, bug spray, extra water bottle. She tossed her keys into the backpack and zipped it.

"Dude, this thing's broken."

Jamie glanced through the windshield. The King of Distractions stood in front of her Jeep, gazing blankly down at the compass.

She climbed out and slammed the door. "Don't use it on the hood. It screws up the magnet."

Noah shrugged and handed her the compass. She slung the backpack over her shoulder and trekked off toward the trailhead. They were going due south three-quarters of a mile, and then it looked as though they'd be off-roading it east through some brush. Jamie noted the BEWARE OF ALLIGATORS sign. Three glossy black crows perched atop it, staring at her.

She smelled something sweet and glanced over her shoulder. "You coming?"

He sucked in some smoke. Shook his head. Jamie knew tromping around in the wilderness wasn't his thing, but he'd seen her excitement when she'd found this posting on the Internet and had figured out this stash was likely to contain something interesting.

"Finders keepers," she said.

He pushed off the hood and trudged over. "It's fuckin' *hot*. Why do we have to do this now?"

Because she had to be back on the island for a shift that started at two o'clock—not that he cared.

"No one's making you come."

He passed her the joint, and she took a drag as he stripped off his T-shirt. She gazed at his tan, muscular surfer's body and remembered why she put up with him. He tucked his shirt into the back of his cargo shorts and pulled his blond dreadlocks back with a rubber band.

"Okay, let's head," he said, taking back the joint.

Jamie led the way over the narrow mesquite-lined trail. She navigated while he clomped behind, muttering at every thorn and sticker burr. He should have been wearing hiking boots like hers, but she was pretty sure he didn't own anything besides flip-flops.

The ground became spongy as they veered east off the trail. Patches of water shimmered through the thinning brush, and she thought of the alligator sign.

"We're nearly to the coast," she said. "This can't be right."

Jamie checked the clue she'd decrypted from the Web

site: *Follow the yellow brick road.* The only yellow she'd seen were the wildflowers along the trail. Was that what the clue meant? Sometimes these clever little hints were more annoying than helpful.

"You lost already?"

She ignored Noah and consulted her GPS again, trying to figure out what she'd missed. She scanned the area. About twenty yards out, the mesquite trees gave way to cattails, then endless marsh. The breeze whipped up, and something foul assaulted her nostrils. A large brown bird soared over them and swooped down at the edge of the foliage. Another followed.

Buzzards.

"There's something dead over there," she said, picking her way through the knee-high grass. Mosquitoes swarmed around her face and neck, and she swatted them away. Up ahead, the reeds rustled, and she saw a flap of feathers. Could it be . . . ?

She took a step closer. The reeds shifted again, and a cloud of flies rose up.

She stopped moving. Her blood ran cold.

"Hey, what is it?"

Her stomach heaved. Her throat closed around the words.

"Jamie? Come on, what is it?"

"It's a girl."

CHAPTER 1

The police station was quiet.

Alarmingly quiet.

Elaina McCord pulled into the empty lot and parked in the space closest to the entrance. She shoved open the car door and got out, sighing at the faint stirring of air. Not a breeze, exactly, but not too far off. For a moment, she stood beside the Taurus to get her bearings.

She scooped her hair off her neck and twisted it into some semblance of a bun. Her poly-blend Filene's Basement pantsuit concealed her holster but didn't breathe. She should have sprung for something silk, but when she'd purchased her career wardrobe, she'd been thinking D.C. or New York. In a million years she never would have guessed she'd end up in Brownsville, Texas—a satellite of a satellite office, a thousand miles from anywhere she wanted to be.

Except today.

Today Lito Island Police Chief Matt Breck had called

Brownsville to request federal assistance in solving a string of homicides. Most likely he was expecting a pair of veteran agents in crew cuts and dark suits.

Instead, he was getting a rookie in a Donna Karan knockoff.

Elaina smoothed her lapels and gathered her determination. She slammed the door shut, locked the car, and hiked up half a dozen wooden steps so a cardboard sign could tell her what she already knew.

The place was deserted.

BE BACK SOON. The black hands on the clock had been positioned for ten-thirty. Elaina glanced up at the sun blazing directly down on top of her. She cupped her hand and peered through the tinted glass door to the darkened offices beyond. The place looked to be shut down.

Who shuts down a police station?

What the hell planet was this?

Elaina huffed out a breath and turned around. Beyond the minuscule lot, a row of tall palm trees bordered Highway 106, otherwise known as Lito Highway because it was the only highway in town and ran the entire twenty-two-mile length of the island. The first two miles, Elaina had discovered, were crammed with motels, restaurants, and surf shops. The last twenty miles consisted of God only knew what. From the map, it looked as though the road disappeared into the Lito Island Wildlife Refuge just south of town. She turned her gaze that way now and saw grass and water and what looked like never-ending acres of swamp.

Or estuary. Whatever.

A weathered wooden deck surrounded the dormant

police station, and Elaina followed it around to the back, taking care not to let her low black heels catch on the uneven slats. The white adobe station house reflected the sun like a mirror. It backed up to Laguna Madre, the bay that separated Lito from the mainland. Elaina averted her gaze from the glare as she made her way to the back of the building. A speck of movement on the water caught her eye.

A boat. Moving in her direction, too, which meant it was either heading toward the police dock or the cleverly named Lito Island Marina just next door.

The boat drew nearer. Some sort of official logo marked the side of it, and Elaina counted at least four passengers standing behind whoever was at the helm. Her stomach tightened as she thought about the fifth passenger, whom she knew would be lying on the floor.

The boat zipped past the police dock before making a wide turn and gliding up to the marina. The wake splashed up through the wooden slats, soaking Elaina's shoes.

Water squished through her toes as she picked her way across the thick carpet of Saint Augustine grass separating the station house from the marina. SUVs and pickups crammed the gravel lot. She spotted two police units and a red Suburban with LIFD painted on the side.

Elaina ducked around the side of the corrugated metal building, passing a leathery man toting an empty crab trap, then a pair of teenagers carrying yellow bait buckets. Next to a humming Coke machine, a man stood smoking a cigarette and watching her. She passed a wooden fish sink and a balding, bearded guy who paused in the act of hacking off a fish head to stare at her. Ignoring all the curious gazes, Elaina focused on the end of the pier.

The boat's captain—Chief Breck?—barked out an order, and a man in a khaki uniform hopped down from the vessel to tie the bowline to a cleat.

Two uniformed men bent down in unison and lifted something off the boat's floor. Elaina watched, shocked, as they manhandled the long black bundle onto the pier, where they laid it out in the sun. Finally, the captain disembarked.

Elaina strode forward. "Chief Breck?"

His gaze shot up and turned instantly suspicious beneath the bill of his LIPD cap. "Yeah?"

She stopped before him and looked up at the guarded expression in his brown eyes.

"I got no comment at this time," he stated.

"Excuse me?"

"You're with the *Herald,* right?" His gaze skimmed over her suit, pausing on her wet cuffs, then snapped back up to her face. "Or maybe you're TV? Either way, I got no comment as of yet, so—"

"I'm with the FBI." Elaina thrust out her hand. "Special Agent Elaina McCord."

His eyebrows popped up, disappearing beneath the hat.

"You called Brownsville this morning?" she reminded him as his baffled gaze dropped to her hand. "Requested assistance?"

His brow furrowed now, and Elaina gave up on the handshake. He looked her over once again. She peered around him at the body bag laid out on the dock. A white-haired man in street clothes stood beside it. The ME?

"Why don't you step on over there?" Breck gestured back toward the building. "Someone'll be with you in a minute."

Elaina gritted her teeth but complied with his request by stepping back a few paces. It wouldn't be wise to piss off the police chief in her first homicide investigation. She crossed her arms and looked on as Breck turned his back on her and exchanged words with his officers.

Smoke wafted over to her. Elaina glanced at the Coke machine, where the man with the cigarette still stood, his shoulder propped casually against the door frame. Something about his steady, penetrating look gave her goose bumps.

She glanced away.

A flurry of feathers erupted as the man at the sink tossed some guts into the water and the seagulls scrambled. A giant brown pelican flapped over to snatch away the prize, then perched on the dock as he gobbled it down.

Elaina glanced around, taking mental notes. The teenagers had disappeared but the crabber still lurked nearby, his arms folded over his chest and his trap at his feet while his attention remained fixed on the body bag. Elaina memorized his face, then scanned the rest of the area for suspects. Some perps liked to hang around and observe the aftermath of what they'd done. Elaina counted nine spectators at the moment, including a shirtless, sun-baked twenty-something with blond dreadlocks. He had his arm draped over a young woman's shoulders, and they watched the end of the pier with morbid fascination.

Elaina checked her watch. She cursed under her breath. Breck and his men stood huddled on the dock, shooting the nonexistent breeze. Elaina felt her temperature rising as the minutes ticked by and the sun glared down.

A large brown bird alighted at the end of the pier and wobbled over on spindly legs to check out the body bag, jabbing at the plastic with a sickle-shaped beak.

Elaina shot past the men and waved her arms. "Shoo! Shoo!" she yelled, and the bird took off.

She whirled around. "*Where* is the body-removal team?"

Breck frowned at her. "The who?"

"The body-removal team! She's baking in there, along with whatever evidence we might recover."

Breck's hands went to his hips. "We're waiting on our ambulance. They got hung up with some sorta accident down at the beach."

Elaina took a deep breath. She felt dozens of eyes boring into her as she straightened her shoulders and tried to calm down.

"When will it be here?" she asked.

"When it gets here. Maynard." Breck jerked his head toward one of the uniforms.

"Yessir."

"Go take Miss McCord over to the station house to cool her jets."

They left her waiting for more than four hours.

Elaina refused to acknowledge the snub. Instead, she retrieved her briefcase from her car, along with her cell phone. She spread her files out across the conference room table and worked diligently, as if she'd gotten up this morning with every intention of spending her Friday afternoon in some backwater police station. By five-thirty, though, her patience was gone. She was hungry and tired. And sticky, too, as the room had no air-conditioning—only a portable fan that circulated the same warm air, over and over. She was about to get up to search for a vending machine when the door popped open. Officer Maynard again.

"Miss McCord? The chief'll see you now."

Finally, an audience with His Highness. Elaina collected her manila file folders and shoved them into her briefcase.

"Right this way, ma'am."

Maynard was shorter than she was, probably five-nine. But he had a trim build and rigid posture that reminded her of the Marines she'd crossed paths with during her twenty-two weeks at Quantico. He led her through the wood-paneled police station and past a sixtyish woman seated at a metal desk beside one of the offices. She was talking on the phone and writing on a pad, a stack of pink message slips piled at her elbow.

Maynard opened the door to the inner sanctum of Breck's office, and Elaina stepped inside. The room smelled faintly of cigars, and the chief sat in a padded leather chair behind a faux wood desk. Arranged in a semicircle around the desk were plastic chairs occupied by people she'd seen earlier at the marina, with the exception of a bald man who held a cowboy hat in his hand. The star pinned to his chest told Elaina he was a Texas Ranger.

"Dr. Frank Cisernos," the white-haired man from the dock said, standing up. "County Medical Examiner."

Elaina shook his hand and introduced herself. She darted her gaze around to the other faces. The young Latino officer smiled at her, but no one else rose to greet her.

Maynard took one of the two empty chairs and gestured for Elaina to take the other. She deposited her briefcase in it and remained standing, then laced her fingers together in front of her so no one would see that she was trembling.

"So, you're here to lend us a hand." Breck leaned forward on his elbows. "Scarborough tells me you're fresh from the Academy."

Elaina tried not to wince. "I graduated last fall." She wondered what else the supervisory special agent had told him. Her boss made no secret of his dislike for her, but he'd finally given her a shot at criminal profiling. Maybe he was coming around.

Or maybe he'd sent her here to fall on her face.

She cleared her throat. "I'm here to provide a criminal profile. Also, I'm authorized to offer FBI assistance with any labs you need." She glanced at the Texas Ranger—who also probably had the clout to fast-track lab work—and knew her stock was sinking quickly.

"A profile, huh?" Breck leaned back in his chair now. "You're gonna tell us about our unsub?"

Everyone's attention settled on Elaina.

"What I have on our subject is preliminary," she said. "I'll need to see photos from this morning's crime scene and I'll need to observe the autopsy. I understand someone from the state crime lab's coming down to assist?"

She glanced at Cisernos, who gave a slight nod.

"And do we know the victim's name?" she asked.

"Nothing confirmed," Breck said. "But for the past half hour, I've had just about every parent whose college kid is down here ringing my phone off the hook. They all heard about the body on the news. Now their daughter's not answering her cell, and they want to know if it's her or not.

"So go on ahead." Breck nodded. "Tell us your profile."

"You said 'nothing confirmed,'" Elaina replied, sidestepping the bear trap. "You mean you have a lead?"

"All I've got for sure is Caucasian female, long dark hair." Breck eyed Elaina's long dark hair as he said this. Then he glanced down at the yellow legal pad on his desk. "She was a mess—we can't even tell her age. But we took a call this afternoon about an abandoned Audi sedan at a boat slip on the north side of town. Car's been there two days. It's registered to Valerie Monroe, twenty-seven-year-old from Houston. There's a purse inside. Driver's license, med school ID, health insurance card. She's a brunette. Car's been impounded, but we still gotta process everything."

"And my supervisor told me the victim was found in the marshes this morning by some fishermen." Elaina looked at the ME. "She was naked and had been eviscerated, apparently, like Gina Calvert back in March?"

"Gina Calvert was found March fifteenth," Cisernos said. "By my estimation, she'd been there at least two days. This new body looks about three days old to me."

"And Gina's body was also discovered in the wildlife park." Elaina's confidence returned as she ran through the facts of the case, which she'd committed to memory months ago. "She'd been injected with ketamine hydrochloride. Her car was found abandoned at a boat slip. Her personal items were left inside."

Breck folded his arms over his chest. "Okay, sounds like you've done your homework, Miss McCord. So tell us about our perp. Who're we looking for?"

Elaina's instincts screamed for her to stop. The prudent thing would be to wait until she had all her facts together. But her face felt warm, her armpits felt damp, and the air in the room was thick with skepticism.

She took a deep breath. "I think the offender is a white male, late twenties to mid-thirties. I think he's bright, but he has an inflated sense of his own intelligence and he's driven by ego. He's most likely attractive, possibly charming, and comfortable approaching women with some kind of ploy. His sophisticated MO shows that he's organized and capable of controlling his impulses. I think he lives on the island, is underemployed, and owns or has easy access to a boat. His hobbies include hunting and fishing. He likes guns. I also think he's probably got some background in law enforcement."

She noticed the startled looks but kept going. "No sign of sexual assault, at least nothing overt."

Breck's brows arched. "Overt?"

Elaina shifted slightly. "Even without rape, I believe these are sex crimes. The knife work is a form of penetration. And this type of offender sometimes can't get an erection, so he substitutes something else."

Breck traded looks with the ranger, and Elaina plunged on so she wouldn't have to answer any questions yet.

"He kidnaps these women, injects them with a chemical to incapacitate them, takes them to remote locations,

and then makes a deep abdominal incision with a serrated hunting knife. He leaves almost no trace evidence
behind, indicating a good deal of knowledge and planning—"

"Now, wait a minute there." Breck held up his hand.
"We only got two victims. You make it sound like we're
dealing with a serial killer."

"I believe we are."

"It could be a copycat. Some domestic murder, staged
to look like the girl from spring break, just to throw us
off."

Elaina tipped her head to the side. "And how many of
those details were released to the media?"

Breck darted an uneasy glance around the room, and
she knew she'd made a tactical mistake by challenging
him in front of an audience.

But he recovered quickly. "And we don't know what
evidence he might have left in that Audi," he added.
"Could be prints all over."

"I'm also referring to Gina Calvert's car. And the
abandoned Mustang found at the boat dock following
the Mary Beth Cooper murder."

The room fell silent. Breck's face was pure astonish-
ment.

"Mary Beth Cooper," he stated.

She nodded.

"From nine years ago?"

She nodded again.

Breck leaned forward now, scowling. "A guy *confessed*
to that crime. He's sitting in Huntsville."

Elaina nodded again.

"You mean to tell me you think they got the wrong

guy up there? He was convicted in a court of law. Someone wrote a book about it, for chrissakes."

"He confessed to a string of murders," Elaina said.
"Investigators have irrefutable DNA evidence he actually committed some of them, too. What I'm saying is, I
think we need to look at Mary Beth's case again. I think
it's related to our unsub." In fact, Elaina believed there
was a good chance Mary Beth Cooper was this perpetrator's first kill.

"The Cooper girl died of traumatic asphyxia," Cisernos said.

Elaina's gaze shifted to the ME.

"Manual strangulation," he added. "I performed the
autopsy myself."

"And as you mentioned in your report," she said, "the
victim had ketamine in her bloodstream at the time of
death. And she'd been stabbed postmortem with a serrated knife."

The room fell silent again. Elaina searched all the
faces for some sign of support. Breck sat with his arms
crossed, looking disgusted. Cisernos frowned. The cops
in the room looked uncomfortable, with the exception
of the young Latino officer, who seemed intrigued. He
sat forward on his chair, watching her, as if waiting to
hear more.

"Well, now." Chief Breck stood up and finally offered
her his hand. "We're glad you could make it up here
today, Miss McCord. I think we can handle things from
here."

After her stellar performance in front of Breck, Elaina
had the urge to go get drunk. She eyed the festive bars

as she drove through town, thinking how nice it would be to pull in and order a double frozen margarita with salt.

Instead, she headed for the bridge. A knot formed in her stomach as she replayed the meeting and forced herself to accept what had happened.

Her first homicide case, her first criminal profile, and she'd totally blown it. No way, no how, would she be invited to observe tomorrow morning's autopsy. Breck had made that clear enough. If she continued to assist on this case at all, she'd have to do it from Brownsville, using whatever reports she could get her hands on. That was if Scarborough didn't yank the case away from her and hand it over to a more experienced agent.

Elaina stripped off her jacket at a stoplight. She gazed out the window at the tourists crowding the sidewalks. Women strolled up and down in shorts and bikini tops. Sunburned teenagers with skim boards tucked under their arms trekked home from the beach. A sign up ahead advertised a vacancy at the Sandhill Inn, where Gina Calvert had spent the final days of her short life.

The light changed, and Elaina hung a left onto Causeway Road, which would take her back to the mainland. As she neared the bridge, she glimpsed Laguna Madre glistening in the evening sun. Catamarans and Sunfish dotted the bay, and Elaina watched them wistfully, remembering the last time she'd been aboard a sailboat. It was out on Lake Michigan, half a lifetime ago. The wind had been frigid, but she had spent the afternoon with a smile frozen on her face because her dad had taken the entire day off.

Her cell phone chimed from its berth in the cup holder.

"McCord," she said.

A brief pause. "Did you get the cigarette butt?"

"Who is this?"

"Bet you've got it tagged and bagged by now." It was a male voice. Low, with a Texas drawl. "I'm right, aren't I?"

Elaina had a flash of the man leaning against the Coke machine. There had been something familiar about him, something that had been nipping at her subconscious all afternoon.

"Who is this?"

"Troy Stockton. I saw you at the marina, Elaina. Very impressive."

Troy Stockton. She drew a blank.

"How did you get this number?"

"I've got lots of numbers. Hey, you really leaving us already?"

Elaina's shoulders tensed, and she glanced in the rearview mirror.

"I'm disappointed," he said. "I wouldn't have pegged you for a quitter."

Elaina surveyed the cars behind her: several SUVs, a convertible filled with young women, a delivery truck of some sort. "Listen, why don't you tell me where you got this number and—"

Click.

Elaina checked the display, but the call was gone. Her incoming-call list read only "Private Caller." She tossed the phone onto the passenger seat.

Stockton. Troy Stockton. The name rang a bell, but the voice had been totally unfamiliar.

Pop!

The wheel jerked right and the car lunged across two lanes of traffic. Brakes squealed. Horns blared. Elaina wrestled the steering wheel as the car skidded off the road.

CHAPTER 2

Cinco Chavez went looking for Troy at the bayside dump where he spent most of his weekends. As usual, the Dockhouse was packed. Cinco waded through the throng near the bar and spotted Troy in the pool room surrounded by smiling women, empty longnecks, and half-wasted oil riggers who thought they were in for an easy buck.

"Wazzup, T?" Cinco claimed a stool next to a threesome of blondes in low-cut tops.

Troy glanced up from the green felt. "Not much." He gave the cue ball a smack and pocketed two stripes.

The big guy leaning against the wall looked pissed. Troy chalked his cue and rounded the table to line up another shot.

Cinco sat on the stool and listened to his stomach growl. Breck had called him in early this morning, and he hadn't had anything besides coffee all day.

"Hey, you eaten yet?" Cinco asked.

Troy didn't take his eyes off the table. "Nope." He tapped the cue ball and waited a few beats as the final stripe dropped into a side pocket.

"Let's go grab some ribs. I'll tell you about the fed."

Troy chalked his cue and surveyed the table. "I already talked to Maynard." He glanced up at his opponent, who was about to lose his roll. "Corner pocket."

But the guy didn't have a clue. He stared down at the layout, unable to imagine how Troy was going to pull off a shot like that when the table was littered with solids. He crossed his arms and sent a smug look over Troy's head to his buddy on the other side of the room.

Troy's eyes sparked at the challenge. Cinco sat back to watch as his friend zeroed in on the shot with total concentration. The room went still.

The stick kissed the cue ball, and it glided across the felt. It bumped off the wall, slid back across the table between two solids, then magically slowed down just as it neared the eight.

Plunk.

The women let out a collective sigh. The roughneck scowled. Troy didn't react at all, except to lean his cue against the table and pick up his beer.

"Maynard tell you about the meeting?" Cinco asked.

"More or less." Troy held out a hand and coolly accepted some twenties. The guys stalked off, bumping into the waitress, who had had finally made it around to pick up empties.

Jamie flashed a smile at Troy. "Get you another beer?"

"Nah, I'm good. Hey, didn't I see you at the marina earlier?"

Jamie's smile faded as she filled her tray with empty bottles. "I saw them bring in that girl." She glanced at Cinco. "I heard she was found on the island, not the mainland. That true?"

"Yep. Mainland is the sheriff's turf, not ours," Cinco told her. "She was found in the park."

"You guys know who she is yet?"

"Not yet."

"So . . . what can I bring y'all?"

Troy handed her the money. "I'm heading out, thanks. Keep the change." Then he turned and gave Cinco his full attention. Meanwhile, the women were busy eyeing Troy's butt.

Shit, when Cinco wanted a woman, he had to work for it. All Troy had to do was show up someplace in faded jeans.

"Man, I need some ribs." Cinco said again. "You want to come hear about the fed or what?"

Troy shrugged. "What's to hear? Maynard said she's a stiff."

"Maybe a little." Cinco recalled the suit, the shoes. But he also remembered the slender body and the clear blue eyes. "Smart, though."

They elbowed their way through the crowd and pushed open the wooden doors at the front of the bar. The air outside smelled like fish and diesel from the shrimp boats that chugged past this stretch of bulkhead all day long.

Troy's car was parked in its usual spot up front. He jerked the keys from his pocket and unlocked it with a chirp. "I gotta work tonight."

Cinco sighed. Very few people knew that behind Troy's laid-back attitude was a workaholic. Cinco had never met anyone who could spend so many hours pounding away on a computer.

"Same book?" Cinco asked.

"Nah, this is something else."

He gave his friend the once-over, noticing the tension in his face for the first time. And suddenly he got it. "You're worried, aren't you?" Cinco asked.

"Why should I be worried?"

Cinco just looked at him.

"Hey, call me after the autopsy." Troy stepped over to the low-slung black Ferrari and pulled open the door.

Cinco shook his head. The man was in denial. "You got problems, bro. Breck blew her off, but Cisernos was listening. I could tell."

"I'm not worried." Troy slid behind the wheel, and the engine purred to life.

He backed out of the space, shifted gears, and roared off.

Elaina stared down at the flat tire.

A blowout. Not a gunshot.

She knew what gunshots sounded like, and this had definitely been a blowout.

So why had she nearly jumped out of her skin?

Elaina yanked open the passenger's-side door and leaned inside the car to switch on the hazards. It was fine. No big deal. She'd never changed a tire before, but there was a first time for everything. If she could handle the Academy, she could handle a freaking flat tire.

She grabbed the owner's manual from the glove box and looked up "Tire, Changing." She flipped to the correct page as the traffic whizzed past her. Stepping away from the road into the weeds lining the highway, she skimmed the instructions. Eight simple steps. Pictures, even. She glanced around at the dimming sky. She'd be out of here in no time.

She walked around to the trunk and popped it open with her key chain. After shoving aside all the gear— flak jacket, evidence kit, emergency flares—she peeled back the carpet.

And stared at the empty, tire-shaped space.

Of course. This was a Bucar—a Bureau car—and someone had obviously made use of the spare already without bothering to replace it.

Sirens sounded behind her, and she felt a rush of panic, followed by relief. Followed by panic again.

Blue and red strobe lights reflected off the Taurus as Elaina slammed the trunk shut. She turned to face her rescuer, who was almost certain to be one of the stony-faced cops who'd witnessed her humiliation in front of Breck earlier.

The police unit rolled to a stop on the shoulder. The driver's-side door opened, and Elaina could just make out a man's silhouette in the white glare of the headlights. Gravel crunched under his shoes as he approached her.

"Ma'am." He stepped out of the headlight beam, and finally she saw his face.

Maynard. Just her luck.

And interesting that he should happen along at this particular moment. Had Breck told him to tail her off the island?

"Looks like you got car trouble."

"A blowout," Elaina said. "I was about to change it, but the spare is missing."

One of his eyebrows tipped up, and she could tell he

was having trouble envisioning her changing anything in a suit and heels.

"Go ahead and pop the trunk," he said. "We'll have a look-see."

"Trust me, it's empty. Is there a service station around here?" She glanced back toward town, but the fading light made it difficult to read the signs along the highway.

"Lemme make a call for you."

"Thank you."

Maynard turned around and went back to the unit. He got inside, and she watched him pull out his radio.

Elaina jerked open the driver's-side door as she adjusted her plans for the evening. She was stuck on Lito Island for the next few hours, if not longer. She retrieved her briefcase, her cell phone, and the gym bag containing her brand-new iPod. She grabbed her purse, where she'd stashed a small paper evidence bag containing a cigarette butt. She thought of Troy Stockton. Was he watching? She glanced up and down the road again.

"Truck's on the way." Maynard trudged toward her car again. "Guy's name's Don, with Don's Automotive. He can get you fixed up and on your way within the hour."

Elaina felt a prick of annoyance. She studied Maynard's face and made a snap decision. "Thank you, but I'm staying."

He frowned. "Staying?"

"Yes." She hitched her purse up on her shoulder. "I'll just need a lift to my hotel."

"And where's that?"

"The Sandhill Inn."

· · ·

Gina Calvert spent the final four days of her life in Room 132, known to hotel staffers as the Sand Dollar Suite. Elaina slipped the key card in the lock, pushed open the door, and stepped into the darkened room. She smelled mildew and lemon furniture polish as she ran her hand over the wall and located the light switch.

The room flooded with a yellowish glow. Elaina took in the simple decor: wrought-iron bed, blue-and-white quilt, bleached oak nightstands. She pulled the door shut behind her and secured the bolt, then the latch. She dropped her bags on the blue chintz armchair and glanced around. On the closest nightstand sat a white princess phone.

Elaina stared at it and felt a wave of dread. She owed her boss an update. Maybe she'd shoot him an e-mail and hope he didn't get it until Monday. That would give her two days to recover from this afternoon's disaster.

She'd underestimated the politics down here. It wasn't just about jurisdiction or expertise. It was about stroking the right egos, playing the game. She should have presented herself as a helpful federal agent, here to observe and lend a hand. Instead, she'd come across as a know-it-all, and Breck had been more than happy to put her in her place.

She pulled out her cell and called her best friend.

"Weaver."

She sighed. Just the familiar sound of his voice made her feel better.

"I'm at the Sandhill Inn," she told him.

Pause. "Didn't they release that crime scene, like, three months ago?"

"I'm spending the night here." She sat down on the

bed and started unbuttoning her shirt. Even the room felt humid. "I got a flat tire."

"So call a tow truck," he said in a low voice. "You're only what, fifty miles from here?"

"Forty."

"Why are you staying, then?"

"Why are you whispering?"

"I'm in the surveillance van with Scarborough and Garcia," he said. "Southwest Bank branch office."

"I shouldn't keep you."

"Forget it. They're both on the phone."

But she felt guilty, anyway. Elaina's partner was possibly the only agent Scarborough liked less than he liked her. It was probably the magenta ties. Her boss was of the don't-ask-don't-tell-don't-advertise persuasion.

"So what happened? Why'd you decide to stay?"

"I don't know," she said. "I guess because they wanted me to leave."

"Atta girl. Hey, you need a ride tomorrow?"

"I'll be fine. I think I'll spend the weekend here, see if I can get anything."

"Good luck. See you in the office Monday."

She felt bolstered, like she always did after talking to Weaver.

Hanging up, she scanned the room again with a fresh eye. It was quaint. Charming, actually. With the right man, the place might even pass for romantic.

Had Gina brought a man back to this room during her brief vacation? Did she pick up strangers at bars? Was she a loner? Most profilers focused their attention on the perpetrator. Elaina—possibly because she was a woman—believed it was just as important to study the victim. If she understood the victim, she had a much better chance of figuring out how she'd crossed paths with her attacker.

Elaina walked into the bathroom and turned on the light. The tiny room had a black-and-white-checkered floor and a claw-footed tub. She caught her reflection in the mirror above the sink. Strands of hair had come loose from her bun, and mascara smudges darkened the skin beneath her eyes. How did women wear makeup in this climate? It practically melted off as soon as she left her apartment every morning.

She unwrapped the soap and scrubbed her face clean. Then she returned to the bedroom and snatched up the carryout menu from the nightstand. She gave it a brief perusal, then called in an order for pepperoni pizza and a two-liter bottle of Coke.

After hanging up the clunky phone, she crossed the suite to the sliding glass door. This room had a view of the beach, according to the hotel clerk. Elaina pulled back the curtains, gazed down at the lock, and sighed. Whatever she'd been, Gina Calvert hadn't been very security conscious.

Elaina slipped off her heels and stepped outside. The sound of breaking waves lured her toward the edge of the patio. A half moon had risen in the east, and she gazed at it for a moment, then turned back to face the suite.

The slider's lock was flimsy but had shown no sign of damage, according to police reports. Ditto the lock on the bathroom window.

Had he come in through the hallway? If so, no

one on staff had seen him. Or if they had, they hadn't reported it. So how had the killer entered her room?

"He came in off the beach."

Elaina gasped and reached for her gun.

CHAPTER 3

He stepped into the light, and suddenly she remembered.

"Troy Stockton," she said accusingly.

"In the flesh." His gaze dropped to her Glock. "Long as you don't blow me away with that thing."

She jammed the weapon back into her holster. "I know who you are. You wrote about the Woodlawn murders up in San Antonio."

He lifted an eyebrow and slouched against the wall beside the doorway. He was half in shadow now, while she was standing in a pool of light.

With her shirt unbuttoned.

"You followed me here," she said, rebuttoning the blouse.

"Nope." He hooked his thumb through his belt loop and watched her.

"How did you know I was here?"

He shrugged.

Either he was following her or someone was feeding him information. Given his line of work, she guessed it was a contact on the police force. Probably Maynard.

She stared at him and hoped he'd shift under the scrutiny, but he didn't. He just stood there, looking nothing like a writer, all tall and broad-shouldered with muscles that bulged beneath his black T-shirt. Where was the pasty skin? Where were the horn-rimmed glasses from his book jacket photo? Must have been a prop, selected to create the illusion of scholarship.

"You decided to stay," he said.

"I'm here for the autopsy."

"You weren't invited."

She crossed her arms, and he shifted his attention out toward the water.

"This beach gets pretty quiet 'long about midnight," he said. "Just couples, mainly. No bonfires anymore, not since the burn ban."

She followed his gaze to the shoreline, where waves churned against the sand. In the moonlight, she could see a cluster of people standing beside a beached kayak. They were sharing a cigarette, and the ember glowed as they passed it around. A few other groups strolled down the beach, probably heading out to the bars.

"He could have walked up to her door without anyone noticing. Maybe she recognized him from someplace, let him right in." Troy turned to look at her. "Or maybe he let himself in."

"The lock wasn't damaged."

His gaze dropped down to her top button, then drifted back to her face. "That lock's a joke."

"How would you know?"

"I've looked at it."

Gina's girlfriends told police she'd gone back to her room alone on the night of her disappearance. And yet the couple in the suite above Gina's had heard muffled voices—a man's and a woman's—in the room beneath them. Who was the man? It was one of the central questions of the investigation.

An investigation Troy Stockton seemed to know a whole lot about.

Elaina pursed her lips. "Are you writing about Gina Calvert now? Another runaway bestseller about slashed-up women?"

The muscle in his jaw twitched.

"You seem to have all the right contacts around here," she said. "Plenty of sources. Probably won't take you too long to crank something out."

His gaze on her was steady. "You figure out why you're here yet, Elaina?"

"I'm still trying to figure out why *you're* here."

Another shrug. "Just thought I'd drop by. Tell you to watch your back."

"Thanks for the tip. But listen—anything I say, whether you hear it from me or one of your friends, is off the record. I'm not here to talk to reporters, and if you quote me in your book, I'll slap you with a lawsuit so fast, your head will spin."

His lip curled up at the corner. "I don't doubt it."

Inside the suite, her cell phone chimed.

"You'd better get that." He straightened away from the wall. "Real nice meeting you, Agent McCord. Good luck with your mission tomorrow."

Elaina got up before dawn. By the time the sky's purple had faded to orange, she'd run four miles on the sand.

Her quads burned. Her lungs tingled. She'd passed Public Beach Access One, Two, and Three. She'd passed a sign telling her she'd entered the wildlife park. She'd passed yet another sign—ENDANGERED BIRD HABITAT—and sprinted on.

All her life, she'd been a runner. *No pain, no gain,* her dad always said. *When the going gets tough, the tough get going.* Or her favorite—which had taken on new meaning since her thirtieth birthday—*use it or lose it.* John McCord was an encyclopedia of clichés. As a child, Elaina had collected the shopworn sayings like prizes from a cereal box, hoping to gain some kind of insight into her taciturn father's personality.

Elaina let her feet slow as she neared yet another sign: TEXAS BIRDING TRAIL. She glanced around but saw no birds—just steep white sand dunes and the endless line of waves attacking the coast.

She scaled the nearest dune for a better vantage point. She ended up with sand in her Nikes and grit clinging to her calves, but the view up top was worth it. Dunes stretched out as far as she could see, and marshes and sky and water. Her hotel and the rest of Lito formed a hazy outline on the northern horizon. Between her vantage point and the town, she saw only a lone fisherman wading near shore and a few squat camping tents.

Solitude.

At least the best someone was likely to find on this island.

Not a bad place to dump a body.

Elaina's gaze shifted to the bay side of the island, where a vast labyrinth of grasses and waterways rippled in the morning breeze.

He *had* to have a boat.

How else could he transport his immobilized victims to dump sites so far off the road? Like Gina Calvert and yesterday's victim, Mary Beth Cooper had been found in a remote marsh, albeit across the bay.

If Elaina had nailed one aspect of the profile, that was it. The killer had a boat.

And if she could find that boat, she could find him.

Troy had his eyes shut and his feet propped on Elaina's patio table when he heard her jog up from the beach. Those soft panting sounds made his blood stir even before her shadow fell over him.

"What are you doing here?"

He opened his eyes and saw just what he'd expected: a flushed, pissed-off woman.

"Waiting for you."

She scowled and glanced at her sports watch. An Ironman. It went well with her spandex top and running shorts, both of which were soaked through.

"How'd you know I was out here?" She leaned a hand flat against the glass door and yanked off a sneaker. Sand cascaded to the concrete.

"I checked." He watched as she emptied the other shoe.

"You checked."

"I told you, that lock's a joke."

She eyed him hotly, and he could tell she didn't believe he'd actually let himself into her room.

He tipped his chair back to enjoy the view. Long, slender legs. Ebony hair, pulled back in a ponytail. All of it covered by a thin sheen of sweat.

"Listen, Mr. Stockton—"

"That's Troy."

"I don't have time for this. I'm late, and I told you, I'm not talking to reporters, so—"

"No, you're not."

"What?"

"You're not late. You already missed it. The autopsy happened last night."

He watched the shock come over her face, next the anger.

"You *knew* about this? Why didn't you tell me?"

"I found out this morning. State pathologist showed up around nine last night. They worked on her for a good four hours. Sent everyone home around one-thirty. Breck and Cisernos are probably still sound asleep, dreaming about all the shit crabs can do to a corpse."

Her cheeks flushed redder. "Is this a joke to you?" She flung a shoe across the patio, and he realized that last comment had been a mistake. He'd meant to needle her, not disrespect the victim.

The second shoe landed with a *clop* beside the door and Elaina sank into a chair.

Troy took his feet down from the table and sat up.

"Great." She rubbed the bridge of her nose and seemed to be talking to herself. "Scarborough'll have me piloting a desk Monday morning. How can I contribute to an investigation when the lead detective won't even talk to me?"

He watched her, weighing the pros and cons of bringing her in. Pro, she was a fed, meaning resources and connections. Con, she was a fed, meaning red tape and other bullshit he didn't want to deal with. Plus, she was a *she,* which wasn't going to win her any brownie points around here. If he aligned himself with her, he'd be signing up for a crapload of trash talk from now until he finished this project, possibly beyond.

Elaina slumped in her chair and gazed out at the water, as if he weren't even there.

"Breck isn't the lead."

She turned her head. Blinked. "What?"

"It's not Breck you have to watch out for. He's the lead, yes, technically, because these last two bodies turned up on the island, which is his jurisdiction. But that ranger you met yesterday, he'll be the one calling the shots now, all the way from Austin. He's got the governor's ear, and if this turns out to be a serial killer at one of the state's most popular beach resorts, you can bet the governor'll get involved, even if only behind the scenes."

"The Texas Ranger. I don't even know his name."

"Doesn't matter," Troy said. "It's his connections you need to remember. Other thing is your boss, Scarborough. He and Breck go way back."

She looked skeptical. "Scarborough and Breck?"

"They were frat brothers at Texas State. I'm surprised he didn't mention that when he sent you up here. And if your boss sent you here, knowing full well how Breck would react, there has to be a reason."

She looked out over the water, those blue eyes hot. He liked the thrust of her chin. She resented being manipulated, but she wasn't about to give up.

"You know, you still haven't told me what your interest is in this case," she said.

He'd known she'd get back to that. "I write crime. And these murders are happening in my backyard."

"Is that all? Proximity?"

He looked into her eyes, and he could see she believed there was more to his motive. She was right.

Troy leaned forward. "If your theory holds water—"

"It does."

"Okay, assume you're right. Then Mary Beth Cooper was one of this guy's first victims. That would mean the man who confessed to killing her was lying, and my book is wrong."

"So you're here to set the record straight?"

"I don't like to be wrong, Agent McCord." He'd bet she didn't, either.

She held his gaze for a long moment, and he saw the first flicker of trust. Then she looked away.

"You seem to know the local politics," she said.

"I grew up around here."

"You seem to be trying to help me."

"Maybe."

She turned to face him. "I won't be a source for you. I've got enough career problems without my boss seeing me quoted in some pulp fiction novel."

"I write nonfiction. It's called true crime."

"Fine," she said. "But I'm off limits to you as a source."

Troy suppressed a smile. *Off limits* had never been part of his vocabulary. "Whatever you say."

"Why did you stop by, anyway?"

He watched her, liking her attitude and knowing he would regret what he was about to do. "Thought you might want a tour."

She eyed him warily. "A tour of what?"

"The crime scene."

• • •

Troy Stockton's boat was flat and narrow, and looked different from all the other flat, narrow fishing boats living at the Lito Island Marina.

"It's black," Elaina said, gazing down at it from the dock.

"So?" He undid the bowline and whipped it into a neat coil, which he tossed on the boat's floor.

"All the other boats are white." She stepped aboard. Everything shifted, and he caught her arm to steady her.

"No law against black." His hand dropped away, and he turned to flip some switches at the helm. Soon the engine grunted.

"Looks like it can go in pretty shallow water."

"Eight inches," he said with a touch of pride.

She looked around for a good place to stand. There weren't many choices, so she rested a hand on the captain's chair as they eased back out of the slip.

"Hold on." He shifted gears, and then they were gliding in the other direction, moving out of the sheltering cove the marina shared with the police dock. Elaina glanced over her shoulder and watched the pier recede. She was going out on a boat with a man she barely knew, without letting her boss or anyone else know what she was doing. Not terribly smart.

She patted her BlackBerry in her back pocket. Her Glock was stashed in the Bianchi holster at her ankle, and if Troy tried anything funny, he was going in the bay.

Elaina shifted, putting some distance between them. She couldn't explain why he made her uneasy. It made no sense, because she spent every day surrounded by macho types—guys trained in firearms, hand-to-hand

combat, and mind games. Since her first day in Brownsville, many of the Bureau, DEA, and Homeland Security
guys had attempted to intimidate her either physically or
by getting in her head, and she'd learned to blow them
off.

But Troy was harder to ignore.

He stood between the helm and the captain's chair,
and she stood beside him, trying not to cling too tightly
and reveal her fear of toppling out of the boat. She
glanced over and noticed his ropey forearms and powerful calves. He was some sort of athlete, obviously, and she
tried to guess the sport.

"You get seasick?" Troy asked.

"No. Why?"

"You look uncomfortable." But he wasn't even looking at her. Those eyes—which were the exact green color
of the bay—were trained on the southern horizon. He
wore cargo shorts and Teva sandals today. His white
T-shirt contrasted with his sun-browned skin, and she
envisioned him on a surfboard.

Why was she even thinking about this? She needed to
focus on the case, not on Troy Stockton. This man had a
reputation. It was coming back to her in bits and pieces.
She didn't usually read celebrity mags, but she had a
vague recollection of flipping through *People* at her den-
tist's office. Troy had been photographed with some gorgeous starlet. That girl from Corpus Christi. What the
hell was her name?

"That was some profile you came up with."

She cut a glance at Troy and saw the smile playing at
the corner of his mouth. She bristled.

"What do you mean?"

"White male. Likes hunting and fishing. Owns a boat. Sounds like half the men on this island, including me." He stared down at her, serious now. "Except for the getting-it-up part."

Elaina felt a blush creep up her neck. "Look, Troy—"

"Here we are." The boat slowed abruptly as he pushed the throttle up, and she stumbled into him. "She was found just over there," he said.

Elaina looked in the direction he was pointing, but saw nothing unusual. Just more grass and water.

"How do you know?"

He tapped his control panel, and she noticed the GPS. "I got the coordinates."

He got the coordinates. From the police, no doubt, who clearly were sharing information with members of the public, but leaving her completely in the dark.

"They got a good set of prints from the victim last night." Troy veered close to the shoreline, and the water was so shallow, Elaina could see grass on the bottom. "They'll run the thumbs through DMV, hopefully get an ID soon."

Elaina thought of Valerie Monroe, who'd graduated third in her class at Baylor Med and had been accepted as an intern at Texas Children's Hospital. She wondered what Valerie's parents were doing at this moment. Most likely they were either en route to Lito Island or already camped out at the police station, waiting for news.

Troy veered left into a narrow inlet.

"We're going in?"

"You want to see it, don't you?"

"Yes, but . . ." She watched him deftly steer the boat through the tight opening. The water wasn't even a foot deep, and she saw ripples in the sand as they skimmed along the surface. "What if we run aground?"

He smiled. "You get out and push."

But they didn't run aground. He tipped up the engine and slowed down, using just enough speed to maintain control over the steering as they maneuvered this way and that through all the channels. She began to doubt that he really knew where he was going.

She spotted something yellow tangled in the reeds. "Look there." She pointed.

"Well, shit." He let the motor stall and then jumped out of the boat and waded over to take a look. "I'll be damned."

"What?"

The boat drifted into the grass and bumped against the bottom.

Troy gazed down at the thin yellow twine but didn't touch it. "They must not have seen this," he muttered. "Or maybe they came in from the south."

"Who came in?"

He looked up. "The crime-scene guys. Breck, Maynard, Chavez. They should have collected all this. It's evidence."

"Evidence of what?"

He trudged back to the boat and shoved it into the center of the narrow channel.

"Of your unsub." He climbed aboard and got them moving again. "This marsh, it's like a maze. I grew up all over this bay, and I get lost half the time. Looks like the killer used twine to mark the route so he could find his way out after dumping the body."

Elaina stared at the twine, struck by the idea.

"And how do we know it came from him?" she asked. "Maybe Breck left it."

"He didn't."

"How do you know?"

"Because." Troy gave her a hard look. "They found it in Gina's case, too. He leaves it every time."

Elaina continued to look queasy, so Troy hugged the coast as he headed back in. He felt her behind him as she silently gripped the chair.

She hadn't liked him poking holes in her profile, but that was too damn bad. Sure, the profile sounded good in theory, but given the demographics around here, it didn't narrow things down a whole lot. Troy had never cared much for mind hunters. Most of them stayed holed up in their basement offices, rattling off psychobabble while the real cops rolled up their sleeves and worked the cases. If criminal profiling was Elaina's thing, she was going to have an uphill battle getting anyone around here to buy into it. Next best thing to fortune-telling, as far as Breck was concerned.

Troy glanced back at Elaina and saw that she still had that uneasy look. Her nose was pink, too, and she'd forgotten sunscreen. She wasn't from around here, evidently, but he didn't know her background. He needed to do some digging and find out just how green a green-horn she was.

She squinted at something up ahead, and he followed her gaze.

"What's going on?"

"Dunno," he said. But as they neared the marina, it

became clear something had gone down during their little sight-seeing cruise. Cars and news vans filled the LIPD parking lot.

"Breck's holding a press conference," Troy guessed, turning into the cove. They glided past the police station, and Elaina turned to stare at the crowd.

Troy pulled into his slip without touching the dock. He hopped out and tied the bowline to a cleat, then held out a hand for Elaina.

She barely glanced at it as she stepped onto the pier without help.

"I hope your police chief knows what he's doing," she said. "If he releases too much detail, he'll compromise the investigation."

"That's one thing you don't have to worry about. The man hates reporters."

"But he talks to you?"

Troy walked across the pier and surveyed the situation. Breck was talking to the media—or more likely, deflecting their questions—from the station house steps. Cinco stood on the sidelines. Troy caught his eye, and he joined them on the lawn beside the marina.

"What's up, Cinc?"

He glanced at Elaina. Then he eyed Troy's muddy sandals and seemed to put together where they'd been.

"Good news and bad news," Cinco said. "We got an ID. Girl's name is Whitney Bensen."

Troy felt Elaina go rigid beside him.

"What about Valerie?" she asked.

"That's the bad news," Cinco told her. "Valerie Monroe is still missing."

• • •

Jamie's stomach clenched as she watched the television. "Are you seeing this?"

She glanced across her apartment to where Noah sat camped out on a beanbag chair beside a pack of Oreos.

"Noah? Are you *watching*?"

But he was intent on his Nintendo DS. "Shit!" He glanced up finally. "What the hell, Jamie? I'm trying to concentrate."

"They identified that victim from the park. And now they've got *another* girl missing. Maybe she's the one we saw on the mainland. I'm calling the cops!"

Jamie lunged for her phone, and Noah shot up from the floor.

"What are you, crazy?" He jerked the phone from her hand. "What are you gonna say, huh? How you were walking along and stumbled into some dead girl and how you *didn't* tell anyone?"

"That was your idea! I wanted to call nine-one-one!"

"Great plan, James. Call the cops out there when you got dope in your car and Ecstasy stashed in your backpack. I'm on fucking probation."

She bit her lip and glanced past him at the television.

"Just chill out, okay? Let the cops handle it."

She looked up into those blue eyes. Which were bloodshot, of course. Why did she get mixed up with these guys? All her life, she'd been a magnet for beautiful, do-nothing men with zero ambition.

"Come on." He kissed her forehead and wrapped those muscular arms around her. "The cops'll figure it out. There's nothing we coulda done, anyway. She was dead, remember?"

Jamie tensed. Yeah, she *remembered*. The image of that mutilated girl had been haunting her for days. She couldn't sleep. She couldn't eat. She was turning into a mental case.

She wrapped her arms around Noah and held on. She felt better somehow.

"What about an anonymous tip?" she said. "I could just stop by a pay phone. Call the sheriff's office."

"Shit, don't you watch TV? They've got surveillance cams, like, everywhere. And they can trace your cell. You call anyone, they'll be at your door in no time. Trust me, okay? Just let it go."

Jamie closed her eyes and listened to the broadcaster drone on. ". . . two vicious deaths in just three months at this sunny coastal paradise . . ."

Make that three deaths. Or four, if this other missing girl wasn't the same one they'd seen. Jamie thought of the corpse, and her stomach turned again.

"You okay?" he asked.

"Fine."

But she wouldn't look at him. She knew what she had to do.

CHAPTER 4

Coconuts had been Troy's favorite fishing hole once upon a time. But blender drinks and half-wasted twenty-year-olds had lost their appeal, and it had been years since he'd set foot in the place. He spotted Cinco bellied up to the outdoor bar underneath a thatched roof. In board shorts and a T-shirt, his friend looked off-duty. But looks could be deceiving.

Troy took the stool beside him and flagged the bartender.

"Anything interesting?"

Cinco shrugged. "Not yet. Place is just getting going, though."

Lito's bikini girls spent their mornings sleeping off hangovers. They hit the beach all afternoon. About an hour after sundown, they'd start working their way down the two-mile stretch of shoreline known as the Strip. Coconuts was the most popular destination by far, dominating the scene with loud music, cheap drinks, and waitresses who wore tops made of actual coconuts.

Troy surveyed the crowd. "How many hits you get on Whitney Bensen's credit card?"

"Two," Cinco said.

"And Gina Calvert was here, too?"

"Spring break," Cinco said. "She spent money here four nights in a row."

Troy nodded. Could be a coincidence. But it was one worth pursuing, which was why Cinco was here on his night off, poking around. Of all Breck's men, Cinco looked the youngest and was the least likely to stand out.

The bartender slid a Dos Equis across the counter. Troy took a swig and pivoted his stool so he could look at the crowd. Half of them were in the pool, where the long swim-up bar gave everyone a chance to check out the goods before making a play.

"You think he's here?" Cinco asked.

"Could be." Troy scanned the faces. Everyone was in pickup mode, but most seemed to be in groups. Fraternity boys, probably down from Austin. Their guy would be solo. Troy was no profiler, but he knew that much.

"So." Cinco tipped back his beer. "Elaina McCord. Not your usual type."

Troy glanced at him.

"Kind of uptight," Cinco said. "Pretty, though. And smart. She's already figured out she needs to make herself useful, quick, or she'll be back to serving warrants and running background checks in Brownsville."

"How do you know what she does in Brownsville?"

"Spent the afternoon with her at the station house, tracking down records. She's putting together a suspect list."

"And you're helping her." Troy shook his head. Not a great strategy on Cinco's part. Breck wouldn't like it. But Cinco was a sucker for a pretty woman, always had been.

"They're combing the bay tonight," Cinco said.

"Who, Breck?"

"And the sheriff. And the Coast Guard. So far, nothing."

Troy doubted they'd find anything tonight—Whitney Bensen was all over the news. But then, maybe this guy wanted to make a splash. Elaina had said he was "ego driven," so maybe he'd like the challenge of dumping another body right under the authorities' noses.

"Breck still hung up on the copycat theory?" Troy asked.

"Not with this other woman missing. Even without the Mary Beth Cooper murder, he's pretty sure we're looking at a serial killer."

Troy frowned down at his beer. Cinco had hit on a nerve, and he knew it. According to Troy's first successful book, Mary Beth Cooper died at the hands of Charles Diggins, a man now serving life without parole in the state pen. Diggins raped and murdered eleven women—mostly Latinas—up and down Highway 77 between Victoria and Brownsville. His territory became known as El Corredor de la Muerte, the Corridor of Death. Diggins claimed to have killed Mary Beth Cooper, and his confession had been so detailed, police had believed him. Troy had interviewed the guy twice up in Huntsville, and he'd believed him, too.

Now Troy was seriously questioning Diggins's story, along with his own judgment. If Troy had detected a lie all those years ago, could he have tipped off investigators before this new rash of killings?

"Anyway, we'll know for sure when the labs come back."

"The toxicology?"

Cinco nodded. "The ranger they sent down, he's got a rush on everything at the state crime lab. Should be something back soon. Media's already made up their minds, though. They're calling him the Paradise Killer."

The bouncer stationed at the beach entrance stopped a slender brunette. Elaina flashed her ID, and he waved her through. Troy turned and watched her walk across the patio.

"If she's got ketamine on board," Cinco was saying, "we're definitely dealing with the same scumbag."

Elaina glanced around briefly before claiming a stool way the hell at the other end of the bar. It was barely five seconds before some beefcake surfer claimed the stool next to her. She smiled up at him, and Troy gritted his teeth.

"T? You listening?"

His attention snapped back to Cinco. "Huh?"

"I said we should have it by Monday. The tox report. Even tomorrow, maybe, if this ranger has enough pull." Cinco's phone buzzed, and he checked the number. "I gotta take this."

Troy's attention veered back to Elaina. She wore a dark green T-shirt and khaki shorts, and she looked more like a Girl Scout leader than a beach bunny. But the outfit wasn't slowing this guy down. He'd noticed her legs, obviously, and that silky dark hair. Kind of hard to miss.

Troy sipped his beer and let his gaze slide over her. Where was her Glock? Maybe she had a backup piece, something small that she'd hidden somewhere interesting. Troy watched her steadily and resolved to find out.

• • •

Coconuts was a predator's playground. And it only took half an hour and two come-ons for Elaina to understand why.

The entire place was designed to make flirting easy and sobriety difficult. Competition permeated the warm, chlorine-scented air as people vied for attention at the swim-up bar, on the dance floor, and around the water volleyball net. For the less active, there was the beach, where a row of lounge chairs had been conveniently arranged in the shadows, away from the music and tiki torches.

It was just the sort of nightspot Elaina's father used to warn her about when she was a teenager. Not that he'd needed to. Elaina had never owned a fake ID, and by the time she was old enough to drink legally, she was more interested in graduating from Georgetown than picking up men.

"Need a refill?" The bartender nodded at the drink in front of her, a frozen concoction called a Señorita-something-or-other. The first guy—Brad—had recommended it to her.

"No, thanks," she said, stirring the drink. It had come in a coconut with a pink umbrella sticking out of it. She'd meant to use the drink as a prop, but then most of it had disappeared without her noticing.

"Hey, I've got a question for you." Elaina smiled at the bartender as he lined up a row of glasses under the taps. "You get a lot of regulars here, or is it mostly tourists?"

He tipped a glass skillfully. "Tourists, pretty much. And rig workers."

"Rig workers?"

"Roughnecks off the oil rigs, out in the Gulf. They come in sometimes, looking to hit on the out-of-towners."

Soft targets, Elaina thought. This place was full of them.

"These rig workers, are they on some kind of schedule, or do they just come and go?"

He shrugged. "I don't know, really. They're just around."

"Are they around tonight?"

He looked past her, out at the pool, as he loaded the drinks onto a tray. "Nah, don't think so. Tonight's surfers and frat boys."

Elaina stirred her drink and looked out over the scene. She took a sip, and her straw slurped. Yummy. Potent, but yummy.

A waitress called in an order and then leaned back against the counter to wait. She sighed deeply and adjusted her coconuts.

"Busy night?" Elaina asked.

The woman rolled her eyes. "Not busy enough."

"I'm Elaina," she said, sticking her hand out.

"Kim." She wiped her hand on her apron and shook.

"Were you on duty earlier this week?"

The waitress lifted an eyebrow. "You mean Tuesday and Wednesday? Yeah. But like I told that other cop, I didn't see anything unusual."

Elaina wasn't surprised Kim had her pegged. Waitresses were an observant bunch.

"What about anything *usual*?" Elaina asked. "What about someone who blended in but something struck you as off? Maybe something minor."

Kim tipped her head to the side thoughtfully as she gazed out at the pool.

Elaina believed their unsub — or unidentified subject — was clever enough not to draw attention to himself. Most likely, he was a smooth talker. Someone who could keep a low profile while he coaxed a woman into his comfort zone.

"I've been racking my brain since that first cop asked me," Kim said. "I didn't see that missing girl around. And nothing stands out. Just the same old same old."

Elaina nodded.

"I'll let you know, though." She smiled at Elaina as she picked up her now-full tray. "You got a business card or something?" She nodded at the bartender. "Just leave it with Joel."

"Sure."

The waitress walked off, and Elaina noticed the fresh coconut sitting in front of her. She took a sip. This one was a virgin, and the bartender winked at her from the margarita machine.

Forget the doughnut shop. The cops on Lito Island should get their freebies here.

"Watch out for those Sweet Señoritas."

Elaina turned around at the familiar voice.

"One'll have you on the dance floor," Troy said. "Two'll have you on your ass."

He was in the same T-shirt and sandals he'd had on earlier, but he wore faded jeans now. His brown hair was sun-streaked and windblown, and it looked as though he'd spent the day out on his boat.

"Thanks for the tip," she said. "What are you doing here, anyway?"

"Same thing you are."

Troy claimed the stool beside her.

"I've got an objective tonight," she told him. "You're not part of it."

He leaned an elbow on the bar and watched her. "Tell me about your objective."

"I need to know if Valerie Monroe frequented this place before her disappearance. Her friends said no, but there's some time unaccounted for."

"You talked to her friends?"

"Of course."

"Sounds like you've been busy," he said. "Not eager to get back to Brownsville, huh?"

Elaina didn't answer that. She sipped her drink and tried to look bored, but inside she felt uneasy. Was she really that transparent? She made a concerted effort not to let her feelings about her job show, but she hated everything about Brownsville: her boss, her assignments, the condescending he-men she worked with serving warrants. It was the same routine over and over: The SWAT jocks hit the door, the men did the investigating, and Elaina was sent off to "keep an eye on the women and children" as if she were a babysitter. As if she couldn't toss an apartment like anyone else. Coming to Lito Island had been her first meaningful assignment since she'd graduated the Academy. It was her first chance to put all those years of study and training to use, her first chance to do something that really mattered.

Troy leaned back on his stool. He lifted her ponytail and sent a tingle down her spine as he read the back of her T-shirt. "You buy that here on the island?" he asked.

"It's from the hotel gift shop." She glanced down at the beer logo on the breast pocket. "Why?"

He looked amused. "You don't speak Spanish, do you?"

"No, why? What does it say?"

"'I've fallen and I can't get my beer.'" He swigged his beer and watched her.

"Well, so what? I needed something that would blend in."

"Good call. But you're gonna have to show a little more flesh, McCord. This is a beach crowd."

"Look," she said, annoyed now, "I'm here to gather information. Do you mind?"

She waited for him to get up, but he didn't budge.

"Tell me about your suspect list," he said.

"I'm not giving you names."

"How'd you come up with it? Maybe I can help you narrow it down. Hell, maybe I even came across one of the names on it when I was researching the Cooper murder."

Elaina twirled her pink umbrella and thought about it. It was probably the rum soaking in, but she was feeling a little looser than she should. "I cross-referenced registered boat owners with the DMV records. Came up with two hundred and eighty-six white males between twenty and forty who live on this island and own a boat."

Troy whistled. "That's a long list."

"Yeah, and you're on it."

He smiled. "Told you."

"Cinco helped me whittle it down. We crossed off guys who are overseas right now, in the military. Some others who'd moved out of the area, that sort of thing."

"Still a lot of folks."

"We're doing criminal background checks, seeing what we can come up with. Our unsub likely has a history of assault or minor sex crimes or both. We hope to end up with just a few dozen names to check out. In the meantime, I want to see what I can get here. Gina and Whitney both hung out at this bar. I have a hunch Valerie did, too."

"You're right," Troy said.

"Excuse me?"

"She was here Monday and Tuesday. She stopped in around midnight. Didn't stay long."

"How do you know that?" she asked.

"I talked to the bouncer on my way in."

"I was about to go interview him," Elaina said, and immediately realized she sounded defensive.

Troy watched her calmly with those sea-green eyes. "The bouncer said he saw her picture on the news today and recognized her."

A chill settled over her as she slowly scanned the crowd. "I bet he's trolling," she muttered.

"Trolling?"

She glanced at Troy, expecting sarcasm. But he seemed genuinely interested.

"Serial killers go through phases," she said. "There's the trolling phase, when he identifies the victim, begins circling. During the next phase, he lures her in somehow, gets her comfortable. Most victims of serial killers don't struggle. They don't realize what's happening until it's too late."

Troy nodded solemnly.

"Then there's the kill, the totem phase."

"Totems?"

"It's the ritual part," she said. "He feels triumphant over the victim, sometimes does specific things to help prolong his feeling of power over her. In this case, I believe it's the mutilation. That's his signature. And maybe he takes something."

"Like what?"

"Maybe a lock of hair or a piece of jewelry. A trophy. A souvenir. Anything that reminds him of it, helps him relive the fantasy." She sighed. "Then the euphoria wears off, he gets depressed, and he starts trolling again. It's a cycle. He won't quit."

"According to you, this guy did quit," Troy said.

"I didn't say that."

"A nine-year gap between Mary Beth Cooper and Gina Calvert? Sounds like a hiatus to me."

"Serial killers don't quit," she said, studying the faces in the crowd. "He probably just went away for a while. Did it someplace else. Now he's back again."

And was he *here*? Right now? Was he flirting with one of these unsuspecting women, laying the groundwork so he could separate her from the pack later? Elaina's attention shifted to the lounge chairs. Couples talking, mostly. A few kissing in the shadows.

"You picked a grim line of work, McCord."

She glanced at him. "Law enforcement?"

"Profiling."

"I'm just an agent," she said. "It takes years to make it into the Behavioral Analysis Unit. I've got the right degrees, but they want people with field experience."

"So that's why you're down here? Field experience?"

"Pretty much," she said, although she doubted that was the only reason. The Bureau had put her at this remote border post, as opposed to one of the major metropolitan areas where so many new agents got their start. Elaina still wasn't sure why. Why here? Why her? She didn't know of a single agent in her Academy class who was less suited for this assignment. But she'd decided months ago to suck it up and make the best of her situation. No one had promised her a job in D.C. or at Quantico. She was going to have to earn it.

Troy tapped his beer bottle against her coconut. "Here's to new experiences, then."

She gazed down into her drink. It was gone again. When had that happened? And she'd thought it had been a virgin, but now she wondered whether it had had a touch of rum in it. She felt a little too comfortable talking to this attractive man she barely knew. She needed to focus. She had work to do.

Troy nudged her arm, and she felt the jolt of it right to her shoulder. "Let's get out of here."

She stared at him.

"Come on." He slid off the stool and took her hand. "It's a half-moon. Good night for a boat ride."

A boat ride? Was he serious? His hand felt warm, and he stroked her palm with his thumb.

And suddenly she remembered. The beautiful starlet he'd been seen with last year.

"You're dating Eva Longoria," she blurted.

"Not last time I checked."

"But you were."

"Eva's married." He tugged her off the stool. She

gazed up at him as he stood there, holding her hand and practically admitting that he hung out with gorgeous celebrities.

"I can't go on your boat with you," she said. "I'm supposed to be working."

"I'm working, too. This is research."

"Research."

He stood so close, she could see the stubble along his jaw, feel the heat coming off of him. For the briefest instant, she thought he would kiss her.

"You really care about this case, Elaina, or are you just passing time?"

"I care." And she realized how much. This case, these women—it was the most important work she'd ever done, and she desperately didn't want to blow it.

"Then let's go." He dropped her hand, and his voice was all business now. "Every badge in Lito County is on the bay right now. You want in on this case, you need to be with them."

"They're looking for Valerie?" She pulled some money from her pocket and left it on the bar.

"Valerie. And that boat you keep talking about." He took her elbow and steered her toward the front entrance. Elaina didn't have a car here. She'd walked up from the beach. Troy must have seen her.

"You think Breck will pull in somewhere to pick me up?"

He glanced at her. "Doubtful."

They passed through a pair of tiki torches and ended up in the parking lot. She heard a chirp, and a pair of headlights blinked. Troy stopped in front of a sleek black Ferrari.

"You've got to be kidding me."

He pulled open the passenger's-side door. "What?"

"It's a Ferrari."

"So?"

"So, I can't ride in that thing with you. I'm a federal agent!"

His brows arched.

"What happened to the pickup truck?" she asked. "The one we rode in to the marina?"

"It's at home. Get in."

Elaina stared at the car. She didn't know how much a Ferrari cost, but it was probably at least a few years' worth of her salary. Or maybe a decade.

"Time's a-wastin'." Troy rounded the back of the car and slid in behind the wheel. The engine made a low, throaty sound.

Did she want to get out on that bay or not? She did. Did she want to beg Breck to pick her up? She did not. So her best option was Troy. He had a boat and he knew his way around.

Elaina eased herself into the car.

CHAPTER 5

Mia Voss watched her friend squeeze through the crowd at El Patio and plunk a pair of enormous piña coladas on the table. She mustered a smile for her. "Thanks."

"Can't get to the islands, we'll bring the islands to you," Alex said.

Mia took a big slurp, giving herself an instant brain freeze. "I don't know what made me think I could get away," she said.

"Hmm, maybe because you haven't had a vacation in years?" Alex supplied. "And you were planning to be gone only a few days?"

"I should have known he'd pull something like this."

Alex stirred her drink. "Hate to break it to you, but your boss is a prick."

"I've had it on the calendar for months. *Months*." Mia shook her head. "And still, the second he walked into my office Monday morning, I knew it wasn't going to happen."

"Where'd he go again?" Alex asked.

"Cozumel. With his new girlfriend."

"Let's hope he gets *turista*." Alex raised her glass.

"I'll drink to that." Mia picked up her fishbowl with both hands and took another slurp. Pretty weak on the rum, but she wasn't surprised. San Marcos was a college town, and watered-down drinks were par for the course at every bar within twenty miles of campus.

Alex leaned forward, and her brown eyes grew serious.

Uh-oh. Now came the real reason she'd invited Mia out tonight. Something was wrong. Alex's fiancé had ditched her. She'd lost her job. She had a terminal disease.

"Okay, don't look now, but there's a *very* hot guy checking you out, about two o'clock."

Mia's gaze shot up.

"I said don't look!"

She jerked her attention back to Alex, but not before getting a brief flash of the man staring at her from across the room.

"Dark hair, leather jacket?"

"Yup."

"He's probably looking at you," Mia said.

"Uh, *no*. Trust me. That high-intensity stare is directed at you, babe."

Mia stirred her drink and flicked another glance at the man. Alex was right. He sat at a table with three other men and a pitcher of beer, but he wasn't paying attention to any of them. His black-eyed gaze was focused squarely on *her*.

Mia tucked a lock of hair behind her ear and wished she'd done something more tonight than pull her strawberry-blond mop into a ponytail. "I think I know him from somewhere." She took a casual sip of her drink.

"You know him?" Alex sounded surprised.

"I don't know his name, but I recognize the eyes."

"Well, he's definitely not a lab rat," Alex said, and Mia shot her a glare. "What? I'm just saying. No way he works at the Delphi Center."

"He doesn't," Mia said. She didn't know all of her coworkers, but she wouldn't have missed this one.

And Alex was right. He didn't look like the men in her orbit.

"Fifty bucks he's a cop." Alex plucked the plastic sword from her drink and nibbled off the cherry.

"Why do you say that?"

"A leather jacket in June? And check out his buddies. Every one of them's packing."

Mia forced herself to look at Alex, but from the corner of her eye she saw the man get up and move toward their table.

"Crap, he's walking over here," Mia said. "Quick, what were we talking about?"

"Your job."

"Anything but that."

"Your trip. Lito Island. How are the beaches down there? I've never been, but I've heard—"

"Hi." A shadow fell over the table, and both Mia and Alex glanced up.

His eyes locked on Mia's. They were so dark, she couldn't tell where the pupils ended and the irises began.

"Caramia Voss, right?"

She opened her mouth to speak, but nothing came out. Alex kicked her under the table.

"Hi." Mia cleared her throat. "I . . . Do I know you from somewhere?"

Alex's phone hummed.

"No. But I know you. Ric Santos."

"Sorry, have to take this." Alex stood up with her phone pressed to her ear. Mia watched in dismay as she headed for the door leading to the bar's patio.

"Mind?" Ric nodded at the chair beside her.

"Not at all."

He sank into the seat and rested his beer glass on the table. Alex's departure didn't seem to bother him.

"So." Mia cleared her throat. "How exactly do you know me?"

"Heard you give a talk about a year ago at the Delphi Center."

"You're a scientist?"

The corner of his mouth curled up. "I'm a cop. San Marcos PD."

Mia stirred her drink but didn't take a sip. She didn't want to get loopy with some guy she barely knew. Last time she'd done that, she'd woken up with a brutal hangover and a crush on Troy Stockton that had taken her years to shake loose.

She pushed the drink away. "It must have been a riveting speech. What'd I talk about?"

He smiled. "Deoxyribonucleic acid."

"I'm impressed. I have coworkers who can't even pronounce it right."

"Hey, I was paying attention." He leaned forward on his elbow and turned his glass. His gaze met hers. "And it was."

"Was what?"

"Riveting."

Yeah, right. She searched his face, looking for signs that he was joking. But she didn't see any. He was a good actor. Or maybe *charmer* was a better word. Yes, Mia worked at one of the world's most elite forensic laboratories, but she had yet to meet a man who considered it much of a turn-on. In fact—with the exception of homicide detectives, who were constantly asking her for favors—most guys avoided the subject of her job altogether. They found it intimidating.

Ric eased closer, and she felt herself doing the same. "So, Caramia—"

"Only my grandmother ever calls me that." She smiled. "It's Mia."

He nodded. "I bet you stay pretty busy, huh? Woman with your expertise?"

"Too busy for my own good."

"How do you mean?"

"Oh, nothing." She rolled her eyes. "My supervisor just loaded me down with work so he could go on vacation." She shrugged. "I put in a lot of overtime, so I guess he figured I could handle it. But honestly? I'm feeling pretty burned out at the moment. The lab's been flooded lately."

"You guys have, what, a hundred scientists over there? Can't you get a hand with anything?"

"Sure, some of it," she said. "It's just, there's this specialty area. It's called miniSTR analysis?"

"Never heard of it. What's miniSTR?"

"Short Tandem Repeats are markers on the DNA strand. Anyway, miniSTR analysis is a somewhat new technique that enables us to get a full DNA profile from a very small or highly degraded sample. I have more experience with it than anyone else in our group, so a lot of that work falls to me. I've been swamped."

He leaned back in his chair and watched her, and she felt a wave of nervousness. Why was she telling him all this? Probably not what he'd had in mind when he dropped into this bar on a Saturday night.

"So." She forced a smile. "What about you? I guess things are quiet around town until fall semester starts up?"

"Not really," he said. "Got a lot of campgrounds in the area. Hiking trails. Tourists getting into trouble."

His gaze flicked over her shoulder, and she knew he was looking at his buddies. She sipped some piña colada and scanned the bar for Alex. Her friend wouldn't leave her here, but she'd definitely make herself scarce for a while so that Mia could soak up some male attention. It wasn't going anywhere, though, because Mia had made the mistake of lapsing into geek-speak.

But then Ric leaned in again, and his dark eyes pinned her. "Listen, Mia. I want to ask you something."

She got a warm little flutter in her stomach. "Yes?"

"Just tell me straight out if you're not up for it." His voice was low and serious, and Mia's imagination took off.

"Okay."

"You watch any news lately?"

"Not really. I don't have a lot of time, so—"

"You heard the media talking about the Paradise Killer? Down on the coast? I've got this cold case," he said, "and I think it might be related."

Mia looked into those intense eyes and heard the faint sound of her ego cracking into a dozen pieces.

"That talk you gave," he continued, "about touch DNA. I think that might really help us out here. You handle some of that at your lab, don't you?"

"We do, yes."

"And some of it's pro bono, right? Cases where there's no budget? Maybe smaller departments?"

"About ten percent of our cases are privately subsidized. We've got grants. And people who donate their time."

Alex appeared at the table, thank goodness, saving her from having to recite the rest.

"Hi," Alex said, smiling.

Mia smiled back and gave her the tiniest shake of the head.

"Did you want to head out soon or . . . ?" Alex glanced at her watch.

"Yes, we should go." Mia jumped up and snatched her purse off the back of the chair. She dug out a business card and handed it to the most attractive man to hit on her in a very long time.

Only he hadn't been hitting on her.

"Call me at the lab," she said cheerfully. "We can talk more about your case."

Elaina tried to ignore the sculpted seat, the cool feel of leather against the back of her thighs. She felt like she was in a cockpit. She glanced out the window as they zoomed down the highway toward the marina. They were much too close to the ground, and she fought the urge to pick up her feet.

"Relax. It's just a car."

Just a car. Right. This man must be very, very wealthy.

But she sensed he hadn't always been. She stole a glance at him. There was something elemental about him—in his speech, his dress, his mannerisms. If she had to guess, she'd say he came from a blue-collar background and had earned what he had.

She needed to find out. He was a source in her investigation. She needed to learn more about him in order to weigh his credibility.

Yeah, that's why she was interested.

He shifted gears again, and she glanced at his thigh in those jeans.

This was ridiculous. His car was having just the effect it was intended to have on women. And she had no doubt that was why she was here.

Elaina looked out her window and took a deep breath. She needed to go running. She needed to exorcise some of this restlessness she'd been feeling the past few days. She'd had sex on the brain lately, and it was Troy's fault. But she was here to work, not socialize.

And he was here to pump her for information he could use in his book. She needed to keep that in mind. Behind all this helpfulness, he had an agenda.

Troy cut a glance at her. "What's wrong?"

She cleared her throat. "Your car. It doesn't smell like smoke."

"So?"

"So, you're a smoker. You were smoking Marlboro Reds at the marina."

He downshifted. "I don't smoke much."

"When do you smoke?"

"When I feel like it."

He whipped into the marina parking lot and slid

into a space beside a sheriff's unit. He got out and came around to open her door. She would have refused his help, but she was fairly sure she'd look like an idiot trying to climb out gracefully.

"We'll take the Supra."

"What's a Supra?"

"Speedboat." He led her down a different pier than the one she'd been on earlier today and stopped at a slip. It was another black boat, but this one had *Salt Shaker* scripted across the side. A lyric from "Margaritaville" popped into her head.

Troy braced a foot on the boat and one on the dock and offered her a hand getting aboard. Then he untied the bowline and hopped in. He checked some gauges at the helm while she surveyed the boat with relief. This one was small and aerodynamic. It had two padded vinyl seats, so she wouldn't have to stand, clutching his chair the whole time. She made herself comfortable in the passenger seat while he backed out of the slip.

Elaina glanced over her shoulder at the darkened marina. The bait shop was shut down for the night, and the only light came from the red glow of the Coke machine. A number of boat slips were empty—people probably out fishing or spending the night on the water.

"Why aren't you using running lights?" she asked over the hum of the engine.

"Don't need 'em." He tapped the control panel, where she saw another high-tech navigation system.

"But what if people don't see us?"

"That's the idea."

She pretended to understand, but she didn't, really.

What good would it do to be invisible if someone could hear them?

"This thing's fast," Troy said. "We can outpace anything on this bay."

They reached the mouth of the cove and he paused to fiddle with the GPS.

She watched him with frustration. She'd never driven a motorboat. She doubted she could even captain a Sunfish by herself. Her father had always manned the rudder of their catamaran while she'd simply followed orders.

Elaina looked north, then south, trying to visualize the map she'd studied. To the north, the causeway lights formed an arc-shaped constellation against the night sky. To the south, the wildlife refuge was a shadowy void. The mainland lay due west, and she saw the flickering spires of the oil refinery in Bay Port, which never seemed to sleep.

"Let's go north," she said. "The boat docks where Gina and Valerie's cars were found are on that end of the island. Maybe he'd come from there."

"Sounds good to me."

She stood up. "And it's my turn to drive."

Elaina was a quick study, and it didn't take her long to catch on to the navigation system. She had a knack for steering, too, and she kept the boat on course, despite the choppiness of the water. Troy had never let a woman drive his boat before, and he decided he liked it. Something about watching Special Agent Elaina McCord take control of all that horsepower really worked for him. He wanted to get her behind the wheel of his Ferrari, too, but that was probably a fantasy. She seemed to have a puritanical streak.

"Is that depth finder broken, or is it really this shallow?" she asked.

He glanced down at the digital display, which showed a mere three feet between the boat's hull and the bottom. "It's accurate. Fact, the average depth of this bay's less than four feet. You could practically walk to the mainland if you had to."

Elaina shifted back some, bumping into him. His closeness seemed to make her edgy, a fact he was finding pretty entertaining.

"And you said you've been boating around here most of your life? So you grew up in Lito?"

"Bay Port," he said. "But my mom worked at one of the hotels, so I spent a lot of time on the island."

"And your dad?"

His dad was a steel-fisted son of a bitch. "He worked on the rigs offshore. You're gonna want to ease left now," he said, changing the subject. "See that channel marker?"

"Not really."

"Just ahead. 'Bout eleven o'clock." He put his hand over hers and turned the wheel.

"I got it."

"That'll take us right up to the causeway. There're some boat docks up and down the coast there, maybe we'll see something."

She followed the markers, which were vague black silhouettes against the moonlit water.

"Almost there," he said as she neared the bridge.

She glanced around, and her ponytail blew against his arm. She smelled good. He'd been buried in work lately, and it had been much too long since he'd spent time around a woman.

"Here, lemme take over a minute." He nudged her aside, and she stepped into the space between the two seats. "You're not bad for a first-timer."

She scanned the horizon. "Seems like we're the only ones out here."

"We're not."

He neared a large cove and slowed down. After cruising the shoreline for a few minutes, he found the spot he was looking for. It was deep enough that they wouldn't run aground and far enough from the shore that they wouldn't drift into the marsh. He cut the engine.

"Now what?" she asked.

"Now we wait."

She glanced around, clearly taken off guard by this plan. She didn't strike him as someone who liked to sit still.

"We just sit here?"

"Relax. Pretend you're on a stakeout." Troy flipped up a seat cushion in back and snagged a frosty bottle from the refrigerated compartment underneath. He held it out for her. "Beer?"

"No. Thank you. I shouldn't drink on the job."

He shook his head. "Can't ride in a sports car. Can't drink." He rested the beer on the side of the boat and fished out a water bottle. He stood over her with it, dripping icy condensation onto her bare thigh. "You sure make a lot of rules for yourself, Agent McCord."

She took the water and looked away. Instead of settling into his seat, he sat on the bench beside her, ratcheting up her tension level. He twisted the top off his beer.

"So tell me how an agent who doesn't speak Spanish gets posted to a border town." He watched her reaction carefully as he tipped back his beer. He couldn't see her face well in the dimness, but her shoulders stiffened.

"I don't know, really."

"You didn't request it?"

"No."

"But don't new agents get some input?"

"Usually." She took a sip.

"And what did you request?"

"D.C., Baltimore, New York. In that order."

She wanted to be near headquarters. She must be serious about this profiling stuff.

She eased her knee away from his, and he smiled. Hell, maybe she'd be good at it. She had him nailed, obviously. But how hard was that? He was attracted to her, and he'd made no effort to hide it.

"And now you're stuck down here, huh? What do you think?"

She watched him for a beat. Then she looked away. "I think it's hot."

"That's it?"

She shrugged.

"Oh, come on. You've been here, what? Six months?"

"Seven."

"In seven months, all you've noticed is the weather?"

He could tell he was pushing her buttons. Maybe she thought sharing an opinion would be like confiding in him. She seemed to prefer keeping people at a distance.

Which was fine with him. He liked a challenge.

She turned to look at him again. "You really want to know what I think?"

"That's why I asked."

"Okay. I think the men around here need an attitude adjustment."

"Is that right?"

"Yes. They have one of three reactions to a woman with a badge: They ignore you, they talk down to you, or they try to get you into bed."

"Hmm," he said, knowing he fell squarely into the last category. "Interesting. And which of those hacks you off most?"

"The talking down," she said immediately.

"Well, I apologize," he said. "On behalf of my idiot Texas brethren. The talking-down thing—I assume you mean Breck and Maynard?"

"And my boss. And the guys I work with, and pretty much every man I've met since I set foot in this state. With maybe a few exceptions."

"Cinco."

She nodded. "Him. And my partner. They're good ones."

"What about me?"

She watched him, and he felt a warm pull of lust. He was definitely going to have to get around her defenses. It might take him a while, but it would be worth it.

"The jury's still out on you. You've got your good points."

"Oh, yeah?"

"You're the only one who calls me 'Agent McCord,' even though I know you mean it sarcastically."

"See, now, I've been stereotyped. I don't mean it at all sarcastically."

"Right."

"God's honest truth. I have the utmost respect for every one of you people who risk your lives to enforce the law."

She tipped her head to the side and watched him. He couldn't see her expression clearly, but he could tell she was skeptical. She didn't know him well enough to know he was serious. He respected the hell out of her chosen profession. Might have chosen it himself if the little problem of his criminal record hadn't kept him out.

She looked out toward the causeway. The water lapped against the side of the boat and they floated for a few minutes without talking. The moon peeked out from behind a cloud, and finally he could see her face. She looked surprisingly peaceful. Maybe she'd just needed to vent.

"This reminds me of Lake Michigan in the summertime."

"You from Chicago?" he asked.

"Mostly. We moved to Virginia when I was in high school."

"Where abouts?"

She closed her eyes and tilted her head back, and he thought she'd missed the question.

"Alexandria," she finally told him.

"That's just down the road from Quantico."

"Yes."

"FBI headquarters."

She had her eyes closed, head tipped back. Expression carefully blank. And he remembered something that had been lodged in the back of his mind since he'd first heard her name.

"Hey, you wouldn't happen to be related to John

McCord, would you? He's a legend up there. Wrote a few books."

"Yes."

Troy sat forward and stared at her. "You're related to Big Mac McCord?"

She sighed.

"Shit, he's your father, isn't he?"

At last, she opened her eyes. She watched him warily, and he knew she was expecting some sort of reaction. Probably the same reaction she got from anyone in law enforcement circles who found out she was the daughter of some hot-shit FBI mind hunter, the man who'd practically invented criminal profiling.

And weren't those some big-ass shoes to fill?

Troy sat back and looked at her. That chip on her shoulder made a little more sense now.

He swigged his beer and glanced away.

"You've heard of my dad," she said.

"Read his books. Saw him interviewed once about the Green River Killer up in Washington State."

The silence settled around them again. The former newspaper reporter in him wanted to pelt her with questions, but she probably got that a lot. So instead, he kept his mouth shut and just watched her. She'd turned to look at the bay.

His gaze wandered from her delicate chin over the swell of her breasts, to linger on those legs. She wore the same Nikes she'd had on this morning, and he wondered again where she'd stashed her gun. And if he'd get a chance to find out.

Now he was having sexual fantasies about Big Mac McCord's daughter.

He reached across her lap. She tensed—then relaxed—as he rested his beer in the drink holder beside her chair.

"It's pretty here," she said quietly.

"Yeah." Troy looked around to appreciate it. The water and the marshes were washed with silver. The breeze felt warm. He'd done some traveling these past few years—Thailand, Patagonia, the Australian Outback. He'd seen some beautiful country, but on nights like this, there wasn't a place in the world he'd rather be than Laguna Madre.

"You ever spend the night out here?" she asked.

"Nah, the mosquitoes get fierce when the breeze dies down. I come out early sometimes, though. Before sunrise. Catch a few fish, watch it get light."

"Sounds nice."

He glanced over at her. A lock of hair blew in her face, and he reached out to tuck it behind her ear. She went still. They stared at each other, her chest rising and falling and their faces just inches apart.

A beam of light flashed in his eyes. She jerked her head around.

"Shit." Troy squinted into the glare of the spotlight. Another boat, not fifty feet out. How had he missed it?

He'd been distracted, that's how. He stood up now and watched the police boat approach them. Elaina got to her feet.

"Breck," he told her as he made out the figures. "A couple others, too."

"Stockton?" the chief yelled. "That you?"

The spotlight beam shifted, and Troy got a good look

at everyone on board: Breck, one of his officers, and some Coast Guard kid at the helm. The guy couldn't have been more than twenty.

"Hey, there," Troy said as they drew up alongside. "Y'all find anything?"

Breck frowned at Elaina, and the younger cop answered for him. "Not yet," he said. "We're still on the northwest shore, though."

"Who's south?" Troy asked.

"That'd be the Coast Guard. And the sheriff's got the west side of the bay. You guys seen anything?"

"Not yet," Troy said.

"What about the bridge?" Elaina directed the question at Breck. "If someone came out here to dump a body and noticed the patrol boats, it wouldn't be a bad place to hide."

"Maynard's got it," Breck informed her.

"We'll cruise this stretch down to the point," Troy said. "See what we can turn up."

Breck scowled. Clearly, he wasn't too happy about their involvement, but the man didn't own the bay.

"Radio if you see anything," he said gruffly.

Troy nodded. "Will do."

The police boat pulled away, and Troy got the engine started again. He set a course from their current position down to Windy Point, which constituted the southern tip of the island.

For a while they cruised without talking. Troy followed an undulating route that mimicked the shoreline.

"That man hates me," Elaina stated.

"He doesn't like outsiders."

"He'd be smart to use me. Doesn't he know I can get him funding for this thing? Maybe even some more manpower?"

"He's got plenty of manpower, at the moment. Sheriff, Coast Guard. He's probably even borrowed a few guys from the neighboring counties."

Elaina shook her head. "Does he see what's at stake here? We've got at least three dead women, probably four. And the time between victims is narrowing."

Troy spotted a bump on the smooth line of the horizon.

"This thing needs a task force," she said. "A coordinated manhunt."

"Look. Up ahead."

She followed his gaze to the south.

"Sit down," he ordered. "And hold on."

"What is it?"

"A boat. South, near the wildlife park."

"What's it doing?" she asked.

"Leaving."

Troy hit the gas, and the boat surged forward. Elaina gripped the side as the wind whipped ruthlessly against her. Spray dampened her face and hair. It soaked through her T-shirt. She strained to see over the pointed hull, which rode high above the water.

"Are we gaining?" she yelled over the din.

"Yes." Troy stood at the helm, his gaze intent on the boat in front of them.

"Should I radio someone?"

"No."

They hit a wave, and she pitched forward.

"Sit down!" he barked, and she did.

What was this guy doing? Why try to outrun another boat, unless you had something to hide?

She reached back and felt the Glock at the small of her back, beneath her T-shirt. She peered over the windshield again. They were definitely gaining. What had once been a dark speck was now a boat-shaped shadow skipping along in front of them. Troy closed the distance until they were parallel with the other boat. Soon they pulled ahead.

"Hang on."

Troy made a sharp left turn, and Elaina grabbed the side. He curved around, then slowed abruptly. Next he flipped a switch, and a thick beam of light shone out across the water. A spotlight. Elaina surged to her feet.

"Damn it."

"What?" she asked.

The shaft of light illuminated a white boat as it slowed suddenly. Then it seemed to stop, but Elaina couldn't be sure. Her ears hummed and her body felt like it was still in motion. She squinted at the boat, at the lone man aboard.

"Goddamn it," Troy said.

"What?"

"A police boat." He switched off the spotlight. "It's only Maynard. We've been chasing our tail."

It was well past midnight when Troy swung the Ferrari into the Sandhill Inn's parking lot.

"Thank you for the ride," Elaina said stiffly, and he could tell she wanted to make a hasty exit.

"I'll walk you in."

"That's not necessary."

"I want to show you something," he said, and got out of the car. Jesus, she was paranoid. What'd she think he planned to do, jump her right there in the parking lot?

"This way," he said, jerking his head toward the side of the hotel.

She hesitated briefly, then followed him past a twenty-four-hour convenience store to a gravel parking lot and a sign that said PUBLIC BEACH ACCESS. They crossed the lot and reached a wooden ramp that arced over the sand dunes. In less than two minutes, they were on the beach in front of the Sandhill Inn.

"You're thinking he might have parked there," Elaina said.

"Might have."

"You're saying he took his own car? I was thinking he walked up from the beach, then used the victim's car to get to the boat dock."

"Maybe he did. But this is another possibility."

She glanced around thoughtfully. "It would make more sense," she said. "The cars have been bugging me. All parked at the boat docks like that, no fingerprints, the victims' clothes folded neatly on the seats."

"Seems staged."

"And too easy," she added. "Like he's leading us to the public docks. When in reality, he could be using another dock entirely. Maybe a private boat slip, either here or on the mainland."

"Could be."

Elaina looked up and down the beach. It was quiet. Just a few stragglers coming home from the bars, some not too steady on their feet.

"Maybe he knocked on her door, tried to lure her out with him," she said. "She might have recognized him from somewhere and said yes. Or maybe she said no, and he got out the syringe. An intramuscular injection doesn't take that much precision."

She was thinking out loud now, and Troy just watched her. He got that feeling again, like he didn't need to be here; she was a million miles away.

"Either way," she continued, "it wouldn't be hard to get a woman off this beach. She could practically be passed out, and she wouldn't look that different from everyone else stumbling home from the bars."

She turned to Troy, and he could see the concern etched on her face. She was thinking about Valerie, who was probably dead by now. And she'd be thinking about the next girl, too. "Breck's going to have to step things up. He needs help, whether he wants it or not."

She looked out at the waves. The breeze kicked up, and she shivered.

"You're wet," he said. "You need to get inside."

"I'm fine."

But she was still shaking, and he stifled the urge to pull her close and warm her up. His thoughts were harder to stifle, though. He wanted to drag her inside and into a steaming-hot shower.

"What do you think Maynard was doing?" she asked.

"Just what he said. Combing the shore."

"Yeah, but why'd he race off?"

"He said he didn't see us." Troy lifted a brow. "What, you don't believe him?"

"I just think he acted funny, that's all. Kind of defensive that we were there. Very territorial."

"Ah, that's just Maynard. Everything's a big pissing war with him."

She rubbed her arms and looked out at the surf, lost in thought again. This woman lived in her head. And it was starting to tick him off.

She turned and looked down the beach. "She played volleyball," she murmured.

"Who?"

"Gina Calvert. I bet she played right on this beach."

Troy followed her gaze to the abandoned volleyball net that was silhouetted in the moonlight.

"Or maybe she played in the pool, at Coconuts." Elaina looked at him. "Gina and the women she came down here with were all on the volleyball team at Trinity College. Gina was a setter."

"How do you know that?"

"It was in the newspaper, back in March."

She'd been following this thing since March? "Long memory," he said.

"I played volleyball in high school. It jumped out at me when I read the story." She looked away again. "It's a social game. Which is ironic, really, because her friends say she wasn't social at all, that she was very reserved, particularly with men. She wasn't comfortable flirting."

He stepped closer. Even in the dimness, he could see the worry line between her brows.

"You're identifying with her, Elaina. You're making it personal. Didn't they teach you not to do that up at the Academy?"

She shrugged. "I'll take any advantage I can get."

"What the hell does that mean?"

"Law enforcement is a boys' club," she said. "I've got the training. I keep up with the physical demands. I'm a decent shot, but not great. My advantage is my gender."

Her words got under his skin, and he wasn't sure why. "How is your being female an advantage when you're looking for some wack job who cuts up women?"

"I can put myself in her shoes," she said matter-of-factly. "I can interview her friends, her loved ones, learn everything I can about her. People tell me things they might not tell some big man with a badge." She gazed out at the water. "I can retrace her steps. Understanding her helps me figure out how she might have crossed paths with her killer. I can help identify this guy by seeing it from the victim's perspective."

Troy crossed his arms, not sure which unsettled him more—the idea of Elaina putting herself in the victim's shoes, or her letting her emotions get so tangled up in this case. "You make it sound like you've got some kind of psychic connection with her."

"I'm just getting to know her, really. It helps my case."

"How?"

Another shrug. "I can tell you, for example, that the man people heard in Gina's room the night of her disappearance—she didn't invite him home from the bar with her. It would have been totally out of character. He had some other reason for being there, some kind of ruse."

She gazed up at him, and Troy saw the moon reflected in her somber eyes. "Okay, you're right. I'm letting it get personal. But I want it personal. I want to know who these women were, not just what I see in their autopsy photos. Everyone keeps calling them 'girls' or 'victims,' but these women have names."

She turned toward the water and shivered again, and Troy's patience evaporated.

"Elaina? Dry clothes. Come on." He took her hand and tugged her up the beach. He half expected an argument, but this time she didn't fight him.

He sent her a sidelong glance as they trudged over the sand. More than dry clothes, she needed to unwind. Her mind and her body needed a break.

"The transportation thing," she said. "It's an interesting scenario. I wonder—"

She halted in her tracks and stared at the inn.

"What?" he asked.

"Someone's in my room."

CHAPTER 6

"Y̲ou probably left the light on."

"I didn't." She moved swiftly over the sand, making a beeline for the ground-floor suite where the lights blazed.

"Hey, wait!" He caught up to her and grabbed her arm. "Someone should check it out."

"What, like a cop?" The look of scorn she sent him would have turned a lesser man to stone.

"That's not what I meant. Just . . . shit, at least tell me you're armed."

She slipped a hand under her shirt and pulled out the Glock he'd seen the night before. "Stay here," she said, and turned around.

Him stay here? Fuck that.

He moved briskly beside her, looking for any movement behind the gauzy curtains. Every light appeared to be on. The glow spilled out onto the patio and Elaina skirted around it as she neared the door. She reached for the handle—

"Whoa, there, cowgirl."

Their heads whipped around. The voice came from

the neighboring patio, where a man sat on a chair in the shadows. He stood up.

"Oh my God," Elaina said. "Is that *you*?"

The man stepped into the light, and Elaina tucked her weapon away.

"You scared the crap out of me!" She threw her arms around him as Troy watched from the shadows. "I didn't know you were coming!"

Boyfriend? Possibly. Dark hair, trim build, about Elaina's age and height. He wore slacks and a dress shirt—no tie—with the sleeves rolled up.

And he was giving Troy a definite "what are you doing out with her at this hour" stare.

"Troy, meet Brett Weaver," Elaina said. "Weaver, this is Troy Stockton."

Recognition flashed across the guy's face, then disappeared. He gave a slight nod.

"When did you get here?" Elaina asked. "Did Scarborough send you?"

An agent. That explained the clothes but not the hostility. Maybe she was sleeping with him.

"Just thought I'd check in, that's all," he said. "I brought you your laptop. And some clothes from your place."

Your place.

Troy couldn't believe it had taken him this long to wonder if she was in a relationship. It didn't matter to him, really, but Elaina was a pretty straight arrow.

And on the subject of straight . . . Troy gave Weaver another once-over. Something about his voice and his body language told Troy that his interest in Elaina wasn't sexual.

Troy propped a shoulder against the wall and focused his attention back on their conversation.

"—but then we got an arrest this morning," the agent was saying.

"You're kidding."

"Downtown branch, just like we thought. Garcia and I made the collar. It was pretty intense."

She beamed at him. "Nice going! Your first big arrest! We should celebrate."

"That's part of the reason I came, actually." He glanced at Troy. "But it's getting late. We can catch up tomorrow, so—"

"Don't be ridiculous. Is this you next door?"

"Yeah. And I let myself into your room, put your stuff on the bed."

"My room was locked."

"That lock couldn't keep out a ten-year-old," the agent said, and Elaina flicked a glance at Troy.

"Well . . . let's have a toast," she said. "I've got a bottle of wine in my room. I'll bring it right over." She turned to Troy. "You're welcome to stay, of course."

Of course. And could the invitation have been delivered with less enthusiasm?

"I'll catch you later." He nodded at the agent, who—despite most likely being gay—was still sending out some of that hands-offa-her vibe. "Nice meeting you. You two have fun."

Elaina lay motionless in bed, but her body still seemed to be moving. The room was dark. Her head was spinning. And each time she closed her eyes, she was back aboard

Troy's speedboat. She could almost taste the brine on her lips as the Supra skipped over the waves.

He'd wanted to come in tonight. If Weaver hadn't been here, would she have let him? A week ago, she would have said no. She didn't sleep with men on a whim.

But something about Troy made her want to bend the rules. Just once in her life, she wanted to be someone besides herself, someone other than responsible Elaina. Serious Elaina. Focused, diligent, ambitious Elaina, who'd forgone a social life to pursue a career with the world's top law enforcement agency.

Where had this weakness come from?

Maybe Gina Calvert had met someone who brought out a similar weakness. Inviting an unknown man home would have been out of character for her—just like Elaina. But that didn't mean it hadn't happened.

Her cell phone chimed just beside her ear, and she snatched it up.

"McCord."

"Y'all polish off that wine?"

She sighed. "What is it? I was almost asleep."

"I've been thinking," Troy said. "You should get a second-floor room. If you plan to be here awhile, that is."

The phone beeped at her, telling her the battery was low. She kicked the covers off and switched on the lamp.

"Do you?" Troy asked.

"Do I what?" She found the charger on the coffee table and jammed it into the outlet beside the nightstand.

"Plan to be here awhile?"

"Yes." She paused, charger in hand, as she realized what she'd just said. Where had that come from?

She'd intended to leave Monday. That's what she'd told Weaver, at least. But she realized now that she had no intention of leaving yet, not until she made progress on this case.

"You need a second-floor room," he said.

"I specifically requested this suite."

"Yeah, and you've had your look around. Now get a different one."

The phone on the nightstand rang. Not a chime or a ringtone, but a shrill clanging noise, the likes of which she hadn't heard in years.

"I'll think about it," she told Troy. "Listen, someone's calling my room. I've got to go."

"Be smart, Elaina," he said, and hung up.

She plugged her BlackBerry into the charger as the princess phone clanged again. She snatched it up.

"McCord."

Silence.

"Hello?"

"Have you found her yet?"

The quiet voice sent a chill through her. "Who is this?" she demanded.

"I'm disappointed," he said. "You federal agents, I thought you'd raise the level of play."

Elaina's chest tightened. This could be a prank. Or it could be real.

Draw him out. Keep him talking. Establish a relationship.

"What's your name?" she asked. The voice sounded muffled, far-away, and she pictured some shadowy figure at a pay phone, talking through a bandanna.

"She's waiting for you, Elaina. This one's special, too. One of my best hides."

His hides? He was hiding them? Or did he mean hides, like hunting hides?

"Where is she?"

Laughter. "Nice try."

"Who are you?"

"Keep looking." The voice was serious again. "Valerie's waiting."

Elaina expected a crowd at Dot's Diner the next morning, but the place was practically empty. She spotted Cinco right away at a red vinyl booth in the back.

"Should I be worried?" she asked, sliding in.

"About?"

"Roaches? Mold? Slime in the ice machine?"

He smiled, his perfect teeth a flash of white against his olive skin.

"We missed the pre-church crowd," he said.

"You guys have a church?" Elaina hadn't seen it, and she'd done a full driving tour of Lito Island yesterday after picking up her car at the shop.

"North end of the island. It's small."

Elaina pulled a menu out from behind the napkin dispenser. "What's good here?"

"Depends how hungover you are."

She glanced up.

"I saw you at Coconuts," he explained.

Then he'd seen her leave with Troy. She wondered what he thought about that. Maybe nothing. She was pretty sure she'd already become fodder for at least a little island gossip, though. Especially after bumping into everyone out on the bay last night.

Practically in a lip-lock with Troy.

What are you doing, Lainey? It had taken Weaver all of two minutes to pick up on the sexual tension between her and Troy, and he was concerned, naturally. *Don't be naive here. The media is* not *your friend.*

"I feel fine," she told Cinco, just as the waitress appeared. Elaina tucked the menu back in its place. "I'll have an English muffin, please. And black coffee."

Cinco ordered something in Spanish and then picked up a file from the seat beside him.

"Here's what I've got." He opened the folder and pulled out a thin stack of papers held together with a binder clip. "Forty-two names, all with violent or sexual offenses dating sometime in the last fifteen years. I put the interesting ones on top."

He slid the rap sheets across the table, and she started thumbing through them. When the waitress returned with coffee, Elaina dropped her arm over the mug shot to block her view. Small-town grapevine and all that.

"Nine aggravated sexual assaults," Elaina said after she left. "Six armed robberies. What's this indecent exposure?"

"Ah, I wouldn't waste much time on him. He's kind of a kook. Likes to streak the crowd at the Fourth of July picnic every year."

Elaina's coffee was strong and hot, with a hint of cinnamon. She sipped it as she neared the bottom of the stack. She'd reached the second-to-last page when she froze—cup in midair—and stared down at Troy's mug shot.

"Aggravated assault?"

Cinco winced. "That was this thing over at the Dockhouse. Long time ago."

She skimmed the info. "He *stabbed* someone?"

"Yeah, but the guy was really out of line."

Elaina just stared at him, waiting for more.

"See, Troy's girlfriend at the time had just won fifty bucks off these guys at pool. One of them started talking trash to her. Him and Troy traded punches. The guy pulled a knife, but Troy took it right off him. Might have nicked him some. . . ." Cinco's voice trailed off and he looked apologetic.

"So now he has a criminal record over a game of pool." Elaina shook her head. *Men.*

"He's really a stand-up guy, though," Cinco said. "Just has a temper."

Elaina flipped to the last page, some thirty-nine-year-old who'd been arrested four times this year for smoking pot on the beach. Naked, evidently.

"Inoperable cancer," Cinco explained. "Hell, I'd be lighting up, too."

Elaina looked up to see Troy towering over their table. Faded jeans again. Black T-shirt. His shaggy hair was slicked back, hinting at a shower, but he hadn't bothered to shave.

"You look worse than your mug shot," she said drily.

Troy slid into the booth and scooted her over.

"Ex*cuse* me," she said as he reached across her to grab a menu.

"Your friend leave?" he asked her.

"He got called in this morning." But not before admonishing her to keep her distance from Troy. Weaver had good instincts about people, and he was protective of the ones he cared about. Sometimes annoyingly so.

Elaina stashed the file beside her purse and pretended

not to notice Troy's warm bulk beside her. Aggravated assault. With a knife, too. It should bump him right to the top of her suspect list, but it didn't. She glanced down at his denim-clad leg beside her. Maybe she was letting her attraction to him cloud her judgment.

But despite his rap sheet, Elaina's instincts told her he was safe. Instincts—plus the fact that she'd been *on* the phone with Troy when she'd received the call from the unsub—had made her scratch Troy off of her suspect list.

The waitress appeared with an English muffin and Cinco's whatever-it-was that smelled heavenly and came with a side of jalapeños.

"Okay, you win," Elaina told Cinco. "What is that, anyway?"

"Migas."

"I'll have the same," Troy told the waitress. "And coffee. Black."

"Here's that other thing you asked for." Cinco slid a single slip of paper across the table.

"Is this the list?" she asked, and Cinco grunted around a mouth full of eggs.

"What list?" Troy asked.

"Window peekers. The vast majority of serial killers start out as Peeping Toms," Elaina said, reading over the addresses and dates. "It's just something I wanted to check."

The incidents were between eight and fifteen years old, just as she'd requested. A report halfway down the list caught her attention. It had occurred a few weeks before Mary Beth Cooper's murder. She glanced at the address.

"Bay Port?" she asked.

"Yep." Cinco exchanged a look with Troy. "Same street where Mary Beth Cooper lived. Thought you might want it."

Uh, *yeah*. "Did the Bay Port police look into this?"

"No idea," Cinco said. "From what I hear, they barely got started on the case when the feds took over. She was connected with the Charles Diggins murders pretty quick there. Most of those victims were Latina, so it was being investigated by the feds as maybe a race thing."

Troy's breakfast arrived and he dug right in. Elaina watched him, wondering how he felt about her putting forward a theory that called his credibility into question. He didn't seem resentful, but he was a tricky man to read.

Elaina tucked the paper into her file. She'd make some calls this afternoon, see if the same family still lived at this address and if they'd mind sitting down with her. It might not go anywhere, but who knew? Maybe whoever had reported this Peeping Tom had gotten a look at him.

Elaina eyed Troy's sausage links as she nibbled her English muffin. She glanced up, and he was smiling at her.

"What?" she asked.

"Hungry?"

"No." She sipped her coffee.

"So let's have it, Cinc." He picked up a sausage and popped it in his mouth. "There any truth to that rumor about a task force?"

Cinco gave Elaina a sheepish look, and she knew she wasn't going to like this.

"There's a task force forming?" she asked.

He cleared his throat. "That's the word."

"Who's on it?" *And why am I the last to know?*

"I don't know yet. Breck's coordinating with the sheriff's office, the Texas Rangers. Looks like everybody's got a hand in."

Except for the FBI agent sent here to work the case. Elaina's temper simmered. This was bullshit. Again.

She rummaged through her purse and jerked a ten out of her wallet. "Excuse me," she said, placing it under her coffee cup.

She made her way to the front of the restaurant and stepped outside as she dialed her boss's number. Only then did she think to look at her watch. Ten-thirty on a Sunday morning. Would he be at church right now? Waking up with some girlfriend? Scarborough had no spouse, no kids. He was a highly demanding boss because personal commitments meant nothing to him.

"Scarborough." The voice was clear and alert. He hadn't been rolling out of bed.

"Sir. It's Elaina McCord. I hope you're not at church."

I hope you're not at church? What an idiotic thing to say.

"What is it, McCord? I'm in the middle of something."

"Right." She cleared her throat. "I'm on Lito Island assisting in the Whitney Bensen homicide. It seems they're putting a task force together, and I wanted to make sure—"

"Relax, you're on it."

She released a breath. "I am?"

"Yeah, this idea of yours about the Cooper connection, it's getting some legs."

"It's . . ." She wasn't sure what to say. She didn't want to discredit her own theory, but since when had anyone been taking her seriously?

"They found another body," Scarborough told her. "Not an hour ago. I just got off the phone with Breck."

Her stomach twisted. "Is it Valerie Monroe?"

"The missing med student, they think. I don't know her name."

"Valerie Monroe. What's the connection—"

"Geography. Killer dumped her in the exact same place as that Cooper girl."

CHAPTER 7

Cinco flashed his badge, and the cop manning the blockade waved him through. He drove past the crime-scene van and wedged his pickup truck into a spot between two sheriff's units.

"You need some shoes?" Cinco asked, eyeing Elaina in his passenger seat. She had on that same outfit from Friday, including the heels. They weren't all that high, but still. "I've probably got some duck boots in back. It'll be muddy."

"Sure."

He twisted around and dug through the crap in the back of his cab: clothes, fishing gear, tools. He handed her some mud-caked boots from the floor. She slipped her shoes off, and he watched—impressed—as she wrestled her feet into his boots without seeming to care about the dirt getting all over her pantsuit. Maybe she only *looked* uptight.

"So what's the protocol here?" she asked.

Or maybe not. "Protocol?"

"Who's in charge of this crime scene? I understand it's a park now? Nine years ago it was just private land transected by a highway."

"Yeah, they got some endangered bird nesting here. Some kind of crane or something. While back, a lot of the bird people pushed to have it made into a nature preserve. I'm not sure who's in charge, to tell you the truth."

She glanced out the window at all the law enforcement types standing around. The friendly Agent McCord from breakfast was long gone. She'd put on her game face.

"You ever worked a homicide before?" he asked.

She glanced over at him. "I participated in a drug raid a few months ago. A guy got shot. Died at the scene."

"This isn't like that," he said, needing to warn her. "I'm not saying you're not up for it or anything, it's just … it's bad, okay? I don't care how long you been on the job, what he does to these girls is bad."

"I know." She met his gaze, and he knew she was prepared. As prepared as you ever could be, but that didn't mean it wouldn't spook her. He'd seen some bad shit over the years, but nothing that compared to this.

He pushed open the door and got out. She followed suit.

"Hey," she said.

He glanced at her over the hood, and she smiled slightly. "Thanks."

"For what?" he asked.

"The boots, and you know, the rest of it."

She ducked under the crime-scene tape and trudged

across the field, right up to the group of men huddled together beside a wooden sign that read BAY VIEW NATURE PRESERVE.

Cinco looked around and tried to get the lay of the land. They were on the mainland side of Laguna Madre, just a few hundred feet in from the bay. The ground looked soft, despite the recent dry spell. A fairly large perimeter had been set up and almost everyone was milling around outside it. Some cops were reluctant to sign into a crime scene and make themselves fair game for a defense attorney down the road. No one wanted to be the jackass who touched the wrong thing and got some scumbag off on a technicality.

A guy Cinco recognized from the Lito County Sheriff's Department walked up to him.

"Hey," he said.

"Hey." Cinco remembered his name, finally. Ketchem. People called him Ketch.

"Man, oh, *man,*" Ketchem said, shaking his head. "This one's bad."

Cinco nodded.

"You never seen anything like it. Swear to God, I nearly booted up my breakfast."

Cinco watched Elaina. She stood beside a crime-scene technician, peering into a ditch.

"Vic's over there?"

"Yup. Guy dumped her in that gulley. Couple inches a water. Fish've been at her. Bugs, buzzards. Damn near everything's had a bite of her. Don't know how they're gonna get an ID."

The image Cinco had been trying to get rid of was back now—Whitney Bensen in vivid detail.

Elaina knelt down and pointed at something on the ground. She waved over a ranger who was standing nearby and exchanged words with him.

"She the fed?" Ketchem asked.

"Yeah."

He grunted something that could have meant anything from "She's hot" to "She looks like a pain in the ass."

Elaina stood up, and Cinco watched her talk to the ranger, then the sheriff. He had to admire her, just wading into the fray like that. She didn't act intimidated, even though he would've thought she would be. The only other woman around lay naked in that ditch, gutted with a hunting knife.

The smell alone had to be unbearable.

"This guy's a twisted fuck." Ketchem shook his head and turned his back on the scene. He looked pretty gray, and Cinco decided he probably *had* booted up his breakfast.

A second crime-scene van pulled up, and two men got out. They opened the back doors, and Cinco watched as they zipped themselves into some white coveralls. One of them took a stretcher from the back and the other grabbed a body bag. A white sedan pulled up beside it. Frank Cisernos. The ME wore khaki pants, a blue golf shirt, and a grim expression. Whatever plans he'd had for his Sunday afternoon had just been canceled. They'd do the autopsy today. Soon, most likely, before the body got any worse.

Cinco wiped his brow with the back of his arm. He gazed up at the sun. Not noon yet, but it was a hundred degrees, at least.

"Fuckin' heat's not helping," Ketchem said.

"Yeah." Cinco glanced over at Elaina, who had to have a strong stomach to be standing there just a few feet from the body.

He won't stop. She'd told him that yesterday as they'd sat in that stuffy conference room pulling together the suspect list. *He'll either get caught or get killed, but he won't stop.*

Cinco gazed up at the white-hot sun again. A pair of buzzards circled overhead, all the time in the world, just waiting for another turn. Meanwhile, he was about to spend the next three hours picking through grass and muck, looking for clues, while the techs spooned that poor girl out of the ditch. Cinco didn't want to be here again. Not today, not tomorrow, not next week. He wanted to nail this guy.

He watched Elaina. She met his gaze briefly, and he knew she felt the same way.

"Come on," he told Ketchem. "Let's do something useful."

Elaina sat in the Taurus and cursed the GPS. "Invalid Address," it told her for the third time. She took a deep breath and keyed in the letters again.

The passenger door jerked open.

"God, don't *do* that!"

Troy slid into the car and pulled the door shut. "Do what?"

She shot him a glare and turned her attention back to the navigation system. "I can't talk right now," she told him. "I'm on my way out."

"Field trip to the mainland?"

She glanced down at the GPS and muttered another curse.

"You don't need that thing," he said. "You got me."

Elaina rested her head back against the seat and sighed. She gazed through the windshield at the inn where she'd spent the past two nights not getting any sleep. Her energy was completely sapped. She felt irritable. It was after eight, but she'd skipped dinner because the mere thought of food repelled her.

"Rough day?"

His voice was quiet, and for some reason her eyes started to sting. *Shit*.

She cleared her throat. "You can't ride in my car. It's against regulations."

"We can take mine."

"Forget it. I'm not pulling up to this woman's house in a Ferrari."

"I brought the pickup."

She glanced at the rearview mirror and saw his black F-150 parked in the row behind them. Her resistance flagged.

She turned to look at him. "Why are you helping me?"

"Damned if I know."

"If you quote me in your book—"

"I won't."

"—I'll be forced to hurt you."

His eyes sparked at the threat.

Elaina looked away. She chewed on her lower lip and debated the wisdom of accepting help, once again, from a ridiculously attractive man who was practically a reporter. There wasn't much to debate. It was a bad idea.

"Come on." He patted her hand and got out of the car.

She sighed again. Then she grabbed her purse from the backseat and shoved open the door.

Her vehicle was a piece of crap. The navigation system inside it was a piece of crap. And she wasn't up for another challenge tonight. She crossed the parking lot to Troy's truck, stepped onto the shiny chrome running board, and hoisted herself inside.

"How'd the autopsy go?" he asked as he fired up the engine.

She shook her head.

"Any chance of getting an ID soon?"

Elaina clenched her teeth as she recalled the ME actually *removing* the skin from the victim's hand to get a set of prints. It had been so decomposed, it had just slid off like a glove, and Elaina almost had to duck out of the autopsy suite and throw up.

She swallowed the bile in her throat now. "Nothing confirmed yet. But we recovered some jewelry. A dragonfly pendant her parents had told us about. We're fairly sure it's her."

"Valerie Monroe?"

"Yes."

Troy pulled onto the highway and headed north, toward the bridge leading off the island. It was getting dark out, and the neon signs were starting to light up at the bars and restaurants lining the road. Tourists crowded the sidewalks, undeterred by some sick freak and his hunting knife.

"Her parents were at the station house this afternoon," Elaina said.

"Valerie's?"

"Yeah." She paused, remembering the woman sitting in that reception room, staring blankly out the window. "I guess no one would give them any news, everyone was avoiding them. Anyway, her father saw my badge and pulled me aside. There wasn't much I could tell him, but I promised to keep him updated, told him we're doing everything we can." A knot formed in Elaina's chest. "I've never felt so inadequate in my life."

The truck filled with silence. As they crossed the causeway, Elaina gazed out over the water. The setting sun made it shimmer with gold, but the postcard-perfect scene did nothing for her. She felt flat.

"Been doing some poking around," Troy said.

She looked at him.

"Some folks in Bay Port remember a rash of break-ins about ten years ago. Someone was rifling through women's underwear drawers, taking stuff here and there."

"Is this on record?" she asked.

"No one ever called the cops. He wasn't taking valuables or anything, so I guess it seemed harmless. And maybe the women were embarrassed about it at the time."

Elaina shook her head. One of those "harmless" break-ins could have turned tragic if some woman had come home and found a man in her bedroom. Cops had a tendency to shrug off panty raids, but those crimes were often warning signs. It was all about patterns of behavior—persistent, disturbing patterns that got worse over time.

At least her father believed so. And Big Mac McCord was known for being right. His conclusions about violent offenders were based on hundreds of jailhouse interviews and years of painstaking research.

Elaina shifted in her seat. Thinking of her dad made her feel anxious. She hadn't talked to him in weeks and she tried to tell herself it was because they'd both been busy. But she was beginning to feel hurt by his lack of interest in her new job. Somehow she'd always thought that when she finally joined the Bureau, they'd have lots in common. But their relationship was as silent now as it had ever been, maybe even more so.

Elaina's mother had been the talker in the family. Julia McCord could go on and on, a mile a minute, in a hyper way that made people uncomfortable. But for all her chatter, she'd never found a way to talk about what really mattered to her—which was one reason Elaina and her dad had been stunned when she'd packed up one day and simply walked out. Elaina had suspected she was unhappy, but she'd never considered that she might leave. It had seemed so unreal. Mothers did not just walk out on their eleven-year-old daughters, their husbands, their lives.

"You okay?"

She glanced at Troy. Straightened her shoulders. "Fine, why?"

"'Cause you look like hell. No offense."

Elaina bit back a retort because she knew he was probably right. She flipped the vanity mirror down to confirm it. The scalding shower she'd taken after the autopsy hadn't helped much. She still looked pale and worn out. She hadn't bothered with makeup tonight and she'd left her hair down around her shoulders instead of pulling it back like she typically did.

"You should eat something," Troy said. "We can stop after this."

"My appetite's on vacation. I just want to wrap up this interview and crash."

He shrugged noncommittally as they took the Bay Port exit just north of the causeway.

Elaina tried to muster some energy. She was investigating here. She needed to pay attention. "Tell me about your hometown. What's it like?"

"You've never been here?"

"Only the refinery," she said.

"Well, that's pretty much it."

Elaina glanced around. This was it? She saw mostly empty fields and a few low buildings up ahead in the distance.

"And how come you've been to the refinery?" he asked.

"I took a trip up here to destroy evidence."

He cast a curious look in her direction. "You wanna explain that?"

"Weaver and I. It was one of our more interesting assignments, actually. We spent the morning filling up a van with coke and marijuana that had been used at trial. Drove up with a police escort. Then supervised everything as TexOil burned it up in one of their jumbo incinerators."

"A full van, huh? Sounds like a party."

"Not really. It took all day, but at least it was a break from the routine."

They drove in silence for a while as Elaina took in the town. She spotted a supermarket, a gas station, a Dairy Queen.

"You and Weaver, you seem like more than just coworkers. You two pretty close?"

She glanced over at him, surprised by the question.

"You could say that. He kind of took me under his wing on my very first day."

She remembered meeting him in the break room. *Special Agent McCord. Welcome to Brownsville.* He'd looked her up and down and smiled. *I see you just graduated from the Academy.*

How'd you know that?

Because you look like Batman. You might want to think about leaving some of that gear at home. Not a lot of runnin' and gunnin' your first year.

Weaver's advice had prompted her to stash her pepper spray and handcuffs and extra magazines in her desk that first day, and she'd trusted his guidance ever since.

Troy slowed as he neared what looked like one of only two stoplights.

"Where do people hang out?" Elaina asked.

"Most head for the island. Not the tourist strip, but the bay side. For shopping, there's Corpus. The nearest steak house is in Brownsville."

The light turned green and he passed a small strip mall with beige awnings that badly needed replacing. A liquor store. A Laundromat. No bank. No Target, no Chili's, nothing that even hinted at coming prosperity. The town had a certain defeated aura about it, as if it had already come to terms with its fate. She glanced at Troy and sensed something. Was it embarrassment? She didn't know him well enough to be sure.

"Cinco says you started out in newspapers?"

He glanced at her. If he was surprised she'd been asking around about him, he didn't let on.

"He didn't say where, though," she continued. "I'm assuming Bay Port doesn't have its own paper."

"*The Lito County Register.* They operate out of that building up there, just past the post office."

Elaina looked past the other stoplight to the plain brick structure just beyond the government building with the telltale flagpole out front. As they passed the *Register* office, she noticed the darkened windows, the empty parking lot. Not exactly a hive of activity.

She glanced at Troy as he hung a left onto a state highway. The simple act of driving through his hometown reinforced her impression that he hadn't come from privilege, that he'd earned what he had. "Bootstrapism," her father would call it. Elaina called it a strong work ethic, something she deeply admired in a man, more than money or fancy degrees or good looks. She'd met way too many men in college and grad school who had been handed everything on a silver platter, and they hadn't impressed her in the least.

She looked at the strong set of Troy's jaw, at his large hand on the steering wheel.

He glanced at her. "What?"

"Nothing."

"Sunday night, things get pretty quiet," he said. "The refinery operates twenty-four-seven. Everything else closes at six, except the gas station and the Dairy Queen. I take it you called ahead to the house?"

Elaina pulled her purse into her lap and flipped open her notepad. "I spoke to someone named Ronnie Dupree."

Troy smiled.

"You know her?"

"She coached drill team up at the high school a couple eons ago. Probably still does."

"She sounded kind of old on the phone," Elaina said.

"That'd be the smoker's cough."

The truck slowed, and Troy turned onto a two-lane road. Elaina didn't see a street sign. Maybe it was good that she'd come here with a guide.

He slowed once again at another turnoff, this one leading into a pocket of one-story brick homes. The houses were fairly spread out, yet they all resembled one another except for the various lawn ornaments.

But "ornaments" was a euphemism. Elaina squinted into the falling darkness and made out a car up on cinder blocks, an overturned swing set, a septic tank. Troy pulled into a driveway, and the headlights swung across a yard dotted with pink flamingoes. He cut the engine, and Elaina heard a bark in the distance. He pushed open the door, and the light above them came on.

She caught his arm. "*I* will conduct the interview," she said sharply. "And whatever she tells us is off the record, as far as you're concerned."

He gave her a "get real" look.

"I'm serious. You need her for a source, come back later. This is my meeting. If you've got a problem with that, stay in the car."

"Truck."

"Whatever."

He leaned closer and rested his forearm on the back of her seat. "Anyone ever tell you you're kinda bossy, McCord?"

"I'm not kidding. I need you to keep it zipped."

He smirked. "I'll do my best," he said, clearly lying.

She slipped out of the truck. An enormous black thing hurled itself at the chain-link fence, and she jumped backward, pressing herself against the truck.

"Easy, there. Just a dog," Troy said.

She tried to ignore the ferocious barks as it lunged, again and again, at the fence lining the driveway. The front porch light went on, and a screen door squeaked open.

"Bear! Knock it off!" A woman with a pile of blond hair leaned outside. She squinted at Troy as he approached. Elaina cut a wary glance at Bear, who was still barking, and rounded the hood to the footpath leading up to the door.

"You from the FBI?" the woman asked Troy.

"No, ma'am. I'm Troy Stockton. Agent McCord's right here."

"Troy *Stock*ton?" She stepped out onto the concrete stoop and fisted her hands on her hips. "Well, my lordy, look at you! It's been years!"

She gave him a heavily lipsticked smile. She had to be at least sixty, but the T-shirt and leggings showed off the body of a much younger woman. She wore white Keds and socks with those little pom-poms on the back, and Elaina wondered if she'd ever been on a drill team herself.

"Troy *Stock*ton." She shook her head. "The famous author. I can't believe it."

He shot a look at Elaina. "This is Special Agent Elaina McCord." He moved aside to make room for her in front of the welcome mat. "Elaina, this is Ronnie Dupree, coach of the Bay Port Wranglerettes."

The woman beamed. "*Former* coach," she said, evidently delighted by this introduction. At last she turned her attention to Elaina. "Nice to meet you. Y'all come on in."

Troy leaned back against the screen door and ushered Elaina inside. She shot him a warning look, which he ignored.

She stepped onto mauve carpet that recently had been vacuumed, judging by the marks. A rose-colored sectional sofa dominated the living room, and on every available tabletop sat a silk flower arrangement. The air smelled like vanilla-scented Glade and cigarette smoke.

"Nice place you got here," Troy said.

"Well, thank you. I like it."

"And is it just you now?"

"Just me and Bear." She smiled at him. "Sabrina's been gone since graduation." She glanced at Elaina. "Can I get y'all some tea?"

"That would be great, thank you," Elaina said.

Ronnie vanished into the kitchen, and Troy ambled over to the mantel and picked up a framed photograph. It showed a blonde in a drill team uniform.

"Sabrina still live in town?" he called into the kitchen.

"She's married, lives in Corpus. I've got three grand-babies now. Can you believe it?"

Elaina heard the back door open, and Bear came tearing into the house.

"Now, you behave," Ronnie scolded him.

The dog trotted into the living room, and Elaina held out a hand for him to sniff. He was some sort of German shepherd mix, she guessed. She crouched down and scrubbed him between the ears.

"You're a dog person."

She glanced up, and Troy was smiling at her.

"You have something against dogs?"

"Not at all. You just seemed pretty scared back there."

"He took me by surprise, that's all. I love dogs." She stood up and tucked her hands in her pockets, much to Bear's disappointment.

Troy was still smiling. "Do you have one?"

"No. Someday, though." Someday when she lived somewhere besides a minuscule apartment and spent more than five minutes a week at home.

Elaina glanced around the room, taking everything in. She liked to conduct interviews in people's homes whenever possible. You could learn so much by seeing the way people lived. Elaina's gaze lingered on the worn green recliner in the corner. The upholstery clashed with the rest of the decor. On the wall behind the chair were several mounted fish.

Ronnie returned with two tall glasses that were already sweating.

"Looks like your husband was quite a fisherman," Elaina said.

Ronnie glanced at her with a startled look.

"I noticed the trophies."

Ronnie turned and smiled fondly at the corner with the recliner. "He loved the water. You heard the term *golf widow*? Guess you could say I was a fishing widow long before I was a real one." She paused. "For years I been meaning to put all that away, but I never can bring myself to do it."

Elaina smiled politely and sampled her tea. It was cold and sugary, and she took another gulp.

"Y'all sit down." Ronnie perched on the edge of a floral-print wing chair and looked at Elaina. "Now, what can I do for you? You said something about a Peeping Tom in the neighborhood? Must be serious to have the FBI involved." A carefully penciled eyebrow lifted. "Don't suppose this has to do with that girl they found this morning at the bird park?"

"Actually, yes," Elaina said before Troy could take control of the conversation. She sat down on the sofa while he continued to stand beside the fireplace. "We're going back and taking a closer look at certain crimes in the area over the past ten years."

"You're talking about the Peeping Tom from ten *years* ago?"

"I believe it was nine," Elaina said, pulling her notepad from her purse. Bear walked over and parked himself on top of her feet.

"Well, that was a long time ago," Ronnie said. "I'm not sure what all I can tell you. I saw him creeping around back there, and I knew what he was up to."

"What was he up to?" Elaina asked.

Ronnie gave her a disgusted look. "Nothing good, I know that." She offered Elaina a white crocheted coaster.

"The police report doesn't mention a physical description." Elaina rested her tea on the table atop the coaster. "Do you recall what he looked like?"

"I didn't get a good look."

"Maybe he was tall? Short? Do you remember what color hair he had?" Elaina held her pen poised above her notepad, but the expression on Ronnie's face had her hopes fading.

"It was dark," she said. "All I saw was a shadow."

Elaina's chest tightened with frustration. She'd known this was a long shot, but she'd been hoping for *some*thing. An incident on Mary Beth's street near the time of her murder was just too coincidental to ignore.

"Can you remember any details at all about that night?" she persisted. "Maybe a strange vehicle parked nearby? Maybe an obscene phone call?"

"I don't remember anything like that."

"What about Sabrina?" she asked, grasping at straws now. "Did she mention anyone bothering her at school or maybe at work? How old was she at the time?"

"She was a senior in high school. She didn't have a job or anything, not with all the time she spent dancing." Ronnie looked at Troy, then Elaina, and seemed to read their disappointment. "All I really recall was seeing some man creeping around the yard. Sabrina never could remember to close her shades when she changed clothes, you know. I saw him out there twice. Second time I'd 'bout had it."

"You'd had it," Elaina repeated. "So the second time, you called the police?"

"No, *first* time, I called the police." Ronnie crossed her arms. "They took their sweet time coming out here, too. By the time they finally got here, he was long gone."

Elaina made a note in her pad and glanced up at Ronnie. "And the second time?"

"Second time, I shot him in the ass."

CHAPTER 8

"You shot him in the *ass*? Like . . . with a gun?"

Elaina glanced at Troy in time to see him shake his head at the stupidity of her question.

"It was my thirty-eight Smith & Wesson," Ronnie said. "I can show it to you if you like."

Elaina made another note in her pad before getting up to go to the back door. Everyone followed, including Bear.

"Where were you standing?" she asked Ronnie.

"Well, lemme think . . ." Ronnie opened the back door and pushed forward the screen, which made a high-pitched screech. Bear bolted from the house.

"Now, see, that was my mistake. He heard the screen and took off."

"Tell me about the shot," Elaina said, looking out over the weedy lawn illuminated by floodlights. "Did you have these lights at the time?"

"Not then," she said. "I put those in after."

"And do you know if you actually hit anything?"

"Sure did. At least I think I did, because I heard a yelp. Real loud and painful-like, back there by the shed."

Elaina looked at the yard, her heart hammering now. This was a good lead. Maybe someone had been treated in a local ER that night for a gunshot wound. It was worth checking into.

If they could pin down the date.

"And did you report this second incident to the police?" she asked, then gave Troy a pointed look, hoping he'd catch her meaning. He did.

"You mind if I have a look around, ma'am?" he asked Ronnie as he started down the back steps.

"Go right ahead." Then she turned to Elaina. "What would they do about it? They didn't give a damn the first time." She gazed out at her yard, where Troy was now prowling around the storage shed with Bear at his heels. "I'll tell you what, raising a pretty daughter alone is no picnic. You have to fend for yourself half the time. That's why I keep my gun handy. That's why I got Bear, too."

Elaina focused her attention on Ronnie again. She hadn't reported the incident, so Elaina needed every detail she could get to narrow down the date.

"Tell me what happened, both before and after you shot at him."

"I had the back door open that night, letting the breeze in," Ronnie said. "The lights were off in here while I was busy in the kitchen. When I walked through the living room, I saw this man leaning against the shed. Perfect view straight into Sabrina's room."

Troy paused at the back corner of the shed. He ran his hand over the wood. He dug into the back pocket of his jeans and pulled out a penlight.

"He was smoking a cigarette, too, and watching her," Ronnie continued. "I remember that now. I thought he might be waiting, I don't know, for us to go to bed or something. It was creepy."

Elaina heard the shed door creak open as she jotted down a note about the cigarette.

"Anyway, I went into the bedroom, got my thirty-eight, then came right back to this spot," Ronnie said. "My mistake was the screen door. I should have just shot right through it, but I pushed it open. He turned tail and ran."

"You fired just one shot?"

Ronnie nodded. "One shot."

She made another note.

"Elaina? You want to come see this."

She glanced up. Across the lawn, Troy emerged from the storage shed. "What is it?" she asked hopefully.

The answer was in his eyes when he smiled at her. "Looks like we've got a slug."

"Can you *believe* it?" Elaina asked breathlessly as Troy backed out of Ronnie's driveway. "A through-and-through bullet!"

He cast a glance at her. Her excitement was palpable; he'd never seen her so revved up.

"I mean, what are the odds?" She flattened her hand against her chest and shook her head. "We might get a DNA sample!"

"It's possible."

"I mean, what a stroke of *luck*."

He cut another look at her. She was sitting there actually grinning. Her smile lit up her entire face.

"Guess it was worth the trip, huh?"

She laughed. "Guess so."

"I gotta tell you," he said, "I thought it was a wild-goose chase."

She shook her head again in disbelief. "I can't get over it. A *lead*. And after today . . ." Her voice trailed off.

"After today, what?"

He glanced over and saw that she'd covered her eyes with her hand and turned away.

Jesus, was she . . . ? "Elaina?"

He heard a quiet sniff.

"Elaina, are you crying?"

She shook her head, but she *was* crying. She wouldn't look at him as she sniffled softly in the seat beside him.

He stared ahead, shocked.

"Sorry," she mumbled. "I don't know what's wrong with me."

He kept his eyes on the road, trying to give her some space.

"God, I *never* cry. This is so stupid. Please don't tell anyone."

He looked at her. "Who would I tell?"

"I don't know, just—" She pressed the back of her hand against her nose. "Just don't write about this, okay? I'll never live it down."

He pulled over near a street lamp and shoved the truck into park. She glanced around, alarmed. Then she looked up at him with those ice-blue eyes that looked bluer than ever right now because she was crying, and he felt a pinch in his chest.

"Elaina. I'm gonna tell you again. I'm not quoting you. I'm not writing about you. I'm writing about this case. *Not* you. So quit being so paranoid."

She looked at her lap and seemed to be trying to rein in her emotions. She nodded. "Sorry." She dabbed her cuff against her nose. "I just feel . . . I don't know. I don't know what's wrong with me today."

"Well, shit, you spent half the afternoon at a murder scene. You watched an autopsy. You talked to a grieving family. Then you spent the evening chasing down leads."

She nodded and looked away. She cleared her throat. "You're right. I'm just tired." She took a deep breath and smoothed her hair back. Then she glanced at the BlackBerry in her lap. "I need to call Scarborough." She punched some numbers into her phone, and he noticed her hands were trembling.

Troy put the truck in gear and pulled back into traffic. She left her boss a voice mail, then dropped her phone into her purse and leaned her head back against the seat. She gazed out the window and seemed calmer.

"I'm just so relieved, you know? I finally did something right."

He glanced over and saw a faint ghost of the smile she'd had a few minutes ago.

It was the smile that worried him. He was almost certain she was in for a disappointment.

"You really think this'll pan out?" he asked.

"What do you mean?"

"The crime-scene techs. You really think Scarborough's going to send a team out there to recover that bullet? And then have it tested?"

Her eyebrows arched. "Of course we'll have it tested. There could be DNA—"

"After ten years?"

"It's possible. What, you think I should *ignore* a piece of evidence like that? It could be our unsub. He could be in the system already."

"I didn't say you should ignore it. I just think you're going to have a tough time getting anyone to look at it in a hurry. Isn't your lab pretty backlogged?"

"Yes." She sounded defensive now.

"You really think this is going to get any kind of priority? A decade-old slug?"

She got quiet and looked out the window. The euphoria had evaporated.

"If your boss gives you any trouble, I know a private lab where you can take it," he said. "You heard of the Delphi Center?"

"Who hasn't?"

"I know a tracer there. She's at the top of her field with DNA testing. I can give her a call for you."

"That won't be necessary. I'll handle it," she said.

"Suit yourself." He cast a sidelong glance at her. "So how'd you know Ronnie was a widow? I assumed she was divorced."

Elaina shrugged.

"No, really. What tipped you off?"

She cleared her throat. "Her living room. Divorcées don't typically put up shrines to their ex-husbands. If I had to guess, I'd say she's still in love with him."

Troy watched her, surprised. First the tears, now the sentimental commentary. Elaina had a soft side that he never would have expected from the no-nonsense FBI agent he'd first seen in action at the marina.

They reached the island, and instead of turning right, toward the Sandhill Inn, he hung a left. Elaina was so preoccupied with her thoughts, she didn't even seem to register where they were going. He pulled into a gas station parking lot.

"What are we doing?" she asked, looking around now.

"Picking up some beer."

"For what?"

"Us."

"I should get back to my room," she said. "My supervisor might call. And I have work to do tonight."

He reached over and rested a hand on her shoulder. His thumb brushed the side of her neck, and his gaze locked on hers. "Don't you think you've done enough today?"

"I still have—"

"Take a breather, Elaina." He squeezed her shoulder. "You're wound so tight, you're like a guitar string about to pop."

She watched him for a long moment. "And having a beer with you is going to cure me of this condition?"

"Can't hurt. Come on, I'm buying."

She looked out the window uncertainly, and he could tell she was wondering where they were going to drink these beers. Her place? His? He just sat there, letting her wonder.

She glanced at her watch. "*One* beer. And then I have to get back to my room."

"That won't be a problem."

As he disappeared into the gas station, Weaver's words of warning came back to her, along with a tiny measure of common sense.

Beer. Man. Moonlight. Elaina knew exactly where this was heading, and she didn't want to go there. Or rather, she absolutely *did* want to go there, but she knew it would be a mistake. This was her first big case. She was at a turning point in her career. It was definitely not the time to have a fling with a stranger, particularly one who could cause her all kinds of professional problems, if he wanted to.

Would he do it?

She didn't know. He'd said he wasn't going to put her in his book, but she wasn't sure she could trust him.

Elaina sighed, annoyed with herself. Why was she feeling this temptation now? She'd gone through twenty-two weeks at the Academy and avoided all the random hookups that were so common among new agent train-ees. Most of the single members of her class had worked hard and played hard. She supposed it wasn't surpris-ing—the predictable result of cramming hundreds of twenty- and thirty-somethings together to sweat and spar and stay up all night studying. The Academy was a pressure cooker, and many saw sex as an effective rem-edy for stress.

Elaina, not so much. She'd sought her physical release on the nine-mile obstacle course, known as the Yellow Brick Road for the painted yellow rocks showing run-ners how to navigate their way through the wooded trail. SUCK IT IN! HURT. AGONY. PAIN. LOVE IT! The signs posted along the trail had been her motivation, her reminder that pain was necessary, that perseverance was critical.

And when the academic pressure had started to build, she'd sacrificed sleep and poured more hours into studying. Week after week, she'd plodded her way through, immune to the subtle come-ons from the men around her. The ability to ignore distractions and focus on a goal had always been one of her best skills.

And now it was failing her.

A trio of girls in bikini tops and cutoffs exited the store and piled into a convertible. Music blared from the speakers as they peeled out of the parking lot and turned onto Lito Highway.

Elaina watched the car fade away and felt wistful. A pang of regret for something she'd lost, but never had. And then the wistfulness disappeared, and she wondered whether each of those girls would make it home safely. Probably they would. But possibly one of them wouldn't.

The door jerked open and Troy slid behind the wheel. He handed her a six-pack of Dos Equis, and the bottles were already slick from the heat. He backed out of the space.

"I just got a text message from my boss," Elaina said.

Troy turned onto the highway and glanced at her.

"He wants me to call him, so I'm going to have to take a rain check."

He didn't say anything as he cruised down the highway in the direction of her hotel. As he neared the inn, he put on his turn indicator, and she realized the flaw in her plan. She didn't want him walking her to her room.

"Actually, could you drop me off next door? At that little grocery place?" She smiled at him. "I skipped dinner, and I need to pick up some things."

He slid a look at her as he passed the hotel. "Appetite's back, huh?"

"Yeah."

He turned into the Quick Mart lot and found a space right in front of the entrance.

"Thank you," she said, pushing the door open. "And for taking me to Ronnie's, too. I really appreciate it. I'll let you know how this thing turns out with the bullet."

"I'll drive you back to the inn."

"No need. It's just next door." She smiled. "Anyway, thanks."

She felt his gaze on her as she entered the grocery store. She blinked at the bright fluorescent lighting and took a moment to get her bearings. She actually did need some groceries. That hadn't been a lie. She snatched up a basket and filled it with the same items that occupied her pantry at home: granola bars, sunflower seeds, pretzels. In the refrigerated section, she grabbed a six-pack of yogurt and some fruit before heading to the check-out counter.

As she walked back to the inn, she congratulated herself on resisting the urge to do something incredibly stupid. It was a wise decision. She should be pleased with herself.

Instead, she felt cranky.

She passed the front desk, nodding at Brenda, the night manager, before walking down the long, carpeted hallway that grew dimmer as she neared the Sand Dollar Suite. The overhead light was out near her door, and she made a mental note to mention it to the front desk in the morning.

She let herself in and switched on the light. The maid had been here, and it smelled like lemons again. She put the grocery bags on the dresser and stashed a few things in the mini-fridge before plugging her phone into its charger. Still nothing from Scarborough.

Troy had been right. All her muscles were tied up in knots. But what she needed more than beer and companionship was a hot shower.

She stood under the scalding spray and thought about her discovery. How would her boss react? With skepticism, most likely. A nine-year-old bullet was a shaky lead at best. And Elaina's request that Scarborough send a team out to recover it from Ronnie's shed could get her laughed out of the office. When her boss had told her that she could offer to fast-track lab work for this case, he'd meant once they'd developed a suspect. Blind DNA tests were not the norm.

But even the prospect of embarrassment wasn't enough to make her ignore the possibility that the through-and-through bullet they'd found tonight might have their unsub's DNA on it. And if that same genetic profile was already in the database . . . She backed away from the thought. She didn't want to get her hopes up.

Elaina squeezed the water from her hair and stepped out of the shower. She dried off, then wiped the fog from the mirror with the towel before wrapping it around her body. Troy was right. She *did* look like hell. She ran a comb through her hair and studied her reflection in the glass. Her eyes were bloodshot. Her skin was a combination of too-pale from hours cooped up in an office and too-pink from her recent adventure on Troy's fishing boat. But who cared, really? She hadn't come to this island to pick up men. She dropped the comb in her travel kit and jerked open the bathroom door.

Her heart lurched. The lamp was on. And Troy Stockton was stretched out on her bed.

"*How* did you get in here?" She stalked over to the bedside.

He gave her an insolent look as he lifted a bottle of Dos Equis to his lips and took a sip.

A warm breeze wafted over her shoulders, and she glanced across the room to the open slider. She strode over to it, dragged it shut, and flipped the latch.

"I told you, I have work to do." She jerked the curtain closed and whirled around. "What are you doing here?"

"Just proving a point." He put his beer on the nightstand, stood up, and sauntered over to her. He rested his hands on his hips and gazed down at her, and she was acutely aware of her damp hair and skimpy towel.

His gaze dropped, then came up again. "Put some clothes on. We're getting you a new room."

"I don't need a new room."

"I'm not asking, McCord. I'm telling. Either you get yourself a new room or you're coming home with me."

Elaina stepped back, clutching her towel. Something dangerous flared in his eyes. "I already requested one," she said, "but there's nothing available on the upper floors right now. The manager said she'd try again tomorrow."

"Did you tell her you're an FBI agent?"

"What does that have to do with anything?"

"Christ, throw your weight around some. Flash your badge."

"It's not a Triple-A card!" She walked over to the dresser and pulled open a drawer. "I'll ask again tomorrow," she said over her shoulder. "Something might have opened— What are you doing?"

He was on the princess phone now. "Brenda? Hey, it's Troy Stockton." A smile spread across his face. "I'm good, thanks. Listen, honey, I need a favor. I'm in 132 with Special Agent Elaina McCord. The FBI sent her here to help out with that murder case."

Elaina huffed out a breath and grabbed a handful of clothes.

"Uh-huh . . . No joke . . . Yeah, she's got a badge and everything."

Elaina rolled her eyes and walked into the bathroom.

"I don't know. Lemme ask her." Troy put his hand over the phone. "Hey, have you ever shot anybody?"

She slammed shut the door.

"I don't think so," she heard him say. "Yeah, just those paper targets. Anyway, she needs a new room tonight. Something on the second or third floor."

Elaina pulled on her jeans and shoved her arms into the rumpled blouse she'd been wearing earlier. She jammed her feet into sneakers, not bothering with socks. Of all the arrogant, heavy-handed—

The door opened a few inches. "I got you all set," he said through the gap.

She yanked the door open and brushed past him. "I can't believe you did that."

"Better pack up." He looked at his watch. "She's meeting us at Room 346 in five minutes."

"You're really infuriating, you know that?"

"So I've been told."

She watched him for a long moment. There was a determined look in his eyes that she hadn't seen before. It told her arguing would be pointless. And she didn't really want to argue anyway when she knew he was right. Some guy who could very well be the killer had the phone number to this room and knew she was staying here.

Troy's eyebrows tipped up. He knew he'd won.

Elaina ignored him for the next ten minutes as she packed her things, exited the Sand Dollar Suite, and rode the elevator up to the third level. The doors were spaced farther apart up here. These were probably larger suites, which was going to be hell on her budget. It probably never occurred to Troy to inquire about a little detail such as room rates.

Brenda stood in front of a room at the end of the hallway. She smiled shyly as Elaina approached with Troy at her side.

"I can't believe you're with the FBI," she gushed. "I don't think we've ever had a federal agent stay here."

"Sorry to be so much trouble," Elaina said as Brenda opened the door.

"No trouble at all." Brenda moved aside and ushered them in.

Elaina stepped over the threshold and froze.

"It's our honeymoon suite," Brenda said when Elaina turned to gape at her.

"I can't possibly stay here."

"It's perfect," Troy said. "Thanks a lot, Brenda."

Elaina closed her eyes and took a deep breath. Then she crossed the enormous room and dropped her bag on the sofa beside the *fireplace*. If this suite cost less than four hundred dollars a night, she'd be amazed.

She pulled open a huge armoire and noted the fully stocked snack tray, complete with gourmet chocolate and roasted cashews. She opened the mini-fridge and discovered an array of miniature liquor bottles, all top-shelf brands.

Elaina turned away and caught a glimpse of the bathroom. It was decorated in the same quaint style as the bathroom downstairs, only instead of the little claw-footed tub, this room had a double shower and a Jacuzzi tub big enough for a swim team.

At a loss for words, she walked to the balcony and stepped out.

Moonlight glittered off the waves as they rolled against the sand. The breeze felt soft on her skin as she leaned against the railing and looked out over the shore. From this high up, she could see all the way to Coconuts, with its flickering tiki torches.

The door slid shut with a *thump*. Troy's boots scraped over the tile as he walked up behind her. His big, warm palms settled on her shoulders.

"Troy—"

"Shh." He started kneading, and as much as she wanted to, she couldn't step away. The pads of his thumbs dug into her muscles, magically homing right in on all those knots she'd been carrying around. Her head sagged forward. How had this happened? She'd done the smart thing tonight, and yet here she was, on the moonlit balcony of a honeymoon suite with Troy.

"Relax," he whispered, and his breath was warm against her ear.

"I can't afford this place."

"I talked her into giving you the same rate you had before."

Those hands continued to work her shoulders, and Elaina closed her eyes. His body eased closer, until his thighs brushed the back of hers. She shivered. He wrapped his arms around her and pulled her against the warm hardness of his chest.

She couldn't let this happen.

She wanted this to happen.

His hands glided up and down her arms, very leisurely, but she could hear her own heart thudding over the hiss of the surf. He kissed her temple, and her nerves jumped.

"You got a boyfriend I need to know about?" His voice was low and warm.

"No."

"Fiancé?"

"No."

His hands slid over hers now, molding her bare fingers to the railing. "Husband?"

"No."

His grip tightened, and she closed her eyes, letting the solid heat of him completely surround her. Then his right hand moved up to her shoulder, and he brushed her hair to the side, baring her neck.

"So why do you keep avoiding me?"

Her heart raced. She wasn't sure she could find her voice. "I just think—"

"You think too much, Elaina."

He nipped her shoulder right where the muscle was tightest, and her breath caught. Her heart hammered as the gentle bite turned into a feather-light kiss that trailed up to her jaw. Slowly, he turned her around and slid his hands up to cup her face. She knew he was giving her one last out. When she didn't take it, he tipped her head back and dove in.

Heat speared through her body as he licked into her mouth. He tasted like lust and beer and everything she'd tried to resist her whole life. He tasted *good*. Her fingers dug into his jeans, and she heard a little sound in her throat. His hands slid down to her waist. His lips were firm and strong, and he kept kissing her, tasting her, and the warm pressure of his thumbs seeped through her shirt. She wanted the shirt gone. She wanted the breeze, his heat. She wanted . . . so many things, it made her dizzy. She arched into him, keeping one hand planted on his hip while the other combed into his hair. She curled her fingers and pulled him closer.

His palm settled on her rib cage, and she realized he'd untucked her shirt. His hand glided over her skin and she started to say something, but he covered her mouth again and swallowed the words and his hand moved up to cup her bare breast. He made a low sound of approval as he stroked the tip of it with his thumb, and she pressed closer.

What was she doing?

She was in a hotel room with a man she wasn't even dating. His body pressed against her, heavy and solid, and all she could think of was how *right* it felt, and how completely natural, and she couldn't believe she'd denied herself one of life's basic pleasures for so long. His hand moved down again, and she shivered and kept kissing him, somehow aware of the buttons of her shirt being plucked open, one by one. And then the breeze tickled over her skin, and a cold wave of panic hit her.

He must have felt her stiffen because he stopped and

looked down at her. She glanced around briefly, but the couples strolling the beach didn't even seem to notice them up here.

"Let's go in," he said.

He knew she wasn't comfortable. She wasn't going to get naked with him right here on this balcony. She drew some air into her lungs and shook her head.

He didn't move. He just watched her closely.

"Not tonight," she whispered.

He eased back, let his hand drop away. The wind moved between them, and the moment disappeared.

And her phone vibrated in her pocket, just to obliterate the mood even more completely. She gazed up at him, and it vibrated again.

"That's probably my boss," she said, refastening her buttons.

Troy didn't move.

"I told him to call me back tonight, no matter how late." She glanced down. Her buttons were askew, so she simply tied the shirttails together. Now she looked about as idiotic as she felt. "I need to go in and take care of this."

"I know."

She watched him. She'd expected guilt. Or at least some attempt at persuasion.

Instead, he slid open the door for her. As she stepped into the dimly lit suite, her phone vibrated again, telling her someone had just left a message.

"I'll call you tomorrow," she said, and he was already at the door. She couldn't read his expression.

"Lock up behind me," he said, and walked out.

The morning shrimp boats were chugging up to the wharf, trailed by a noisy flock of scavengers, when Brenda pulled into the driveway. She got out of her car and heard the sound of news radio. He wasn't asleep yet? That wouldn't be good.

Instead of going inside to fall into bed, she tentatively approached the garage, where her husband had been spending so much time lately. She smelled gun oil and cigarette smoke as she stepped through the doorway.

"Hi," she said.

He was at his workbench, hunched over a pistol, and he didn't look up.

She went farther into the room, sidestepping a crate of the MREs he liked to take on his camping trips. "Guess what happened tonight."

No response. His hands moved briskly, disassembling, reassembling.

"I met a real FBI agent. She's staying with us. She's been there since Friday, and here I didn't even know till now. It's a woman, but still. I knew you'd get a kick out of it."

Not a word. Only the click and slide of the parts coming together over the sound of the radio. He dropped the pistol on the newspaper in front of him and jabbed a finger at the stopwatch.

Damn, he'd been timing himself.

He glared up at her.

"She showed me her badge and everything," Brenda said, trying to distract him. "She's here investigating those murders. Knows Chief Breck. She said she'd help keep an eye on things at the inn."

Elaina McCord hadn't said that, but she may as well

have. What sort of law enforcement person would stay at a place and not help guard it? Plus, Brenda had given her the honeymoon suite.

He picked up the gun and aimed it at her. A chill went straight to her heart.

"Put that away. You know I hate those damn things." She stared into the black hole. "Do you even have the safety on?"

He watched her steadily, his eyes expressionless, like a shark. She hated it when he looked that way.

Snick.

She jumped slightly, and he laughed.

"No bullets," he said.

Brenda backed out of the room. She couldn't talk to him when he got like this.

He touched the stopwatch again and started taking the thing apart.

CHAPTER 9

The headline screamed out from the stack of newspapers sitting beside the counter: PARADISE KILLER STRIKES AGAIN. Mia lifted a paper from the stack and put it beside the register.

"And something to drink with that?"

She glanced up at the cashier. "Yes, I'd like a tall nonfat—"

"Just the paper, thanks." An arm reached around her and slid a bill across the counter.

She turned around.

Ric Santos held up a cardboard cup. "Tall nonfat latte?"

"Your change, sir."

"Thanks." He scooped the change off the counter, tucked the newspaper under his arm, and led Mia away from the coffee bar. "I got you some breakfast, too," he said, depositing a small brown sack on a nearby table. He pulled out a chair and looked at her expectantly.

"How did you get here?" Mia asked.

"Drove, same as you."

"But how'd you get *in*?" She stared at him, taken aback by his appearance at this coffee shop on the ground floor of the Delphi Center. This lab had tighter security than most military bases.

"Sit down." He nodded at the chair.

She sank into it and looked at what was spread out before her on the table. A newspaper, two coffees, and a paper bag containing—she peeked inside—chocolate almond scones.

He sat down in the chair beside her and leaned forward on his elbows. Those brown-black eyes pinned her, and she was suddenly self-conscious about her white lab coat and messy ponytail. She'd put in two hours already this morning before coming downstairs for her nine o'clock coffee break.

Mia's gaze narrowed as she took in the details of his appearance—the starched white shirt, the rolled-up sleeves, the dark slacks.

The gun and badge plastered to his hip.

He was dressed like all the homicide detectives she worked with, and she realized he'd been a bit vague when he told her he was a cop.

And she also realized it was no accident he'd wandered into this particular coffee shop on the ground floor of her office building at nine o'clock sharp.

"You've been checking up on me. You found out my schedule." She nodded at the cardboard cup in front of her. "You even found out my coffee preference, what I like to *eat*."

He leaned back in his chair now and looked at her. "Does that bother you?"

"Actually, yes. And what bothers me more is that you came here in person. I told you to call me. Don't you think this is a little presumptuous, Detective Santos?"

"Ric."

She arched her brows, waiting for an answer.

"Let me ask you something," he said. "How many detectives call you in an average week?"

Dozens. They'd all managed to get the number of her direct line somehow. And they all wanted updates on their lab work. She didn't fault them for their dedication, but if she answered every one of their phone calls, she'd never get any work done. For this reason, she had all outside calls directed straight to voice mail.

"I needed to talk to you," he said simply. "I thought I'd have better luck doing it in person. I'll forget your coffee preference, though, if it makes you feel better."

She shook her head, feeling foolish now. He'd bought her breakfast, after all. And at least he'd had the courtesy to catch her on a break, instead of having her called down from the lab.

She picked up the latte and took a sip. One Splenda. His detective skills were impressive. "So what is it you want from me?"

He let the question hang there, and for a moment she was back at the bar, flirting with this man and thinking he was flirting with her, too.

"Rumor has it you're the best DNA tracer they have working here. I've got a cold case." He tapped a long brown finger on the newspaper in front of her. "I think it might be related to what's happening on Lito Island."

"Why don't you talk to the investigators down there about it? I saw on the news that they've got a task force put together. Even the FBI's involved."

"I called them already. Man in charge—police chief by the name of Breck—he's not interested in my theory."

Mia tipped her head to the side and watched him. "It's pretty shaky, I'm guessing?"

"Not shaky, just unsubstantiated," he said. "That's why I need you."

"How cold is your cold case?"

"Five years."

Mia sighed. "And I assume you've got DNA evidence?"

"I think so, yes."

She waited for him to elaborate. So far, this was sounding shaky to her, too.

He leaned forward now on his elbows. "You ever been out to Devil's Gorge?" he asked. "Rugged country. About ten miles west of here. Some of the best views in central Texas."

"I'm not much of a hiker."

He nodded. " 'Bout five years ago we had two college girls go missing from there. Separate incidents. They went out hiking and were never seen again."

"Never seen at *all*? Not even their remains?"

"Nothing."

"So where's your DNA evidence? Do you have the suspect's clothes or something?"

"We don't have a suspect," he said. "At least nothing solid. Just some flimsy leads that never went anywhere."

"And what is it you want me to analyze?"

"In both cases, the victim's clothing was found in a trash bin not far from the trailhead. I don't believe those girls undressed themselves."

Mia watched him. Her talk months ago in front of an audience of police officers had alluded to the JonBenet

Ramsey case and how DNA from the girl's tights was used to eliminate her father from the suspect list.

"Touch DNA," Mia stated. "That's what you're looking for, right?"

Ric's gaze locked with hers, and she recalled why she'd been so taken with him back at the bar.

"Mia, I've got two missing college girls, and not a lead in five years. I've got no bodies, no suspects, and no budget. If you want to know the truth, what I'm looking for is a miracle."

Elaina pulled into the driveway and double-checked the address. This couldn't be it. She'd expected a beachfront fortress, some sort of architectural wonder built to withstand hurricanes and make a statement about its owner's wealth.

This place made a statement all right, just not the one she'd expected.

She stepped out of the car and onto the cracked driveway. She slammed the door and gazed up, marveling at the spindly-looking stilts. The modest wooden bungalow perched atop them looked as if it would blow away in the next tropical storm.

The black pickup was parked under the house, beside a closed garage. She eyed the line of dusty windows. If she wiped the grime away and squinted through them, would she see a Ferrari 360 Modena housed inside?

Her gaze was drawn to the sand dunes just beyond the house. She heard the crash of waves and the distant screech of seagulls, and over all of it, the faint sound of country music.

"Troy?" she called out, walking past the pickup.

No answer.

She followed the music and was halfway up a flight of wooden steps when her breath caught.

"Wow."

Emerald-green water. Sugary white sand. The coast stretched out before her, and she stood there a moment, letting the wind tangle her hair and wondering what it would be like to wake up to that view every day.

"You lost?"

She glanced around but didn't see him. "Where are you?"

"Down here."

She descended the creaky steps and spotted him beneath the shadow of a tall palm tree. He stood beside a primitive wooden fish sink with a green hose rigged to it.

"I didn't see you," she said, approaching him.

But she saw him now. Shirtless and sun-browned and slick-skinned, he looked like an ad for cologne.

Until he took a handful of fish guts and tossed them in a bucket. His fingers were bloody. Sun glinted off the blade of his knife.

"You've been fishing," she said—another brilliant conversation starter.

His gaze settled on her a moment. Then he went to work on the fish again, peeling the spine away with a skillful flick of the wrist.

"What did you catch?"

"Snapper. Couple of specks." He dropped the fillets into a cooler near his feet. She stepped closer and glanced down at the translucent strips of meat lined up on a bed of ice.

"Nice haul."

He rinsed blood off the knife, then his hands, before drying the blade on his cargo shorts and tucking it into a leather sheath. Then he tossed it on the work surface, right beside a half-finished beer.

She remembered how he'd tasted last night, and her cheeks heated. Her gaze drifted to his chest.

He sipped his beer and watched her. She could tell from that smug look in his eyes that he knew the direction her thoughts had taken. And yet he just stood there, taunting her with everything she'd turned her back on last night when she'd told him no.

She shifted her attention to the cooler and cleared her throat. "So . . . that's a lot of fish. What do you use for bait?"

He rested his bottle on the table and stepped forward. "You here for a fishing lesson, McCord?"

"No."

"What *are* you here for?"

She swallowed. "You said you know someone at the Delphi Center."

If he was surprised by her answer, he didn't look it. "Your boss thinks you're wasting your time," he said.

"Yes."

"You're going around him."

"Yes."

"And you want me to help you." He was taunting her again, and her temper bubbled.

"Look, do you know someone or not?"

He crossed his arms, which made it almost painful to keep her attention focused on his face. "I know someone. She's a DNA tracer."

"Will she talk to us? Soon? Time's of the essence here, and—"

"She'll talk to me."

"Good."

They stood there, looking at each other, and she realized now what an amazingly *bad* idea this was. She shouldn't be going around her boss. She shouldn't be pursuing dead-end leads. And she definitely shouldn't be spending any more time around this jaw-droppingly sexy writer, who in all likelihood was going to sink her career by putting her in his book.

And yet here she was, begging him for help.

He stepped closer again, and her breath stopped.

"Where's the slug?" he asked.

"In my car. I went over there this morning and got the whole piece of wood, so it's still embedded."

"It's barely ten. You've been busy."

"Cinco helped me."

Something flickered in his eyes, then disappeared. Jealousy? She wasn't really sure.

"I'll take you," he said, and then she was sure.

"Good," she said. "But this time I'm driving."

Elaina was ticked off at him again, and Troy remembered his mother's advice about the wisdom of letting someone else win an argument every now and again.

"You know, we saved a couple hours this way."

She glanced up from the file she'd had her nose buried in for the last two hundred miles. "What's that?"

"My car," he said. "It's a lot more efficient than that wreck you drive."

"That has less to do with the car than the fact that you've been doing ninety since we left the island."

"No use wasting a good engine."

She rolled her eyes.

"What're you reading, anyway?" he asked.

"Stuff for work."

He shot her an expectant look.

"Trust me," she said. "You wouldn't be interested."

"I'm very interested. It's had your undivided attention all morning." Between that file and her BlackBerry, she'd hardly given him a second glance.

Not the reaction he was accustomed to getting from a woman. Particularly one he'd tried to seduce just a few hours ago.

She sighed and shoved a pencil into her hair. There was already one up there, holding all those silky dark strands in a sloppy knot. Very naughty librarian.

"It's a study on recidivism," she said. "The tendency for certain types of offenders to repeat their crimes after release."

"No shit? They've really got a word for that? And here I thought some people were just lifelong fuckups."

She looked at him. "You're making fun of me."

"You're not the only one who's read a few books, McCord."

"Sorry. I didn't mean to be patronizing." She gave him a tentative glance. "I hate it when people do that to me."

"Forget it. I'm just trying to get a rise out of you. When I insisted on driving, I was thinking you'd be better company."

She closed the file and put it on the floor by her feet. She was in that ugly suit again today, but she'd removed her jacket and kicked her shoes off after the first hour, and the sight of her bare toes was driving him crazy. Cherry-red polish. Who would have expected Elaina McCord to have cherry-red toenails?

"So," she said. "Tell me about the Delphi Center."

He could tell she was just making a stab at conversation, but he appreciated the effort. "You know the background?"

"Something about a wealthy oil heiress whose daughter was murdered?"

Troy nodded. "Sarah Hayley Jones. The lab was founded by an endowment from Jones after her daughter was raped and murdered by a convicted sex offender. He was in the system already and had been on an eight-year crime spree before the murder happened, but the rape kits were sitting around collecting dust." Troy veered around an eighteen-wheeler, and Elaina clutched the door. "If any of them had been tested sooner, the guy could have been picked up before he killed Vanessa Jones. When the old cases started to come to light, her mom gave her entire fortune to start the Delphi Center. Ninety-two million dollars."

"That's a lot of rape kits," Elaina said.

"One of the lab's missions is to help clear the backlog of untested DNA samples. The whole idea behind the place is that the best predictor of future violent behavior is past violent behavior. These offenders keep offending. Think you'd call it recidivism."

She ignored the jab. "I guess that explains the name, then? Wasn't the Oracle at Delphi a Greek prophet?"

"Not bad. Sounds like you been to college."

"So what's your connection to the place? How do you know this Mia Voss?"

"I've known her a couple years now," he said, "ever since she started working there."

Elaina eyed him across the car, and he could tell she sensed she wasn't getting the full story. But the super-condensed version was all she was getting, at least from him.

"What?" he asked as she continued to stare.

"It's really amazing," she said. "It's not so much what you say but what you *don't* say that I find myself wondering about."

"You're talking in riddles, McCord."

"Uh-huh. Well, don't worry. I'm not interested in your torrid past."

"Not even a little?" He pretended to look hurt, and she rolled her eyes.

Then she picked up the file from the floor, tucked those pretty feet up next to her on the seat, and resumed her reading.

Mia Voss had strawberry-blond hair and freckles to match, and she in no way resembled Elaina's precon-ceived notion of a DNA specialist.

"It's how old?" she asked, gaping at Elaina from across her office. The room was small and cramped, and about as well-lit as a broom closet. When Mia had shown them in here, she'd called it "cozy."

"About nine and a half years," Elaina told her.

Mia leaned back against the counter and turned her dismayed expression to Troy. "And we're talking about an *outdoor* storage shed? This thing's been exposed to the weather?"

"Actually, we got pretty lucky there," Troy said. "The bullet's embedded deep in the two-by-four. Elaina had the entire piece removed, checked it in with your evidence clerk. It's waiting for you downstairs."

Mia shoved her hands in the pockets of her lab coat and took a deep breath. "Well, at least you didn't dig it out with a pocketknife." She shot a look at Troy, and Elaina remembered seeing a pocketknife in his hand as he'd stood in Ronnie's yard. He must have thought better of the idea.

"Gimme some credit," he said now. "And yeah, we know it's a long shot, but we at least need you to try."

"This case is important," Elaina added, and Mia looked at her.

"It's the Paradise Killer thing, isn't it?"

Elaina started to spout a variation of her typical "No comment" when Mia held up a hand.

"No, wait. Forget I asked," she said. "You can't tell me the details, and I don't want to know, anyway." She turned and grabbed a sticky note from a pad sitting beside a formidable-looking microscope. She jotted something on the paper and passed it to Elaina. "But in case that *is* what you're investigating, I should give you this name."

Elaina glanced down at the paper. "Ric Santos, San Marcos PD?"

"He's investigating several cold cases he thinks might be related. He tried to talk to the police chief down there, but apparently the guy wouldn't give him the time of day."

Elaina's temper simmered as she slid the note into her pocket. Chief Breck wouldn't know a lead if it conked him on the head. And *she* was supposed to be the one in need of field experience.

"How long until we can expect a result?" Troy asked.

"Oh, I don't know. Given my current caseload, I'd say I'll definitely have something for you by next Christmas."

Troy gave her a baleful look that for some reason set Elaina's teeth on edge.

"Aw, come on now," he said. "You're not gonna make me beg, are you?"

"I'll do everything I can," Mia promised. "But I should warn you not to get your hopes up. A nine-year-old DNA sample—especially one that's been exposed to the elements—isn't exactly the ideal specimen for testing."

"Just do the best you can," Troy said. "We don't expect you to work miracles."

Mia raised an eyebrow skeptically as she showed them to the door.

"You have time to give Elaina a quick tour?" Troy asked. "She's never been here before."

Mia smiled apologetically. "I have two hundred and twenty-three unread e-mails in my in-box. Sorry, but I hardly have time to breathe today."

"We'll show ourselves out," Elaina said, but Mia continued to retrace their steps back toward the elevator. Visitor's badge or not, Elaina got the impression she wasn't allowed to just wander around this place unaccompanied.

But oh, how she would have liked to. She'd noticed the list of departments in the lobby: Trace Evidence;

Ident—that is, fingerprints; Questioned Documents. Osteology was in the basement. Elaina had always had a fascination with bones, and the Delphi Center had one of the top forensic anthropology departments in the world. One of their staffers, Kelsey Quinn, had given a lecture at the FBI Academy while Elaina was there. The men in the audience had been so busy drooling over the woman's looks, they'd probably missed most of her presentation. But Elaina hadn't, and she'd come away highly impressed with Dr. Quinn's expertise.

Elaina followed Troy and Mia down the corridor. They passed a long window with a double helix engraved on it. Beyond the glass, a handful of lab-coated workers stood at tables, peering into microscopes.

"How many DNA specialists do you have working here?" Elaina asked.

"There are six on my team," Mia said. "Then there's my supervisor, who's in charge of divvying up the cases. He's on vacation right now, though, so I should be able to sneak you onto the schedule."

They passed another series of windows, and Elaina saw a room filled with computers.

"That's Digital Imaging and Cyber Crimes," Mia said. "It's a growing department. We've had a lot of Internet fraud come in lately. We're also seeing a spike in online child predators."

They neared the elevator bank and passed a row of doors. Elaina stopped short. A picture tacked to a bulletin board caught her eye. She stepped closer and saw that it wasn't a picture, after all, but a square yellow sticker, like someone might put on a car. The image on it was a stylized purple dragonfly, exactly like the pendant that had been recovered from their latest victim at autopsy. Elaina had thought the dragonfly pendant was just an unusual piece of jewelry, but maybe there was some significance to it.

Beside the dragonfly picture was a Far Side comic and a clipped-out review of a sci-fi movie. Elaina read the placard on the door beside the bulletin board. BEN LAWSON, PH.D.

"What is it?" Troy asked.

She glanced over at Mia. "This Dr. Lawson. Is he an entomologist?"

"That's downstairs with botany," Mia said. "We call it our Plants and Ants section. Why?"

"I was just wondering—" She nodded at the picture. "This dragonfly design. I think I've seen it before."

"You'd have to ask Ben about it," Mia said. "He works Cyber Crimes. I can give you his e-mail if you want."

"Thank you."

They stepped inside the elevator and Mia pressed her palm to a panel before selecting the ground floor. Elaina couldn't believe the security here. It was tighter than Quantico, or at least it seemed to be.

"So it's back to the coast, then?" Mia asked. "Or will you guys be in town for a while?"

"We've got to get back," Troy said, dodging the thinly veiled inquiry as to whether he and Elaina were a couple. He definitely had a past with this woman; Elaina could tell just from her body language.

The doors dinged open and Mia led them to the spacious lobby where they'd checked in. Troy leaned in to kiss her, and she offered him a cheek. To Elaina, she held out a hand. "Special Agent McCord, it was nice meeting you."

"You, too." They shook hands, and then Elaina dug out a business card. "Thank you for your help today. If you don't mind sending me that e-mail address for Dr. Lawson?"

"No problem." Mia tucked the business card into the pocket of her lab coat. She looked from Elaina to Troy and back to Elaina. "And I should stress again my concerns about your case. That sample's probably much too degraded to tell us anything useful." Her eyes grew somber. "But I'll do what I can. I read about those women in the paper, and what happens to them . . ." She shook her head. "Anyway, if you *are* working on the Paradise Killer thing, you should call Detective Santos. He might be a better lead for you than that bullet."

The afternoon sun blazed down on the highway, turning the endless yellow stripes into wavy lines. Troy blinked and tried to shake off the daze. He turned up the air-conditioning. When he spotted a gleaming silver truck parked up ahead on the shoulder, he pulled over.

Elaina glanced up from her file. "What are we doing?"

"I'm hungry." He shoved open the door. "Time for a break."

She got out and followed him to the truck, picking her way across the uneven gravel in those ridiculous shoes.

"What do they have here?" She squinted at the menu board, which was in Spanish.

"Pork tamales. And any kind of taco you could want—meat, cheese, peppers, whatever."

"What are you having?"

"All of it."

Elaina ordered a veggie taco and then wandered to a nearby fruit stand. Troy joined her back at the car.

"Are you finicky about your upholstery?" she asked.

"No."

"You sure? Because this orange—"

"Get in, Elaina."

She lowered herself into the seat, and he shook his head as he started the car. He drove about a quarter-mile up the road and pulled over beneath a live oak where they'd have some decent shade.

She checked her watch, then glanced around. "Where are we, exactly?"

"Halfway through the Rio Grande Valley. Passed the King Ranch about an hour ago."

She gazed out at the citrus groves. The trees were lined up in neat rows. He'd always thought they looked like leafy green soldiers.

"It's pretty," she said.

"You've never been here?"

"I don't get out of the office much. If I do, it's generally to help serve a warrant somewhere in Brownsville."

Troy chomped into his taco and watched her. He could tell from the little crease in her forehead that something was bothering her. Given her priorities, he figured it had to do with her job.

"Trouble at work?" he asked.

She glanced at him. Hesitated. Probably debating whether to open up again.

"You really want to hear about it?" she asked.

"Sure."

She pulled an orange out of the paper sack, obviously stalling.

"Totally off the record, Elaina. This is just you and me."

"Okay. I think Scarborough's just biding his time."

"Until what?"

"Until he can get rid of me," she said. "New agents are on a twenty-four-month probationary period. I think at the end of mine, I'm going to be out of a job."

"Why would he want to get rid of you?"

"I'm not sure, really. It's just a feeling I get." She dug a fingernail into the orange and stripped back the peel.

"You're probably right, then."

She glanced up, looking surprised by his answer. "You think so?"

"Well, you're pretty intuitive. If that's your read on the guy, it's probably dead-on."

She didn't say anything as she peeled the orange, making a little pile of rind on the napkin in her lap. She separated a section, and a bead of juice slid down her arm.

"You really think I'm intuitive?"

"From what I've seen, yeah. And your hunch about Diggins was right, even though most people thought you were way out on a limb there."

"It wasn't a hunch, really." She licked a drop of juice from her wrist, and Troy's pulse picked up. "It was a theory, based on careful study of all the facts in the case."

"And what made you take a look at the case? It had been closed for years. They had a confession. The entire legal system bought his story. I bought his story. Everyone except you."

She shrugged. "It just didn't fit, that's all."

"What didn't fit?"

"The victimology."

"You mean because Mary Beth was Caucasian? Serial killers don't always stick with one ethnic group."

"I know." She glanced up at him as she peeled another section. "I'm talking about who these women were. And the circumstances of their abductions."

He watched her, curious to hear what she had to say. He'd met few people who knew as much about the Diggins case as he did.

"Diggins picked low-risk targets," she said. "Prostitutes and strippers who worked the bars and truck stops along the interstate. Because he was a long-haul truck driver, he knew the area well." She glanced up from her orange. "Are you aware he has a near-genius IQ?"

"One thirty-five," Troy said. It was one of the most interesting aspects that Troy had discovered during his research. The man had had a chance to go to college on an academic scholarship, but he dropped out his first semester and eventually became a truck driver for a farming supply company. "What's your point?"

"My point is, Diggins was underemployed. He could have done a lot of things, but what he *chose* to do was a job that gave him a chance to troll for vulnerable women within his comfort zone. By all accounts, his victims willingly got into his car. Mary Beth Cooper was a veterinary assistant last seen setting out on a nature hike. Even though her remains were found near some of the others, it still didn't add up for me."

"So it *was* a hunch."

She carefully removed another section of orange and popped it in her mouth. "I guess, yeah, it started that way. I believe we're dealing with a similar sort of unsub now. Whatever job he has is just a job, but the murders are what he considers his true occupation."

"When I interviewed Diggins," Troy said, "he referred to the murders as 'his work,' almost like he was creating art or something. It was twisted."

"This guy's just as twisted. If you study the crime-scene photos, you'll see what I mean. He's making some sort of point to us. Law enforcement, the public, who-ever. Or at least in my *opinion* that's what he's doing. We won't know until we find him."

Troy looked at her with admiration. "You have your dad's knack for seeing patterns. Maybe it runs in the family."

She shot him a look that he couldn't read.

"Your dad encourage you to go into profiling?"

"No."

"He encourage you to apply to the Academy?"

"No." The orange had her full attention now. Clearly, there was some sort of tension between her and her father, but she didn't want to talk about it. And she never talked about her mother at all. Maybe she'd had a rocky upbringing. Hell, who hadn't? Troy was way more interested in who she was now.

He watched her, realizing how much he liked talking to her. He wasn't used to being able to discuss his work with anyone, much less a woman.

She took another bite of fruit. She had juice on her bottom lip, and he battled the urge to lean over and lick it off.

"Don't let this guy Scarborough smack you down,"

he said. "You've got good instincts. You're going to be a top-notch agent someday."

She glanced up, clearly startled. "Thank you."

And she didn't even give him crap for the "someday" part. She knew she wasn't there yet. But she had potential. She had a promising career ahead of her.

Too bad she was going to spend it in some windowless basement office at Quantico. With a little experience under her belt, she could be a good field agent.

Troy finished his taco and crunched the tinfoil into a ball. "So did you always want to join the FBI, or did you just kind of fall into it because of your dad?"

That got her hackles up. "No one just *falls* into becoming an FBI agent. The acceptance rate at the Academy is—" She stopped and looked at him. "You're baiting me, aren't you?"

"Got me." He smiled. "I like watching you get all riled up. Like that day at the marina."

"I knew you weren't just some casual bystander," she said. "You were watching me like a hawk from the moment I stepped onto that dock."

"See what I mean? Good instincts."

"You're lucky I've eliminated you from my suspect list. You fit the profile to a T, right down to your abnormally high level of interest in this case."

"Honey, I've got an abnormally high level of interest in a lot of things. Including bossy federal agents with sexy toes."

She cast him a wary glance. "I don't get you. How can you think about sex all the time when there's a murder investigation going on around you?"

He unwrapped another taco. "I've spent my whole career knee-deep in murder investigations. I had to learn to compartmentalize, or I'd never relax. You should try it. Work-life balance and all that crap."

"Well, you're ahead of me career-wise," she said. "Right now I'm just trying not to get fired. Work-life balance is down the road."

She got quiet then and nibbled another bite of orange. "What about you?" She glanced at him. "Did you always want to be an investigative journalist?"

She probably didn't realize she'd just given him a compliment. When he'd first met her, she'd accused him of writing pulp fiction.

"When I was a kid," he told her, "all I could think about was leaving home. Never occurred to me to write anything besides my name on the job application at Tex-Oil."

She didn't comment. He was pretty sure she knew all about his background, but she didn't have the guts to admit she'd checked him out.

"How'd you go from working on oil rigs to the *Lito Country Register*?"

Okay, so she was gutsier that he'd thought. And he was tempted to tell her the truth—that the editor at the *Register* had given him a chance he didn't deserve by offering him a job on the sports desk, and that the man had been both a mentor and a father figure to Troy until he died last year of a heart attack. But that sounded sentimental as hell, and Troy wasn't about to tell her any of it.

"Well, let's see, I got arrested for stabbing some drunk in a bar. Had a big mess on my hands, could have gone to jail. But the D.A. cut me a deal, and I knew I'd been given a second chance. I promised myself I'd take advantage of it, stop pissing my life away between rigs and bars like my old man."

"Guess you made good on your promise," she said.

"Guess so."

She nibbled another bite, and he gave up. He leaned over and kissed her. She started to pull back, but he combed his fingers into her hair and held her in place, taking advantage of the fact that her hands were full of orange. She tasted sweet and tart and even better than last night when she'd been so nervous. He felt her give in. She kissed him back, tangling her tongue with his, the sweet with the spicy, and her mouth got hot.

She jerked back and stared at him. Her breathing was uneven.

"It's yours," she said.

"Huh?"

"Your phone." She nodded at the console.

Troy cursed and snapped up his cell phone. "What?"

"Yo, man, you anywhere near a TV?" Cinco's voice yanked him back to reality.

"No, why?" He glanced at Elaina, who avoided eye contact with him as she collected bits of orange peel that had fallen on the floor.

"There's a news conference in ten minutes. Breck's leading it."

"What's the news?" Troy asked, sensing it was going to be bad.

"They IDed the victim from yesterday, and it's not who we thought."

"It's not Valerie?"

Elaina's gaze shot up.

"Who the hell is it, then?"

"This is a Houston girl," Cinco said. "Dropped out of college about two months ago. Been kickin' it down here ever since. Her parents didn't even know she was missing until they got the call from Breck."

"Shit," Troy muttered as another ringtone filled the car. Elaina's this time—maybe that Santos guy calling her back.

"Hey, you two getting back here anytime soon?" Cinco asked. "I don't know what Elaina told Breck, but she's been gone all day, and people are starting to notice."

Troy glanced at her in the seat beside him. Her face had gone pale.

"Who is this?" she asked the caller.

"We're on our way," Troy said.

"Pen. I need a pen." Elaina jerked her purse into her lap and pawed through it.

He reached over and pulled one of the pencils out of her hair. She snatched it from him, then dragged the file folder into her lap and started scribbling.

"What is that? What does that mean?" Her fingers whitened as she clutched the phone. "Hello? *Hello?*" She pulled it away from her ear and scowled at the screen. *"Shit,"* she hissed. "He did it again!"

"Did what? Who was that?"

She gazed down at the note she'd written and shook her head. "I can't believe this. I don't know what this *means.*"

"Who was it?"

She glanced up. "The man who called me. I think it's him."

CHAPTER 10

"*Him* as in the killer?"

"I can't be sure," she said. "He talks about the case, but he's so vague."

"You mean he's called you before?" Troy gripped the steering wheel and leaned across the seat. "Elaina?"

She glanced up. "What?" Then back at her notes. "Yes, he's called before. But I'm not sure who he *is*. Do these numbers mean anything to you?"

Troy clenched his teeth and looked at her. She'd cut him out. Why hadn't he expected it? He wasn't a cop. She didn't owe him information. But he'd thought she trusted him.

Not enough to tell him some freak was calling her, apparently.

"Do they?" She shoved the file folder under his nose, and he forced himself to pay attention.

"What is this?"

"He rattled off these numbers. And said, 'Valerie's still waiting.' Maybe he's full of bull."

"Could be." Troy shook his head. "But he could be legit. Cinco just called. The woman they autopsied yesterday was IDed as a college student from Houston. Valerie Monroe's still missing."

"Oh my God."

"When did you last hear from this guy, Elaina?"

"He called my room earlier." She looked down at her notes again.

"Which room?"

"My hotel room," she said absently. "What are these numbers?"

"Elaina." Troy's patience was unraveling. "*Which* room?"

She finally met his gaze. "The first one."

"He hasn't called you since you moved?"

"No."

"But he got your cell number somehow. That can't be an easy thing to get. It's not like you're listed in the phone book."

"No, but I've given my number to a lot of people," she said. "Practically everyone I've interviewed here. I told them to call me if they thought of anything that might help the case. But that doesn't matter nearly as much as what this man *said*. He told me Valerie's waiting."

Her gaze locked with his, and he could practically read what she was thinking. How would the caller know Valerie was still missing if he wasn't the killer?

"Maybe he's just some jerk who likes toying with a federal agent." Troy tried to sound hopeful, but it wasn't very convincing. "Cinco said there's a press conference about to happen. Maybe word leaked out that the most recent Jane Doe isn't who they'd expected, and this guy's using that info, trying to pull your chain."

Elaina looked at her notes again. "I think it's him.

And I think he's playing games with me. Taunting me. He used that phrase again. 'She's my best hide.' "

Troy cursed and stared out the windshield.

"Wait a second," she said, and he heard the note of dread in her voice. "I think I know what this means. These are coordinates."

"Coordinates?"

She glanced up. Her eyes were intense, alert. But not nearly frightened enough for someone who'd just received a call from a serial killer.

"Longitude and latitude," she said. "GPS coordinates. It's like we thought—he's playing games here. And he just handed me a big clue."

Mia leaned over her worktable, careful to position the tape precisely along the elastic waistband of the running shorts. When the clothes came from a perpetrator, she took samples from the inside of the collar, the armpits, the inside of a hat—any area that rubbed against skin and was likely to absorb sweat. When the clothes came from a victim, her best bet was the waistband.

"Another rape kit?"

Startled, she glanced up to see Kelsey Quinn standing in the door of her laboratory. The forensic anthropologist was in her typical uniform of jeans and a T-shirt. The brown patches on her knees told Mia she'd been toiling in the dirt this morning, probably at one of the older excavation sites on the grounds. Besides being a world-renowned forensics laboratory, the Delphi Center also had the macabre distinction of being one of the world's top decomposition research facilities.

"Not exactly a rape kit," Mia said, "although it's

possible she was raped." She resumed her task, pressing the adhesive side of the tape to the waistband, then carefully lifting it away. "These clothes were recovered from Devil's Gorge. I'm trying to get skin cells of the perpetrator."

"Assuming there was one," her friend said from the doorway. "I got your message. I take it those clothes are from one of the missing hikers?"

"That's right."

"And you're looking for touch DNA?"

"Yep." Mia carefully laid the tape beside the other strips she'd already collected. "If he removed these shorts from the victim, he probably deposited skin cells on the elastic. The other hiker's shorts are made of spandex, which isn't as conducive to this sort of testing."

Kelsey leaned against the door frame but didn't venture into the room. She knew Mia wouldn't appreciate someone breathing down her neck while she examined evidence. Tracers tended to be neat freaks, a trait born of many hours spent on witness stands explaining to defense attorneys that blood, semen, and other evidence was not the result of contamination in the lab.

"And what's the razor blade for?" Kelsey asked.

"That's my backup method. In case the tape fails to lift any skin cells, I'll gently scrape the fabric and see what I can get. I can do it later." Mia raised her eye shields and leaned back against the counter behind her. "What do you have for me?"

"I looked through our records and made a few phone calls," Kelsey said. "No human skeletons recovered from Devil's Gorge in the past five years."

Mia sighed. "I figured as much. My detective seems pretty thorough."

Kelsey lifted an eyebrow. "*Your* detective?"

"The detective who brought me this case," she corrected. "Ric Santos with San Marcos PD. I figured he checked on any skeletal remains. I was thinking, though, maybe someone found a partial. Is there a record of any human bones at all from that area? Both missing hikers are female."

"Closest thing is a long bone that came into my office about six months ago. Some rock climbers found it near an abandoned campground."

"But . . . ?" Mia sensed a dead end.

"Microscopic examination showed osteons lined up in rows."

"I know you're going to tell me what that means."

"Osteons are small, circular bone structures. In humans, they're scattered randomly throughout the bone cortex. In animals, they tend to be found in rows. The bone was an animal femur, probably from a small cow or a deer. It's usually pretty easy to tell what I'm dealing with just by looking at the context—deer don't have fingers, people don't have hooves, that sort of thing. But if it's a single bone, maybe carried somewhere by a scavenger, I usually have to look at it under a microscope to be sure."

Kelsey nodded at Mia's worktable. "So it seems the missing hikers are still missing."

"Well, thanks for checking."

"Hope your evidence there yields something better." Kelsey smiled slyly. "I've met Ric Santos. I wouldn't want to disappoint him, either."

• • •

Elaina's heart sank as she gazed down at the map. "This place is *enormous*."

Troy handed her a plastic bag and started the car again. "Eighty-five thousand acres," he said as he pulled out of the gas station parking lot.

She studied the outlines of Laguna Madre National Wildlife Refuge. "It looks pretty untamed, too," she said. "The entire southeast boundary looks like inlets and coves."

"It is. What did Breck say?"

Elaina set her jaw and gazed out the window. "Pretty much the same thing he said when I told him about the first call. It was a prank."

"He really believes that?"

"I don't know what he believes," she said sourly. "Evidently, the tip line has had hundreds of pranks since the day it was set up. He says this is probably more of the same."

"Yeah, but none of those pranks came in on an investigator's cell phone."

"I pointed that out." She refolded the map so that the section showing the wildlife reserve was on top. "But did he listen? No. Unless I come up with something, and I quote, 'solid,' this tip doesn't merit anyone's time."

She looked out the window. In the last twenty minutes, the scenery had gone from fertile farmland to scrub brush mixed with pockets of wet. They were nearing the coast.

She cast a sideways glance at Troy. He had a strong profile. He was only thirty-five, but he had faint lines at the corners of his eyes, probably from so much time spent in the sun. She liked the lines. They made him seem wise beyond his years.

She looked away. She could feel herself falling for this guy. With every day, with every minute they spent together, she could feel herself letting go of that hard-won control, letting her emotions take over. She took a deep breath and summoned her courage.

"Listen, Troy." She cleared her throat. "You brought up a good point earlier. One I've been thinking about."

"What's that?"

"Work-life balance and all that 'crap,' as you called it." She looked at him but couldn't read his expression. "The fact is, I have no life. I can't. At least not right now. Maybe someday, but for now, I really need to focus on what I'm doing here. I can't mess up. I can't afford mistakes. There's too much at stake—not just for me, career-wise, but for this case and these victims. I can't be distracted and miss something important."

He smiled, but he didn't seem amused. "So I'm a distraction, huh? And here I thought I was helping you."

"You are. You have." She looked at the map in her lap. "I want you to know I appreciate it. Your taking me to the Delphi Center and introducing me to your friend, and giving me the lay of the land down on the island—"

"But you don't want to sleep with me."

"No. I mean, we hardly know each other."

"And you don't do flings, is that right?"

Her stomach tightened. "That's right."

"And you don't need any distractions."

"Yes."

"Okay, no problem."

She looked at him. Was he serious, or was he teasing

her again? She couldn't tell, so she was going to go with
serious.

The car filled with silence. She looked at the map in
her lap. She looked at Troy. "Are you still up for this?"

"You mean now that you've told me you're not going
to jump me in return for my services as a tour guide?"

She chose to ignore that. "I understand if you need
to get back. We've been gone all day. I can always come
back tomorrow—"

"Bad idea. Eighty-five thousand acres of marshland
isn't a great place for you to be wandering around alone."

"I could bring someone. Maybe Maynard or Weaver."

She saw the muscle in his jaw tighten. "I'll take you."

"Are you sure?"

"Yes."

"Because you've already given up your whole Monday
and—"

"You really want to lose a day on this thing just because
you're afraid you can't control yourself around me?"

She blinked at him. "I can control myself."

"Good. That makes two of us. Now, quit asking
whether I want to be here. I'm here. Let's get this done."

Now she was the one to get annoyed. "I'm just pointing out that you're about to drive this nice car of yours
into a swamp. And then we're on foot, from the looks of
it. And it's got to be ninety-five degrees outside."

"One-oh-one," he corrected. "And yes, I'm up for it.
It's you I'm worried about. I picked up some stuff for you
at the gas station."

Elaina lifted the bag from the floor and poked through
it. Water. Sunscreen. Flip-flops. She pulled out a pair of
pink hibiscus-print shorts and glanced at him.

"Are we going to a luau?"

"That was all they had," he said. "You're going to melt in those pants you've got on. And forget the heels."

They passed a sign for the reserve, and Troy turned onto a narrow road.

"You're wearing pants," she pointed out. And cowboy boots. And a black T-shirt that was sure to absorb heat.

"Jeans breathe. Whatever synthetic stuff that suit is made from doesn't."

"We should have taken *my* car," she said pointedly. "I've got tactical pants and ATAC boots stashed in the trunk."

"ATAC boots?"

"All-Terrain, All-Conditions. I started keeping them with me for just this type of emergency."

"Looking for bodies in a swamp? You do this a lot?"

"It's his pattern," she said.

Troy rolled his Ferrari to a stop beside a wooden guardhouse and paid the awestruck attendant a few dollars. They entered the park and followed a narrow road that curved south. Troy kept glancing at the phone in his hand. They'd been using his for navigation because Elaina's didn't have nearly as many bells and whistles on it.

"According to this, we're about three and a half miles from where we want to be," he said.

"And we're about to run out of pavement."

Her prediction proved correct as the road veered west, away from their destination.

"I need a place to park," he muttered. "Somewhere not too soft."

Elaina pointed to some scrub brush sitting on a gentle rise to their east. He found a gap in the foliage and eased into the space between.

She glanced around warily. "Are you sure this is the best place to—"

"Yes." He leaned across her, popped open the glove compartment, and pulled out a pistol, which he tucked into the back of his jeans.

She didn't ask if he had a permit for it. She didn't want to know. After he got out of the car, she kicked off her shoes, slipped off her belt—along with the holster attached to it—and shimmied out of her pants. The shorts he'd bought were hideous, but at least they had belt loops. She transferred her weapon and slipped an extra magazine into her pocket, alongside her cell phone.

She climbed out of the car, and the humidity settled over her like a blanket. They'd parked in the shade of a few scraggly bushes, but the land all around them was baking beneath the late-afternoon sun. Bushes and patches of water dotted the grassy prairie. In the hazy distance, she saw the blue-gray line that would be Laguna Madre.

"You think we'd be better off by boat?" Elaina asked.

Troy glanced up from his digital map. "Not according to this. Plus, it's low tide."

"Which direction?"

"About three miles south."

"That doesn't sound too bad."

He gave her a look that told her she had no idea what she was talking about. Then he tromped around the back of the car, and she saw that he'd managed to scrounge up a gym bag from somewhere. He took the plastic bag from her hands and stuffed the water bottles into the duffel. Then he squirted a big glob of sunscreen into his palm.

"This has insect repellent in it." He handed her the bottle. "Put some everywhere you can reach."

He crouched at her feet and began slathering her legs. She focused on covering her face and neck. When her legs were finished, he rubbed the extra lotion over his face and hooked his arms through the duffel like a backpack.

Elaina checked her watch. "Just after five," she said.

"I figure we got three hours." He scanned the horizon. "Keep your gun handy."

"You think he's out here?" Elaina asked. She'd thought of that, too. Maybe this was some sort of ambush.

"I'm more worried about gators," he said.

"Gators?"

"And keep an eye out for snakes."

He set off to the south. Elaina adjusted her weapon and fell into step behind him.

Laguna Madre National Wildlife Refuge
N 26° 13.681 W 097° 20.005
6:25 P.M. CST

She mostly watched her feet as she tromped over the uneven terrain. The ground was sandy, with sharp blades of grass jutting through. Sticker burrs were everywhere, and she kept stopping to pluck them from between her toes.

Troy had set a brisk pace. She discovered the footing was easiest if she stepped into the big impressions made by his boots. She had to stretch her legs to do it, though, and after the first half hour, her breath was coming in shallow pants.

In. Out. Slow. Down. She forced her lungs into a rhythm that matched his footsteps.

Sweat and sunscreen seeped into her eyes. She ignored the weeds clawing at her calves. She ignored the mosquitoes buzzing around her ears and nose. She kept her gaze on the ground, and whenever possible, stole a glimpse of her surroundings.

"You see anything?" she asked.

"Nope."

She didn't, either. But, then, she hadn't had as much opportunity to look.

Perspiration streamed down her back and legs. Her shirt glued itself to her body. The grass became taller. The sand became damper. Eventually, it wasn't sand at all, but mud, thick and warm, that oozed between her toes. With every step, she fought the suction that tried to hold on to her shoes. The plastic straps chafed against her skin.

She glanced backward. The bushes where they'd parked were a dark green dot now. They were in a sea of grass and muck.

"Need a drink?" Troy glanced over his shoulder at her.

"I'm good."

But she wasn't good. She was winded. Breathless. As if the air was too heavy to enter her lungs. It didn't make sense, because ever since her college days at Georgetown, she'd been an avid runner. She'd handled the jogging trail through Rock Creek Park with all its rises and dips—no problem. And since moving to Texas, she'd run nearly every day in an ongoing effort to keep up with all the jocks surrounding her. She should be able to handle a zero-grade hike without breaking a sweat.

In. Out. In. Out.

Of course, she always ran in the mornings, before seven. She wasn't used to this oppressive heat, to this hot, pungent air that was almost too thick to breathe.

She blinked the sweat from her eyes and glanced around. She was supposed to be investigating here. But she saw nothing out of place—nothing besides herself and Troy and their two long shadows tromping across the marsh.

Another gust of hot air. Another cloud of mosquitoes. She tried not to think about it. She concentrated instead on Troy's footprints. She listened to his breathing. It was steady. Even. If he could do this, so could she.

He checked his phone again. "Not much farther," he said. "Keep your eyes peeled."

Grass. Mud. Sun. The occasional long-legged heron picking its way through the marsh. Troy saw no sign of a human, either living or dead. Only endless acres of cord-grass and brackish water.

He glanced over his shoulder. Elaina's cheeks were bright pink. Her shirt was soaked through. Her calves were covered with scratches and slime.

"Water break." He slung the pack off his back and unzipped it.

"I'm fine. Let's go. We're running out of daylight."

"Drink, Elaina." He shoved a water bottle at her and dared her to argue. She didn't. Instead, she tipped her head back and chugged, and he got his first good look at all the welts on her neck. He fished the sunscreen from the bag and handed it to her.

"I don't think it's working," she said.

"It's better than nothing. And you're getting eaten alive. This place is a breeding ground."

She passed him the water, and he guzzled the rest, then stuffed the empty bottle back in his pack. Elaina slathered lotion on her neck and face. Troy scanned the horizon. They'd reached their destination an hour ago and had been searching the area in a spiral pattern ever since.

They'd found zilch.

"Maybe you were right," she said, and wiped her brow with her cuff. She'd rolled her sleeves down after the first hour, probably to guard against mosquitoes. "He's probably just some loser trying to jerk my chain. I'm sorry I dragged you out here."

He flashed a look at her. "I'm not."

"Why on earth not?"

"Look around you. Tell me what you see."

She did a slow three-sixty. They stood ankle-deep in water, surrounded by marsh. Crabs scuttled around their feet. The sky was orange on the horizon, darkening to bloodred, then purple. A V-formation of pelicans soared, toward the setting sun.

Troy watched her eyes and waited for the spark of recognition.

"It's the same as the others," she said. "It's the type of place he'd pick—a scenic nature area that's a pain in the butt to get to."

"Yep."

"And it's federal land, which means if he *did* put her here, the FBI takes over the case. More gamesmanship."

Troy nodded. "That's what I think, too. This isn't a prank. We're just too late. Valerie's been missing almost a week. Whatever was left of her has been scavenged and scattered by now."

He consulted his phone again. It was running low on juice, so he powered it off and shoved it in his pocket. "We'd better head back," he said. "We've been out here too long already. We'll be hiking in by penlight if we don't get a move on."

Elaina glanced around, and he could tell she wasn't ready to give up. "Fifteen more minutes."

Somehow he'd known she would say that.

She trekked west, toward the sunset, her gaze intent on the ground in front of her. Troy followed, ignoring the blisters covering his feet. Water-filled cowboy boots weren't his top pick for hiking.

She stopped short, and he bumped into her.

"Look there," she said.

"Where?"

She pointed up ahead, to something shiny that caught the light. They both moved toward it at the same instant. It was a plastic box. Olive green. Not much bigger than a shoebox. The sun glinted off the hooks of a bungee chord that someone had wrapped around it, probably to hold it shut.

"What do you think's inside?" Elaina asked, and he heard the dread in her voice.

"Only one way to find out." He crouched down beside it.

"But crime-scene protocol—"

"This isn't a crime scene," he pointed out. Not yet, anyway. But he didn't want to waste time on formalities. The box could be full of fishing tackle, for all they knew. He unhooked the bungee chord and pulled on the lid.

"It's stuck," he said.

"Want me to try?"

He glowered up at her. Then he shifted to the other side and tried a different angle. Elaina knelt down next to him. She smelled like sweat and sun block, and her hair blew against his forearm as he gripped the plastic top.

A soft sucking noise. The gentle *pop* of a seal breaking. He pulled the lid back—

"Toys?" Elaina gazed down into the box.

Troy lifted up a plastic bag that looked like it contained something from a kid's Happy Meal. A plastic puppy dog. "Looks like it."

"Is that cereal?" She pulled out a mini-sized box of cereal, the kind sold at convenience stores. "Special K," she said, and picked up something else. "And beef jerky. What's all this stuff doing in the middle of a swamp?"

Troy lifted a plastic Baggie containing half a dozen white pills. "Now, this looks a little more interesting." He read the typewritten label.

"What is it?"

"Esteroides," he said. "Steroids."

"Those are illegal."

"Here, yeah. But not at your friendly neighborhood pharmacy just south of the border. Drugstores in Matamoros do a booming business in controlled substances." He picked up another Baggie, this one containing a hand-rolled cigarette.

"Is that a joint?"

"Yep." He opened the bag and sniffed. "Smells good, too."

Elaina rolled her eyes. "Terrific. We've stumbled into

some kid's secret stash. Another great lead." She stalked away from the box and scanned the horizon. She turned around and plunked her hands on her hips. "This sucks. It's almost dark and we haven't found—"

"*Stop.*" Troy's gaze homed in on the long black ribbon gliding between her ankles. "Don't move."

"What?"

"Water moccasin."

Her gaze dropped. She yelped. But to her credit, she didn't move a muscle. Troy crouched there, motionless, as the snake eased close to him with its head out of the water, then veered away.

"Omigod. Omigod. Omigod. I hate snakes."

"Good thing he's leaving."

"Is it poisonous?"

"Yep," he said. "Cottonmouth."

She clasped her hand to her stomach and stepped backward. "Omigod, I nearly— *Ah!*"

She fell backward and landed on her butt with a splash. She glanced around, looking dazed. She lifted her hands up, and they were coated in muck.

Troy dropped the lid back on the plastic box and trudged over to help her.

"*Damn* it!" She got a panicked look on her face and started flailing around.

"You okay?"

"No!" she wailed. "My phone!"

She fished her BlackBerry out of the water. It was covered in sludge. She fumbled with it and jabbed at the buttons.

"It's dead!"

"So get a new one." Troy stepped closer to her and spied something tangled around her shoe.

"This had evidence on it! I needed that telephone number to trace in case that phone call wasn't a hoax."

"It wasn't," Troy said grimly.

She glanced up from the muddy phone. "How do you know?"

"Because." He crouched down and untangled the yellow twine from her flip-flop. "You just tripped over the killer's calling card."

Elaina picked her way through the mud almost totally by feel. Troy's penlight cast a thin beam on the ground before him. She focused on the light and the tiny strip of grass and water it illuminated. She would have given anything for one of those huge Maglites her father had always admonished her to keep in her car, but that, like dry feet and a gallon of Gatorade, was a fantasy.

The air smelled like rotting vegetation. It hummed with mosquitoes and who knew what other insects. The sun was long gone, and they hadn't found Valerie or any sign of her since the yellow twine. With nothing but a penlight, they had little hope of finding anything unless they literally tripped over it.

"You took some forensic science classes up there at Quantico, right?"

She followed close behind him. "Yeah."

"Any idea how long it takes for a body to decompose in this kind of marsh?"

She'd been working it out in her head. "Well, most of the cases I studied were from the Body Farm in Tennessee. But I've been reading up on the Delphi Center.

They've got a farm up there, too, and their findings are more applicable to this sort of climate. According to— *Ouch!*" She shook her foot, and Troy turned the light on it. He snatched a baby crab off her toe and tossed it away.

"You okay?"

"Yeah."

"Here, hold on to me." He took her hand and tucked it into the waistband of his jeans, just inches away from the pistol he'd put there. They continued their trek.

"You were saying? The Delphi Center?"

"They did an interesting comparative study," she said.

"Do tell."

"Are you making fun of me again?"

"No." He stopped briefly and glanced around. The moon hadn't risen yet, and they were using the distant arc of lights on the Lito Island Causeway to navigate by.

"Well, in Tennessee, it can take days or even weeks for scavengers to skeletonize a sixty-pound hog. A few hours north of here, an animal that size can be picked clean in just twenty-four hours by the native bird species. Add in the effects of water and increased humidity, and I'd say we could be looking for mostly bones at this point."

"A canine unit would help."

"Yes." Elaina let the word hang there without adding the rest.

"That's assuming you can get anyone to understand the significance of the yellow twine," Troy added.

"Yes."

Elaina curled her fingers inside his jeans. His body felt warm against her hand, and his T-shirt was saturated with sweat. She knew his boots couldn't be comfortable, and despite his silence on the subject, she was pretty sure he'd suffered about as many bug bites as she had.

"Water break?" he asked.

"Let's just get there. You want to try that phone again?"

"No use. Once it's dead, it's dead. I have a charger in my car, though. We can juice it up and call your boss again."

Elaina had tried him earlier and only gotten voice mail. She glanced around at the inky blackness. Fireflies twinkled here and there, providing an interesting show, but not much in the way of guidance.

"This is so weird," she whispered.

"What?"

"Being out here. No lights. No phones. Just the marsh and the sky."

"That's the way God made it."

She hiked in silence for a while, digesting that. Did he believe in God? After studying and writing about some of the most depraved murderers of the last two decades? Elaina had grown up believing in God, but she hadn't given it much thought lately. She believed in the opposite, though. She believed in evil. She knew monsters were real. She'd seen their handiwork up close. She'd heard their voices as she'd pored over the transcripts of their jailhouse interviews with her father. She knew there were people out there—walking, breathing, stalking people—who were capable of unspeakable cruelty. People who simply had no soul.

She wondered what it felt like to spend your last moments with a person like that. What had Mary Beth Cooper felt? And Whitney Bensen and Valerie Monroe and this new woman from Houston? A lump rose in her throat, and she tightened her grip on Troy's belt.

"Do you think—" She paused, feeling self-conscious about the question now. Scientifically speaking, she knew the answer. But she wanted Troy's take on it.

"Do I think what?"

She cleared her throat. "I've been wondering about the ketamine," she said. "Do you think he does that for a reason? Besides controlling them?"

"How do you mean?"

"I mean, do you think they ever wake up?" Her skin chilled as the words left her mouth. "Do you think they realize what's happening when he starts the cutting? Do you think that's part of his thrill?"

Troy didn't say anything. The only sound was the monotonous *slurp glop* as the mud sucked at her shoes.

"I think it's possible," he finally said.

She took a deep breath. "I do, too."

"But the thing to remember is—"

She bumped into the solid wall of his back. "What?"

"Shh."

"What is it?" she whispered.

He dropped down, yanking her with him. Her knees sank into mud. He took her chin in his hand and turned her head to face due east.

"There," he whispered in her ear. "Someone's over there. I saw a flashlight."

Elaina strained to see what he meant. She reached for her weapon and felt Troy do the same. Gradually, she managed to make out the figure—a black shadow against the sky that was almost as dark.

It was a man. Average height. Stocky. Not twenty yards away. He moved toward them.

In his hand was a gun.

CHAPTER 11

"FBI! Drop your weapon!"

The figure froze at her words. Elaina's heart slammed against her breastbone as she knelt there, aiming her gun at the shadow. She felt Troy beside her, his pistol raised alongside hers.

"I'm a cop," the man called out.

"Drop the gun!" she shouted. *"Now!"*

He crouched down slowly and placed something on the ground. Then he stood, lifting his hands above his head. She and Troy stood, too.

"I'm a cop," he repeated. "Lito Island PD."

"Cinco?" Troy asked.

"Troy?"

Elaina's breath whooshed out. She lowered her arms.

"What the hell're you doing?" Troy demanded. "You damn near got your head blown off."

Elaina's hands shook as she reholstered her Glock.

"What're y'all doing out here?" Cinco shined a flashlight in her face as she approached him. Then the beam shifted to Troy.

"I got a phone call," she told him. "Anonymous. Possible location of Valerie Monroe's remains."

"GPS coordinates, right?" The beam moved back to her again.

"Breck told you?"

"No," Cinco said. "I got a call like that, too. She gave me the location, almost to the square foot."

"You mean you found something?" Troy asked.

"Your caller was a *she*?" Elaina cut in.

"I found something," Cinco said. "Not sure what it is, yet. Got the area taped off. Cisernos is on his way out here to tell me what we're looking at."

"What does it *look* like we're looking at?" Elaina asked.

Cinco shook his head. "Well, shit, I'm no expert. But looks to me like a leg."

Elaina stood beside the portable spotlight and watched a member of the evidence-response team deposit a bone atop the white sheet.

"Is it human?" she asked.

He glanced up. "Appears to be." He swatted at the cloud of insects swarming around the surgeon's light attached to his headband. "Looks to me like a tibia. We'll need to consult a forensic anthropologist to be sure."

"Got another one."

Elaina turned and saw the dog handler approaching from the east. His black Labrador, Ike, had alerted on twelve other bones in the past hour. So far, no skull. Elaina met the dog handler's gaze and asked the question with her eyes.

"Sorry, ma'am."

She sighed. It was entirely possible they might never recover the full skeleton. Elaina dreaded the thought of breaking that news to the victim's family. A vision of Valerie's father filled her mind. He was wrecked and grieving as his wife stared out the window of that police station. He'd looked at Elaina with his watery blue eyes that could have been her own father's, except that her own father never cried.

You have any children, Ms. McCord?

No, sir, I don't.

Well, when you do, you'll know what it's like to have your heart ripped out.

"McCord!"

She turned and spotted Scarborough standing beneath the open-sided tent that had been set up to sort evidence.

"Sir?"

"Over here. Someone you need to meet."

Elaina crossed the muck, tugging at the hem of her flowered shorts as she went. She was covered in grime, head to toe.

Scarborough wore his typical slacks and dress shirt, but his sleeves were rolled up to the elbows. His gaze skimmed Elaina, then he gave a curt nod.

"This is Special Agent Bob Loomis. He's taking the lead on this."

Elaina traded nods with the man. She was pretty sure no one wanted to shake her hand at the moment.

"Loomis has seen your profile. He's got some ideas of his own to add. Fill him in on what you know."

"Sir?" She gazed up into her boss's piercing gaze.

"About your mystery caller," Scarborough said, and then stalked off.

Elaina shifted her attention back to her new acquaintance. Tall. Paunchy. Wedding ring. She put him in his mid-forties.

"I read your profile," Loomis said. "It didn't mention an accomplice."

"That's right. I don't think he has one."

"In that case, how do you explain the female who called Officer Chavez?"

"She could be anybody," Elaina said. "Someone walking down the street who accepted a few bucks just to talk on the phone for him."

He paused for a moment. "Chavez said she sounded agitated."

"It's also possible she found the bones out here. That would make most people agitated. Maybe she'd heard about these murders on the news and didn't want to get involved beyond reporting her find."

"With GPS coordinates?"

Elaina swallowed. Loomis had a point. It was a strange coincidence. And she couldn't explain it, except to say that whoever the caller was, Elaina didn't believe she was the killer's accomplice. They were dealing with a lone perpetrator, of that she felt sure.

"This box you found earlier," Loomis continued. "The one with the toys. Any idea if it's connected in some way?"

"Nothing solid," she said, and immediately regretted her choice of words.

"What do you have, McCord?"

"Just a theory, really. It could be nothing."

"Or it could be something."

She hesitated. "I was just thinking about the cereal box."

"The bran flakes?"

"Special K," she said. "That's a street name for ketamine hydrochloride. Also, Kit Kat, Vitamin K, Cat Valium. It's commonly used as an animal anesthesia, but it's also a club drug. Maybe it's just a coincidence, but so far, all the victims have had ketamine in their systems."

He crossed his arms and looked at her, and she stood there, clasping her hands together to keep from scratching the itchy welts up and down her neck.

"It's my understanding that the tox results aren't back yet on the most recent autopsy—the girl from Houston," he said. "And I hear she was pretty decomposed. We may never know what drugs, if any, she had in her system."

"Actually, we should," Elaina said. "The ME was instructed to look for ketamine. He took a vitreous sample from the eye."

"How do you know?"

"I attended the autopsy."

This seemed to come as a surprise to him. He tipped his head to the side, and she couldn't tell whether it was respect or skepticism she saw in his gaze.

"Well, you're right, then. If she had ketamine in her system, we'll probably find traces. You think she did," he stated.

"I'd be surprised to learn otherwise. All the other victims have had it. It seems to be his drug of choice."

He looked at her for a long moment. In her peripheral vision, she saw Troy approaching. He must have just finished giving authorities his formal statement.

"You understand this case is ours now, don't you?" Loomis asked her. "Besides this one turning up on federal land, we know we've got a serial killer on our hands, and it's time we stepped in."

Elaina waited. Where was he going with this? Everyone knew the Bureau had taken over. That particular piece of news accounted for the resentful looks she'd been getting tonight from Breck and the sheriff and especially Cisernos, who had responded to Cinco's request, only to be told his services weren't needed; the FBI had taken charge.

"I've been tapped to lead up this investigation, McCord. You're new. You're green. Letting you anywhere near this thing is probably a mistake."

She saw Troy edge closer, probably wanting to hear the rest of it. Elaina wanted to hear it, too. She sensed a "but" coming. Despite the sweat and the mud and the Hawaiian shorts, it was possible this man actually took her seriously.

"But you're already involved," Loomis said, "so we're going to go with it. You're a part of this case, and I've got a task for you, starting right now. That is, if you're up for a challenge."

Troy was waiting when Weaver exited the station house. He watched the agent walk across the blindingly white caliche parking lot. Three in the afternoon, and the man still wore a jacket. His only nod to the triple-digit temperature was his slightly loosened tie, which happened to be purple. Not a great choice for spending the afternoon with Lito Island's finest.

If Weaver was surprised to find Troy out here leaning

against his car, he didn't show it. He stopped beside the battered Taurus and pulled out his keys.

"Hey, I think you dinged my car," he said.

Troy scowled at the sedan. It was a heap, just like Elaina's. "I can't believe you guys drive these things."

"We took a vow of poverty. What can I do for you, Mr. Stockton?"

"Troy. And you know exactly what you can do for me."

"I don't know where she is," Weaver said.

"Bullshit."

"Okay, I know exactly where she is, but I'm not going to tell you."

"Why not?"

"Because she's got a difficult job to do, and she thinks you'll distract her." The man's gaze dropped briefly, and he lifted an eyebrow. "I can understand her concern."

Troy gritted his teeth. "She's off trying to track down that ketamine."

Weaver didn't say anything.

Troy crossed his arms. "I was standing right there when Loomis asked her to do it. That's where she's been all day, isn't it?"

Weaver just looked at him.

"Is she aware she's being set up for failure?" Troy tried to keep his voice neutral, but some of the anger slipped through. He'd been mad as hell since Elaina had turned to him last night and politely ordered him to leave the crime scene. Searching high and low for her since eight this morning hadn't improved his mood any.

"You underestimate her," Weaver said now.

"What's that supposed to mean?"

"Elaina knows she's being set up. How could she not? It's been happening since she joined our office. She's doing the only thing she can do."

"Which is?"

"The impossible. Walk into a hostile environment. Provide a profile nobody wants. Track down the origins of a drug that can be obtained by any kid with a computer. She'll do everything they ask her to, and more, and that's how she'll prove herself. And she doesn't need your help, however much you'd like to give it to her."

Troy's gaze narrowed on the agent's face. He caught the disapproval in his eyes, and something else, too. Disgust.

Weaver thought he was using her.

And maybe he was. Maybe this was about sex and Troy's perverse attraction to a woman who'd made it clear she didn't want him around.

Or maybe not. Troy wasn't sure really. But he knew he was pissed at her, and knowing she was off somewhere on a fool's errand—*alone*—when she'd caught the attention of a serial killer wasn't something he could let go.

"I'll find her," he told Weaver.

"She'd be happier if you didn't." He opened the door and slid behind the wheel. The car coughed as he started it, and then he looked up at Troy. "But if you *do* find her, I suggest you stay out of her way. She doesn't need any more stumbling blocks right now."

"Stumbling blocks?"

"Oh, you know, like seeing her name on the news, having her professional reputation trashed in the media."

He slid on a pair of mirrored aviators. "Don't cause problems for her. You won't like the result."

Troy laughed. "Are you threatening me?"

"You *were* listening. Good. Now, do us both a favor and leave Elaina alone."

CHAPTER 12

In a loose-fitting sundress, Birkenstocks, and a string bikini, Elaina blended in with all the other drug tourists wandering the side streets off Mercado Juarez. And yet four hours into her mission, she had nothing to show for her efforts but a purse full of pills and sore feet.

Elaina scraped the hair off her damp neck and twisted it into a knot. She unzipped her purse and pulled out the crude map the cabdriver had drawn for her in exchange for a generous tip. She'd managed to locate all three *veterinarias,* but her inquiries had elicited nothing more than blank stares and shaking heads. Ditto her inquiries at the many *farmacias* she'd tried.

The stench of sweaty bodies and car exhaust wafted toward her as she turned a corner and stepped back onto a busy street. Pedestrians streamed up and down the sidewalks, pausing to haggle over brightly colored blankets and silver jewelry. Elaina passed an ice cream kiosk, a ceramics shop. She passed a rack of Western boots and inhaled the scent of freshly cured leather. She stepped around a little old lady sitting on a blanket in the middle of the sidewalk, her hand-painted crosses spread out around her. The woman called something after her in Spanish. Elaina turned to look and smacked into something solid.

"Oh!" She glanced up at a barrel-chested young man exiting a store.

"'Scuse me," he said, and tipped his cowboy hat.

She noticed the sign painted on the window. FARMA-CIA. This place was three times bigger than all the other spots she'd visited. And she'd struck out with the animal places, so why not try?

A group of older couples filed out, probably retirees from Texas stocking up on cheap meds. Elaina held the door open for them and then slipped inside.

A large box fan stirred the air. In contrast to the oven-like conditions outside, the store's interior was a comfortable eighty-five degrees. Elaina's shoulders relaxed as she glanced around to get her bearings. Tables piled with T-shirts. Cheap liquor. Giant coolers brimming with ice and beer. And on the back wall, a long white counter with hundreds and hundreds of little boxes and bottles stacked behind it.

She made a beeline for the counter, mentally rehearsing her lines as she went.

A muscle-bound twenty-something and his girlfriend were hunched over the counter reading the labels on several little white bottles that Elaina guessed contained steroids. She sidled up next to them and caught the eye of an idle clerk.

"*Hola.*" Elaina smiled at the middle-aged woman, who wore a lab coat but probably had nothing in the way of medical training. "*Tiene Viagra, por favor?*"

"Sí, sí." The woman plucked something off the shelf behind her and placed it on the counter.

Elaina smiled. *"Gracias. Y tiene ketamina?"*

The woman looked blank.

"Er, Ketaset? Ketalar?" She went through the other medical names she'd gleaned from the Internet chat rooms she'd visited last night. Not a glimmer of recognition.

Elaina sighed and took out her wallet.

"Oxies?" asked the woman.

Elaina shook her head.

"Percs? Vicodin?"

She shook her head again, and the woman rang up her purchase. Elaina left the store with a knot of frustration in her chest and another batch of pills she didn't need.

"You looking for some K?"

She turned around. The couple that had been at the counter was leaving the store now.

"Do you know where I can find some?"

"El Toro," the man said. "They're pretty chill about selling it without a script, too. Take a left at the corner." He slung an arm over his girlfriend's shoulder. "And if you want something to do tonight, come to Boingo's."

"Boingo's," she repeated.

"It's on the beach," the girl added. "We heard it's cool."

"Thanks," Elaina said. "I'll check it out."

They sauntered away, and Elaina headed for El Toro. She'd expected another pharmacy but found a veterinary supply store instead. In the window were several cages containing emaciated dogs, a tired nod to the store's supposed purpose. She repeated her polite inquiry, and this time, the clerk placed a small glass vial on the counter in front of her.

Elaina picked it up and looked at it. The chemical she held in her hand could put a cat to sleep. Could send ravers into a "K-hole." Could subdue a victim for murder.

"Esta bien?"

She glanced up at the clerk, a grandmotherly-looking woman with soft brown eyes and a friendly smile. Elaina nodded, and excitement surged through her as she opened her purse.

After paying for the ketamine, she slid a crisp hundred-dollar bill from her wallet, and the clerk's eyes widened. Elaina unfolded a piece of paper containing twelve mug shots—the top twelve candidates on her suspect list. All fit her profile. All had violent criminal histories. All had traveled to Mexico in the past year.

"Conoce algien de eso foto?" Elaina asked. *"Una cliente aqui?"* It was the phrase she'd been rehearsing in her head all day but hadn't had a chance to use. *Do you recognize anyone from this photo? A customer here?*

She moved the page across the counter, and the woman glanced down at it.

"Sí."

Elaina slid the hundred toward her but kept her finger on it. The woman cast a wary glance over her shoulder, and Elaina held her breath, praying that whomever she was worried about wouldn't come waltzing out here.

She turned back to Elaina and started to say something.

A lab-coated man stepped through the curtain. His gaze locked on Elaina's and instantly turned suspicious.

Elaina glanced at the clerk again, but her face had become a blank mask. Reacting on instinct, Elaina scooped her hundred and her mug shots into her purse, along with her purchase. The man eyed her coldly from behind the counter as she left the store.

Elaina wove her way back toward the main strip, more deflated than ever. She'd been so close, and the lead had just disappeared. Maybe she'd go back later. But she had a hunch the woman wouldn't be nearly as willing to help her.

Elaina sighed. It was now dusk. Her energy was spent. But worse than her fatigue was the feeling of failure that seemed to grow heavier with every step.

All last night she'd stayed awake, cruising chat rooms and Internet sites. She'd learned more about the rave scene than she'd ever imagined possible, including where and how to buy practically any club drug out there. She'd learned that Troy had been right—Matamoros offered a cornucopia of legal and illegal meds, provided someone knew where to look. And Elaina had no doubt their unsub knew precisely where to look.

He'd been here. Elaina felt certain of it. She just needed someone to ID him. Ketamine was available on the Internet, yes, but she didn't believe the unsub would want to leave a paper trail, not when he could get the drug cheaply and anonymously down here.

She took a right, then a left, weaving her way through all the shops and kiosks. They'd begun to blur together, an endless parade of ponchos and leather goods and brightly colored piñatas.

She stopped short. A familiar image caught her eye. A yellow-and-purple sticker on the window just up ahead.

She approached the dragonfly and stared at it, just to be sure. It was the same design as she'd seen on Dr. Lawson's bulletin board—a design remarkably similar to the pendant she'd seen in the morgue.

Elaina's pulse quickened as she peered through the glass window. An Internet café. Young people lounged around low tables and pecked away at computer keyboards. The familiar, high-pitched buzz of a coffee grinder reached her ears.

She stepped inside and smelled the tantalizing aroma of fresh coffee. She wasn't sure what she was doing here besides taking a break, but she couldn't just walk by. She needed to know what that symbol meant. And her system was screaming for a jolt of caffeine. She dropped her bag onto a table and sank into a chair.

"Get you something?"

Elaina looked up into the twinkling eyes of a young waitress. She spoke and looked like an American, and her purple braided pigtails made Elaina think of a punked-out Pippi Longstocking.

"An iced coffee, please," Elaina said.

"Anything to eat with that?"

"No, thanks. But I have a question for you. That sticker on your window. Do you have any idea what it means?"

She followed Elaina's gaze. "The dragonfly?"

"Yes."

She shrugged. "Beats me. I think one of our day-trippers put it there."

"Day-trippers?"

"You know. Backpackers. Hikers. Tourists who like to trip."

"Oh. Got it."

"They come over the bridge every day. Some stay. Some don't. Some of them wear T-shirts sporting that dragonfly. I'm not really sure what it means." She smiled. "Sure you don't want anything to eat?"

"No, thank you."

Elaina turned to stare at the sticker. The symbol meant something, something important. She just didn't know what.

When the waitress came back, Elaina had her photo lineup out on the table.

"Listen, could you help me with something? I'm down here looking for someone. Have you seen any of these guys around? Maybe they're day-trippers?"

The woman placed the iced coffee on the table and gazed down at the photos. She gave Elaina a wary look. "Those are mug shots."

"They are."

"I guess that makes you a cop, huh?"

Elaina didn't say anything. She just watched Pippi as her wheels turned. To cooperate, or not to cooperate? Elaina could tell she recognized someone, or it would have been a split-second decision.

Come on, Pippi. Give me a break here.

The woman's eyes slid to the bottom row of faces. "I don't know," she said.

"Sure you do. All these guys have been through here recently," Elaina said, although she didn't know that for sure. "You've probably seen at least a few of them."

She bit her lip. She darted her gaze around the room. Elaina held her breath.

"This *one* guy . . ." She pointed a black fingernail at

the bottom left mug shot, and Elaina's pulse jumped. Noah Neely. The kid with blond dreadlocks who'd been hanging around the marina that first day. "He was staying at the youth hostel across the street around spring break."

"Spring break? Of this year?"

"I think." She glanced around the room again, obviously nervous. A man in a red baseball cap near the door was staring at them, but he looked away.

"I don't know his name." She shook her head. "He was in here a lot, though. Cheap tipper, too. I remember that."

After chugging her coffee, Elaina left the waitress a huge tip, along with a business card. Reenergized, she slung her purse over her shoulder and headed for the hostel. Finally, a solid lead. Not only did Neely fit her profile, he'd been present at the marina when the sheriff had brought in one of the victims.

Some perpetrators like to watch the police work. Some even insert themselves into the investigation. Her father's words echoed through her head, and she felt a renewed sense of confidence.

At the hostel, check-in required a twenty-dollar deposit and no ID.

"Cheets?" the manager asked her.

"Excuse me?"

"*Cheets?* You want *cheets?* For your bed?"

"*Sí, gracias.*"

"Ten dollar."

Elaina passed him another bill. Then she pulled her crumpled map from her purse and flattened it out on the Formica.

"You know of any *veterinarias* near here?" she asked. "Besides these?"

He gave her a knowing look. "Ten dollar."

Elaina handed over another bill. He took a ballpoint pen from behind his ear and drew an X several blocks from the main square. "Here," he said. "Cheap *drogas*."

At last she was getting somewhere. She felt heady with excitement as she stuffed her wallet back into her purse, along with her room key. She suspected she'd have roommates, and she intended to pump them for information.

"Gracias," she said. "I'll be back for those sheets."

Outside, she was once again surrounded by noise and heat. She wended her way through the side streets, trying to follow the map. Darkness was falling. Some of the shopkeepers were shutting down for the day, packing up merchandise and pulling aluminum doors down over their storefronts. Elaina kept walking. Four more blocks to go. The distance between storefronts increased. The sound of traffic near the square diminished. No *veterinarias*. No *farmacias*. Not even a trinket shop, just empty doorways punctuated by foul-smelling garbage cans and graffiti.

Elaina's skin prickled. She wasn't in a tourist neighborhood or anything like one. She needed to go back.

She turned around and saw a brief glimpse of red in a doorway. She hesitated, then kept going. Gone were the college kids, the backpackers, the sun-browned women with their dresses and straw hats. She gripped the strap of her purse and set her sights on a distant intersection. Cars. Stoplights. If she could just get there—

Ssst. Ssst.

The sound came from behind her.

Ssst. Ssst.

She walked faster.

Ssst. Ssst.

Forget the intersection. There was a T-shirt shop two blocks up. If she could make it there—

A man stepped into her path. Dark. Bulky. A red ball cap pulled low over his eyes.

CHAPTER 13

Elaina's heart skittered. She tried to step around him, but he blocked her way.

She moved without thinking—upward thrust to the jaw, knee to the groin. A surprised grunt, and he went down. Her brain screamed *Run!* at the same instant something seized her arm and wrenched it behind her back. He grabbed her around the waist, and panic set in as her heels scraped over the pavement. He was dragging her into an alley. She bucked and kicked. Her face struck brick. Pain and shock rocketed through her. She saw a glint of metal. Felt the purse being ripped from her arm. Then a hand was in her hair, yanking her head back and exposing her neck. Something cool and hard pressed against her skin.

Her eyes stung. Hands groped her. Too many hands, pulling, tearing. *Too many, too many, too many.* She heard a shrill noise and realized it was coming from her. Her cheek was pressed against the brick, and then a knife slid into her field of vision. Sour breath in her face. Words she didn't understand. Something burned at her temple.

She tried again to kick, but her heel connected with nothing but air.

Everything jerked backward. She landed on the concrete, and pain zinged up her spine. Grunts, groans, curses. She scrambled to her feet as one of her assailants raced off. Red baseball cap. Her purse in his hand.

"*Run,* Elaina!"

She stumbled backward, into the wall, and gazed down at the twisting pile of bodies in the middle of the alley. *Troy.* He cursed and struggled underneath her attacker.

She jumped on the man. She hooked an arm around his neck and jerked against his windpipe with all her might. The guy tried to pull her over, but she tightened her hold. Troy rolled out from under him. The man got to his feet, taking Elaina with him. Troy's fist smashed into his face with a sickening crunch. Then a flash of metal. He made a swipe with the knife, then another. Troy leapt back, and the man exploded from her grasp. He shot down the alley and disappeared around a corner.

Elaina stared after him, gasping. Her mind reeled. She whirled around, searching for other threats. Trash cans. Doorways. A flutter of movement as a woman ducked into a building and slammed the door.

"Elaina."

She flinched at the touch and spun around.

"You're bleeding." Troy took her arm and towed her toward the noise and lights of the tourist zone. He pulled her into an empty alcove where a bare lightbulb shone down from above a door. She glanced around for any sign of the two men, but they were long gone.

Troy took her face in his hands and turned it. "Shit, he

got you." His thumb moved over her cheek. The skin at her temple burned, and she remembered the blade.

Something fierce glinted in Troy's eyes. The pulse at his neck throbbed. His skin was slick with sweat, and blood trickled from his lip. She could almost hear his heart pounding right in front of her. Or maybe it was her heart.

"You all right?" he demanded.

Her legs felt like noodles all of a sudden. He must have seen it in her face because he clutched her shoulders.

"Elaina?"

"I'm okay."

His gaze on hers was intense. "What was in the bag? Did you lose your gun? Your badge?"

"My gun . . ." Her mind swam. She looked over his shoulder and tried to get control of her thoughts. "I left all that in my safe, at the Sandhill Inn. My bag had—" Her brain went blank. What had been in there?

"Where's your passport?" His voice snapped her back to reality.

She glanced down. A thin cord. She fished the travel pouch from inside her dress. They hadn't gotten it. She felt the outline of her passport inside it. "It's here. I didn't have it in the purse. It's right here."

"Good." He took another look at her temple and his expression hardened. "Let's go." And then he pulled her out of the doorway and down the street. She stepped in something wet. She looked down at her feet and realized her sandals were gone. Probably back in the alley. She glanced around. They were nearing the tourist area again. Some of the shops had closed down for the day, and music drifted from all the restaurants and bars now filling in with tourists.

She spotted an armored vehicle on the corner up ahead. Beside it stood two uniformed men holding assault rifles. Troy seemed to spot them at the same time she did.

"Should we—"

"No," he said. He glanced around, then tugged her into a nearby store. It was open to the street, the displays crammed in front to lure passing tourists. She watched mutely as Troy grabbed a T-shirt off a table and snagged a water bottle from one of the ice bins.

"Come on."

He handed her the shirt and pulled her into a stream of pedestrian traffic.

"Wipe your face up," he said. "We're almost there."

Elaina pressed the shirt to the side of her head. When she pulled it away, it was crimson with blood.

He'd cut her. That asshole had cut her with his knife.

Troy stopped at an alley. Someone approached them, and Elaina recoiled before she saw that it was just a kid. Troy spoke to him in rapid Spanish and paid him some money, evidently for guarding his pickup.

The shiny black Ford was parked just up the alley, and she'd never been so glad to see a vehicle in her life. The passenger door was sandwiched right up against a building. Troy pulled open the driver's side and held her arm as she climbed in. She crawled over the console and had barely settled into the seat when the engine growled to life, and Troy maneuvered out of the alley. Then they were on the street, cruising past all the shops and bars and brightly lit restaurants.

She leaned back. Her shoulders sagged. She gazed down at the bloody T-shirt in her hands.

"Clean that up as best you can," Troy said. "We don't need any questions at the border checkpoint."

Elaina picked up the water bottle from the console and twisted off the top. Her hands were shaking. God, her knees were, too. She squeezed her thighs together and tried to make them stop. She took a deep breath.

"You got a car down here?"

"It's at a garage," she said, "just north of the bridge." She'd heard stories of American cars in Matamoros getting towed, and tourists having to buy them back for obscene amounts of money, so she'd walked the bridge and taken a taxi into downtown.

Troy turned again, and the bridge spanning the anemic-looking river came into view. No traffic snarls at the moment—just drunken yahoos in sombreros clogging the sidewalks.

She doused the T-shirt with water and tried to clean up her face. It stung, but she wasn't sure she wanted to look at it. Troy's reaction hadn't been good. Would she need stitches? She tried to imagine herself with a Frankenstein scar down the side of her face.

Shit, he got you. He'd cut her. What else would they have done if Troy hadn't shown up?

She'd done okay against the first one. Better than okay—she'd had him on the ground. She could have just run. She hadn't anticipated the second guy.

She should have.

And then the hands were back, groping and pulling at her. Fear shot through her, so raw she could smell it.

"You okay?"

She glanced at Troy. He seemed so calm. So in control behind the wheel of his pickup.

"Elaina?"

"I'm fine. Just—" Shaken. Nauseated. Rattled to her bones. "Just flustered a bit."

His gaze hardened. He focused his attention on the road. There were several lines at the checkpoint and he chose the shortest one.

She busied herself cleaning up the blood. It gave her something to do with her hands. She glanced over and realized he needed cleaning up, too.

"Here." She reached over, hesitated for a moment, and then dabbed the wet shirt against the side of his mouth. He didn't flinch, even though it looked as though he'd taken a solid punch in the jaw.

Elaina pushed away her guilt and resettled herself in her seat. By the time they reached the checkpoint, she looked more like a disheveled tourist than a woman who'd just been assaulted with a deadly weapon. At the American side, she half listened as Troy exchanged casual pleasantries with the border police. Elaina clenched her teeth against the pain and leaned her injured temple against her hand, trying to look bored. The last thing they needed was to be pulled over and detained for questioning.

The officials waved them through, and she gazed at the side mirror as the checkpoint receded behind them. She closed her eyes and felt a flood of relief.

Troy cranked up the a/c and turned a vent to face her.

She swallowed the lump in her throat. "I need to pick up my car. It's at that garage up there on the right."

He glanced at her. "And the keys?"

The keys. She closed her eyes and cursed mentally. "In my purse. I'll have to come back tomorrow with a spare." Why hadn't she tucked her key inside the pouch with her passport and that extra bit of money?

She looked at him again. "How did you find me?"

"It's not too big a town."

"But how did you know I was down there?"

He glanced at her but didn't answer.

"I spotted you outside the café," he said. "But then you disappeared. Took me a few minutes to track you down again."

She heard the edge in his voice, and didn't want to think about the scene in that alley. She dabbed the T-shirt against her head. The bleeding seemed to have stopped. She peered into the side mirror and tried to see the cut.

They were in Brownsville now. She recognized the buildings, the exit for her apartment. A sign for a hospital appeared, and Troy skated across several lanes of traffic.

"What are you doing?" she asked.

"Taking you to a hospital."

"No."

He flashed a look at her. "You've got a fucking gash on your face, Elaina. You need medical attention."

"It's just a scratch."

He glared at her.

"Have you been to the ER in Brownsville?" she asked.

"No."

"Well, I have. It's a zoo, especially at night. I'm not setting foot in that place."

His jaw tightened. He shook his head.

"Just take me to a drugstore, I'll get a butterfly bandage."

Another glare. She ignored it and gazed out the windshield.

The truck filled with silence as he took the highway leading to Lito Island. Elaina shifted her attention out toward the gulf. Soon the arc of the causeway lights came into view. He was doing ninety now, and an hour-long drive had been cut in half. He turned onto the causeway. When they were on Lito Highway, he took the first turn into a supermarket parking lot.

"Lock the doors," he ordered.

He got out of the truck and walked briskly into the store.

Elaina locked the doors. She leaned her head back against the seat and took a deep breath. She would not cry. She would *not* unravel in front of him again.

She looked down at herself. A splatter of blood decorated her breast, and one strap of her dress was torn. The bikini she'd worn beneath her sundress to blend in with the tourists was bloodied, too, but she didn't have a change of clothes. She ripped the second strap to match the first, then tied the two ends behind her neck in a halter. She gulped down the water and took a few deep breaths. By the time Troy exited the store with his cell phone pressed to his ear, she looked halfway normal.

He passed her a grocery bag, and she stowed it at her feet beside the soiled T-shirt.

"So," he said as they turned onto the highway. "What else was in that purse of yours? Anything important?"

Her mind felt clearer now as she recalled the contents.

"Some money, my sunglasses. Retin A, Cipro, Viagra, ketamine."

He slid a glance at her. "Big afternoon."

"Yep."

"Cell phone?"

"I haven't had a chance to get a replacement," she said. That was one bit of good news. At least she wouldn't have to walk into her office and explain how she'd lost a second Bureau phone in twenty-four hours.

They drove down the highway, and she gazed out over the marshland. The stars were out now. It seemed so quiet, so peaceful. And just a few miles south of here, everything felt like a war zone. The silence took hold as she let herself be mesmerized by the landscape. The marshes raced by—black shadows interrupted by glimmering fingers of water. She glanced around and realized he'd passed the inn. They were almost to the wildlife park.

"Hey, where are we going?"

"No more arguments." He turned off the highway and onto a gravel road. *His* gravel road. He was taking her back to his house. Something flashed in the side mirror, and she looked over to see a pair of headlights. Her pulse leapt.

"Someone's behind us."

"I know." He pulled into his driveway and cut the engine. A sleek black Lexus pulled up alongside her. A man got out. He wore slacks and a black golf shirt. He carried a briefcase. Moonlight glinted off his completely bald head.

"Who's that?"

"Javier Lopez. Good friend of mine." Troy pushed his

door open, and the interior light came on. He gazed at her across the console, and she saw it again—that fierceness she'd seen in the alley. "He's a doctor, and he's here to take a look at you. And I meant what I said about arguments, Elaina. I'm fresh outta patience tonight."

Troy had never minded the sight of blood, but watching Lopez sew up that gash in Elaina's face had made him want to puke. He sat on his deck now, staring out at the surf and waiting for Elaina to finish up whatever she was doing in his bathroom.

Six stitches. That was it. It could have been worse. It could have been a *lot* worse if he hadn't been combing a nearby street when he'd heard that scream. The panic in it—along with his absolute certainty that it belonged to Elaina—had made his blood run cold.

He picked up the bottle from the table and refilled his glass.

The door slid open and he turned to see Elaina step outside. She padded across the deck in her bare feet. They'd been torn and bleeding earlier, but she'd cleaned them up.

"What are you drinking?" she asked.

"Tequila."

"Is it any good?"

"You've never had tequila?"

"Not by itself." She glanced around and seemed to hesitate before taking the chair closest to his. "Just in margaritas."

He scooted his chair around so that it faced hers. He reached out and tilted her chin up so he could see her wound in the moonlight. Six tiny black sutures. The skin at her temple glistened where Lopez had put ointment on it.

"You're going to have a scar."

"Probably."

He let his hand drop away. For a long moment, he just looked at her and saw that same hint of fear he'd seen earlier. He was glad to see it. She *needed* to be afraid. She needed to learn some caution and not go flashing her creds in places where cops had unnaturally short life expectancies.

At the same time, though, he hated that look in her eyes. Anger churned in his gut as he took in her scraped cheek, her bruised arm. Fearless Elaina, who didn't run when he told her to. Who waded through swamps looking for dead girls. Who spoke to desperate parents when everyone else with a badge wanted to run and hide. She still wore the torn purple dress with the blood on it, and Troy knew that if he had the chance right now, he would kill both those fuckers with his bare hands.

She broke eye contact with him and looked out at the beach.

He went inside the house to get another glass. When he came back out, he poured some tequila and slid it in front of her, then sank into his chair, facing the water.

She lifted the glass and looked at the amber liquid.

"It's from Jalisco," he told her, and then watched in amazement as she tipped her head back and poured it down her throat.

"Well, shit, that's one way to do it."

Her eyes slammed shut. She bent over and made a sound like a gagging cat.

"Laina?" He pounded on her back. "Hey, you okay?"

She shook her head vigorously, and he couldn't help it—he started to laugh.

Her head snapped up and she wheezed something at him.

"You're supposed to sip it, not shoot it. This stuff's three hundred bucks a bottle."

She winced and shuddered, and he tried to soothe her by stroking her back.

"It's awful," she gasped.

"You just have to get used to it."

"Why would you want to?"

He laughed again and combed her hair back from her face. It felt soft and cool, and he liked the way it lifted in the breeze. She cast a wary glance at him.

"Guess it's an acquired taste." He picked up his glass and sipped. "Want something else?"

"I'm fine," she said, and glanced at her watch. "Anyway, I should be getting back. You mind giving me a ride to the inn?"

"Happy to," he lied, but then he didn't move. Neither did she. After a drawn-out silence she leaned back in the chair and closed her eyes.

He looked out at the water. The surf rolled against the shore, and he heard the distant sound of rap music from one of the nightclubs not too far down the beach.

"Feels nice out here," she said.

"Yeah."

"Cooler than it's been."

"Yeah."

"Thank you for helping me."

She put it out there casually, but he knew she didn't feel that way about it. She opened her eyes and looked over at him. "I would have been in trouble if you hadn't come. I'm not sure what would have happened." She turned her glass on the table and looked away.

"Seemed like you were doing okay at first," he said. "Don't know what you did to that baseball cap guy, but he was in some serious pain when I got there."

"Knee to the groin," she said.

"Nice."

"It was the other one." She shook her head. "I didn't even see him. He came right out of my blind spot. I can't believe I let it happen. It was one of the first things they taught us at the Academy."

She shook her head again, and he could tell she was disappointed with herself.

And he knew what he should do here. She needed a friend tonight, a drinking buddy. If he had a decent bone in his body, he'd rise to the occasion and stop fantasizing about getting her into bed. He took another sip of tequila.

"Don't beat yourself up," he said. "You just need to keep training. Take a break from the office every once in a while. Sharpen up your fighting skills instead of your pencils."

"I've definitely spent too much time at a desk."

"Then get out there, do some more training. It's part of being a good field agent. Only way to learn how to fight is to practice."

She gave him a wry smile. "And I suppose you've had plenty of practice?"

"You should know."

She'd seen his entire rap sheet, seventeen years' worth of bar brawls and disorderlies and public intoxication charges. He hadn't been arrested in years, though. He'd cleaned up his act.

It startled him to realize he actually gave a damn that she knew it.

She poured a splash of tequila into her glass.

"You go to Mexico a lot?" she asked.

"Now and again."

She took a tentative sip and winced. "That where you learned Spanish?"

"Nah, I learned it growing up. Cinco's house, mostly."

"You guys were friends? He seems younger than you."

"He is." Troy tipped his glass and let the taste slide over his tongue. "He's got four older brothers, though. He's fifth. *Cinco.* Anyway, his oldest brother was my best friend growing up. Spent more time at their house than mine."

"Must have been nice, growing up with all those people around."

"Yeah, sometimes."

"Our house was so quiet." Another little sip. "I'm an only child. And my dad was always working. Plus, I was sort of a loner."

"I can picture that."

"Ha. Thanks a lot."

"You seem like you'd have been serious, even as a little kid."

"I was."

"And what about high school?" he asked.

"What about it?"

"That's when you moved to Virginia, right? I bet that was a tough time to move."

"It was okay," she said. "But you know, having a dad who's an FBI agent doesn't exactly do wonders for your social life. Most of the guys I knew were intimidated. Every time I went out, I came home to a big interrogation. 'Where were you?' 'Who were you with?' 'Where'd you go after that?' It used to drive me crazy." She shot him a skeptical look. "Are you really interested in all this?"

"Yes." He tossed back another sip.

"Anyway, I didn't really come out of my shell until college. No, actually, I should say grad school."

He swirled his drink and leaned back in his chair. Grad school. Troy hadn't even gone to college. It was one of the major differences between them and definitely not his favorite topic. But still, it was nice talking to her about something besides a murder investigation.

He glanced at her and saw that she was giving the blue agave another chance. "So what happened in grad school?"

She rolled her eyes. "I fell in love. Or at least I thought I did."

"You thought you were in love, and then . . . ?" He waited for her to fill in the blank.

"He was a law professor. She was his T.A." She took a gulp, and this one seemed to go down easier than the rest. "And yes, I'm fully aware of what a cliché that is. What can I say? He was a cheat, and I was an idiot."

"Love makes people stupid." Troy downed the rest of his drink and offered her the bottle. She nodded, and he filled up their glasses.

"How do you know?" she asked.

"Just what I hear."

They stared at the sky, and his buzz started to kick in. They didn't talk for a while, just drank and listened to the waves. It felt good. This was one of his favorite pastimes, but usually he did it alone.

"You haven't asked about the ketamine."

He'd known it was too good to last. He turned to look at her. "What about the ketamine?"

"I bought some. No prescription necessary. It's entirely possible our unsub is buying his supply at a *veterinaria* just over the bridge."

"Great. Now what?"

"I don't know. The clerk there started to ID someone from my photo array, then clammed up when her manager walked in."

Troy closed his eyes and muttered a curse.

"I did, however, find a waitress who could ID one of my suspects as being a frequent customer right around spring break. First thing tomorrow, I'm going to see if we can get some surveillance on him."

"Elaina." Troy leaned forward on his elbows. "You think it *might* be possible your undercover operation is the reason you were attacked?"

She looked at him.

"Don't you know you can't just go waltzing down there, trying to pull some sting op with the local vendors? Shit, drugs are a serious business here. You're lucky you didn't get a bullet in your brain."

Troy tipped back his glass. Forget driving. If he took her home at all tonight, it was going to be a half-mile walk down the beach.

"It's okay to ask for help," he said. "You don't have to be Superwoman all the time."

He could feel her tension now. He glanced over at her. She was pissed off at him. Again.

"You don't think I can do my job?"

"Don't get defensive. That's not what I'm saying. I'm saying I would have gone with you. Purely as a friend, not a reporter," he added when she sent him a wary look. "Weaver would have gone with you, too. Or Cinco or Maynard. Law enforcement is a team effort. You have to ask your teammates for help when you need it."

She didn't reply, and he wondered if she'd heard this advice before. She could stand to hear it again, obviously.

"At the very least, next time take someone who speaks Spanish. Someone who can fish for information without ticking people off."

She stood up. Here it came. The big *adios*.

She surprised him yet again by picking up her drink and taking it to the wooden railing. She rested it there and looked out over the beach.

"I think you're right," she said, and the words were almost lost on the breeze.

He got up and joined her, resting his glass beside hers.

"I get this feeling all the time that so many people expect me to fail," she said. "Sometimes I even think they *want* me to fail. My boss. My coworkers. My own father." Her hair blew around her face, and she gathered it up and twisted it into a knot. "I guess I'm distrustful of people's motives. I don't think they really want to help me. I think I need to do everything myself. Prove to everyone that I'm capable."

She looked at him, and he saw the vulnerability in her eyes. She gazed back out at the beach. "You want to know the worst thing about tonight?"

He watched her closely. She was letting her guard down. Slowly, but surely, she was doing it. And it had only taken countless hours alone with her and half a bottle of Don Julio.

"What was the worst thing about tonight?"

"I felt completely helpless. My whole life I've spent trying to get away from that feeling. Ever since my mom walked out."

She shook her head. "I think about how hard I worked at the Academy, all the weapons training, the hours of sparring. And it only took two thugs with a switchblade about one minute to reduce me to a defenseless, terrified woman in that alley." Her voice wasn't quite steady now, and he knew she was revealing a side of herself—a weakness—that she usually kept hidden. A lone tear slid down her cheek, and she quickly swiped it away. She looked out at the water, and he had the urge to wrap his arms around her and say something protective and comforting. But he sensed she wouldn't want the usual weepy-female treatment. Hell, he didn't want to give it. If either of those guys had pulled a gun, Elaina would likely be dead right now. And her death would barely make the news—just one more casualty in the border wars. She knew it, too. She knew just how close she'd come to being a statistic.

She took a deep breath, and Troy watched her get her composure back. She shivered, and he hoped it was just because of the cool breeze.

"Sorry," she muttered. "Too much information, right?"

"No."

"Must be the tequila," she said. "I'm not usually this chatty."

"I like you chatty."

She went back to the table and got the bottle. She poured a few fingers into his glass, then hers.

Troy pushed the last of his prurient fantasies out of his mind. She was trying to get good and drunk, and he didn't blame her. She'd been through a trauma tonight. She felt emotional. And if he manipulated the situation to his advantage, he deserved to end up in the seventh level of hell.

She took another sip and held the glass up to the moonlight. "Is this stuff really three hundred dollars a bottle?"

"That's if you smuggle it in. Retail, it's more."

"That's ridiculous," she said, and took a gulp. "Wasteful. I can't believe I'm drinking it. Every sip is what, twenty bucks?"

She wanted to change the subject, and he was happy to oblige her.

"Depends on your definition of wasteful," he said. "How much is a line of coke?"

"I have no idea." She shot him a peevish look, like the Elaina he knew, and he felt reassured that she was back in control. He wasn't about to have a soggy drunk on his hands.

"How much is a Louis Vuitton purse?" he asked. "Or an iPhone? Or a pair of Bulls tickets?"

"Okay, okay, I can see your point. I love basketball." She cast him a sidelong glance, and he saw the faintest trace of a smile now. Progress.

She turned to face the water. For a few minutes, she got quiet and he tried not to notice how pretty her neck looked with her hair pulled up like that.

"I can't believe you live on the beach," she said. "Do you ever wake up and look out the window and have to pinch yourself?"

"No."

"Really?"

"I grew up on the bay, so being surrounded by water's pretty normal for me. I think I could swim before I could walk."

She sighed wistfully. "I've never been skinny-dipping. It's on my list. Or it was."

He looked at her for a second, not sure he'd heard her right. "What list?"

"My 'Things I've Never Done But Secretly Want To' list." She glanced at him. "When I joined the Bureau, I crossed a lot of stuff off it."

"Why's that?"

"Well, anything illegal is out. Plus anything ethically questionable."

He turned around and leaned back against the railing, enjoying the conversation now. "What's unethical about getting naked in the ocean?"

"I'm not sure." Another sip. "Probably something. Oh, yeah. Public indecency."

"What if you own the beach?"

"Do you own this beach?"

"No, just hypothetically."

"Then it wouldn't be a good idea," she said.

"It's a great idea. It feels good. You should go sometime. Hell, go now if you want to. I won't tell anyone."

"Really?" She grinned. "Would you go with me?"

Would he go skinny-dipping with her? She didn't even have to ask. But he looked at her, smiling at him in the dimness, and he realized just how very, *very* inebriated she had to be right now. Time to take her inside and tuck her in on his couch with a glass of water nearby. And he knew that was the dead last thing he was going to do.

"Never swim alone," he said. "That's my motto."

"Oh, you're not serious. I can tell." She poured another shot of tequila into her glass. Troy watched her, and something tightened in his gut.

Her gaze met his as she brought the glass to her lips.

"Better watch it, Elaina." His voice was low and dark now, and her eyes widened slightly.

"Why?"

He eased closer and watched the uncertainty flicker over her face. He nodded at the bottle. "You think you drink enough of that tequila, I won't touch you?"

She put the glass down. "No."

"Don't mistake me for a nice guy."

She gazed up at him, her eyes big and luminous in the moonlight. "I know you're not a nice guy." She swigged the rest of her drink and plunked the glass down defiantly. "This is for me."

"How's that?" He put his hands over hers, trapping them against the railing as he eased his body against hers. A taunt. A threat. A promise. It was up to her.

"It's my liquid courage." She gave him a cautious smile, and her voice was barely a whisper. "The way I feel around you scares me to death."

CHAPTER 14

He stared down at her but didn't move. Finally, she rose up on her toes and kissed him. That was all the invitation he seemed to need, and the next instant his mouth was on hers—hard and taking.

His hands moved into her hair, holding her head in place while he opened her up to him. He tasted like the tequila they'd been drinking, and her tongue started to tingle. She curled her fingers around his neck and just tried to keep up. He was an amazing kisser. She had a faint thought that he was probably much better at sex than she was, and she was way out of her league. And then his hands were on her hips, gripping them, pulling her up, off her feet, and planting her on the railing. She wrestled her mouth away and glanced back and felt woozy.

"I got you," he said huskily, and took her mouth again and his fingers dug into her hips, and she knew that he did have her and she wasn't going anywhere except where he wanted her to. He pushed her knees apart with his body and settled into the space between and turned his attention to planting kisses in a line down her jaw and her neck.

She hooked her ankles behind him and tipped her head back. The breeze wafted over her and she was basking in moonlight and it felt wonderful and she breathed up at the sky.

"Hold on," he whispered, securing her thighs tight around his sides as he let go of her hips and slid his hands to the back of her neck. A little tug at the ties of her dress, and the fabric dropped to her waist. Her gaze met his as she felt another tug and her bikini top fell, too. She saw his eyes heat and she shivered, more from the way he looked at her than from the breeze tickling over her skin. And then his big, warm palms slid around her back and pulled her closer at the same time his mouth found her breast.

She closed her eyes. She let the sensations wash over her—the night and the cool air and the hot, delicious suction of his mouth. She'd never felt this way, like she could just float away and let sensation take over, and she gave into it and tilted her head back and used her legs to hug him closer. Through the fog, she heard laughter and then a *whoop* from the beach below.

He picked her up and set her on her feet, and she grasped for her bathing suit and the fabric of her dress.

"What?"

"We got company." He took her hand. He grabbed the bottle of tequila with the other hand and pulled her toward the house.

His house. She looked at the house now. She looked at him. He must have seen her hesitation, because he pulled her close and gazed down into her face and asked her a question with his eyes.

She answered by kissing him, still holding her clothes to her chest, and even though their hands were full, the kiss went on and on, and finally he stepped back and gave her a little yank toward the door.

Inside, the air was cooler. He put the tequila down on a table inside the door, and she paused to let her eyes adjust to the gloom. He pulled her through the living room, and she watched his tall, dark shadow and her heart did a little jump. *This man. This beautiful, sexy, fascinating man wants me.* She stumbled behind him toward the bedroom wing, and her mind started to swim again, and she knew it was the liquor and the dizzying prospect of what they were about to do together. That low, deep throbbing that had started outside intensified now as he pulled her down a narrow hallway. And then they were in the dark cave of his bedroom and his hands were on her again, tangling in her hair as he kissed her and walked her backward across the room.

She reached for his jeans, pulling him closer and loving the feel of the denim under her hands. Her top was gone now—lost somewhere along the way—and the hardness of his chest pressed against her bare breasts. She wrestled the shirt off him, greedy to touch him now, like he was touching her. She wanted to feel his skin and the solid contours of his body. He lifted his arms to help her, and the shirt disappeared. She paused and blinked at him. The outdoor light seeped through the blinds and cast pale lines across his body. He could have been an ad for jeans or cologne or sex, and just looking at him made her breath back up in her lungs.

He smiled slightly, as if he heard what she was thinking. She knew he'd had many other women before her, and something twisted inside her, but she ignored it and let him pull her into his arms. He guided her back until her thighs bumped up against his bed. He stopped kissing her long enough to push the dress down her legs until it was a heap on the floor. And then she was standing there in only her yellow bikini bottoms, and he was kissing her and murmuring things as his tongue explored her mouth and his hands explored her breasts and hips and thighs.

Heat gathered between her legs and the room started to spin and his hands were on her and she felt like she was in the center of an erotic dream. She knew it would end tomorrow, but right now all she wanted was for him to keep touching her and making her feel this magnetic *pull* of desire, stronger than anything she'd ever felt. *I've never done this.*

"What's that?"

She opened her eyes and gazed up at him and realized she'd spoken out loud.

"This," she whispered.

"Huh?"

"A one-night stand."

He stared down at her in the dimness. "Guess we better make it count, then." He pulled her against him and kissed her roughly until her lips were numb and her legs started to quiver. And then he leaned her back onto the bed, and she felt the cool slide of the bedspread beneath her skin. He pinned her to the mattress, and the hard, heavy weight of him settled right between her legs. She whimpered and tried to roll her hips. He moved down her body, licking a path to her navel as he went, and she felt his thumbs slide into her bathing suit. He peeled it off, and it landed with a *swish* somewhere on the floor, and she lay there, holding her breath. The room started to spin, and her mind registered his hand cupping her heel and the light kiss against the top of her foot—first one, then the other. Her body felt tingly everywhere. She heard him shucking off his jeans. She felt his skin against hers and the rasp of his stubble over her body as he made his way back to her mouth. And then he was *in,* without warning, and she cried out.

He went still. He brushed her hair out of her face and rested his forehead against hers and it was damp with sweat. She clutched him to her, felt the tension in his muscles. And then he pulled back and braced his weight on his hands and started the long, powerful strokes she'd been craving since their very first kiss. She moved under him. She tried to keep up. But she was swimming in water that was much, *much* deeper than she'd ever imagined. Her mind was reeling, and her nerves, and her *heart,* and she wrapped herself around him and tried to hold on. Her muscles burned. Her vision blurred. She clung to him and tried to make it last and last and last, and she never wanted it to stop.

"Now," he said against her ear, and then the wave broke, and she arched against him, and he made one final, powerful plunge and collapsed on top of her.

Mia was fantasizing about a glass of wine and a hot bubble bath when she whipped into the parking lot of her apartment building. She gathered the groceries off her front seat and immediately sensed that she wasn't alone.

She scanned the lot, searching for any sign of trouble. Nothing. No shadows between the cars. No quiet grumble of an idling engine. She slung her purse over her shoulder and told herself she was being paranoid—an occupational hazard given the amount of time she spent around blood stains and rape kits.

She pulled her Mace from her purse as she strode purposefully toward the stairs leading to her one-bedroom apartment.

The hair on the back of her neck stood up. She darted her gaze around. Something moved in her peripheral vision. She glanced at the pickup parked closest to the mailboxes.

Inside the truck, an arm reached up and adjusted the mirror.

She halted.

The door swung open, and the light inside the cab came on. Mia's heart lurched as a man climbed out. He slammed the door and moved straight toward her in the darkness.

She hurried for the stairs.

"Mia?"

She glanced over her shoulder.

His strides lengthened. "Hey, wait up!"

She lifted the Mace. He lunged out of the shadows and ripped the tube from her hand.

She shrieked to wake the dead.

And realized it was Ric Santos standing in front of her. He smiled. She swung back her bags and knocked him in the ribs with a week's worth of Coke Zero.

"You *jerk*!"

He laughed.

She hit him again, harder, eliciting a curse in Spanish this time.

"What are you doing skulking around out here? I nearly Maced you!"

"I know." Another lady-killer smile like the one she remembered from the bar.

She stalked off toward the stairs. She'd stomped up half of them when she heard his footsteps echoing on the metal below.

He caught up to her and took the plastic bags from her hand. Now she was totally disarmed, so she shot him a venomous look.

"It's nearly midnight. You should know better than to creep up on women in parking lots." She stopped in front of her unit, and he propped a shoulder against her door frame as she fumbled with her keys.

"In my defense, I didn't creep," he said.

She glanced into his laughing eyes and felt her cheeks warm. He was right—he hadn't really been creeping. And she'd left a message for him earlier, so she shouldn't have been that surprised to see him. But then, she hadn't expected him to show up at her home.

She opened her door. He followed her inside, and she flipped on the light switch in the foyer.

"Some people use the phone to communicate. You should try it."

But he was too busy glancing around her apartment. She remembered the mess she'd left it in this morning and decided not to turn on any more lights. She also decided not to be embarrassed that she'd spent her evening working and grocery shopping.

He walked into the kitchen and flipped on a light switch, then set her groceries on the counter. He plunked her tube of Mace on the bar dividing the kitchen and living room.

"You're worried about security," he said.

She tossed her purse on the sofa and walked over. "So?"

"So that's good. You ever thought about getting a handgun?"

"How do you know I don't have one?" She slid a six-pack of soft drinks into the fridge and looked up at him. He was in her kitchen. She'd never expected to be standing in her kitchen talking to this man tonight.

"Do you have one?" he asked.

"God, no."

"Why not?"

She snatched a grocery bag off the counter and put some Lean Cuisines in the freezer. "Same reason I don't have an iron."

His eyebrows lifted.

"If I had an iron, I might actually iron something."

He leaned back against her sink and watched her. She tossed the empty bag on the counter, and his gaze dropped, and in that brief instant, she discovered two things: Ric Santos was a breast man—not that she'd met many men who *weren't,* but she definitely noticed his look of male appreciation at the sight of her snug-fitting T-shirt. She also discovered he had either manners or self-control, because he refrained from staring. An amazing number of men didn't, which was why she wore a lab coat practically every second she was at the Delphi Center.

She got a cup down from the cabinet and filled it with ice. "Would you like a drink?" she asked. "I've got some wine somewhere."

"No. Thanks, but I can't stay long," he said. "I just stopped by to find out what's up. You called me twice, so I'm guessing you finished the tests."

She filled her glass with water. "Not yet. I was calling about the victims' clothes."

She'd thought he looked intense the last time she'd talked to him, but that was nothing compared to the way he was looking at her now.

She cleared her throat. "I examined all of the items under a stereomicroscope and I had several interesting findings."

"Such as?"

"Were you aware that each shirt has a puncture hole on the upper-right shoulder?"

His brow furrowed. "What, you mean like a stab wound?"

"I mean something much smaller. The kind of hole that would be consistent with a twenty-five-gauge needle. The sort someone might use to inject someone with a drug."

"*Both* victims' clothes?"

"Yes." She took a sip of water. "In each case, there was a very small amount of blood left on the inside of the garment at the site of the hole. I'm testing both blood samples, but my guess is it'll come back as belonging to the victims. You said both women are already in the database?"

He nodded. "Their families submitted DNA samples

to the missing-persons index years ago, hoping for a match someday. So far, we've had nothing."

"Well, it gives me something to compare the blood to. If the blood isn't theirs, you'll be the first to hear about it."

"Puncture holes." Ric rubbed his jaw. He badly needed a shave, and Mia wondered if he hadn't been home since yesterday, or if he was one of those men whose beards grew quickly.

"I read in the paper about the Paradise Killer," Mia ventured. "Investigators say they believe he's drugging his victims. Women at bars are being cautioned about leaving drinks unattended, stuff like that."

"Ketamine," Ric muttered, staring at the floor now. He was thinking about his case. Mia had seen this before with many of the homicide detectives she knew. They had this remarkable ability to focus. Mia could relate. She tended to block out everything when she peered into one of her microscopes.

"I had one of our toxicologists examine the clothing," she said, and Ric looked up. "That *is* what he found— trace amounts of ketamine hydrochloride in both cases."

Ric crossed his arms and watched her without speaking. She wasn't sure what she read in his expression, but it seemed a lot like respect. To her dismay, she felt a flush of pride.

"So," she said nervously, and she knew she was in trouble here. Allowing herself to care what this man thought of her was an extremely dumb idea. But she also knew it was too late—she cared not only about his opinion of her, she cared about his case.

"Anyway, I thought you'd want to know," she said. "Your two missing hikers are definitely connected, and there's a strong chance they're linked to the Paradise Killer, too." Actually, she had more to tell him, but she wasn't prepared to do it yet. She didn't want to share the rest of the test results until she got confirmation from one of her colleagues at the Delphi Center.

Ric was watching her now with a gleam in his eyes, and her stupid heart fluttered.

"You realize what this means?" he asked her.

"What?"

"You just resurrected a dead investigation."

CHAPTER 15

She heard screaming.

The noise pierced through the fog and penetrated her brain.

Elaina opened her eyes. Then squeezed them shut again to block out a thousand tiny daggers. Too much light. Too much noise. The high-pitched screams were coming from outside. She squinted at the window as the sound continued.

Seagulls.

She sat up. She was in Troy's bed. He was sprawled out beside her, completely naked and completely conked out. She glanced around. Tangled sheets. Discarded blue jeans. A scrap of yellow peeking out from under the bed.

The pain intensified as her brain began to process. How late was it? She looked around for a clock, but her gaze got hung up on Troy. He lay on his stomach, his muscular back rising and falling with his rhythmic breathing. Slowly, she pulled the sheet away from herself and eased out of the bed. The floor creaked under her foot. She froze. She glanced at him, but he was dead to the world. She took a tentative step, then another.

She scooped her yellow bikini bottoms from the floor, grabbed her dress, and slipped out of the room.

The hallway was dim. No outside windows. She crept past the bathroom where Dr. Lopez had stitched her up last night and avoided even a glimpse at the mirror. She crept into the living room, where she stepped into her bathing suit bottoms and pulled the dress over her head. It fell to the floor, and she stood there, blinking down at it. A vision of the dark, stinky alleyway slammed into her.

Don't think about it. Don't think at all.

She hastily pulled the dress up and tied the torn straps. She spotted her travel pouch on the coffee table and grabbed it, then remembered she had no shoes. It didn't matter; she'd walk back on the beach. She crossed the living room and slid open the door.

The sky was a painful, brilliant blue, and the mid-morning sun shimmered off the water. She clamped her hand over her eyes and stood there a moment, waiting for the nausea to pass. Seagulls screeched at one another, and she steeled herself against the noise as she padded across the deck to retrieve the other half of her swimsuit. As she walked toward the wooden stairs, her gaze landed on an empty bottle and two bar glasses sitting beside the hot tub that was built into the deck.

She stopped and stared at it. She remembered Troy, his hair slicked back from his face, his gaze, dark and sensuous, as he'd lifted her out of the bubbling water and set her down on the deck. He'd pushed her knees apart and—

Oh. My. God. Her legs went weak. Her skin tingled. She bit her lip and pictured him just a few rooms away, stretched out across his bed. She could go back there right now and crawl in with him. She could do it. But she shouldn't. She should leave. That was the definition of a one-night stand—no morning after.

Wasn't it? She thought of him, bracing himself above her, gazing down at her in the shadows.

The door slid open, and she jumped at the sound.

He stood there in only a pair of shorts. Their gazes locked.

She didn't breathe, didn't move, except for the brief instant when her attention veered to the staircase beside him. It was just a millisecond, but he caught it anyway, and his expression hardened.

"It's for you," he said, and thrust out his hand.

She stared blankly down at his phone. "It's . . . what?"

"Weaver. For you."

He took a step forward and handed her the phone, then turned and went back inside.

She looked down at the cell phone. Her heart was thudding now. Her hands shook slightly, and she didn't know if it was the aftereffects of alcohol or Troy or the realization that one of her colleagues had called her on his phone.

She put it to her ear. "Special Agent McCord."

A slight pause, no doubt as Weaver absorbed this strangely formal greeting. Why had she said that?

"Thought I'd catch you before you came into the office," he said, and *his* voice was surprisingly formal, too. "I'm with a Detective Ricardo Santos from the San Marcos Police Department. He's been trying to reach you. Any chance you could meet us on the island after your meeting with Chief Breck?"

Her meeting with Chief Breck? It took her a full two seconds to realize the detective must be standing right there and Weaver was covering for her.

"No problem," she said, and glanced down at her clothes. "I'll . . . um, just be another half hour or so."

"Good. Why don't we meet up at that coffee place across from the hotel?"

"Fine. Thank you."

They disconnected, and she took a wistful look at the stairs. So much for her attempt at a coolly casual exit. She should have known she'd be bad at this.

She opened the door and went back inside to return Troy's phone. Footsteps sounded in the hallway, and then he was crossing the living room, wearing jeans, a white T-shirt, and Teva sandals.

She held his phone out to him. "That was Weaver." She said, and instantly realized he knew this already.

His eyebrows tipped up as he shoved the phone in his pocket.

"I'm late for something. I have to go."

He walked into the kitchen and grabbed a set of keys off the counter.

"I can walk," she said. "It's just down the beach."

Instead of answering, he strode past her and into the bedroom part of the house. He came back with a pair of pink flip-flops dangling from his fingers. He held them out to her.

She clenched her teeth with annoyance as she took the shoes from him and slipped them on her feet. He was already out the door.

He chose the pickup, thank goodness, and had the engine started when she climbed in.

"Thank you for the ride," she said.

He slipped on a pair of sunglasses and said nothing as he backed out of the driveway and took the road back to the main highway. The silence hung there in the air, and she glanced uncomfortably around the cab. Her gaze landed on the clock.

Nine-twenty? She'd missed half the morning. Her stomach clenched with anxiety as she tried to remember what she'd intended to do this morning. A call to Loomis to arrange surveillance for that suspect. Another call to Dr. Lawson. And Santos, although she could scratch that off the list now because he'd obviously come here to see her. He must have something important to share. And here she was, late and exhausted and hungover beyond belief.

She glanced at Troy, silent and hostile behind his mirrored sunglasses. She'd known last night was a bad idea. She'd known it from the first shot of tequila, and she'd done it, anyway.

He pulled into a McDonald's drive-through, and she listened, astonished, as he ordered two Egg McMuffins and two large coffees. He paid for the food and shoved the cups in the console, then handed her one of the sacks.

"What's this for?"

"Breakfast."

Her gaze narrowed on him. She dropped the bag on the floor and looked out the window. "I'll pass, thanks."

He shrugged. "Suit yourself."

He pulled back onto the main highway and drove the rest of the short distance to her hotel. He pulled up to the front door and braked, but didn't even bother to put the truck in Park.

A bitter lump lodged in her throat. She knew what he was doing, and she wanted to hit him.

Instead, she gathered her things and climbed out.

"Thank you," she said as she closed the door.

She turned and walked into her hotel, carrying a cup of McDonald's coffee and wearing another woman's shoes.

The thousand daggers had morphed into a pair of hammers at her temples by the time Elaina walked into Dot's Diner. With much reluctance, she removed her sunglasses and scanned the room for Weaver. She spotted the familiar back of his head on the other side of the restaurant. The dark-haired detective seated across from him looked up as she neared the table.

"Detective Santos? Elaina McCord." She held out her hand. The detective gave her a firm handshake while checking out her face.

"Holy crap, what happened to you?" Weaver asked.

She slid into the booth beside him. "It's nothing," she told him.

"Nothing?"

"Just a few stitches."

"Did Troy have something to do with that?" Weaver demanded. "I swear to God, I'll kick his redneck ass right back to the trailer park."

Elaina shot him a "drop it" look as she took a menu from behind the napkin dispenser. Her stomach did a flip-flop the instant she opened it.

"Who's Troy?"

She glanced across the table. Detective Santos was watching her.

"No one," she told him. And then to Weaver: "I got into a little scuffle in Matamoros yesterday. It's really no big deal."

"I thought you were checking out veterinary clinics," he said. "Don't tell me you went down there alone."

"Troy was with me. We ran into some thugs but squeaked out okay." The waitress showed up, and Elaina quickly changed the subject. "Water, please. And a cup of coffee. Black."

She felt both men watching her as she tucked the menu away and pulled a notepad from her purse. She knew Weaver was busy noticing every detail of her appearance, from her still-damp hair to her slightly rumpled shirt and slacks, which she'd planned to iron in her hotel room the night before, but as of twenty minutes ago had still been draped over an armchair.

She glanced across the table at the detective, who—despite a long drive from San Marcos—managed to look much more professional than she did in his button-down shirt and slacks.

"So," she said crisply. "Detective Santos. Your department sent you down here? Does that mean you have something relevant to our case?"

He watched her for a moment, and she felt herself being sized up. "It's Ric," he said. "And I've got two linked cases. Two women who went missing up in Hays County."

"*Two* linked cases? That's a huge break." Elaina turned to Weaver. "What did Loomis say?"

The waitress reappeared with coffee and water. Elaina lifted the glass and downed half the water in one sip.

"He was noncommittal," Weaver told her. "He's not

convinced, but at least he's not dismissing it out of hand."

She turned her attention back to Ric. "Tell me about your cases."

"Both college students," he said. "They disappeared from separate nature trails where they'd gone hiking alone. Their bodies were never recovered, but we found their clothes. According to a tracer at the Delphi Center, it looks like they were injected with a shot of ketamine hydrochloride, upper right arm."

Elaina leaned forward. "When were the abductions?"

"February five years ago. Both victims had told their roommates they planned to spend the day hiking at Devil's Gorge."

"Where's that?"

"About ten miles west of town. It's a state park. There's some endangered bird that nests there, I think."

"And it's your jurisdiction?" Elaina asked.

"No, but the college is. These two girls knew each other from the Wilderness Club, so we were originally looking at a campus connection. And when it became clear we had two missing students and zero leads, the sheriff's office was more than happy to let us keep it."

"Nature trails." Weaver looked at Elaina. "It's an interesting pattern."

"Pattern?" Ric asked.

"All the victims either disappeared from or were found in some sort of nature reserve," she told him. "As a matter of fact, I think every one of the places is some kind of bird sanctuary."

"Maybe our unsub is a bird-watcher," Weaver said.

The waitress brought plates of food that the men had

obviously ordered earlier, while they were waiting for Elaina. She gulped down the rest of her water and asked for a refill.

"You should try the *migas*."

She glanced across the table and met the detective's gaze over his plate of greasy eggs and sausage.

"Knock that hangover right out," he said.

"I'm fine, thanks." She took a sip of coffee and turned back to Weaver. "I don't think he's a bird lover. He's more of a hunting type."

"Why do you say that?" Ric asked.

"His weapon is a serrated hunting knife. And he literally *hunts* women. I believe he selects his targets, stalks them, and ultimately kills them. It's like a sport to him. I also believe he's intelligent, underemployed, and either has some background in law enforcement or wishes he did."

"A wannabe cop?"

"Possibly. He's been meticulous about not leaving behind evidence, with the exception of some yellow twine that can be found at any hardware store. He seems to know police procedure. He's taunting the authorities. It's possible he's even inserted himself into the investigation already, maybe as a helpful witness or something."

"You sound like a profiler," Ric said.

Elaina didn't comment. She aspired to be a profiler, but officially, she was just an agent. A new one at that.

"How is he taunting authorities?" Ric asked.

"I've received some calls from him."

His eyebrows tipped up at this. "You personally, or the police?"

"Me personally."

"We've traced each of them to disposable cell phones," Weaver added.

Ric was frowning now, obviously not happy to hear she'd been singled out by the killer.

"So you came all the way down here," Elaina said, redirecting the conversation. "Did you bring any leads for us?"

Ric forked up a bite of sausage. "I've got three banker's boxes in my truck. Every one of them's filled with files and photographs and interview notes that never went anywhere. Thought I'd sit down with some of you guys and see if any common names pop up. That is, if you're working a suspect list."

"We are," Weaver said. "Unfortunately, it's much too long. Our challenge has been figuring out where to focus." He turned to Elaina. "Your trip south of the river help give us a hand with that?"

"Actually, it did." She told them about the man the waitress had identified.

"That doesn't mean he was down there buying ketamine," Ric pointed out. "He could have just purchased it online."

"True," she said, "but this would have been much easier. And no paper trail. Given the amount of effort he's spent trying not to leave behind DNA or fingerprints, I think he'd much prefer not to leave a paper trail."

"What's the name again?"

"Noah Neely," she said. "Twenty-seven. Shares an apartment with a couple of guys over near the wharf."

"Twenty-seven is pretty young," Ric observed. "You're saying he started when he was in his early twenties?"

"Earlier than that," Elaina said. "If he killed Mary

Beth Cooper, too, that means he's been active since he was eighteen."

Ric looked skeptical again, and Elaina shifted uncomfortably. For a serial killer, this guy was on the very young end of the spectrum.

"Did you tell Loomis about this?" Weaver asked. "And why are you looking at me like you're about to need a favor?"

"I do," she said.

"Uh-oh."

"Detective Santos is going to be busy poring over the case files today."

"It's Ric," he repeated. "And I wouldn't mind both your help with that. We're talking thousands of pages of material."

"Gee, I'd love to," Weaver said, "but I get the feeling I'm on stakeout duty."

"You are," Elaina said. "But the good news is we've got some help."

Weaver looked at her expectantly.

"Officer Chavez offered to lend a hand," she said. "He's part of the task force," she explained to Ric. "He drives a dinged pickup with tinted windows. It'll fit right in on the fish docks."

"That means Ric and I are in the Beast?"

"Sorry," Elaina said, knowing she was sentencing him to hours upon hours of unair-conditioned gloom in an FBI surveillance van. "Maybe you could spread the files out in back, cull through them and compare notes while you keep an eye on the suspect. And we'll be taking turns. Cinco and I can take whatever shift you guys don't want."

Ric looked from Elaina to Weaver, and she could tell he realized he wasn't dealing with the A-team. "What's the rest of the task force doing today?" he wanted to know.

"Some of them are on the mainland, interviewing staff at the two parks," Elaina said. "Another few agents are back in the Brownsville office working the phones and running down more background on the victims' last days."

"And here we are at the beach." Weaver sighed. "How come I feel like I've been relegated to the Island of Misfit Toys?"

"Maybe because you have?"

"Meaning what?" Ric asked.

"Meaning the powers that be think we're all chasing down dead-end leads," Elaina said. "They're letting us do it, but the heavy lifting is taking place elsewhere."

"And what do you think?" Ric asked.

"I think you just brought us a major break," she said. "I think your hikers are connected to our latest victims, and if we can solve one case, we can solve them all. So who cares what everyone else thinks? Let's just suck it up and get working."

After the meeting ended, they stepped out of the restaurant into the blazing brightness of the parking lot. Elaina slid on sunglasses, and Ric walked away to take a cell-phone call.

"What are you doing, Lainey?"

She tore her attention away from the detective and looked at Weaver.

"What do you mean?" she asked, although his worried expression told her precisely what he meant.

"Troy. You said you were going to stay away from him."

Her stomach knotted, and it wasn't just the nausea returning. Every time she thought about the way things had gone with him this morning, she felt sick.

"I can't talk about this right now," she said. And she couldn't. She felt too raw. Why on earth had she convinced herself she could sleep with a man without getting her emotions involved? For someone with a psychology degree, it was an incredibly stupid move. But she hadn't exactly been thinking with her head last night. More like her libido.

"I'm not going to say 'I told you so,' " Weaver said.

"You just did."

"Okay, but don't make me say it again."

The knot in her stomach tightened. *Don't let it happen again*—that was what he meant. And she had no intention of letting it happen again.

But then, she'd had no intention of letting it happen at all until she was standing half-naked on his deck. And even looking at it now, in the brutal light of day, she still wasn't sure that if she could go back and do it over again, she'd do a single thing differently. How crazy was that? Despite how miserable and embarrassed and amazingly stupid she felt this morning, she still wanted the man. *Still*. She still wanted his hands and his arms and the way he'd looked at her so intently last night, as if she were the only woman in the world.

"Lainey?" Weaver was watching her with concern now, and the guilt kicked in. He was the only friend she had down here—a fact she needed to remember.

"I hear you."

"You *say* that," he told her, shaking his head, "but I don't think you're listening."

CHAPTER 16

Cinco mopped the sweat from his brow and glanced at the woman sitting next to him. She was that shade of greenish-white someone got right before they heaved up their lunch. She'd been that way for hours, though, so he didn't actually think she'd do it, but still, she looked bad. The heat and the rotten fish smell wafting over from the docks probably weren't helping any.

"Long night?" he asked.

She looked over at him but didn't answer. It was none of his business. Which told him exactly what sort of long night it had been.

She stared through the windshield at the run-down apartment building two blocks up, where nothing had happened for the past five and a half hours.

"Too much tequila," she said, confirming his suspicions.

"Troy likes that shit. Me, I'm good with beer. Maybe some Jack and Coke sometimes, but you can keep the Don Julio."

She kept her gaze trained on the apartment building and managed to put up some kind of invisible wall. She didn't want to talk. Which was fine with him, but, shit, they'd been here forever and he was bored out of his skull, and he needed something to take his mind off the hundred-degree heat.

"Soon as this shift ends, you should go get some *migas*," he said.

She glanced at him.

"Or Pedialyte. If you can stand the taste."

She unbuttoned the cuffs of her shirt and rolled her sleeves up, finally, after more than five hours. Cinco couldn't imagine how she'd waited this long. He was in a short-sleeved T-shirt and he was broiling, so she must have been about to pass out. The right sleeve went up, and he noticed the bruises on her arm. Four little ovals, all in a line. Troy's mom used to get marks like that.

"Heard you got jumped down in Matamoros."

She looked at him. "Where'd you hear that?"

"Some of the guys."

She sighed and looked away.

"Happened to me once."

Her head whipped around.

"I was about seventeen," he said. "I'd been down at the bars. Was heading back for the bridge, couple guys came at me in this alley. Busted my nose. Grabbed my wallet. Scared the shit out of me, too, I'll tell you that." He looked into her pretty blue eyes. "It could happen to anybody."

She turned away and shifted closer to the door. He knew body language, and this was another NO TRESPASS-ING sign. Well, damn, at least he'd tried. He pictured the stitches lined up on the side of her head. Had she just thought she could show up like that and no one would notice?

"You ever get used to it?" she asked. "You know, the physical part of the job?"

"You mean like arrests and takedowns?"

"Yeah." She turned to face him, and she seemed like just a regular woman now. His sister. His mom. Not some hotshot federal agent.

"A little," he said. "But there's always that adrenaline rush, you know? It's a good thing, being afraid sometimes. Keeps you careful."

She looked out the window. "I wasn't being careful. I was walking around, so absorbed with my case, I forgot to think about what was around me."

She was opening up, and Cinco was glad. He liked her. Not that he planned to make a play or anything. Troy had dibs. But he'd gotten used to her, and he wanted her to feel comfortable here in his town. He wanted her to respect him as a cop, too, even though she had a federal badge and probably half a dozen degrees on him.

She took her water bottle from the cup holder and finished it off.

"You ever want someone to go down there with you, just let me know."

She glanced at him, and he could tell she thought he was just saying it, maybe to be polite or something. But he didn't offer stuff like that unless he planned to follow through.

"I mean it," he said. "I can show you around. Teach you some of the local slang."

"You'd teach me Spanish?" She looked surprised at this.

"If you want to learn, sure. You live here, right? You may as well pick it up. I'm happy to teach you some, at least enough to get by."

She looked at him, and he started to get uncomfortable. Did she think he was hitting on her?

"Thank you," she said. "That's a very generous offer."

He was definitely uncomfortable now that she'd gotten all formal like that. She probably *did* think he was hitting on her.

"I've been taking lessons," she went on. "You know those tapes? But it would probably go faster with a real teacher. I'd appreciate the help."

Cinco's phone rang, saving him from more gratitude. He handed the binoculars to Elaina and fished the thing out of his back pocket.

"Chavez."

"Yo, it's me. You're staking out that apartment, right?"

"Yeah," he told Troy.

"Word is, there's something about to go down."

"Where'd you hear that?" Cinco asked.

"Maynard. Is Elaina with you?"

"Yeah." He glanced over at her. She looked disinterested, but she was definitely eavesdropping.

"I want you to watch her back."

Cinco caught a glimpse of someone in the side mirror. The FBI guy. Weaver. "She's right here. You want to talk to her?"

"No. Just keep an eye on her."

"Will do."

They disconnected just as Weaver walked up to the window. Cinco noticed he'd been pretty stealthy, too, probably trying not to be seen by anyone in that apartment.

"I come bearing gifts," the man said, and handed Cinco a cell phone. "Elaina, that's for you. Programmed with the same number you had before in case your mysterious friend wants to get in touch again. Scarborough is about to call and give you instructions."

Cinco passed her the phone.

"Instructions for what?" she asked.

"He'll explain." He looked at Cinco. "I have a present for you, too. You're invited to the party. Come in your favorite Kevlar."

Elaina's eyes widened. "But where—"

The phone in her hand rang, cutting her off.

"That'll be Scarborough," Weaver said. "He'll explain everything."

Elaina stood beside the minivan, blinking sweat from her eyes as she stared at the map Scarborough had spread out on the hood. It showed a satellite image of Noah Neely's apartment, which was just around the corner from the alley where the tactical team had gathered.

"We got a corner unit, one entrance, two north windows, one south, and no balcony." Scarborough drew an arrow with his pencil. "Loomis and his team go in here, south stairwell. You guys hit the door, get everyone under control. Where's Chavez?"

"Sir?"

"You said there're two males inside at this time? Noah Neely and somebody else?"

"That's right."

"Okay, I want the second four-man team covering the

north stairwell leading to the parking lot." Scarborough scanned the faces around him, pausing briefly on Elaina. She wondered if she looked as hideous as she felt. Her stomach churned, her skin felt clammy, and the Kevlar vest seemed to be flattening her lungs.

Scarborough's gaze veered back to Cinco. "Landlady says the unit next door is vacant, but the rest are occupied. Any intel on the neighbors?"

"A woman walked up several hours ago with a toddler," Elaina put in. "I didn't see them leave."

Scarborough lifted his radio unit. "Anyone entered or left the premises, last six minutes?"

"Negative," said the agent on point.

"Okay, I want Callahan on that door." He tapped the map with his pencil. "That's Unit 23. Make sure no one pokes a head out to see what's going on. This needs to be a straight in-and-out job. We grab him up, take him in for questioning."

"And the friend?" someone asked.

"We'll talk to him here, run his ID. He checks out, he's free to go. Here's our man, people." Scarborough held up an enlarged mug shot. "He recently failed a piss test, and his probation officer said he wouldn't be surprised if he was tweaked out on something today, so expect the unexpected." He passed the picture of Noah Neely around, but he didn't need to. Neely was memorable. The waitress in Matamoros had remembered him. Elaina had remembered him from the marina. A park ranger and a bird-watcher from Laguna Madre National Wildlife Refuge had remembered him, too, which was why they were here right now. Both witnesses had picked his picture out of a photo lineup and reported seeing him on a hiking trail the day after Valerie Monroe went missing. That trail was less than a mile from where the last set of remains was found, remains that just this morning had been positively identified as Valerie's.

Elaina studied Neely's mug shot, although she'd memorized it days ago. His hair looked ropey and dirty. He had bloodshot eyes and dilated pupils. More than anything, he simply looked wasted. He didn't seem like someone capable of kidnapping and savagely murdering six women. But psychopaths didn't necessarily walk around with swastikas tattooed on their foreheads.

"McCord? You with me?"

Her gaze snapped up to Scarborough. "Sir?"

His brow furrowed. Then he turned his attention to the rest of the team. "Okay, let's move." And then to Elaina: "A word, McCord."

The teams loaded into the two minivans. Elaina's heart thudded as she stepped over to talk to her boss.

"You look like shit, McCord."

"I'm fine, sir."

"Next time you're sick, call it in. This is a tactical operation. We don't need a weak link in the chain. You got me?"

"Really, I'm fine, sir." Her chest tightened as she gazed into Scarborough's cool gray eyes and knew she'd already lost the argument. "Just a bit warm from doing surveillance."

He looked at her for a long moment. "All right, you can stay. But hang back while the teams hit the door."

Elaina's heart sank, and she knew what was coming next.

"You can go up afterward and interview the tenants.

Talk to that mom in Unit 23, see if she remembers any-thing funny about her neighbor."

"Yes, sir."

"And next time you're sick, take the day. Don't come dragging ass into the middle of an operation and putting your teammates at risk."

He turned his back on her and climbed into the front of the nearest minivan. The side door stood open, and Elaina felt her cheeks flush as she noticed all the other agents sitting inside, looking pointedly away. They'd overheard all of it. She swallowed the bitterness in her throat and climbed in. It was packed with men and gear, but Cinco squeezed himself against the wall and made room for her. Before she'd even wedged her butt in next to him, they were moving.

Shake it off. Concentrate. She dried her sweaty palms on her pants as the van careened around a corner and came to a halt in front of the suspect's building. The door slid open, and everyone emptied into the street, attract-ing startled looks from nearby pedestrians. Elaina hus-tled to the side and watched the two teams set off—guns drawn—to fulfill their objective. Her chest constricted, and she knew it wasn't just the vest. She should be with them, but once again she was on babysitting detail. The only difference this time was that Scarborough had been right to put her there.

She walked over and waited at the bottom of the stairwell. Footsteps thudded above her, and she heard a sharp rap on the door. She held her breath, dreading the sound of gunshots. Instead, she heard mumbled voices, the squawk of a radio. Minutes later, the heavy clomp of boots as the dazed and confused suspect was led down the stairs between Loomis and Callahan. Noah Neely wore cargo shorts, sandals, and a pair of handcuffs, and he winced at the sunlight as Loomis led him to the waiting police unit.

Anticlimactic.

Like most of the other ops she'd had the privilege to be involved in.

Elaina watched the car roll away. She loosened the Velcro straps on her vest and took a deep breath. Time to haul her buns upstairs and conduct some interviews.

A girl loitering beside the building caught her eye. She wore a bikini top and cutoffs, and she couldn't have been more than eighteen. She sucked on a cigarette and looked Elaina up and down.

A breeze floated by, and the flowery fragrance of dryer sheets chased away the fish stink. Elaina glanced over the girl's shoulder and saw a pair of machines filled with tumbling clothes.

New plan.

She walked up to her. "Hi."

The girl squinted at Elaina through a stream of smoke. Her expression said she'd been there, done that, and she was neither impressed nor intimidated by law enforcement.

"You live here?" Elaina asked.

She lifted a shoulder neutrally.

"Do you know that guy who just left?"

The girl smirked as she dropped the cigarette on the ground and crushed it under her cork-heeled sandal. "'Left.' That's good. Looked to me like got arrested."

"You don't seem surprised."

"Bound to happen sooner or later." She crossed her

arms over her flowered bikini top, and Elaina noticed the heart tattoo peeking out from her left triangle.

"You know Noah?"

"Everybody knows Noah. I never bought anything from him, though, so don't get any ideas."

Elaina leaned a hand on the railing beside the stairs. "He get a lot of company?"

She smiled slightly. "When he's around."

"Have you ever seen him bring any women home?"

She tipped her head to the side and looked at Elaina. "What happened to your face?"

"I got mugged."

"Cool."

"Not really."

A buzzer sounded in the laundry room, and the girl glanced over her shoulder. She looked at Elaina again and seemed to decide something.

"There's this one girl. She's here a lot. I don't know her name or anything."

Elaina's fingers itched to pull the notepad from her pocket, but she didn't. "You remember what she looks like?"

A shrug. "Like everybody."

"Like you?" Caucasian? Blond? Tan and skinny?

"I don't know. Brown hair, I think. She's not that pretty. I think he mostly likes her for her Jeep."

"She drives a Jeep?"

"A Rubicon. Blue. Great beach car. Noah's a surfer, so . . ." She sighed. "I've got to go. Too bad about your face. Maybe you should use your gun next time."

"Thanks," Elaina said. "I'll have to remember that."

• • •

Elaina elbowed her way through the crowd at Coconuts, doing her best not to get sandwiched between all the sweaty bodies and frothy cups of beer. She spotted Cinco at the bar, dressed in board shorts again and pretending to be a surfer.

"She here yet?" Elaina asked, taking the empty stool beside him.

"Haven't seen her."

"I checked the volleyball courts. Nothing."

"She'll show." Cinco tipped back his beer, and Elaina tried not to cringe. "It's her night off. And this is the place to be."

Elaina could see why. Bare skin. Bouncing breasts. Swimsuit-clad women leaping and diving into the sand after balls. Volleyball Night at Coconuts was a pickup scene to top all pickup scenes, and it beat the hell out of whatever else was happening on Wednesdays.

Or so Elaina had heard. But then, she should probably develop another source for island info beside Brenda. The clerk at the inn didn't seem like someone who would be clued into the rave scene that Elaina was pretty sure operated beneath the radar of most islanders, including Chief Breck.

Elaina glanced around and sighed. She'd finally taken Troy's advice and bared a little skin in order to blend in with the crowd. The other agents out in force tonight . . . not so much. Elaina had spotted all five of her colleagues from the Brownsville field office—all cleverly disguised in khaki shorts, Hawaiian shirts, and deck shoes—in less than two minutes.

"Sweet Señorita, is it?"

She glanced up into the warm brown eyes of the bartender. John? Joe?

"No, thanks, Joel. Just a water, please."

He arched his eyebrows, and she realized her mistake. She needed a prop.

"A virgin," she amended. "And I mean straight fruit juice." If she so much as sniffed a shot of rum or tequila or any other liquor tonight, she was done for.

Cinco was watching her, seeing too much. He knew she'd been out with Troy last night, and it was quite possible he'd been given a detailed account. Elaina's brain flashed to the hot tub, the bed, the box of condoms on Troy's nightstand. She felt her cheeks warm.

Did every cop on the island know? Cinco didn't seem like a gossip, but Elaina was a realist. As the sole female member of the task force, she was bound to attract some salacious comments.

Joel slid a glass in front of her, and it was filled with something thick and red.

"My secret hangover cure."

She glanced up at him. "Do I look that bad?"

He smiled. "I can spot a hangover a mile away."

She sniffed the glass. Something tomatoey. Elaina's stomach clenched. Her head started to pound. She just wanted this day over. She took a tentative sip as she searched the faces again, looking for her target.

"So'd you see the interview with Noah Neely?" Cinco asked.

"No. Did you?"

"Heard about it," he said. "They say this kid's a tomb."

"I'm not surprised. He's been in the system before."

"Yeah, you can tell. Took him about three seconds to ask for a lawyer. We won't get shit out of him now."

"You're right." Which was why they needed the girl-friend. Elaina scanned the female faces again. This time her attention got hung up on a very familiar man. He sat at the other end of the bar beside some blonde in a halter top. She was talking and smiling. He leaned closer to hear what she was saying, and Elaina felt a punch of jealousy so strong, it knocked the breath out of her.

"You looking for someone?"

She tore her gaze away from Troy and stared up at Joel.

"Seems like you're looking for someone tonight. I know a lot of people around here, so . . ."

"Jamie Ingram," Cinco put in, as Elaina seemed incapable of speech.

Less than twenty-four hours. Less than one *day*. And suddenly the consequence of what she'd done crashed down on her like an anvil. She had no claim on him. Not now, not ever. She'd let her guard down, and all she had to show for it was a punishing hangover and a growing sense of shame. How could she have been so stupid?

"She's on one of the volleyball teams," the bartender was telling Cinco. "They played earlier and won. They'll be back in a while."

"Hey, there she is."

She forced herself to follow Cinco's gaze across the pool, where a quartet of young women were walking. They wore red, athletically cut bikinis that showed off toned abs and muscular buttocks. One of the four was the owner of a blue Jeep Wrangler Rubicon.

"Which one is she?" Elaina asked, because she had

yet to meet anyone who looked at all like their driver's license photo.

"Girl closest to the pool," Cinco said. "You want me to come with you?"

"No. Thanks." This woman worked at some bar where Cinco hung out, which meant he had a conflict of interest. Elaina would conduct the interview herself. She got up from her stool.

And cut a glance at Troy, still immersed in titillating conversation. She ignored the sting and set off to salvage what was left of an exceedingly crappy day.

CHAPTER 17

"Jamie Ingram?"

She looked up from her group of friends. "Yeah?"

"Could I talk to you a moment?"

Four pairs of eyes stared up at her curiously. They were seated in the sand, stretching out before their next match.

Jamie's gaze moved from Elaina's stitches to her friends, then back to Elaina again. "What about?" she asked.

"It's kind of private, if you don't mind."

She shrugged and stood up, and Elaina led her to a pair of empty lounge chairs near the tiki torches. It wasn't the quietest spot on the beach, but she wanted some light so she could read this girl's facial expressions.

Except she wasn't a girl. She was twenty-three. Old enough to know better than to get involved with the wrong guy.

They sat down, and Elaina could feel the woman checking her out. Elaina adjusted her bikini top. She wore it beneath an untucked, unbuttoned cotton blouse that concealed the Glock in the holster at the small of her back.

Jamie's gaze lingered on the frayed cuffs of the shorts Elaina had created just a few hours ago from a pair of jeans.

"You're a cop, aren't you?" Jamie asked.

"Why do you say that?"

"I don't know. Why else would you want to talk to me?"

Elaina watched her eyes. She looked wary. Curious. But not nearly nervous enough for someone who had taken part in a murder.

"My name's Elaina McCord. I'm a special agent with the FBI."

Jamie pulled back slightly. "What's going on?"

"Are you aware that your boyfriend's been taken in for questioning?"

Her startled expression was Elaina's answer. "What'd he do now?"

"What do you think he did?"

Her lips tightened at this, and Elaina knew she needed to watch her step here.

Elaina leaned back on her palms and looked up and down the beach. "I used to play volleyball," she said. "I was a hitter. You?"

She waited a moment before answering. "I'm a setter mostly. But four-on-four, we do some of everything."

Elaina nodded. "And your boyfriend likes to surf?"

Jamie looked at her cautiously. "Surf, skim board, wake board. He likes water sports."

"And he likes to party, too, I take it?"

She didn't say anything.

"He gets down to Mexico a lot. You ever go with him?"

"How would you know how much he goes to Mexico?"

Elaina smiled gently and waited for her to grasp the gravity of the situation. She saw the fear bloom in Jamie's eyes when she caught on.

"Two arrests for possession," Elaina said. "One for assault. You sure you want to invest your time with a guy like that?"

Jamie glanced down and toyed with a bracelet on her wrist. It was like one of those Livestrong bracelets, only purple instead of yellow.

"You like to hike, Jamie?"

She glanced up.

"I know Noah does. I know he was seen by two witnesses at the Laguna Madre National Wildlife Refuge last week. The day after a young woman went missing, as a matter of fact. He wasn't alone."

Jamie swallowed. Elaina could feel the tension coming off of her.

"He's a memorable guy," Elaina said. "I think it's the hair. Personally, I remember him from the marina the day they brought in the remains of a butchered girl. He wasn't alone then, either. You were with him."

"I didn't do anything wrong."

Elaina looked at her. "You didn't do anything right, though, did you?"

She looked defiant now, and Elaina switched tactics. "How old are you, Jamie?"

She hesitated a moment, probably wondering if it was a trick question. "Twenty-three."

"That's two years older than Gina Calvert. You know who that is, don't you?"

The defiant look faded, and Elaina continued. "She

played volleyball, just like you. Probably right on this beach. And then she disappeared. Do you know what happened to her?" Elaina paused and watched her face closely. "It was so horrible, they couldn't even put it on the news, did you know that? Imagine how her parents must have felt, learning what happened to their little girl."

Jamie glanced over her shoulder now, clearly desperate to get back to her friends. "Look, I really need to—"

"We can do this here or at my office," Elaina said. "It's your pick."

She looked down at her lap. Dance music thumped from the speakers nearby, making even the chairs vibrate. Elaina waited.

"We were hiking," she said finally.

"Where?"

"One of the trails near the alligator pond."

"What day?"

She met Elaina's gaze. Bit her lip. "June fifteenth. About one o'clock. We were *hiking*, okay? That was it. We didn't put her there." Jamie looked down again and fidgeted with her bracelet. The silence stretched out, and Elaina waited for her to fill it.

"I should have called the police earlier. I know that." Her voice wobbled now. "But we were scared, all right? You would be, too."

"You're right, I would."

Jamie shook her head. "I don't know who would . . . do something like that. To anyone. Even an animal. God, it was just . . ." She shuddered. "It was sick. But it wasn't me. Or Noah." She had a plea in her eyes now. "You have to believe me. He wouldn't hurt anyone."

"His record says otherwise."

A whistle sounded, and Jamie glanced backward. The volleyball match was starting, and her team was waving her over.

"I need to go now."

Elaina watched her, trying to read her face. She looked scared and flustered, and Elaina believed her when she said she wasn't involved. Whether her boyfriend was involved was another matter, but Elaina's gut told her no. His age, for one thing. And his whole demeanor. Whoever masterminded these killings was sharp. Clever. Capable of gamesmanship and staying one step ahead of the police. Noah Neely wasn't capable of passing a piss test.

"I'm going to be in touch," Elaina said now. "We need more information from you about what you saw that day."

Jamie nodded.

"And if you have plans to leave town, I strongly suggest you change them."

She nodded again and stood up. "I understand. You're wrong about Noah, though." She fidgeted with her bracelet again, and Elaina noticed the dragonfly on it. Her heart skipped.

"What happened to that girl—it wasn't him who did it," Jamie said. "You're looking for someone else." She started to step away, and Elaina caught her wrist.

"What is that?" she asked.

Jamie frowned at her, and Elaina released her arm.

"That design on your bracelet," Elaina said. "What does it mean?"

"Nothing. It doesn't mean anything." Another whistle sounded, and Jamie glanced over her shoulder.

"But what—"

"It's just a bracelet," she said, and dashed away.

Troy watched Elaina return to her stool to debrief Cinco and some other members of the task force. Very low profile, all of them gathered around like that. Elaina had mastered the local attire, but the other agents may as well have been wearing neon signs. Troy shook his head with disgust as they conducted their little powwow. If their perp, whoever he was, happened to be here tonight, he no doubt would have aborted his plans by now or moved on to better hunting grounds.

Elaina paid her tab. He watched her say her good-byes, knowing from the way she avoided even a glance in his direction that she knew good and well he was here. Maybe she'd sensed him. Troy could relate. He'd felt her presence the instant she'd set foot in the place in those frayed denim shorts that showed off her legs.

He caught up to her on the beach.

"Knocking off early?"

She kept walking. "I'm going to bed."

He wisely swallowed all the crude comments that popped into his mouth. "How you feeling?" he asked instead.

"Fine."

Yeah, right. She looked like someone fighting off a migraine and losing, and he would have bet money she hadn't put any grease in her system to combat that hangover.

She picked up her pace. He matched her stride without effort.

"You know, you're barking up the wrong tree with Jamie Ingram."

She didn't respond.

"I've known that girl since she was a kid, and she's not involved in this."

"Oh, really?" she said. "And what about her boyfriend? Is he one of your playmates, too?"

"He's a burnout. Used to be a competitive skater, but far as I know, he hasn't done a lick of honest work in years. He's not your killer, though."

She kept going.

"Think about it, Elaina. You're looking for someone shrewd. Above-average intelligence and highly motivated. That kid isn't motivated to get up off the couch."

She stopped and turned to face him. "Since when did you become a homicide investigator?"

"I think I know a little bit about criminals. I *have* written a few books on the subject."

"I'll let you know when we need your expert advice."

She was in Ice Queen mode. And if he hadn't been up with her half the night, he might have bought into the act.

"You're pissed off at me," he said, and she rolled her eyes. "You should be. I was a jerk."

She started to walk away, but he caught her arm and turned her around to face him.

"I've never set out to make a woman feel cheap before. I guess it worked."

She looked out at the water. "Let's just forget it. It doesn't matter."

"It matters to me," he said. He should have acted

cool and aloof—like she had—but catching her trying to sneak out of his house had made him hotter than hell. And he'd done what he always did when he was hotter than hell—he'd turned mean.

Elaina shook off his arm. "Let's both agree it was a mistake, okay? Let's move on."

He watched her, trying to read her expression in the dimness. "Move on, as in what?"

"As in, let's go back to being . . . friends or . . . professional acquaintances or whatever it is you want to call what we were before I spent the night with you."

He eased closer. She moved back fractionally, and for an instant, her gaze dropped to his mouth. She was remembering last night, and he saw the moment she realized she'd given herself away.

"Friends?" he said. "You really think that's possible?"

"Of course I think it's possible. Don't you?"

Not a chance in hell.

"Sure," he said. "We'll try it your way."

"Really?"

"Yeah, why not?" He stepped back from her.

She hesitated a moment, then started backing away. "Well. Good night, then. I'll see you . . . whenever."

"'Night, Elaina." He nodded. "Be sure to lock your doors."

Elaina watched the pretty receptionist pick up the phone and prayed that Mia was in today.

"Mia, it's Sophie, down in the lobby."

Elaina breathed a sigh of relief.

"Yeah, I've got a visitor here for you. Ms. Elaine McCord."

"It's Elaina." She nudged her ID across the counter again, hoping the woman would notice the three big letters up at the top. The security at this place bordered on ridiculous.

"Okay, I'll tell her." She hung up the phone and graced Elaina with a movie-star smile. It was the same expression she'd worn when she'd informed her that Dr. Lawson wasn't answering his phone, and no, it wouldn't be possible for Elaina to just swing by his office and poke her head in.

"Dr. Voss will be right with you," she told Elaina now.

"Thank you."

"If you'll just clip this on." Another smile as she passed Elaina a visitor's badge.

After donning her label, Elaina wandered over to the window and gazed out at the perfectly manicured grounds. A group of buzzards circled in the distance, and she shuddered to think what sort of feast had caught their attention today. This place was strange, no doubt about it. She wondered what nearby ranchers must think of the new neighbors with all their Greek architecture and rotting corpses.

An elevator dinged open, and Mia strode across the lobby. She wore the lab coat Elaina recognized, along with a curious expression.

"Elaina. What a surprise." Her gaze darted around. "Is Troy with you?"

"Not this time, no."

"I just called him yesterday with an update." A little crease formed between Mia's brows. "He didn't tell you the results won't be ready until later this week?"

"He must have forgotten to mention it. Anyway,

that's not why I'm here." Elaina glanced at the receptionist, who was pretending to be busy on her computer
while she listened to every word. "Do you mind if we
talk in your office?"

Mia hesitated just for a moment. "Not at all."

Elaina followed her to the elevator. "I hated to call
you down here," she said when they were out of earshot,
"but the receptionist wouldn't let me through, and I
really need to see Dr. Lawson."

"Ben?"

"Is he in today, do you know? His out-of-office
message said he'd be back yesterday, but he still hasn't
answered any of my e-mails or phone calls."

"I have no idea," Mia said, "but we can take a look."
She cast Elaina a sideways glance. "So you're not here
about your DNA test?"

"Not specifically, why? Do you have any news?" Elaina
held her breath. A DNA profile, or better yet, a hit in the
CODIS database, was slightly more concrete than the
dragonfly lead. But pressure was mounting, and Elaina
was taking her leads wherever she could find them.

"Nothing yet," Mia said as the elevator stopped at her
floor. "Like I told Troy, I'll be in touch as soon as I know
anything."

Elaina stepped out of the elevator behind Mia and
felt a prick of annoyance once again. "Is there some reason you're communicating all this through him? It's *my*
name on the evidence receipt, if I remember right."

Mia smiled politely over her shoulder. "I planned to
contact you, too, as soon as the results were ready. But
Troy's called repeatedly to check, and his name is on the
invoice, so—"

"What invoice?" Elaina stopped and stared at her.

"The invoice," Mia said. "The bill we'll be sending out for your lab work. Troy told me the FBI hadn't approved the expense."

Elaina clenched her teeth and tried to mask her irritation.

"These tests are expensive," Mia went on. "And Troy was happy to pay for them. Why? Is there a problem?"

A problem? Not really. Elaina hadn't been looking forward to personally footing the bill, but it was a control issue. Now Troy would have the results before she did, and he was practically a reporter. She never should have let him get involved.

Of course, without his involvement, no one at the Delphi Center would have made time for her in the first place.

"Don't let it bother you. Troy likes to pay for things." Mia smiled, and for some reason it got under Elaina's skin. "It's his way, I think."

"Whose way?"

Elaina turned to see a petite brunette standing at her elbow holding a cardboard coffee cup in each hand.

Mia's face brightened. "Alex, have you met Elaina McCord? She's with the FBI."

"No kidding? Nice to meet you. I'm Alex Lovell."

"Alex works with Ben in Cyber Crimes." Mia turned to the woman. "Have you seen him around? Elaina needs to talk to him about a case she's investigating down on Lito Island."

Alex passed Mia one of the coffee cups. She was staring at Elaina now with open curiosity. "I saw him downstairs. He was right behind me in the coffee line. Lito

Island, huh? You must be investigating that serial killer." And then to Mia: "Isn't that what Troy's working on?"

"I was just telling Elaina she shouldn't let it get to her how he pays for stuff," Mia said. "He's funding some lab work for her, but didn't tell her he was picking up the bill."

"That's Troy for you. It's a pride thing with him." Alex tilted her head to the side. "How well do you know him, anyway?"

Elaina drew back. "I, er, we haven't known each other long." She looked from Mia to Alex. Why was she explaining herself to these nosy women?

Mia crossed her arms. "I'm guessing he never told you, then? About his role at the lab here?"

"What role?"

"He helped fund the place," Alex said matter-of-factly. "Donated just over a mil." She shot Mia a look. "Not that that would pay for more than a few of your microscopes, but hey, for most of us working stiffs, it's a respectable chunk of change."

Elaina stared at Alex, thinking she'd heard her wrong. Over a *million* dollars?

"I can see he forgot to mention it to you." Alex exchanged another look with Mia. "How surprising." She turned to Elaina. "Still waters run deep with him. Just FYI."

Elaina stood there, completely at a loss for words. Was it her imagination, or did *both* of these women have a past with Troy? Elaina's head began to throb.

"There you are." Mia's gaze flicked over Elaina's shoulder. She turned around to see a young man striding toward them.

"Ben, meet Elaina McCord." Mia nodded in Elaina's direction. "And now I've really got to get back to work. I'll give you a call as soon as I have something, all right?"

"I should get back, too," Alex said. "Good luck with your investigation. I hope you nail the bastard."

They turned and walked away, and Elaina shifted her attention to the man standing beside her. He wore washed-out jeans and a T-shirt, and his wire-rimmed glasses made him look just old enough to vote.

Elaina shoved the surreal events of the last five minutes out of her mind. *Focus.*

"I'm Special Agent Elaina McCord, with the FBI."

The wunderkind smiled at her. "The Dragonfly Lady. I was just about to call you."

CHAPTER 18

Ben ushered her into his office and plunked his enormous cup of coffee on the desk, amid stacks of files and paperwork. He moved a tower of books off a side chair and nodded for her to sit down.

"Sorry about the mess." He sank into an ergonomic-looking desk chair and smiled at her across the piles. "I've been out for two weeks on vacation. Not that it ever gets very clean around here. So you're really an FBI agent?"

"I really am." Elaina glanced around. Ben Lawson's broom closet was only slightly larger than Mia's and had the same number of windows—none. The only light emanated from a silver laptop computer on the other side of his L-shaped desk and a purple lava lamp sitting atop a bookcase in the corner. Also atop the overstuffed bookcase was a collection of plastic action figures.

"A real, live FBI agent." He smiled again and she got the impression he was making fun of her.

"Do you have an issue with FBI agents?"

"Not at all, it's just we don't get too many around here. You guys have your own lab up there at Quantico. Of course, ours is better, but what can I say? We're David to your Goliath.

"Your message said something about a dragonfly. Are you sure you don't have me confused with Dr. Pritchard?"

"Dr. Pritchard?" Elaina asked.

"Our entomologist." Another smile. "He knows everything you always wanted to know about bugs but were afraid to ask."

Elaina nodded at the door to his office. "That dragonfly sticker you have on your bulletin board. What does it mean?"

"It's a symbol." He shrugged. "Symbols are open to interpretation. It can mean anything you want it to."

She leaned forward impatiently. "Listen, Ben. I'm working a murder investigation. I don't have time for games here. I need to know what that dragonfly stands for."

The spark of amusement vanished from his eyes. He pushed his glasses farther up the bridge of his nose. "A murder investigation."

"That's right."

He rubbed his jaw, looking serious now. "Wow. That's heavy. And you're sure the dragonfly is connected?"

"I think so, yes. Two of the victims were wearing jewelry with that dragonfly on it. And I've seen it several other times during the course of the investigation."

He sighed. "Well, it looks like you're going to have to make time for games, then."

"Excuse me?"

"The dragonfly. It symbolizes a game." He leaned his elbows on the desk and looked at her intently. "Are you familiar with geocaching?"

"No."

"It's a popular sport. It's kind of like treasure hunt-ing, only you find the clues on the Web and use a GPS to locate the treasure. Sort of like a high-tech scavenger hunt."

Elaina's pulse picked up. "Never heard of it," she said. "You say this is a sport?"

"Absolutely." A sheepish grin. "Although, admit-tedly, it tends to be played by computer geeks. But some of us are athletes, too. You'd be surprised."

"And it involves GPS coordinates?"

He swiveled in his chair and reached for his com-puter. His hands moved over the keys with impressive speed, and suddenly the screen turned purple. "Well, if you haven't heard of geocaching, I'm assuming you're not familiar with the sport's redheaded stepchild." The purple faded to black, then red, then back to purple again, and suddenly a yellow dragonfly appeared on the screen.

Elaina leaned forward. "What's that?"

"Also known as extreme caching."

The words "Xtreme $$$ing" appeared at the top of the screen above several blanks. He quickly keyed in a user name and password.

"You're a member," she said.

"I guess you could say that." The screen went black, and then white text scrolled up in a way that recalled the beginning of *Star Wars*. "It's not really a club, per se. But not just anyone can participate. You have to crack a few codes just to get in the door. And then there are certain guidelines."

"What are they?" Elaina's gaze was riveted to the

screen, although the words were too far away for her to read.

"Well, take regular geocaching," he said. "It's fairly easy to play if you have the right equipment. Basically, an Internet connection and a GPS, and you're good to go. At least for the easy hides."

Hides. The word sent a chill through her.

Another blank came up, and Ben entered in some numbers. "It's a family sport. It's fun. Safe, as long as you pay attention to the difficulty ratings and use a little common sense. The sport has a number of different off-shoots, but this one is pretty hard-core."

The screen turned purple, and a silver list appeared. Elaina stood up and walked around the desk so she could read over Ben's shoulder.

"What is that?" she asked.

"A list of caches in this zip code."

"But it's gibberish."

"That's part of the game," he said. "Everything's encrypted, even the list of hunts you can choose from."

"How do you break the code?"

He turned and grinned up at her. "I could tell you, but I'd have to kill you."

She frowned. "I'm serious. How do you—"

"Okay, take this one here. It's a simple substitution code." He pointed at the text, which looked like nonsense to Elaina. Ben pulled a sticky note from his desk drawer and jotted down the words. Then beneath each one, he wrote a different word. "See? Solve for the square root of sixteen, and that tells you to move down the alphabet four letters. This one's easy, but some of them involve riddles or algorithms. Looks like this cache is hidden in a state park not too far from here. Every heard of Devil's Gorge?"

Elaina stared down at him. "Just recently, as a matter of fact."

Ben entered the decrypted words, and some GPS coordinates popped up on the screen, alongside several icons—handcuffs and a kite.

"That was a simple code," he said. "These two clues here look tougher to crack, though. But even so, I bet this is a pretty popular cache, given what's inside it."

"How do you know what's inside it?"

"The pictures. See? Handcuffs mean you can expect some sex toys."

"*Sex* toys?"

"I told you, this game's hard-core. If it were a movie, it'd be rated R, at least. There's a subversive element to it. The more difficult and dangerous it is to get to, the better." He turned back to the screen and pointed at the other icons. "The kite lets me know there's probably some pot in there, too. You know, 'high as a kite'? There are icons for pills, toys, comic books, porn. Pretty much anything you can imagine."

"So people can just show up and find this stuff? In a public park?" Elaina shook her head. "What's to stop someone from raiding the stash?"

"They have to find it first." He smiled. "That's where the sport comes in, really. These things aren't just sitting around. And you may find this difficult to believe, but there's an honor code among cachers. If you take something, leave something. It's that simple. You can take what you want, but you're expected to leave something of equal or greater value behind."

Elaina folded her arms over her chest and watched Ben. He was an admitted computer geek and a cyber cop. He was a quasi–law enforcement officer, and this was his hobby?

"I know what you're thinking." He swiveled in his chair and looked her straight in the eye. "And I don't waste my time on the drug caches. I mean, what would be the point? The Delphi Center does random testing on all its employees. I worked my butt off to get a job here, and I'm not going to jeopardize it for a weekend trip."

"What *do* you waste your time on?"

He smiled. "At the risk of completely blowing my cover as a normal guy? I'm into X Men."

Elaina stared at him blankly.

He sighed. "I can see you're not a geek." He nodded at the bookshelf beside her. "*X-Men*. The comic book? I collect the action figures."

She eyed the toys lined up on the bookcase with relief. He was out there, but maybe less so than she'd originally thought.

"These caches," she said. "What do they look like?"

"Anything, really. Some of them get really inventive. They might be camouflaged to look like a rock or a plant. It's part of the creativity. But more often than not, they're just boxes that have been painted flat brown and hidden. Ammo cans are a favorite. Some of the original cachers were gun enthusiasts and survivalists. We get a lot of NRA types. Some law enforcement buffs."

Elaina could almost hear her heart pounding. Gun enthusiasts and law enforcement buffs. "You said ammo cans. What about an airtight plastic box secured with a bungee cord?" She remembered Troy opening it in the swamp.

"That sounds right," he said. "Why, did you find one?"

"At one of the crime scenes."

"You're serious? You weren't putting me on about the murder investigation?"

"No." She gazed at the nonsensical words displayed on the screen. "And I'm beginning to think maybe the killer is hunting these treasure hunters." She glanced at him. He was wide-eyed now, and she realized she'd said too much. "It's just a theory. I don't really know for sure what the connection is."

"Whoa. That's just . . ." He turned to look at his computer. "Wow."

"Is there any way to know who goes out and visits these sites?"

"Well, these boxes don't contain logbooks, like normal caches. Like I said, the sport is pretty underground. You wouldn't really want your name written down in a box with some of this contraband, would you? But online is more open because it's sort of a gated community. Lots of people jump on to log their finds."

"Show me what you mean."

He clicked into a new screen and pointed to it. "Most people post comments after they visit a place. 'Major bushwhacking involved,' for example. Or 'Excellent hide.' There's a lot of dialogue back and forth, but no spoilers. Ruining someone's hunt is considered a major party foul."

"I see." Elaina skimmed the list of comments. The

participants had screen names like Moun10 Bkr and HunnyBooT and MadDawger. "Would you be able to track someone, maybe by their screen name?"

"It's possible," he said. "But it would take some doing. This sport has hordes of followers, especially around here."

"Why around here?"

"San Marcos is a college town. So is Austin. Anywhere a lot of young people converge, you're likely to find a big community."

Lito Island definitely qualified as a place young people converged—it was the spring break capital of the state.

Ben's phone rang, and he snatched it up. She saw him check his watch and could tell by his conversation that she'd made him late for something. He needed to get back to work, and Elaina needed to get back to the island.

But not before she completed her mission.

"I can see you're swamped here," she said after he ended the call. "You've been gone two weeks, and I'm sure your workload didn't miraculously disappear while you were on vacation."

"Sure didn't." He leaned back in his chair and watched her. His tone was glib, but his face looked far more serious than it had when she'd first walked in here.

"I need your help," she said.

"How did I know you were going to say that?"

"Because you're smart." It was an obvious attempt at flattery, but she was inching toward desperation. "I'm going to give you a list of the seven victims, along with the locations where they were last seen and where their remains were found. I need you to find out if there's a concrete link to this treasure hunting."

"*Seven* victims?"

"Yes," she said. "And those are just the ones we know about. He's working so fast now, we can hardly keep up with him."

Ben watched her for a moment. "Do you know their user names?"

She scoffed at him. "I don't even know for sure that they were involved in this game, or whatever you call it. But this connection keeps cropping up, and it needs to be explored. Can you do it?"

He smiled slightly, but the amusement was long gone now. "Exploring in cyberspace is my specialty."

Elaina gazed down at the files fanned out across the bed. Two boxes down, one to go, and still she and Ric Santos had found no piece of evidence to link anyone in the missing hiker cases to any of the suspects on her list. Files blanketed the bed, the sofa, the coffee table. Elaina had volunteered her suite as a workroom—what else was she going to do with all the space?—and she and Ric had put in a good four hours together this evening. But they'd had no luck, and finally the detective had excused himself to his first-floor hotel room to catch up on e-mails from his office. Elaina, meanwhile, had plodded on.

She rubbed her tired eyes now and stared down at a typewritten statement taken by the San Marcos police officer who'd interviewed a roommate of one of the missing women. She was in the Wilderness Club, the roommate had reported. She liked to hike and rappel and mountain bike. She frequently went for all-day treks alone on the nature trails near San Marcos.

Wise idea? No. A straight-A student with a major in

biology should have known better. But Elaina had studied enough murder cases to know one of the problems with young people was that they considered themselves invincible. Those terrible things on the news—those things happened to other people, not to them. Not to privileged young women just months shy of graduation with their whole lives ahead of them. They had always been, and always would be, the lucky ones.

Until suddenly they weren't.

The officer's report contained no mention of any sort of high-tech treasure hunting. No mention of any computer games. No mention of any special equipment—such as a GPS—that the hiker might have habitually carried along. Had she been searching for a cache the day that she'd gone missing? Or had she simply been out enjoying the scenery? Maybe someone had spotted her on a trail, closed in for the kill, and then planted her remains somewhere, possibly near a cache site. And yet her remains had never been found.

Elaina hadn't figured out what was going on, but she felt certain the killer viewed it as a game. Seven women dead, maybe more. A quiet rage fermented inside her as she thought about someone getting off on that.

A knock at the door, and she glanced at the clock. Just after ten. It might be Ric, back for more file sifting. Or maybe it was Troy.

Elaina climbed off the bed and walked over to check the peephole.

Brenda.

She undid the latch and pulled open the door.

"Here we go!" Brenda beamed at her, and Elaina

glanced down at the tray laden with chocolate-dipped strawberries, a bowl of whipped cream, and a bottle of champagne.

"I think you have the wrong room," Elaina said.

Undeterred, Brenda eased past her and ferried the tray over to the coffee table, then glanced around for an empty surface. She spied a place on the minibar and set down her load.

"It's our champagne turn-down service," she announced proudly. "It's part of the honeymoon package. I tried to bring it the other night, but you were out, so . . ." Her voice trailed off, but not before Elaina detected a hint of I-know-your-little-secret in her tone. She realized there was only one good reason the island gossip broker would personally deliver this tray to her door instead of asking someone else to do it.

"This isn't my honeymoon," Elaina said.

"Well, I know *that,* but you may as well enjoy." She smiled brightly. "It's included in your room rate."

"But I thought—" And then she remembered Mia's words today, and her mouth clamped shut.

"Would you like the turn-down service, too?" Brenda nodded at the bed, which was awash in papers.

"That won't be necessary." Elaina forced a smile as she ushered her toward the door, snatching her phone off the table as she went. "Thanks for stopping by."

When she was gone, Elaina jabbed Troy's number into the phone.

"Champagne and strawberries? Is this your idea of a joke?"

"Come again?"

"I'm in the honeymoon suite," she said. "And strangely, the staff seems to think I'm paying the *honeymoon* rate here."

"You're telling me someone brought champagne to your room."

"Yes!"

"And you're complaining?"

"Yes! I didn't give you permission to pay for my hotel room. *Or* my lab tests. Just what are you trying to prove here?"

"Nothing," he said.

"I don't need your money, Troy. And what am I going to do with all this champagne and strawberries and whipped cream?"

"I can think of plenty of things you could—"

"I'm putting this room on *my* credit card. And please don't pick up any more bills behind my back." The princess phone jingled, and Elaina eyed it hotly. Now what? Were they sending up a masseuse? She clicked off with Troy and grabbed up the clunky receiver. "Hello?"

"Hi, it's me, Brenda. I just got down to the lobby and noticed your car in the parking lot. You left your lights on."

"It's someone else's." Elaina had pulled in before six o'clock, and she hadn't been using headlights.

"Gray Ford Taurus? Row closest to the building?"

Elaina huffed out a breath. "I'll be right down."

She slammed down the phone, slipped her feet into the nearest pair of sandals, and headed down to the parking lot, where she found her dinged-up Ford sitting in the front row of spaces, locked tight as a drum.

With the headlights on. Maybe she'd turned them on when she'd swung by the Brownsville office and used the parking garage.

"Going someplace?"

She glanced up to see Troy crossing the lot toward her. She opened the car, switched off the lights, and headed back to the inn. "To bed."

"Want company?"

She shot him a glare as he held open the door for her.

"Just thought I'd ask." He smiled. "How goes the investigation?"

Elaina ignored Brenda's interested gaze as Troy stepped into the elevator with her.

"I spent the day at the Delphi Center, talking to some friends of yours. Mia and Alex? Your name came up. I'm sorry you weren't there."

He winced. "I'm not."

The elevator doors parted, and Elaina tried to mask her annoyance as he escorted her down the hallway. She opened her hotel room with a key card and walked into the suite.

Troy stood just inside the door, staring at the paperwork that blanketed nearly every surface. "Looks like you've been busy."

"Ric and I spent tonight culling through files."

"Who's Ric?"

"Homicide detective down from San Marcos." Elaina dropped her keys back in her purse and turned to face Troy. "Mia mentioned him, remember? Looks like his cold cases are linked to the murders down here."

"What's the connection?"

"Ketamine," she said. "And something else I just

learned about today at the Delphi Center. It's this game—"

"Extreme caching."

"You know about it?"

"Talked to Jamie today, and she filled me in. I stopped by to update you."

"You interviewed our witness?"

"You got a problem with that?" Troy propped his shoulder against the wall.

"As a matter of fact, yes. She gave a formal statement just this morning about finding Valerie Monroe's body. She's part of this investigation."

"Good reason to talk to her," he said.

"You're walking a fine line here, Troy. Researching a book is one thing. But this is an *active* case. We don't need outside interference—"

"What are you doing tomorrow?"

She stared at him. "Tomorrow."

"Tomorrow. Day after today. 'Bout eight hours from now."

"I've got a task force meeting." She gestured to the floor. "Then I need to finish going through these case files with Ric."

"Let him go through his own case files." He pushed off the wall. "I've got a lead for you."

"What is it?"

"Came from Jamie," he said. "You might say it's from the underground."

"I'm on duty. I can't just shirk my responsibilities to go off on some treasure hunt with you."

"You really think the break you need is going to come from these old papers?"

"It could," she said. "There might be a name. Maybe a common witness, a common suspect—"

"Then let Ric find it. What time's your meeting?"

"Eight."

"I'll pick you up at nine-fifteen." He reached for the doorknob. "Dress for the heat."

CHAPTER 19

E laina awoke to the bleat of her new phone. She
squinted at the clock. Nothing good ever came of a
phone call at 4:42 A.M.

She dragged her cell off the nightstand. "McCord."

"It's Loomis. Meet me at the marina in ten minutes.
We've got another missing girl."

Nine minutes later, Elaina slid into a parking space
between an LIPD cruiser and a Taurus nearly identical
to her own. She scraped her hair into a quick ponytail
and joined the huddle of men beside the bait shop.

"That was at oh three hundred," Loomis was telling
the group.

Elaina scanned the faces and recognized about half of
the task force.

"The apartment was unlocked," Loomis continued.
"She entered and found the subject's purse and cell
phone sitting on a kitchen counter. No sign of the subject. That's when she called the police."

Cinco met Elaina's gaze across the huddle. He was
dressed just as she was in khaki tactical pants and ATAC
boots, with a sidearm secured to his belt.

"About fifty minutes later," Loomis went on, "a patrol officer doing a routine drive-by noticed the white Kia Spectra parked here at the marina with the driver's-side door open. Upon investigation, he discovered a pair of women's sandals and a red Speedo bathing suit folded on the front passenger seat."

Elaina's stomach pitched. Her gaze veered to the white car on the other side of the lot, and her feet started moving. A man in an LIPD uniform was standing guard beside the still-open door. Elaina ducked her head down and looked into the vehicle.

A red two-piece swimsuit. Identical to the one Jamie Ingram had been wearing last night.

"Jamie called it in."

She turned to see Cinco walking up behind her.

"Who—"

"Friend of hers on the volleyball team." His eyes were solemn. "You remember the tall one?"

"Brunette?"

"Her name's Angela Martinez. She's twenty-four."

"You know her?" she asked, somehow reading the answer right there on his face.

"We went to high school together."

"McCord? Chavez?"

They turned around, and Loomis gestured them over. "McCord, you're with me, covering the wildlife park. Chavez, go with Maynard. You two know this coastline better than we do. He's gassing up the patrol boat."

Elaina glanced around. "Is this everyone? It feels thin."

"It is," Loomis said. "We've got a few agents on their way from Brownsville, plus a couple at the apartment complex. They'll join the foot search when they wrap up there. Hopefully, we'll get a canine unit out here before too long."

"And Chief Breck?"

"He's on the bay already, with the sheriff and a couple deputies. Okay, people." Loomis raised his voice to address the group. "Angela Martinez has brown hair, brown eyes. Five-ten, one-forty. She was last seen less than five hours ago at Coconuts bar. This girl's tall and athletic, so let's hope she puts up a fight. Now, everyone get moving. She might still be alive."

Troy dropped the boxes at his feet and used his key card to unlock Elaina's door. No sooner had he pushed it open than a man stood in the doorway, glowering at him.

And holding a Glock in his right hand.

"Ric Santos?"

"Who the hell are you?"

"I'm Troy," he said, and the glower intensified. "Wanna give me a hand?"

Troy picked up the first box and shoved it at the detective. The man paused briefly, then returned his gun to his holster and took the load.

"What is this?"

Troy picked up the second box and followed him deep into Elaina's suite. It was just as messy as it had been last night—more so, actually, given the unmade bed. Noon, and the maid clearly hadn't been by yet. Or maybe she had, but the detective had sent her away.

"I'm bringing you two boxes' worth of research into the Mary Beth Cooper murder." Troy deposited his carton on the floor beside the sofa. Ric did the same. "Consider it a donation to the cause."

"You've investigated the case?"

"You could say that. Elaina tells me you guys have set up shop in here, comparing notes. Figured it wouldn't hurt to go through this stuff, too."

The detective regarded Troy skeptically. "How come you're not out beating the bushes with the rest of the task force?"

"I would be," Troy said, "but the entire marina's been declared a crime scene, so I couldn't get my boat out. And the wildlife park is off-limits to civilians today."

"You're not a cop?"

"I'm a writer."

The detective's brows arched in surprise.

"True crime books," he added. "These boxes represent eight months' worth of research into Mary Beth Cooper, including crime-scene photos, autopsy reports, and jailhouse interviews with the man who confessed to killing her but turned out to be full of shit. Do you want this or not?"

Ric gazed down at the boxes and rested his hands on his hips. He looked exhausted, frustrated, wrung out. "I want it," he said anyway.

"Thought so." Troy peeled the lids off the boxes and tossed them on the sofa. "So what about you?"

The detective pulled the first manila folder from one of the boxes and glanced up. "What's that?"

"Why aren't you out beating the bushes with the rest of them?"

"They've got plenty of boots on the ground. Figured

I might be more help doing brain work instead of leg work."

"Feds wouldn't let you onto their task force, huh?"

His eyes darkened, and Troy knew he'd guessed right. "Hey, you planning to help here? Or you just dropping off?"

"I can help." Troy's gaze skimmed over the ocean of files and paperwork. "Lotta information spread out in here. Is it as bad as it looks, or you and Elaina got some kind of system?"

The detective picked up a yellow legal pad from the coffee table and tossed it at him like a Frisbee. Troy caught it.

"Yeah, we've got a system. And it's worse than it looks."

N 26° 12.375 W 097° 10.701

Elaina plowed her way through the cattails, ignoring the blisters and the scratches and the merciless sun. The first two she pushed out of her mind by concentrating on the ever-changing terrain and devising a path. The last was harder to ignore, especially when her jaw muscles went slack and her scalp grew cool and tingly with sweat. She was approaching heat exhaustion. With every shiver, she knew it. And yet she felt completely incapable of a rational response. She needed water, yes. And shade. But Loomis and Callahan were just ten feet ahead, and she'd be damned if she prevented her team from scouring its designated quadrant of swamp.

"Tell me about Cinco Chavez."

Elaina's gaze cut up and to the right, where the task force leader was forging ahead through the tall reeds.

"What about him?"

He tossed a look at her over his shoulder. "What's your read there?"

Elaina's poached brain somehow caught his implication. "You mean my read on him as an officer?" No, that wasn't what he'd meant.

"Your read on him as a suspect."

She flicked a glance at Callahan, who'd taken on the role of pace setter for their little expedition. He didn't react to the question from Loomis, but he was much too close not to have heard him. Evidently, the team leader's theory didn't come as a surprise to him. They were grasping at straws now, and she guessed it was because their prime suspect had an alibi for last night. An agent had tailed Noah Neely home from his interrogation and surveilled his apartment until the call came in about Angela. A quick check had revealed Neely to be asleep in his bed at the time, which pretty much eliminated him from their suspect list, provided Angela's disappearance couldn't be attributed to a copycat.

So now the latest and greatest suspect was *Cinco*?

"I think . . ." Elaina struggled for a response. "Frankly, I think that's crap. Sir."

"He knows Martinez," Loomis countered. "He knew the Cooper girl, too. They grew up in the same neighborhood in Bay Port." He glanced back at her. "You aware of that?"

"Yes, but he would have been six*teen* at the time of Mary Beth Cooper's murder. That's much younger than the profile—"

"He lives on the island, just like you said. Likes to hunt and fish, has access to boats. He's got the law enforcement background, plus the inside skinny on everything happening around here. And the kicker—he supposedly took that phone tip with the GPS coordinates from Noah Neely's girlfriend."

"You think he lied about—"

"I think he's been up to his eyeballs in this thing from the get-go. More than any other cop here, including his boss. You aware he was the first responder to the Gina Calvert crime scene?"

"Yes, but that doesn't mean—"

"And he's been at Coconuts bar almost every night for the past two weeks?"

Elaina's legs were Jell-O, her skin clammy. "You're suggesting he's been trolling? Under the guise of searching for the killer?"

"I'm suggesting he's always in the wrong place at the wrong time. Or the right place, however you want to look at it."

Elaina stepped into a hole, and lukewarm water filled her right boot. She took a few steps back and veered toward Callahan, who seemed adept at finding what little firm footing there was in this mud pit. The tide had gone out since last night, leaving acres and acres of soggy marshland that would have been accessible by boat at three o'clock this morning.

"You've spent more time with Chavez than any of the rest of us," Loomis pressed. "Tell me what you think."

Elaina took a deep breath. She needed to be objective. After all, she'd shared her geocaching lead with him, and he hadn't outright laughed. Yes, he'd looked at her like she was crazy, but at least he'd heard her out.

It had been Callahan who'd smiled. Smugly. While

looking away. And she'd known her theory was going to be the topic of much discussion among members of the task force later.

Let them tear into her. At least they'd be giving her theory some thought.

"Well?"

Rivulets of sweat slid down her spine. She cleared her parched throat. "I think Officer Chavez is solid. Dedicated. Eager to lend a hand, but there's nothing more to it than his devotion to the job." She sounded like a sappy toast at some retirement dinner. "Anyway, his age doesn't fit the profile, and I've seen nothing to make me think he'd be capable of this level of violence."

The men fell silent in front of her. The sun's rays beat down, and the chorus of cicadas surrounding them escalated to a deafening buzz. Elaina tipped her head back. Noon had come and gone, and the sky was nearly bleached white by the unyielding sun.

A distant bird caught her eye.

She knew that bird. She knew its swirling, circling pattern. She stopped short, just as the buzzard swooped down and disappeared behind some foliage.

"There," she said, and her lungs constricted.

"What? Where?" Loomis turned to look at her.

"A buzzard. There." She pointed at the distant clump of cattails. "It's feeding."

Troy had a crick in his neck and a renewed sense of loathing for the sick bastard who'd killed all these women.

He glanced across the room at Ric Santos, who was buried in old police reports.

"I covered the Woodlawn murders up in San Antonio

years ago," Troy said, and the detective looked up from his paperwork. "Crossed paths with a special agent Rey Santos with the VICMO squad up there. Any relation?"

"He's my brother."

Troy thought he'd seen a resemblance. "Elaina's got a theory this unsub may have applied to the FBI," he said. "I know the applications in this region go through the San Antonio field office. Could your brother—"

"She already asked," Ric said. "He's checking it out, said he'd probably have something by tomorrow."

The door to the suite opened, and Weaver trudged in, looking battered and fried. Elaina followed. Her glassy-eyed gaze drifted over the room, paused briefly on Troy, then moved to the minibar, where an unopened bottle of champagne sat in an ice bucket. She crossed the room, plunked the bottle onto the counter, and walked out with the bucket.

Weaver dropped into an armchair.

"What happened to you two?" Ric asked.

"Heat index of ninety-nine-point-nine million." He tossed his shades on the coffee table, revealing pasty white circles above lobster-red cheeks.

"You guys ever heard of sunblock?" Ric asked as Elaina slammed back into the room. She went straight into the bathroom and closed the door.

Troy looked at Weaver. "What's wrong with her?"

The agent's worried, bloodshot gaze settled on the door, and Troy heard the shower go on.

"She found the body." Weaver sighed heavily. "It wasn't pretty."

Ric cursed. "Time of death?"

"Early this morning, they think. We missed her by a few hours."

Another curse from Ric.

Troy got up and snagged Elaina's duffel bag from the floor. It felt empty. He pulled open dresser drawers and gathered up clothes, then grabbed an Evian from the mini-fridge.

"God, I'm whipped," Weaver said. "Anyone up for a burger? All I've eaten today is a granola bar."

"You guys should hit the diner across the street." Troy crossed to the bathroom and tapped his knuckles on the door. "We'll catch up with you there."

He opened the door and slipped inside. Elaina was on the floor of the shower, her knees hugged to her chest as the water pelted her back. Beside her was the ice bucket.

Troy dropped her clothes in the sink and pulled open the glass door. He crouched down next to her, and she turned her head just enough to see him.

"Go away," she mumbled.

He pried the ice cube out of her hand and replaced it with the bottle of water. "Drink this." Then he moved her hair aside and rubbed the ice cube over her neck. Her back was pale, in sharp contrast to her neck and arms, which were brick red.

"Please go away." She rested her forehead on her knees and hunched into a tighter ball.

His jeans and boots grew damp from spray. At least she'd had the sense to take a cool shower instead of a hot one. He grabbed another ice cube and rubbed it between her shoulder blades. She didn't say anything. After a few minutes, she turned to look at him. Her face was pink, her lips chapped. Scratches marred the skin of her arms.

"We were too late," she said.

"I know."

Her gaze held his, and he read a world of emotions he knew she'd never talk about. At least not right now. And it was all he could do not to pull her into his lap. But she'd shut down if he did that. She'd shrink into her shell, like a hermit crab, and never come out.

She closed her eyes and turned her head away. "I need to be alone."

He stood up and stepped out of the shower. "Five minutes, Elaina. Then we're meeting everyone across the street for dinner. Finish that water."

She didn't argue, and he wouldn't have listened to her if she had. He slipped out of the bathroom and found the suite empty. He sat on the bed to wait, resisting the urge to go out on the balcony for a cigarette. Ten minutes ticked by, but he heard movement behind the door, so he didn't hassle her. Finally, she stepped out of the bathroom in the shorts and T-shirt he'd selected. Her freshly combed hair hung damp and loose around her shoulders.

"Ready."

He held the door open for her and followed her down the hall. Her gait this evening was stiff, her shoulders slumped. She looked like a casualty of the Boston Marathon, and he half expected her to sway into the wall as they walked down the corridor.

"You okay?" he asked.

"Fine."

He shook his head but let it go as they made it down to the lobby and crossed the highway to the diner.

"Who's coming?" she asked listlessly.

"Ric. Weaver. Whoever's around."

"Cinco and Maynard?"

"I have no idea."

Was she worried about walking in with him? He couldn't have cared less, but he wasn't sure she wanted to advertise their relationship.

Relationship. Troy cut a glance at her as they neared the entrance. He wasn't quite comfortable with the word, but he couldn't come up with a better one.

She glanced up at him. "What?"

"Nothing." He yanked the door open, and she flinched at the arctic blast of air-conditioning.

"It's *freezing*."

"You'll get used to it." He spotted Ric, Weaver, and Cinco around Dot's large corner booth. They watched him and Elaina approach the table. All three looked unhappy, particularly Weaver, who somehow managed to rake Troy over the coals with a three-second glare.

Elaina slid in beside her partner, and Troy followed.

"I was just telling Ric about the apartment," Weaver said.

The waitress appeared, and they ordered Cokes and hamburgers all around. Troy asked for a chocolate milk-shake.

"What about the apartment?" Elaina asked.

"No sign of forced entry," the agent reported. "Door was unlocked. Purse on the counter this time, wallet out."

"Contents?" Ric asked.

"Driver's license, insurance card, photos, health club card, twenty-five dollars cash. None of the victims' wallets look to have been pilfered."

"And her car?" Ric asked.

"At the marina," Cinco said. "Along with her clothes."

"So you're thinking he keeps a boat there."

"Actually, no," Weaver told him. "He parks the victim's car at a different dock each time, and we think it's a diversion. The theory is, he has a boat someplace else, maybe a private slip somewhere."

"Timing's tight," Cinco said. "Angela was at Coconuts at least until one-thirty. I saw her myself. Assuming he followed her home from the bar, he would have had to kidnap her, take her out on his boat, kill her and dump her in the wildlife park, then go back and plant her car at the marina, all before three-fifty."

"What happened at three-fifty?" Ric asked.

"Patrol officer called in the abandoned Kia," Cinco said. "Door was open. Angela's clothes were inside."

The waitress arrived with the drinks, and silence settled over the table as everyone unwrapped straws and started slurping. Everyone except Elaina.

"Your missing hikers," Weavers said to Ric. "Were their valuables stolen?"

"Backpacks, clothes, car keys—all that turned up in a trash can not far from the trailhead. Their cars were in the parking lots, right where they'd left them, according to witnesses."

"So he probably found them on the trails, versus kidnapping them at their homes and taking them there," Troy said. "Why the change in MO?"

"Who knows?" Ric said. "Maybe being near the water changed things for him. He wanted to throw a boat into the mix."

"Pretty bold move," Weaver said.

"What, using a boat?"

"That, but also the kidnapping. It multiplies the number of potential witnesses. Also increases the odds of leaving evidence behind."

Troy glanced at Elaina. She was staring at her plastic cup, tracing a pattern in the condensation with her index finger.

"What's your take, T?"

Troy's gaze snapped to Cinco.

"Why go to their apartments and hotel rooms?" Cinco asked him. "Why not just take them straight from a bar to the dump site?"

"Who knows?" Troy said. "Maybe a bar is too busy. You ever seen the parking lot at Coconuts after last call? It's a meat market. Besides, there's been no sign of forced entry, so he's probably got some sort of ruse. Something that gets them to open the door for him." Troy eyed everyone at the table. Ric looked most interested, and Troy had come to realize over the past six hours that the detective was obsessed with this case.

The food arrived, and everyone busied themselves with ketchup and mustard. Elaina nibbled a french fry.

"But why a bar instead of a hiking trail?" Weaver said around a mouthful of food. "In the most recent five cases, all the victims have spent their last evening at the same bar."

"You're sure about that?" Ric asked.

"We've got their credit-card activity, along with eye-witness accounts. Every one of them was at Coconuts the night of her abduction. It doesn't make sense. I mean, if he wants to do his thing in a nature preserve, why not just lie in wait and spring himself on some hiker?"

"He works at night," Elaina said quietly.

"What's that?" Cinco asked.

"The mutilation. The part he considers his *work*—all that happens at night, under cover of darkness. Women don't generally hike at night, and he couldn't just grab them and carve them up in broad daylight."

She leaned back against the booth now and looked out at the restaurant, avoiding all the gazes at the table. Weaver frowned at her.

"What happens now?" Ric directed the question at Weaver, who—for lack of a better candidate—seemed to be the designated expert on the workings of the FBI's task force.

"There's a press conference scheduled for tonight," the agent said. "Loomis and Breck at the podium, feds and locals playing nice for the cameras. Autopsy happens"—he glanced at his watch—"right about now, as a matter of fact."

Troy slid Elaina's water glass in front of her. "Hydrate," he murmured in her ear.

"The autopsy won't produce much," Weaver said. "We already know the victim's identity, plus the cause and time of death are pretty evident this time." He shook his head. "What I'd really like to do is round up every last surfer and frat boy at Coconuts tonight and hook them up to a polygraph."

Elaina pushed her plate away and pulled Troy's milkshake in front of her. She took out the straw and licked ice cream off the tip.

Troy's gaze scanned the restaurant, looking for out-of-towners mixed in with all the locals. Tonight was tourists, mostly, along with a few media-types, easily identifiable by their loosened neckties and wilted dress shirts. Evidently the Paradise Killer wasn't having quite the negative effect on tourism the governor had anticipated when he'd sent a Texas Ranger down to lend a hand. Troy had hardly seen that guy all week, and the feds had clearly taken over.

He glanced at the fed beside him, relieved to see her working on his shake. It wasn't as good for her as water, but at least it would put some sugar in her system.

What had she seen today? Or maybe it was the thought of how close they'd come to saving Angela Martinez that had put that haunted look in her eyes. She wasn't going to sleep tonight. Troy had dealt with that kind of insomnia. He knew a cure for it, too, but he doubted she'd let him show her.

She pushed the cup away and leaned back against the booth. She looked out across the restaurant, and suddenly her dull expression was replaced by alarm.

"Uh-oh."

"What?" Troy gazed out the window facing the Sandhill Inn. A man and a woman walked up the sidewalk together and entered the hotel. The woman, Troy would have known anywhere. The man, he vaguely recognized.

"I wonder why they're here," Elaina said.

"I have a feeling we're about to find out."

CHAPTER 20

"What are you doing here?"

Mia whirled around at the familiar voice and gazed up into a pair of brown-black eyes. She immediately went on the defensive.

"I'm checking in," she said crisply.

"Yes, but why?"

"Um . . . so I can have a bed for the night?" Mia accepted a pair of key cards from the clerk with the over-teased hair. She glanced back again and watched the muscle tighten in Ric's jaw. Clearly, he didn't want her here, and she found that interesting when for the past week he'd practically been pleading for her help.

She turned and handed one of the key-card envelopes to Ben, who was waiting beside their heap of luggage. The techie looked innocuous as always in his T-shirt and faded cargo shorts, and Mia could tell Ric had just this instant realized they were here together.

"The entire task force is booked here," Ric said. "Do you realize that?"

She arched her eyebrows at him.

"You're not *on* the task force," he pointed out.

Ben eyed the detective curiously, probably wondering what his problem was. Mia was wondering the same thing.

"I didn't realize being on the task force was a prerequisite for booking a room." Mia turned a smile on Elaina, who'd just stepped into the lobby. Troy followed behind her, along with a young Hispanic man and a slightly older guy who seemed to be impersonating a sunburned raccoon.

"Mia." Troy sauntered over, planted a kiss on her cheek. "Decided to join the party, huh?"

Elaina shot him a reproachful look, while Ric glared at him.

"Dr. Lawson, right?" Troy held out a hand to Ben. "Think I've seen you at the Delphi Center."

Ben shook hands with Troy while Mia studied all the faces. Everyone looked either bleary-eyed or weather-beaten, and she could see this investigation was taking its toll.

"I hope to hell y'all didn't come down to hit the beach," Troy said.

"Actually, no." Mia felt the weight of half a dozen expectant stares, including the desk clerk's. "We're here to work, not play. I think we've got some leads for you."

Twenty minutes later, everyone was assembled together in the honeymoon suite. Elaina had just finished stacking files against the wall in a futile effort to make enough space for everyone. Between the people and the paperwork, it was a full house.

"Which do you want first, good news or bad?" Mia asked from the sofa.

"Bad," Elaina and Troy answered in unison. She shot a look at him across the room. He was leaning casually against the wall, but the tension in his shoulders told her he felt anything but casual. Elaina was edgy, too. Mia and Ben's arrival had given her a jolt of energy, and she was impatient to hear the news they'd brought. But whatever it was seemed to necessitate a computer, and so Elaina had busied herself tidying up while Ben had plopped down on the sofa and powered up his laptop. Now she perched on the sofa arm beside him and waited.

"Okay, here's the bad news." Mia took a deep breath. "The man you're looking for isn't in the database."

Elaina bit her lip. It had been a long shot. She'd known that. But she hadn't realized until this moment how much she'd been expecting to get lucky. She'd let herself entertain the idea that if she could just get hold of a DNA sample, the illustrious Dr. Voss would work magic with it.

She'd been expecting a miracle—just like Mia warned her not to.

Elaina looked at Troy. She knew he read the disappointment in her face, and she felt embarrassed for being so naive.

He shifted his attention to Mia. "You ran the profile through the state *and* national databases?" he asked.

"Yep," she said. "He's not in CODIS, which means either he has little or no criminal history, since standards vary from state to state, or if he *has* been swabbed for whatever reason, his sample hasn't been processed yet. Which is entirely possible, by the way, because everything's so backlogged. Problem is, that doesn't help you ID him."

Elaina huffed out a breath. "Okay, what's the good news?" And it had better be good. She needed, desperately, for something positive to come of this hellacious day.

"The good news is obvious, isn't it?" Mia said. "We actually got a profile. From a nine-year-old bullet and a five-year-old pair of running shorts. Both pieces of evidence yielded a sample. An itty-bitty one, but still."

Elaina watched her, momentarily dazed by her use of "itty-bitty," which she hadn't expected from a scientist. But then her tired brain processed the rest of Mia's statement.

"What running shorts?" she asked.

"From the missing hikers." Ric turned to Mia. "You got touch DNA." He folded his arms over his chest and smiled at her. "Goddamn, you did it, didn't you? I *knew* you could do it!"

Elaina felt a twinge of jealousy. Never in her life had a man looked at her like that—like he truly respected her as a professional.

"Let me get this straight," Troy said. "You put together a DNA profile from some skin cells left on a pair of shorts?"

"Ric had the missing women's clothing," Mia said. "He correctly deduced that the victims hadn't undressed themselves. And when their attacker pulled off their clothes, he left behind trace amounts of perspiration on the elastic bands. He wasn't wearing gloves, apparently, and when people commit crimes, their hands often sweat from nervousness. So we look for perspiration, maybe some shed skin cells, in order to recover DNA."

Across the room, Cinco whistled. "Man," he said. "You can get a profile from a few cells?"

"The sample was small and also degraded due to its age." Mia looked at Elaina. "As was the case with your through-and-through bullet. But I used PCR to amplify both samples and—"

"Back up," Weaver said. "PCR?"

"Polymerase chain reaction." Mia paused, and Elaina could tell she was trying to dumb it down for her audience. "It's a method of augmenting what you have. Think of it as using a molecular Xerox machine to copy what you need for further testing. Anyway, the DNA samples matched at ten loci, which is only a partial profile, but it's still useful. That's a match in the genetic pattern at ten specific places on the chromosomes."

"Which means?" This from Ric.

"It means the likelihood of these two samples coming from different individuals is practically nonexistent."

"The FBI standard is thirteen matching loci," Elaina said. "Ten won't stand up to scrutiny in a courtroom, but it's enough for a lead."

"Absolutely," Mia said. "For investigative purposes, this should help you a lot."

"We can flesh out our profile," Elaina added, getting excited now. "The man we're looking for was in Bay Port nine years ago, trespassing at the home of Mary Beth Cooper's neighbor, just a week before Mary Beth's murder, which I believe was his first kill. Then four years later, he spent an extended amount of time in San Marcos."

"Why extended?" Weaver asked. "Maybe he was passing through."

"More likely, he kills in his comfort zone," Elaina said. "So he was comfortable up there, knew the trails around

Devil's Gorge, at least well enough not to get caught. I'm willing to bet he's native to this area, either Bay Port or Lito, moved to San Marcos for a few years, and now he's back, living and working on the island. A history like that helps us narrow the suspect list."

"I can check driver's license records," Cinco offered. "See what comes up."

"What about Ben?" Troy asked.

All eyes turned to the cyber cop, who was tapping away at his keyboard. "I'm ready whenever you are."

"Let's hear it."

"Okay, I plotted out all the locations where victims have been found, along with the last known locations of the missing hikers." He hit a few keys, and a Google Earth map came up on his screen. Everyone gathered around the sofa to watch over his shoulder.

"Don't forget Angela," Cinco said quietly.

Ben glanced up. "I just added her. Elaina e-mailed me the coordinates from the discovery site this afternoon." He pointed to the screen. "The red dots are the victims."

He zeroed in on the Lito Island wildlife refuge until they were looking at aerial photographs of actual trees. Elaina recognized the gravel hiking path she'd been on early today. It petered out about a third of the way into the park, leaving the inhospitable wetlands the task force had combed on foot.

"Here's the most recent site," Ben said, and zoomed out to an aerial view of the whole park. "Here's where Gina Calvert was found. And Whitney Bensen. Now watch this." He hit a button, and three yellow dots appeared, not far from each of the discovery locations.

"What're those?" Weaver asked.

"Cache sites," Elaina blurted.

Troy looked at her. "This is what I wanted to show you today before you got sidetracked. Jamie told me she and one of her friends stumbled onto one of these caches close to where that spring breaker was found."

"Cache sites?" Weaver asked. "You want to translate that?"

Elaina explained about the dragonfly lead and the Web-based game being played by Jamie and her friends.

"You think Angela was involved?" Cinco asked.

"I'm not sure," Elaina said. "We know that several of the victims played this computer game. Could be the killer sees women on the trails and targets them later. Or maybe he selects them at Coconuts, then takes them out near the cache sites and leaves them for other players to find."

"Why would he do that?" Ric asked.

"Shock value," Elaina said. "Maybe he likes the idea of some unsuspecting hiker stumbling onto what he's done, like Jamie did. As for the kill itself, I believe it gives him a sense of dominance. That's part of his thrill. He selects the target, controls when she goes under, controls the dosage of ketamine and how likely she is to wake up while he's cutting her. Maybe she begs for her life and he gets off on that, too. It's all about control with this guy."

"But what's his motive?" Ric asked. "What sets him off? We have a murder nine years ago, two five years ago, and now this new rash of homicides."

"Motives aren't always cut and dried," Elaina said. "You can't necessarily look at the crimes and say, 'Hey, he's killing women who remind him of his domineering mother' or something. Every psychopath is different, but most grow up with a deep-rooted desire to commit violence. It usually manifests itself through inappropriate behaviors at an early age."

"Torturing animals, starting fires, bed wetting," Troy said.

"Those," Elaina agreed, "and also lying, blaming, manipulating. Callous disregard for others. As they grow up, they have increasingly vivid fantasies about violent acts. Then one day there might be a triggering event, and they give in to the impulse. In Mary Beth Cooper's case, I believe he followed the Charles Diggins murders in the media. They were happening right in his backyard. Maybe he felt envious, wanted to try his hand at it. He finds Mary Beth, disables her with the ketamine, and has a knife close by for the mutilation he wants to do. But maybe he misjudges the dosage and loses control of the victim, and in a panic, he strangles her and then stabs her. His crimes since then have been more methodical, more carefully planned and carried out. But they were still probably prompted by some triggering event. Maybe he lost a job, got rejected by a lover, something like that. Whatever it was set him off, and now he's escalated."

The room had fallen silent. Elaina looked around and had a flashback to her disastrous first meeting with Chief Breck. She should shut up now. She needed to remember that not everyone grew up with John McCord as a father and heard phrases like "homicidal triad" and "postmortem interval" tossed around the dinner table.

She looked at Ben's computer. "What else did you find?"

He tapped a few more keys, and Elaina recognized the Xtreme $$$ing Web site. "I've been researching the victims, too," Ben said. "Although, without knowing their user names, it's tough to tell whether they were in on the game."

"I can find out about Angela for you," Cinco said.

"That would help. Anyway, what I *did* find were three different individuals who just happened to visit each of these seven cache sites over the last six years. They all posted comments about their finds."

"You can trace that?" Troy sounded skeptical.

"When you're online, you leave a trail. It's almost impossible to move around undetected—sometimes it just takes a while to track someone down. Which is why I have a job. I'm in the process of tracing those user names back to actual e-mail accounts and then hopefully getting a court order to get their identities handed over by their Internet service providers."

"What are their screen names?" Elaina asked.

"So far I've got MoonMan4, BabyJane, and Grim-Reefer."

"The last one sounds promising," Troy said.

"Yeah, I thought so, too." Ben entered some words, evidently decoding the gibberish listed on the screen. GPS coordinates appeared, alongside several icons.

"How did you do that?" Elaina asked.

"That one was a plus-six code." Ben glanced up at all the blank stares. "Solve a math problem, get a positive six, and so then I add six to every number in the posted coordinates, which gives me the *actual* coordinates of the cache. This cache is entitled 'Dead Drop,' which I thought was interesting."

"No kidding," Weaver said. "*That* sounds suspicious. How long will it take you to find out the identity behind that user name?"

"Depends," Ben said.

"Did you say 'Dead Drop'?" Elaina's pulse was racing now. "That's a spy term." She glanced at Troy. "You leave a package at some predetermined place, at some predetermined time, and the two parties involved never have to have a live meeting."

From Troy's look, Elaina knew he could tell where her mind had gone.

"Robert Hanssen did that," Troy said. "At that park in Virginia, right?"

"He used a plus-six code, too," Elaina said, a little dizzy now. This was too big a coincidence. It *wasn't* a coincidence. It was more gamesmanship. More toying with the FBI. "Maybe he's leaving the victims near the cache sites for us to find. A literal dead drop."

"I'm afraid I'm lost," Mia said. "Robert Hanssen was that FBI agent who spied for the Russians, right? You're saying Hanssen used GPS coordinates?"

"Hanssen's plus-six code had to do with timing," Elaina said. "For example, if he told his contact to pick up a dead drop on January second at three P.M., the message actually meant to do a pickup on July eighth at nine P.M. See? He added six to everything. A lot of people think he was paranoid, but he was the most successful spy to ever work for the FBI."

"You think the unsub chose this code on purpose," Troy stated.

"I think he likes to believe he's smart," Elaina said. "He considers himself in the same league as someone who eluded the FBI for more than twenty years."

"Let's get back to what we *know*," Weaver suggested, turning to Ben. "Where is this cache site?"

"This is one of the caches within the Lito Island wild-life park," Ben said. "Actually, it's the one closest to the victim who was found earlier today, Angela Martinez. It shows here that the cache contains porn, some weed, a flyer—"

"What's a flyer?" Elaina asked.

"It's a roving treasure. In concrete terms, it's just an aluminum dragonfly pendant with a serial number on the back of it. Hence, the dragonfly symbol you keep noticing everywhere. When you discover a flyer, you can log onto the Web site, enter the serial number, and find out where it's headed. You're supposed to either move it along on its journey or put it back where you found it."

"What kind of journey?" Troy asked.

"Anything," Ben said. "Maybe someone has their flyer following their favorite band around the country. Or maybe someone wants their flyer to get from New York to L.A., or attend the X Games, or visit every Major League Baseball stadium. The possibilities are endless."

"If the killer planted it, he might be telling us where he's taking his next victim," Troy said.

"Maybe," Ben said. "But the only way to know is to track down the cache, find the pendant, and enter the serial number on the Web site to see where it's going."

"You can't find out on the computer?" Elaina asked.

"Unfortunately, no," Ben said. "That's part of the backward nature of this particular game. It's all a secret. You get a hint of what you're looking for from the icon, but you actually have to get your hands on the cache to know for sure what's there."

"So, what are we waiting for?" Elaina asked. "Let's go find it."

"Hang on there, Road Runner," Weaver said. "You want to look for it *now*? It's dark outside. The park is closed off to traffic. And you've been up since four this morning, traipsing around in the mud."

"Wouldn't work, anyway," Ben said. "These things are hard enough to find in the daytime. By flashlight, it'd be hopeless. We should wait for sunrise."

"I'll go," Troy said.

"It's a crime scene," Weaver reminded him. "No one's going in there without signing the crime-scene log and getting past whoever's guarding it, which I believe is someone with the LIPD."

Everyone's attention turned to Cinco.

"I'll check it out," he said.

"You can borrow my GPS," Ben offered. "You ever done this before?"

"No," Cinco said. "But how hard can it be?"

CHAPTER 21

After tossing the case around for a while longer, the group dispersed for the night. It was agreed that Cinco and Elaina would hit the park at first light, with the guidance of Ben's GPS and whatever clues he could decrypt from the Web site. The plan meant she might miss the task force meeting, but she'd worry about that later—she didn't want to let this lead wait.

Elaina grabbed a bottle of water from the mini-fridge and glanced at the balcony. An orange ember glowed near the patio table. She opened the sliding glass door and fisted a hand on her hip.

"You told me you didn't smoke much."

"I don't," Troy said from the shadows.

"So why are you smoking now?"

"I'm agitated. Helps me think."

"Giving yourself lung cancer helps you think?"

He turned to look at her. "You gonna come out here and sit with me, or just stand there acting like my mother?"

Elaina stared at him. He rarely mentioned his parents. From what little Cinco had told her, she'd gathered they were divorced, like hers were, and that he kept up with his mom but never spoke to his dad. Elaina was just the opposite. And having a dysfunctional family herself, she was tuned in to other people's weirdness.

Troy flicked an ash on the tile. "Take a load off, Elaina. You've had a crap day."

She stepped onto the balcony and sank down on the end of the lounge chair. She turned her attention to the beach. The surf was up tonight, pounding rhythmically against the sand. She liked the sound. Maybe she'd sleep with the door open tonight.

"I think you're right about Mary Beth," Troy said. "I think she was his first kill."

Then again, maybe she'd sleep with the door closed and locked, and her Glock resting on the nightstand.

She shifted her gaze to him. "It's really bothering you, isn't it?"

"Damn straight. I spent two years on that book. I've got file cabinets full of research on the Charles Diggins murders. I should have known Mary Beth didn't fit."

"The FBI didn't see it, either."

He didn't say anything, which she took to be something of a jab at the Bureau's competence.

"Anyway, we see it now," she said. "The thing is finding him before he does it again."

It sounded so simple. And yet, with each day that ticked by, Elaina felt more and more discouraged about their chances of success. Over and over again, they'd been too late. Why would tomorrow be any different? Or the next day? She thought of Angela Martinez, and her throat tightened.

"You okay?"

She glanced over at him. "Fine."

He stared at her in the dimness. "You should learn to lie better. Might come in handy."

For a while, she didn't say anything. The waves rolled against the sand as her conversation with Loomis echoed through her head.

"Do you think he's a cop?"

Troy sucked in a drag and watched her. "Why do you say that?"

"I don't know, really. A combination of things."

"Such as?"

"He's very good at avoiding detection. I mean, he's meticulous. No hair, no prints, no DNA."

"Mia got DNA off those shorts," he said.

"Yes, and that's probably because touch DNA wasn't widely known about five years ago. These new cases have yielded nothing in the way of forensic evidence. We've searched the cars, the crime scenes, the victims. No trace evidence. Don't you think that's weird?"

"Well, that in itself should tell you something."

"And the phone calls," Elaina said. "His mocking the FBI. Leaving Valerie on federal land like that—it's as if he wanted to make sure the Bureau got involved. I think he's playing games with us."

"You're saying he's a law enforcement groupie?"

She paused to chew on her statement before she said it. "I'm saying more than that. I think he's one of us. Or at least he tried to be. Maybe he's a washout from some police academy, possibly even Quantico. If he got rejected or fired, that could be a major triggering event."

"What makes you think Quantico?"

"Just little things, really. The plus-six code, which

could be an allusion to Robert Hanssen, who screwed over the FBI. And that other clue Ben showed us just before he left. That one from the cache hidden in Devil's Gorge."

"The one that said, 'Follow the Yellow Brick Road'?" Troy asked.

"Yes."

"What about it?"

"The Yellow Brick Road is a nickname for the obstacle course at the Academy. It's the bane of every NAT's existence."

"NAT?"

"A New Agent Trainee," she said. "Otherwise known as 'gnat,' which is about how small you feel while you're there. About how I'm feeling right now, too."

"Don't beat yourself up, Elaina. You've been working harder on this than anybody. Hell, if it weren't for you, we wouldn't even know about the extreme-caching angle. That could lead to an actual *name*. You told Loomis about it, right?"

Elaina sighed.

"What'd he say?"

"He looked at me like I'd told him I was a member of the Flat Earth Society. I think he thought it sounded wacky. Maybe it did." She rubbed her eyes. "God, I can hardly even remember the conversation now. It was so damn hot. I could barely see straight."

Quiet laughter from the shadows. "You probably did sound wacky."

"Thanks for the vote of confidence."

"Try him again tomorrow. Show him the Web site. It's pretty hard to argue with the theory once you see the aerial map."

"Maybe you're right." Elaina shifted her attention to the waves and rubbed her arms. Now she felt chilly. Just a few short hours ago, she'd felt like she was standing in a frying pan.

Troy dropped his cigarette on the tile and crushed it out with his boot. He took something off the table and stood up.

"You're leaving?"

"Nope." He walked over and eased a long leg over her chair, then lowered himself behind her.

All her nerve endings snapped to attention. She felt the brush of his fingers as he twisted her hair into a rope and tucked it in front of her right shoulder. She heard a soft sucking noise, and then he tossed something on the ground.

"What is that?"

"Aloe." His palms closed over her upper arms, and electricity zinged down her spine. His hands felt cool and slick, and he slid them up and down with gentle pressure.

"Where'd it come from?"

"Gift shop downstairs." He massaged the gel into her skin, rubbing little circles over her sore tendons with his thumbs. The breeze kicked up, and she shivered.

"Feels cold."

"I know." He squeezed more aloe into his palms and gently kneaded the feverish skin at her neck. His touch was light enough not to hurt, but firm enough to send little darts of awareness throughout her body.

She gazed out at the waves, remembering the view from his deck. She closed her eyes and focused on his hands moving over her skin. The throbbing started, deep and low in her body. How could she have such a weakness for this man? All he had to do was touch her, and she was willing to forget everything that mattered and just step into that sensual place where her mind shut down and her body took over and he watched her with that heated look in his eyes. She wanted him to look at her that way again. She wanted to spend the night with him again, and many more nights to come.

She sighed softly, and his hands stilled. For a moment, all she heard was the waves hissing and the rapid pounding of her own heart.

He picked up her hair and let it fan across her back. Then he stood up and stepped away from the chair.

"What are you doing?"

He gazed down at her, and she couldn't read his face. "Trying this your way, remember?" He scooped the tube of aloe off the ground and handed it to her. "Drink plenty of water tonight."

He stepped to the door and glanced back at her. "And be careful out there tomorrow."

"I will."

Brenda pulled into the driveway, tired beyond belief from working another night shift. She was sick of the hours, but the pay was good, and they needed the money. And it wasn't as if she was missing out on much at home. When her husband wasn't working late, he was holed up in that damn garage, or out on one of his drives or fishing trips. And anyway, she liked people. She liked to watch the comings and goings at the inn. It beat the hell out of thinking about her crappy marriage and her nonexistent sex life.

She stepped through the back door and almost tripped on the giant duffel bag in the middle of the laundry room floor.

"What the—" She glanced up and into the kitchen. The entire floor was covered with boxes and Army surplus duffels. Spread across the breakfast table was the gun collection, even the ones her husband never took out of the safe.

"What the heck is going on?" she asked as he walked into the kitchen with a box full of ammo.

"We're moving."

She stared at him.

"Get packed. We leave Monday morning, right after you pick up your paycheck."

She couldn't talk. She could hardly think. Her brain was working just enough to comprehend the tone of his voice. She'd heard it before. It meant he'd made up his mind, and there was no changing it.

He dumped the box on the table, and Brenda watched him wordlessly as he sorted boxes of bullets. She thought of her tomato plants. She thought of the new wallpaper she'd just put up in the bathroom. She thought of the Sandhill Inn and the friends she'd made there.

She stepped over the duffel and into the kitchen. "But . . . but I like it here."

"Too bad."

"Why do we have to move again?" Desperation filled her as she glanced around the kitchen and realized it was done. He'd already decided, without talking to her— same as when he'd packed up their little apartment and announced that they were moving to San Marcos.

"I don't *want* to move. I'm sick of moving!" She could

hardly see him now through the blur of tears. "I like my job, for once. I like this *place*."

"Shut up and pack." He wouldn't even look at her as he loaded his handguns into a bag.

"No." A blanket of calm settled over her as the word left her mouth. She wasn't going. Not this time. Not for him.

His eyes came up. They were flat again, and an icy finger of fear tickled her spine. She'd pushed too far.

He rested the gun on the table. He walked over. Brenda eased back, against the cool flatness of the wall, and tried to melt into the Sheetrock.

"I'm sorry," she whispered. "I didn't mean it. I'll go. Of course I'll go."

He stopped in front of her. His big hand closed around her neck, cutting off the words. Cutting off the air. She tasted blood in her mouth as she bit her tongue and the hand squeezed.

"I'll say it once more, so listen good." The grip tightened, and her eyes started to burn. "I'm leaving Monday. And you're coming with me."

CHAPTER 22

"All right, you're looking for anything out of place," Ben said into the phone.

Mia adjusted the air vent to face her. She checked her watch. Then she lifted her thighs, trying to unglue herself from the leather seat of Ben's Pathfinder. She couldn't believe she was sweating this much at only ten in the morning.

"Look for natural objects sitting in unnatural ways," he continued. "Parallel sticks. A pile of rocks. Maybe even just one rock in a place you wouldn't expect to see one."

Mia surveyed the marshland stretched out in front of them. Ninety-six hundred acres. A lot of ground to cover. Even with GPS coordinates, she wasn't confident Elaina and Cinco were going to find an inconspicuous brown box. But Ben seemed to think there would be clues scattered about, just to keep the game interesting.

A movement in the side mirror caught Mia's eye. A gray pickup pulled over behind them on the shoulder, and Mia recognized the driver even before he climbed down and approached her window.

"Yeah, something like that," Ben said. "Uh-huh . . . That's what I mean."

Mia rolled the window down, and Ric leaned an arm on the roof of the car. He wore a gray T-shirt today and jeans. *Jeans,* in this searing heat.

"What are you doing out here?" he demanded.

"Helping." She nodded at the police cruiser stationed at the entrance to the wildlife park, about a quarter-mile up the road. "They wouldn't let us in, so we set up this little call center. Ben's on the phone with Elaina right now, walking them through it. They told Cinco they're releasing the scene this morning, but I'm beginning to have my doubts."

Several news vans were pulled over beside the road-block, filming the officer turning cars away. The foot-age would probably accompany their breathless updates about the Paradise Killer's latest strike.

She shifted her attention to the detective looming over her. Ric's disapproval was nearly as palpable as the humidity.

"What is your problem, anyway?" she asked.

"My problem?"

"Yes, your problem." She needed to get this off her chest; it had been bugging her since last night. "You approach me in a bar, practically beg me to help you. You show up at my work, my home. I bust my butt running evidence for you, I come down here to share my results, and you treat me like I've got the plague or something."

He shook his head and looked away at the media vans.

"That's it, that's it!" Ben gave Mia a thumbs-up.

She closed her eyes with relief. *Finally.* They'd been out here for hours.

"You should go home, Mia."

She glanced up at Ric.

"You're not on the task force. You have no business being down here."

She laughed. "*Un*believable! And are you on the task force?" She already knew the answer—she'd discussed it with Troy.

"I'm a trained police officer. You're not." He leaned closer, and she saw the dark intensity in his eyes. "Have you noticed how many women are part of this investigation?"

Several mosquitoes flew into the SUV, and Mia tried unsuccessfully to shoo them out. "I don't know. A few?"

"One." Ric said. "Elaina McCord. That's it."

"Yeah. And?"

"And do you know what's been happening to the *one* female investigator working this case? She's been getting phone calls from the unsub. He's fixated on her."

Mia stared up at him. "What are you suggesting, exactly?" Surely he didn't think Elaina was personally in some sort of danger. She was an FBI agent, for heaven's sake.

"I'm suggesting you go back to San Marcos."

"Damn it!"

Mia turned to look at Ben, who was gripping the steering wheel now, shaking his head.

"What?" Mia asked, but he wasn't listening. Whatever was happening on the other end of that phone had his full attention.

"Mia? You hear what I'm telling you?"

She gazed up at Ric now and saw more than hostility in his eyes. Was it concern? Was he actually worried about her?

"I'm leaving tomorrow," she told him. "As planned. Two heads are better than one. And ten heads are better than two. You got me involved in this thing, and now that I am, I'll do whatever I can to help."

Elaina strode through the cubicles and tried to shrug off the curious stares of her colleagues. Flak jackets were one thing, but agents didn't typically roll into work wearing running gear and looking as if they'd just undergone a chemical peel. Elaina stopped at her cube and shuffled through the message slips and sticky notes littered across her desk. She quickly logged onto the computer and checked her in-box. She found dozens of items that needed her attention, but no word from Special Agent Rey Santos in San Antonio.

"McCord."

She glanced up to see Loomis standing beside her cube. His starched shirt and tie were a marked contrast to her own flame-broiled appearance.

"Glad you stopped by," he said. "We need to talk."

Elaina replaced the phone. Loomis jerked his head toward a nearby conference room, and she followed him without comment. *Glad you stopped by?* Since when was Loomis in charge of her schedule? Yes, she was on his task force, but she was pretty sure she—like everyone else in this building—still answered to Scarborough.

"Have a seat," he said, and she couldn't stop herself from taking a furtive look at her watch. "Am I making you late for something?"

"No," she lied, and lowered herself into a chair.

He leaned back in his seat. "We missed you at the task force meeting this morning."

"I was at the wildlife park. Officer Chavez and I—"

"I know, I know." He waved her off. "The geocaching thing. I heard you struck out."

"Not exactly. We found two of three caches listed on the Web site, but both were empty, unfortunately. I had the Evidence Response Team collect them for processing."

He gazed at her with a look that was part annoyance, part disbelief.

"Since joining this team, you've missed two task force meetings."

Elaina held her shoulders rigid and forced herself not to squirm. "I was investigating—"

"You were investigating a lead, I know. But you're part of a team, McCord. Or at least you were. And it's not your job to go blazing out on your own to Mexico and wherever else, chasing down dragonflies and buried treasure. We do things as a unit around here." His gaze veered to her stitches. "Part of that's for your protection."

Elaina swallowed the lump in her throat. "I'm sorry. Did you just tell me I'm *no longer* on the task force?"

"That's correct."

She surged to her feet. "But that's not fair! You haven't even listened—"

"*You* haven't listened. Or followed direction. Or shown common sense. Hell, just this morning you took a POI with you to a closed crime scene."

"Cinco Chavez isn't a person of interest," she protested. "I told you—"

"That's my call, not yours. You're off, McCord."

"But—"

"Save your breath." He stood up now, too. "It's not my decision, and even if it was, I wouldn't change it."

She stood there, stunned. "Whose decision is it?"

And then her question was answered when Scarborough stepped into the room. Loomis traded looks with the supervisory special agent, then cast a last baleful glance in Elaina's direction before walking out the door.

Scarborough took Loomis's place at the conference table. He reached over and snapped shut the mini-blinds on the window facing the bullpen. Elaina's stomach plummeted.

"Sit down," he said.

She sat.

The seconds ticked by as he pinned her with a stern expression. He leaned back in the chair and propped an elbow on the table.

"Special Agent McCord." His voice oozed disapproval.

"Yes, sir."

He cocked his head to the side and watched her. "Do you know how many years I've got in?"

She floundered for a response. "Years you . . . No. No, sir, I don't."

"Twenty-three. Last ten of 'em here, too." He tapped his knuckles on the table. "That's three more years than your father had before he retired to write his books, you realize that?"

Her stomach filled with dread. A vague impression she'd had since the first day she'd walked into this office began to crystallize.

"I'm sorry, sir, but what does my father have to do with this discussion?"

He gazed at her for a few endless seconds. "Something interesting happened right before you showed up here last fall. I got a call from Quantico. Were you aware of that?"

Elaina opened her mouth, but nothing came out. What had her father *done*?

"Someone very well-connected in this organization strongly *suggested* that I encourage you to rethink your career choice."

"That you . . . what?"

"I was told to weed you out, McCord."

Elaina couldn't move. She couldn't speak. She could barely breathe.

Scarborough leaned back in the chair, watching her. "You know, some folks think this office is like the Wild West. They're not too far off, really, when you consider some of the shit we're dealing with. Quantico usually gives us a lot of latitude, and I like it that way. What I *don't* like is some pencil pusher calling me up and telling me how to run things. And as it turns out, the call wasn't really necessary because you've been doing a pretty good job of getting weeded out all by yourself."

He flipped open the file sitting in front of him, and Elaina noticed it for the first time. She held her breath.

"Some notes from your field supervisor," he said. " 'The agent is highly intelligent, has strong organizational skills, and shows great attention to detail.' "

Elaina cleared her throat. "Thank you. Sir, I—"

"It also says here that you're a loner, that you're headstrong, and that you have a tendency toward insubordination."

Elaina clamped her mouth shut.

"Loomis is even less impressed than that. He thinks you're a liability to this office and is suggesting a letter of censure in response to your behavior since you joined his task force."

Her mind reeled. A letter of censure would follow her around for years, making it virtually impossible for her to join an elite team within the Bureau. She heard her dreams of becoming a profiler being crushed like a tin can.

"That's Loomis's take," Scarborough said. "I'm inclined to hold off."

She blinked at him. "Why?"

"Because of this lead you developed. The computer game. Loomis thinks it's screwy as hell, but we're dealing with a man who disembowels women for fun. I'd be surprised if he *didn't* have a screw loose. Anyone with a map can see there's something to the theory."

She held her breath, waiting.

"You might say your ability to think outside the box saved your ass this time." He flipped the file shut. "The letter of censure's on hold for now, but you're done with the task force. I want you off that island and back at your desk by Monday morning."

"But I was planning to go to Coconuts tonight. To help with surveillance."

"Forget it—that's his trolling ground. And we've got more than enough men assigned to it."

She opened her mouth, but he cut her off with a look.

"That's it, McCord. You're off the task force. Even if Loomis wanted you on his team—which he doesn't— the unsub's fixated on you. He's reached out to you about his last three kills."

"He didn't call about Angela," she rushed to say. "I haven't heard from him in days."

"Are you sure? No odd phone calls? No notes on your windshield or slipped under your door?"

Elaina froze. She thought of the incident with her car the other night, when she thought she'd left the lights on.

"Maybe he's taking a breather, then, but it won't last long." Scarborough pushed the file away and crossed his arms. "Anyway, he's toying with you, and I'm not planning to dangle one of my agents out there like bait. Dismissed."

"But, sir—"

"Dismissed, McCord. I'll see you here Monday."

CHAPTER 23

Mia waded through bar patrons, searching for Elaina McCord. This place was packed tonight, but the woman had to be here somewhere.

An icy drizzle of beer landed on Mia's shirt. She gasped and looked up to see a man grinning down at her from beneath his baseball cap.

"'Scuse, me." He toasted her with his cup. "Didn't mean to do that."

Yeah, right.

Mia was about to tell him off when she spotted Elaina on the other end of the volleyball court, standing beside a group of agents.

"Hey, you want a drink?" the beer-slosher asked.

Mia ignored him and plowed her way through the crowd. Elaina was deep in conversation with Weaver, who looked extra grim this evening, despite his don't-worry-be-happy attire. Elaina, by contrast, was dressed kick-ass agent style in a black pantsuit and white shirt.

Elaina pretended not to notice her, and Mia waited patiently for her to look up.

"Is it true?" Mia asked.

Elaina traded looks with Weaver before responding. "Is what true?"

"That you're off the case."

"It's true."

"I can't believe it! How can they take you off?"

"They can do whatever they want," Elaina said, and glanced at her watch. "Anyway, I need to get going."

She wouldn't make eye contact, and that—more than anything—told Mia she was near the breaking point. "Wait." Mia clasped Elaina's arm, obviously startling her. "Just . . . let's have a drink, okay?"

"I really can't."

"Just for a minute. Before you go."

Mia claimed a bar stool a few spots down from Weaver, who was eyeing her curiously. They probably thought she was a little nutty, and maybe she was, after spending the past five nights burning the candle at both ends. Mia's nerves were frayed, so she had at least an inkling of what Elaina was feeling.

Elaina sighed. One more glance at her watch, and she took a stool. "A Coke, please," she told the bartender.

Mia ordered a margarita, and Elaina watched her impatiently.

"So did you want to talk about something in particular, or . . . ?" She waited for Mia to fill in the gap.

Mia watched her for a moment, and then she *got* it. Her fuzzy view of the taciturn special agent suddenly sharpened.

"You don't have a lot of girlfriends, do you?" Mia asked.

"Excuse me?"

"You're extremely direct. And you don't like to chat." She shrugged. "It's just an observation."

Elaina cast an annoyed look at the bartender, as if wishing he'd hurry up with their drinks.

Mia reconsidered her take on the situation. Maybe this was a Troy thing. Maybe Elaina had picked up on something from her and Alex and was on the defensive about it.

Elaina met her gaze now. "What is it you wanted, exactly?"

Or maybe she was just prickly.

"I wanted to see if you might try to stay on," Mia said.

"It's not my decision."

The drinks came, and Mia stirred hers thoughtfully. "You realize you're the only woman on this case, don't you?"

Elaina sipped her Coke and looked away.

"And you realize you're the only one who believes in this Web angle, right? If you leave, who's going to follow up on that?"

"That's not my call. I'm off the team."

Mia rolled her eyes. "This is your brainchild, Elaina. You convinced Ben. You convinced me. You even convinced Ric, and now you're leaving? Why won't you fight for your case? I think you're on to something here, and now it's going to fall by the wayside."

"It won't fall by the wayside."

"How do you know?"

"Because," she said, her voice tight with suppressed emotion, "at this very moment my vehicle is on its way to the lab. The unsub left me a note two nights ago— the GPS coordinates where Angela Martinez was found. Only, I didn't realize what he'd done until it was too late to help her."

Elaina downed the rest of her Coke and plunked the glass on the bar. She started to reach for some money, but Mia stopped her.

"He left a note in your *car*?" she asked.

"Yes." Finally, Elaina looked at her, and Mia recognized the emotion swimming in her eyes: guilt.

Mia pulled a credit card from her purse. "Don't take that on, Elaina. It's not your fault. You did everything you could."

Elaina snorted. "That's crap. If I'd done everything I could, she'd be alive right now. This guy tried to give *me* a message, and I was too blind to see it."

Mia watched her with a sick feeling in the pit of her stomach. Ric was right. The killer was fixated on her.

"I think your boss is right," she said now. "You should step aside. Your colleagues can handle this one without you."

Elaina glared at her. "You want to know how they're handling it? Look around this place." She gestured to the agents standing around in khaki shorts and deck shoes. "It looks like a freaking Land's End photo shoot. And you want to know who they interviewed this afternoon? Cinco Chavez! I swear to God—" Elaina pinched the bridge of her nose and turned away.

The bartender returned with a credit card and a receipt. Mia glanced down and slid the card back. "That's not mine," she told him. Then to Elaina: "They're really interviewing *Cinco*?"

"Yes."

She lowered her voice. "As a suspect?"

"Yes! Forget that there's *no* physical evidence connecting him to these crimes. Forget that he's been in the presence of *other law enforcement officers* when some of the victims went missing." She glanced around and seemed to realize this wasn't the time or the place for this conversation. "Anyway, *yes* I'm definitely off the task force, and *no* I don't think my colleagues will handle it. Anything else you want to discuss with me? Hey, how about our shared interest in Troy Stockton? Maybe that would be a little more comfortable. I thought he was great in bed, but the morning after sucked. What was your experience?"

Mia gaped at her.

Elaina took a deep breath and blew it out. From the corner of her eye, Mia saw Weaver watching them with a pained look on his face.

"I just love girl talk," Elaina said, sliding off the stool. "We should do it again sometime."

Elaina was at his house. Or Weaver. Or someone else who drove a piece-of-shit Taurus, but Troy hoped it was Elaina. Five minutes ago he'd wanted nothing more than a cold beer, a hot shower, and about ten hours of sleep, but as he trudged up the stairs, the sight of Elaina sitting on one of his deck chairs looking out over the water changed his mind. So did the little black overnight bag parked beside his door.

She got up and walked over. "You're home," she said.

She wore her hair pulled back in a smooth ponytail. Troy took in the black suit, the badge, the gun plastered to her hip. She wasn't dressed for Coconuts, and he knew the rumor he'd heard from Maynard was true. She was off the task force, which meant that she was leaving.

Something sharp twisted in his chest.

"May I come in?" she asked, and her voice was loaded with politeness.

In answer, he unlocked the door and jerked it open. Then he picked up her bag and gestured her inside.

His house was dark, but he didn't bother with lights. He tossed her duffel on the sofa and emptied his pockets onto the kitchen table: wallet, cell phone, tape recorder.

She stood beside the door, looking uncomfortable as she glanced around the house.

She took a tentative step toward him. "Where were you today?"

"Road trip."

"Road trip where?" Another tentative step.

"Huntsville," he told her. "And I need to shower."

He felt her behind him as he walked toward the back of the house. "Talked to Cinco," he said, stripping off his T-shirt and tossing it on a chair in his bedroom. He turned to look at her. She'd never looked as *agent* as she did right now, and he couldn't believe she was back at his house.

"How is he?" she asked.

"Pissed." He sank onto the bed and pulled off his boots. "It wasn't your idea, was it?"

"I can't believe you'd even say that."

He flung a boot into the corner. Then another. "Thought maybe you sold them on your cop theory."

She folded her arms over her chest. "I'm off the task force."

"I heard." He stood and gazed down at her. She didn't look too broken up about it, but Troy knew better. There was a reason she'd come here. She needed something from him, and it had nothing to do with the case.

She broke eye contact with him and stepped toward the door. "Well." She cleared her throat. "I should let you shower."

He walked into his bathroom, turned the shower to scalding, and spent ten minutes scrubbing away the scum of humanity that seemed to cling to him every time he set foot in that prison.

He yanked a towel off the rack and wrapped it around his waist. His bedroom was empty now. He pulled on some jeans and found Elaina in his kitchen, standing before an open refrigerator. She'd taken her jacket off and rolled up her sleeves.

"You shop like a bachelor," she told him.

"I am a bachelor." He reached around her and grabbed a beer off the top shelf. "If you're hungry, I can order a pizza."

"I'm fine."

She closed the door, and then they were standing there alone in his darkened kitchen. He popped open his beer, then leaned back against the counter and watched her over the bottle as he took a sip. Her gazed dropped to his bare chest, then slid back up again. She was uneasy here, nervous. And he didn't mind because he knew she was struggling to keep her emotions in check, which meant she *had* emotions where he was concerned.

He had emotions, too. They were bound up in a big, tight knot in the center of his chest. Mainly anger, with some lust mixed in. But mostly anger.

She stared at him through the shadowy room. Moonlight streamed through the window above the sink, outlining her silhouette. His eyes were drawn to the badge and the gun at her hip.

"Tell me about Huntsville," she said.

"I interviewed Diggins again."

She tipped her head to the side.

"I needed to see where he got his information all those years ago. About Mary Beth."

"And?"

"Turns out he overheard one of the guards talking about it after he was taken into custody. One of them had a buddy who worked the crime scene. That's where he got his details."

Her eyebrows arched. "He told you that?"

"Yep."

"Impressive interview skills."

He shrugged. "Tools of the trade."

"Still, it's impressive."

He looked at her Glock, then met her gaze again. The silence stretched out. He stepped forward and she eased back slightly.

"What are you doing here, Elaina?" He leaned a palm on the counter beside her, and she looked up at him.

"I don't know."

He moved closer and brushed the cold lip of his bottle against the place on her neck where her pulse thrummed. "Yeah, you do."

She shivered and closed her eyes, and he brushed the icy wet bottle against her breast. He heard her sharp intake of breath. He rubbed the bottle over her nipple, and it made a wet mark on her crisp white shirt.

"Tell me why you're here." He held the bottle against her as he slowly, one by one, plucked open the buttons on her shirt.

Her eyes drifted open, and she gazed up at him. He

rested the beer on the counter and parted her shirt with his hands and found the pale lace bra she wore beneath all those unisex clothes. She'd put it on for him. He knew it. And it was an unbelievable turn-on.

"You want something," he murmured in her ear, and slid his finger up to trace the lace. "Elaina?"

"I just—"

He kissed her. Roughly. Because he didn't want to hear her excuses. He wanted honesty for once. He wanted her naked and honest and open to him without all the bullshit. He wanted *her*. Now, before she suited up again and went back to her home and her life and her goddamn career.

He kissed her deeper, longer, harder, sliding his hand down and dipping his fingers inside her pants, and he heard her breath catch.

"Tell me what you want, Elaina."

She tilted her head back and gazed up at him. "You," she whispered, and he touched her where she was soft and hot, and she pressed against him. "Please, I want you."

CHAPTER 24

Troy pulled her into the bedroom, and she was barely inside before he had her shirt off and her bra unfastened. This was happening so fast this time, and she hadn't even been drinking.

"Wait," she said, fumbling with her belt. She jerked the buckle open, and saw the glint in his eyes as she took off her badge and holster and placed them on his dresser. He reached behind her and loosened the rubber band at the nape of her neck, so that her hair spilled freely over her shoulders. He eased her back onto the bed and he rested his knee on the mattress as he reached down to slip off her shoes.

Thunk—one hit the floor. *Thunk*—the other followed. He moved over her, tugging on the hook of her slacks as he kissed her mouth, her chin, her throat, and made his way down her body. He stopped at her navel, and she felt the slide of fabric as he pulled her slacks off her legs. And then it was just his warm breath against her skin and the sandpaper feel of his chin as he continued down, down, until he was on his knees at her feet. He lifted her calf and kissed the arch of her foot, and she nearly leapt off the bed.

"Ticklish?"

She tried to jerk her foot away, but he held it firmly by the heel.

"Cherry red," he murmured, massaging her arch with his thumb. "It's been driving me crazy."

She propped up on her elbows and watched him and began to get dizzy as he rubbed her foot. God, his hands felt good. He pressed his thumb against her arch and she felt a surge of heat deep within her body, and she squirmed on the bed while he looked at her. He made his way back up, trailing kisses over her calf, her knee, her thigh.

"This, too." He kissed the little satin rosebud below her navel, and she shivered under him. "It's so girly."

"What?"

He moved slowly up her abdomen, and she lost the ability to process whatever he was saying. He molded his mouth over her breast and pulled. "Don't get me wrong." Another pull. "I like it. A lot." And then he focused on what he was doing, and she held his head against her and wrapped a leg around him so he wouldn't get distracted again. His weight on her and his warm skin and his hard muscles under her palms were making her heart hammer until she thought it would pound right out of her chest.

"Troy."

"Hmm?" He kept doing that thing with his mouth, and at the same time she felt his hand sliding over her stomach.

"Oh my God, *Troy.*" She reached back, for the night-stand, for the drawer she remembered from last time, even though she had no idea how she remembered anything when her head was spinning and every nerve in her body was on the verge of combustion.

The drawer. She couldn't reach it. *"Troy."*

He lifted his head and seemed to see what she was after and leaned over her to grab the box of condoms. She took advantage of his distraction by shimmying herself down the mattress and reaching for his jeans.

He pushed himself up, off the bed, and quickly stripped off his clothes. Her heart skittered at the sight of him in the dimness. She remembered this, too, and felt a warm flush of anticipation.

He stood there staring at her, and she could tell he liked what he saw. He liked *her.* He wanted *her.* And it wasn't about tequila this time, or beer, or anything else. A little bubble of happiness expanded inside her as she stared up at him and watched him want her. He looked dark and intent, and no one else had ever looked at her that way, and she wanted to capture the image and keep it in her head forever.

He slipped the strap down her shoulder and pulled off her lacy white bra—the one that he liked, a *lot,* but that he now tossed carelessly onto the floor beside her shoes. Her panties followed, and then he quickly covered himself and climbed back on the bed. She lay back without breathing and braced herself as he pushed her legs apart, and then he filled her, and every nerve in her body screamed out.

"Oh, God," she gasped, and clung to him as tightly as she could and urged him into that fierce, addictive rhythm she'd been craving since their first night together.

And then it was back. Again. And she pulled his head down to kiss her as his body pounded into her. She couldn't get enough of him. She'd never get enough of him. If she lived to be a hundred, she'd never get enough of the intense, abundant feeling of making love to this man.

He propped his weight on his arms and looked down at her, and in his heavy-lidded gaze she saw the same indescribable pleasure she was feeling. She reached up to comb her fingers into his hair.

And then he kissed her. Deeply. Roughly. And in a way that told her that she *wasn't* alone, that this wasn't just about alcohol or sex, and that he was feeling it, too. She pulled him closer, as close as she possibly could, and tried to block out the single coherent thought flashing through her brain, but it wouldn't go away.

I love you. And that blinding realization was followed by a wave of wonder and euphoria and, most of all, fear.

"Elaina." He wrenched his mouth away and gazed down at her, and she knew what he was trying to tell her, what his look meant. It wasn't love, but it was something good, and she tipped her head back and lost herself in the explosive, vibrant moment when they fused themselves together and reality spun away. Time seemed suspended as tremors shook her and she held on to him with every fiber of her being.

Slowly, she opened her eyes to see him gazing down at her. The side of his mouth lifted in a smile, and he rolled onto his back, pulling her with him. He settled her against his chest and sighed deeply.

Her pulse thrummed in her ears. She loved him. But

did she really, or was that just her hormones yelling at her? She didn't know. In a rush of panic, she sat up to look at him, but his eyes were closed, and he looked like he was sleeping.

Sleeping? Already? She started to move off the bed, but he caught her wrist.

"Lay back." He tugged her against him, never opening his eyes.

She nestled her head against his chest, and he wrapped his arms around her, and for a while she just listened to his heart thudding and felt the steady rise and fall of his breathing.

She was in trouble here. She knew that. This wasn't a one-night stand anymore, but it was a far cry from a committed relationship, and she'd fallen in love with him. Tears welled in her eyes, but she blinked them back. What was she doing? She shouldn't trust this man. She shouldn't trust any man, not even her own father. To Elaina's horror, she started to cry.

He went rigid. She felt him lift his head to look at her and she squeezed her eyes shut, but her hot, wet tears leaked onto his chest.

"Hey," he whispered.

She shook her head. She didn't know what to say to him.

"You want to talk about it?"

She shook her head again.

He tucked her under his chin and kissed the top of her head, and somehow the utter sweetness of the gesture made her feel even worse. She had to stop. She had to get control of this.

He stroked his hand up and down her side, and Elaina

took a deep breath and just focused on that. After a few minutes, she'd regained her composure. Then his hand stilled, and for a long time neither of them moved, and the only sound was the quiet hum of the air conditioner down the hall.

Her father had betrayed her—the one person she'd always trusted in her life—and it felt strange and surreal and just *wrong*.

Her world had been knocked off its axis. Her career was in jeopardy. And the work she cared about more than anything had been taken away from her.

And what had been her brilliant response to this predicament? She'd sought refuge in the bed of a man who would never love her. And then she'd cried all over him.

She needed to get out of here. She needed to go home to her drab, lonely apartment, where she could deal with it all in private.

But that wasn't what she wanted. She wanted to stay here with Troy, the one thing that felt real and solid and warm in her entire universe.

He squeezed her shoulders. "I've got an idea," he whispered.

"What?"

"Let's go swimming."

She turned to look at him. "I don't have a swimsuit."

"You'll like it better that way."

Troy awoke in an empty bed with the seagulls screaming outside his window. He sat up and glanced at the clock. Almost eight. He glanced at the dresser, and a chill settled over him.

He spent a few moments clenching and unclenching

his teeth. Then he threw on some shorts and went in the kitchen, where a quick glance around confirmed that she was gone. Again.

Only this time she'd taken the trouble to leave coffee. Troy poured himself a mug. He took it out onto the deck and looked out over the beach where just a few hours ago he'd persuaded Elaina to break a couple laws with him. He took a sip of coffee. It was strong enough to wake the dead, and he took another sip.

He spotted her on the shoreline. She was all forward motion—none of that side-to-side arm shit so many women did when they ran. She'd learned how to run on the beach, too, and she moved barefoot across the wet, hard-packed sand. She was speed and intensity, and his heart lodged in his throat as he watched her eat up the beach with those powerful legs.

She sprinted past his house, then slowed and stopped. She wore only shorts and a running bra that fit her like a second skin, and he couldn't take his eyes off her as she braced her hands against her waist and arched back to suck down big gulps of air.

He joined her on the sand. "How far'd you go?"

She glanced at him, still good and winded.

"Six miles," she gasped.

"Not bad."

She shrugged.

"Didn't see your stuff inside."

"It's in the guest bathroom." She wiped sweat from her brow with her forearm. "I didn't want to be in your way."

He looked at her and felt the overwhelming urge to do something very physical to her very soon.

"You up for some more?" he asked.

"More what?"

"How 'bout we start with some sparring?"

"Defensive tactics?"

He thought about Mexico and Diggins and the psycho who was obsessed with her. "You can never be too prepared," he said.

She nodded. "All right, you're on."

Troy was a boxer, evidently. As soon as she saw the weights and the punching bag in his garage, it made sense. He'd been fighting and scrapping all his life, and he was still doing it, only he'd turned it into exercise.

They stood on the mat between his weight bench and his car, and Elaina glanced around.

"How often do you work out here?" she asked.

"Every day."

He lunged. She brought her knee up almost instantly, but he got her into a headlock.

"You hesitated," he said. "Never do that. Didn't they teach you that at—"

She dropped to her knees, jerked him off balance, and flipped him onto his back. She planted a knee on his chest and shoved her arm against his windpipe.

He smiled, and she eased back a fraction. "That's good," he said. "I like you on top."

She started to get up, but he pulled her down and kissed her. She was sweaty, but he didn't seem to care, and he held her there and kissed the hell out of her. There was something fierce about him this morning. An urgency. Or maybe she was the one feeling it because of all the tension coursing through her life. But wherever it was coming from, she went with it, tangling her fingers in his hair and grinding her body against him and kissing the hell out of him, too.

Something creaked, and they both glanced up. Elaina stared in shock at the man looming in the doorway.

"*Dad?*" She scrambled to her feet.

Her father's familiar blue eyes raked over her. His icy gaze settled on Troy as he got to his feet beside her.

Her father took a few steps into the room, and Troy reached out to offer a handshake. "Mr. McCord? Troy Stockton."

Her dad stood motionless, and Elaina's cheeks flushed with embarrassment. After an excruciating pause, he shook Troy's hand. "I know who you are." He turned to her. "Elaina, I need a word."

She stared at him. He'd flown more than a thousand miles for a *word*?

"About what?" she managed.

He gazed at her with that impenetrable look she'd known all her life, and she realized he wasn't going to have this discussion in front of an outsider.

Troy seemed to realize it, too. He squeezed her hand and looked her in the eye. "I'll let you guys talk," he said, and left the room.

She watched the empty doorway as the sound of his footsteps receded up the stairs. She didn't hear the door slide open, which meant he was on the deck, and she wondered if he could hear them.

She turned back to face her father. "How did you find me?"

He looked amused. "I'm retired, not brain dead."

Elaina walked to the garage's back door, which faced

the beach. Troy had propped a big box fan there, and she switched it off. The room went silent except for the distant sound of the surf. Elaina turned her back on the view and crossed her arms as she watched her father, and a bitter lump formed in the back of her throat.

"You look different," he said, eyeing her stitches.

He didn't look different at all. He wore a version of the same pinstripe suit she'd been seeing her entire life. His only acquiescence to the heat was the missing tie, which she guessed was in his pocket.

"I've been following your case," he said.

The bitterness swelled. "It's not my case anymore. Scarborough took me off."

"I can't say that I'm sorry." His voice was measured. Even. And he'd carefully neglected to mention whether he'd had anything to do with Scarborough's decision.

Elaina looked out at the water. She'd known her father hadn't wanted her to become an agent. But she'd chalked it up to protectiveness and assumed he'd deal. Like anyone.

But he wasn't anyone, he was John McCord—a man used to getting his way and bulldozing everyone who stood in his path. The Bureau was packed with people like her father. Smart, competent, confident people who were accustomed to being right all the time and who didn't like hearing the word *no*.

"If you came here to talk me into quitting my job, you can save your breath," she said.

"That's not why I came."

She looked at him expectantly.

"I came to apologize. I should have let you go your own way." He stepped closer to her until they were just a few feet apart. "I didn't realize you really had it in you, Lainey. I thought you'd take after your mother."

His words were like a knife into her sternum. For a moment, she stopped breathing.

He stepped closer, tipped his head to the side, and studied her carefully, as if really *seeing* her for the very first time. "I'm beginning to think you're more like me, though."

She stared at him, not sure she could speak. She didn't even try, and after a few seconds, he reached into his jacket and pulled out an envelope.

"This is a plane ticket to D.C.," he said. "For Wednesday morning. You have an interview at Quantico Wednesday afternoon with the head of BAU."

She blinked at him.

"A spot opened up on his team, and he'd like to talk to you about it."

She stared down at the envelope, as though looking at it might make it more real. "But I thought I needed more field experience—"

"You would, normally," her dad said. "But this position's designed for newer agents. They're looking for fresh ideas, people who haven't succumbed to groupthink."

She glanced up at him warily. Was he being honest with her? She didn't know anymore.

"I figured you might not want to stay with me, so I booked you at the Westin Hotel in Alexandria." He stepped closer and put the envelope in her hand. "It's a great opportunity."

"It's a *safe* opportunity," she said.

He slipped his hands into his pockets and sighed.

"You're my daughter, Elaina. Someday when you have kids of your own, you'll understand."

The words of Valerie Monroe's father came back to her as she stood in Troy Stockton's garage with waves from the Gulf of Mexico crashing against the sand behind her. It was the most bizarre conversation she could remember.

"Anyway, it's up to you, of course."

"Of course."

He bent over and kissed her forehead, and she forced herself not to flinch, but John McCord, expert on body language and so many other things, caught it anyway.

He stepped back. He cast a look around Troy's garage, lingering for a few disapproving moments on the black Ferrari. And Elaina knew if he uttered so much as a single syllable about Troy, she was going to snap.

Instead, he nodded and stepped toward the door. "Take care of yourself, Elaina. Let me know what you decide."

CHAPTER 25

Elaina sat in her nondescript apartment, leaning back against her nondescript sofa as she hunched over the papers spread out on her nondescript coffee table.

I thought you'd take after your mother.

All her life, she'd been desperate for any kind of honest, candid words from her father, and when he finally gave them to her, they sliced her to the bone.

He thought she was a quitter. He thought she was weak. Despite years and years and years of demonstrating otherwise, he thought she was incapable of committing herself to a goal and seeing it through.

Elaina reread the same paragraph in the same police report she'd read three times before. *No sign of forced entry. No sign of struggle. Officer noticed victim's wallet sitting open on the kitchen counter . . .*

She got up from the carpet and shook out her stiff legs. There was no concentrating today. Ever since Troy had dropped her off at the office this morning with a guarded look in his eyes and a halfhearted kiss, Elaina had been unable to keep her focus.

She had the interview.

She hadn't landed it the way she'd expected—she hadn't landed it at all, in fact; someone had landed it for her. But still, she had it. It was hers. And she'd be stupid to turn her back on the opportunity she'd always dreamed of, just to make a point with her dad.

BAU. The profiling unit. Some of the sharpest minds in the country, and *she* had a chance to work with them on the very toughest cases of her time.

Elaina's gaze drifted to the Xerox-copied photograph of Valerie Monroe's remains. Elaina didn't need the photograph, because she'd seen the remains herself, and the image was engraved on her brain.

Elaina walked into her kitchen and glanced at the clock. Nearly eleven. Her pizza was late. She filled a glass with water, and the reflection in the window above the kitchen sink captured her attention.

Her hair was messy, her cheeks sunburned. Her snug-fitting sports bra revealed her muscular arms and—good God, was it *really*? Yes, it really was—a hickey Troy had given her last night when they'd gone skinny-dipping together. She remembered him nibbling on her shoulder and then her neck and then her mouth as both he and the waves had rocked her into oblivion.

Who had she become over these last couple weeks? She looked nothing like the crisply dressed, determined agent who'd arrived at the Brownsville office so many months ago. Her father was right—she'd changed.

The phone rang. She retrieved the BlackBerry from her purse and checked the number. Weaver.

"Did you see the list?" he asked, and she heard the excitement in his voice.

"No, where is it?"

"Ric's brother faxed it to the office. He got every applicant who's applied to the Bureau through the San Antonio field office over the last five years."

"I asked for ten years. Is there any way——"

"*Two* applicants were highlighted," Weaver cut in. "First one's Joel Etheridge, originally from Bay Port. He was thirty-one when he last applied, which was five years ago. He was living in San Marcos back then."

Joel Etheridge. She'd heard that name before, but she couldn't pinpoint where.

"You ready for the other one?"

Her stomach tensed. "Who?"

"Greg Maynard."

"As in *Officer* Maynard? Of the LIPD?"

"You got it. This guy's got a bug to join the Bureau, apparently. He's applied twice, been rejected both times."

Elaina's doorbell rang, and she went to answer it as a motive started to take shape in her mind. Some types of psychopaths would lash out when confronted with rejection.

"When did he first apply?" she asked.

"May, two years ago. Then again last fall."

"And Joel Etheridge?"

"January, five years ago."

"That's right before the hikers went missing."

"Yeah, I noticed that."

"Hold on a sec." She peered through the peephole at the pizza delivery man. Actually, "boy" was more accurate. He looked as though he might have ridden over on his bike.

She swung the door open and accepted the warm,

aromatic box from him. It nearly burned her hands. "Thanks," she said, setting it on the coffee table.

"I need to see your credit card," the boy said, "to verify the number."

Elaina went to get the card from her wallet and turned her attention back to Weaver. "Why do I recognize the name Joel Etheridge?" she asked.

"LIPD interviewed him way back in March. He's the bartender at Coconuts. He gave a statement about seeing Gina Calvert with her friends at the bar on the night she disappeared."

"He doesn't have a criminal record," she said.

"Neither does Maynard."

"Any particular reason Etheridge's application was rejected?" She showed the pizza guy her credit card, then wrote in a tip and signed the receipt.

"Hmm, probably because, according to this, he had no college degree, no military service, and no particular language skills. Take your pick of reasons."

Elaina locked her door behind the delivery kid. "He shouldn't even have bothered applying."

"No joke. Anyway, I called LIPD. Maynard's on duty tonight. We need to track him down, pronto. He was supposed to be staking out Coconuts with some of the other locals from the task force, which sounds just a little too convenient for me."

She checked her watch. "How soon can you meet me over there?"

Pause. "I thought Scarborough pulled you off."

"How soon?" She shoved her credit card back inside her wallet.

Her stomach dropped out.

"Elaina, are you sure that's a good idea?"

She stared at the card.

"Elaina? You there?"

"I'm here," she said. "And I know what he's doing."

Troy spotted Elaina's clunker the instant she turned into Coconuts's parking lot, which was emptying rapidly. She pulled into a space near the entrance, and he strode over to meet her.

"Your theory's right on," he said as she climbed out of the car.

"What are you doing here?" She glanced around the parking lot as she slammed the door. "And where is everyone? I thought they closed at two."

"Sundays, they close at midnight. And you were right about the credit-card swap. He keeps a stash behind the cash register. A rainbow of colors, from practically every bank you can imagine. Each one of them's under the name Jenny Etheridge."

"Who's that?" she asked.

"Could be his mom. His sister. His cat. How the hell do I know? Point is, Weaver told me your theory, and I think you're right: He snags the victim's card, then gives her back one that looks identical except for the name and number. Most of these women are half-tipsy, probably don't even notice, just slip the card into their wallets and go on their way."

"I saw it happen to Mia last night," Elaina said, clearly alarmed. "She's not here, is she?"

"She went back to San Marcos."

"And where's Joel Etheridge?" She moved for the entrance, but Troy grabbed her arm.

"He's gone already. The waitress I talked to said he lit out of here not long after closing."

"You don't think—"

"That's exactly what I think."

"Troy?"

He turned around to see Kim, the waitress, hurrying toward him from the main entrance of the building. She glanced nervously over her shoulder and then handed him a stack of receipts.

"Thanks, I owe you big." Troy immediately started sifting through them.

"I could lose my job for this. What's all this about, anyway?"

"Do you remember any female customers talking with Joel tonight?" Elaina asked.

"No one in particular. Why?"

Troy weeded out the female names and handed the rest back to Kim. "Sixteen women paid by credit card tonight. You sure that's it?"

"It was slow. And anyway, it's usually the men who pay." She cast a nervous look at Elaina. "What's going on?"

He handed Elaina the women's credit-card slips and turned back to the waitress. "You sure you don't remember *anyone* talking with Joel tonight? Someone he might have been interested in?"

"Joel's married." She looked confused. "And it was just a regular night, until you showed up."

"Oh my God, Jamie's in here." Elaina looked up at him, eyes wide.

"I know." He turned back to Kim. "Did he seem interested in Jamie Ingram at all? Or anyone else at the bar?"

"He was talking to that volleyball player a little. The one whose friend got killed?" The waitress looked at Elaina. "She was at the bar with her boyfriend and some other people, but she seemed down. Not really into it. I think Joel was trying to cheer her up."

Elaina's gaze locked with Troy's. "We need to find her. Now."

Jamie sat in her beanbag chair and gazed up at the ceiling. She'd finally done it. After five months. She'd known she needed to do it for almost that long, but she'd never managed to find the courage. Until tonight.

What the fuck's your problem tonight, James? You're being a real bitch.

She'd put up with month after month of half-truths and laziness and outright mooching, but it was that one oblivious comment that had sent her over the edge. She was done. He was history. And instead of feeling sad or lonely or even angry, she felt absolutely nothing at all.

What was wrong with her? She hadn't cried a single tear since she'd found out about Angela. She'd picked up the phone that day. She'd heard the words. But it was like none of them had any meaning. The words were just separate little letter combinations, rattling around in her brain, with nowhere to go.

A knock sounded at her door, and she turned to look at it.

Noah? Not likely. Fighting for something he wanted wasn't his style. And, really, he'd only sort of wanted her.

She'd known that all along, she just hadn't let herself admit it. She closed her eyes and felt ashamed. Where was her self-respect?

Another knock, harder this time. Jamie got up and went to the door.

"Who is it?" she asked as she looked through the peephole.

"Hey, Jamie, it's Joel. You left your credit card at the bar."

He held her card up between two fingers and gazed straight at the peephole. His eyebrow lifted in that sexy way he had when he flirted with women around the bar. Jamie's pulse sped up. Tonight he'd been flirting with her. And for the first time in days, she actually felt something that wasn't nothing.

She undid the latch and swung open the door.

"We need a police unit at all sixteen of their locations, ASAP," Elaina told Weaver over the phone.

"That's going to be a tall order. LIPD consists of six officers, one of whom we don't trust. And I just spoke with Loomis. The four agents we have on island tonight are only in two vehicles."

Elaina squeezed her eyes shut and took a deep breath. Troy's Ferrari rocketed down the highway, en route to Bay Port, where Troy thought Jamie lived, even though she had a job on the island. In the driver's seat beside her, Troy juggled his phone and the gearshift as he talked to Cinco, who was running down Jamie's home address.

"Call Ric," she said, on a burst of inspiration. "He's up to speed. And what about the Lito County sheriff? Maybe he can send—"

"Ric is in San Marcos," Weaver said. "His chief called him back to organize a search for those hikers' remains near the cache sites."

"I hadn't heard."

"The other problem is where to send people," Weaver continued. "We have names, but some of these women are likely to be out-of-towners here on vacation."

"We need to check hotels," Elaina said. "We'll start with the ones closest to Coconuts. We can get someone over there to look at guest registers."

"We don't have the manpower," Weaver said practically. "We need to prioritize this list."

"Jamie Ingram is at the top. We're getting her address right now. After that, any woman traveling alone."

"I got it," Troy told her. "It's 561 Lowland Road, Apartment C. That should be just over the causeway, second exit heading north."

Elaina repeated the directions for Weaver.

"I just saw a sign for that exit," he said.

"Then you're ahead of us. Call me after you get there."

They hung up, and Elaina glanced out the window as restaurants and motels and surf shops raced by. Troy gunned it through a yellow light, but then had to slam on the brakes as a group of teenagers darted in front of the car. Elaina jerked forward, and Troy's arm shot out to catch her as she bumped her chin on the dash.

"Sorry."

"Just go," she said after the kids had passed. Troy floored it, and she counted the stoplights until the road leading off the island. Three more to go.

"You get any notes today?" he demanded. "Voice mails? Text messages?"

She glanced down at her phone, which she'd already checked twice. "Nothing."

"Call Ben. If this guy's planning something tonight, he might have hinted about it on the Web site. Or in one of the chat rooms."

Elaina scrolled through her call history until she found Ben's number. She pressed Redial, and closed her eyes to pray.

CHAPTER 26

T roy blew past the speed trap on the other side of the causeway, wishing for once to get pulled over so he could pick up a sheriff's deputy. No such luck. It was 1:13. Plenty of time for Joel Etheridge to knock off work and get his ass over to the home of his newest target. Troy only hoped Weaver or Cinco had somehow managed to beat him there.

Elaina's phone rang, and she answered it instantly. A white-knuckled pause, and then she glanced at him, and he knew it was bad by the look in her eyes.

"She's gone," she told him.

"You mean not home or . . . ?"

"Her purse is there. So is her Jeep. But her front door's unlocked, and she's nowhere."

"We need a vehicle description. What's this guy driving? He's on his way to a boat dock somewhere, and we need to find him before he gets there."

But Elaina wasn't paying attention. She was consumed with her phone. "No credit card at all? We have her receipt from the bar." She glanced over at him. "Our theory's panning out. All the victims had credit-card charges at Coconuts, but credit cards weren't found with their personal belongings. I think he takes the dummy card, along with the real one, just to cover his tracks. And Jamie's Jeep is there, which means he probably leaves their cars at a public boat dock after the fact, to mislead police."

Troy clenched the wheel. If he was planting the victims' cars, that made it all the more likely he was using his own car to transport the women and using a private dock.

"What's Joel Etheridge's address?" he demanded. "We need to get over there."

Elaina nodded at him. "You heard that?" Pause. "Okay. *Damn it.*" She glanced at Troy and shook her head. "All right, call me back."

"What is it?"

"Turns out Etheridge lives not far from the police station, and Cinco just went by. No one's home," she said gravely. "He's got a boat slip right on the bay, but the boat is gone."

Jamie heard bees. She gazed up at the inky blackness and heard them buzzing all around her.

Where am I?

She squinted up at the darkness and tried to make sense of it. The bees. The buzzing. The bumping and bouncing against something hard and cool beneath her back. *Where am I?*

She sensed someone beside her. The shadow moved, hunched over her, and she tried to focus on the face.

"You're awake." It was a low, male voice, and the buzzing nearly drowned it out.

He turned away, then back again. Something closed around her upper arm. One of the bees stung her. And then everything faded out.

Elaina gripped the door as Troy whipped into the marina parking lot and screeched to a halt. Her phone tumbled to the floor, and she snatched it up, checking desperately for a message she might somehow have missed.

"Anything from Ben?"

"Not yet," she said. The tracer was on his computer right now, trying to decipher the latest posting by Grim-Reefer. Late this afternoon, he'd announced a new cache within the zip code that encompassed Lito Island. The GPS coordinates were encrypted, of course—all part of his game.

"We should take two boats," Elaina said as Troy reached across her and popped open the glove compartment. "That doubles our chance of intercepting him."

Troy glanced at her, and for a second she thought he was going to refuse to let her drive one of his toys.

"Good idea," he said instead. "You take the fishing boat." He handed her a key with a little foam bobber on it, and Elaina eyed it suspiciously.

"You want me in the slow boat," she said as he collected a second boat key, along with his pistol. "The Supra's faster. You said so. You're trying to beat me to him."

They got out of the car, and Troy looked at her over the top of the Ferrari. "Elaina, gimme a break. The Supra's harder to drive. And dangerous if you don't know the bay."

"I know exactly what you're doing. Let me remind you that I'm trained to apprehend criminals."

"Not this kind, you're not," he said, and as soon as the words were out, she could tell he wanted to take them back. He turned away from her and cursed vividly.

"Don't try to sideline me on this, Troy. I'll never forgive you."

He spun back around to face her. "He eviscerates women, Elaina! He makes a sport of it! I don't care how much goddamn training you've had. Your father's right—you don't belong anywhere near this asshole."

"And what are you planning to do? Walk up to him and make a citizen's arrest?"

He shoved his pistol into the back waistband of his jeans, and she knew exactly what he was planning. He intended to end this whole thing tonight, if he got the chance.

"I'm taking that speedboat," she said firmly. "I'm going after Jamie, I'm going after this subject. And if you get in my way, I'll arrest you myself."

The seconds ticked by as she held his gaze.

"Fine," he snapped. "We'll take the speedboat, but I'm driving."

N 26° 14.895 W 097° 12.055

Troy scanned the horizon, looking for any indication of another boat. He saw no sign of life, not even the wild kind, as he neared the northernmost boundary of the 9,600-acre preserve.

He glanced at Elaina, who stood beside him, gripping

the windshield in one hand and her phone in the other. She wore some kind of military pants and hiking boots, and her Glock was holstered securely at her side.

"Anything from Ben?" he asked.

"Nothing," she said. "He promised to call as soon as he cracked the code. Got a text from Weaver, though. Loomis has requested a hostage rescue team from San Antonio."

"Good move," Troy said. A team like that would probably come with a chopper and searchlights, which would enable them to comb the entire coastline in a matter of minutes. But how soon could they get here?

Troy stared out over the horizon. Even with a nearly-full moon, it was difficult to see much. Shiny ribbons of water wove their way into the marshlands. Troy searched for the widest channel, which led into the heart of the wildlife park.

"Pretty high tide," he commented.

"Is that good?"

"Just means it's easier to get in and out of here by boat."

The channel came into view, a silvery roadway, cutting through the reeds.

"Decision time," he said. "We either go in or not. If he's in there already, this is our best shot of catching up to him. If he's not here yet, we're stuck in a maze and he could zoom right past us on his way to Windy Point or someplace."

Elaina glanced around, as if the shadowy void would offer some kind of clue.

"Do you hear that?"

"What?" But as he said it, he heard what she was talking about—the faint, high-pitched buzz of a boat engine. Troy shut off the motor. "It's coming from the north. Let's see where it's going and then we'll follow."

He pulled Elaina into a crouch and hoped the silhouette of his boat didn't stand out against the sky. But the moon was dodging in and out of clouds, making visibility spotty. Someone would have to be really lucky—or really observant—to notice them here.

The noise grew louder. "Not a lot of horsepower," Troy said. "Sounds to me like a skiff."

"That means we're faster, right?"

"Yeah, but he's smaller, lighter. He can go places we can't." As soon as he said this, a tiny white light blinked into view. Troy made out the shape of a boat with a light at the bow and a person-shaped lump at the stern. It was too dark to see the person clearly. What Troy *did* see were a couple of fishing poles glinting in the moonlight.

Was this their guy? Or just some night fisherman looking for a place to cast a line?

The boat slowed and veered left, and Troy muttered a curse.

"What?" Elaina asked.

"He's turning into the marsh."

Elaina's pulse raced as Troy glided slowly through the ever-narrowing channel, using only the moon as a guide. He'd even turned off the navigation system to ensure the greenish glow wouldn't attract attention.

"You think he can hear us?" she asked.

"Not as long as he's moving."

The skiff slipped in and out of view as it meandered through the cattails deeper and deeper into the marsh.

They'd made a mistake by taking *Salt Shaker*. But she'd thought this was going to be a race, not a game of hide-and-seek.

Did he know they were here? Was this some sort of ambush, or was he simply going about his sick work, business as usual, completely unaware that he was being pursued?

"Close in on him," Elaina said. "If it turns out to be nobody, we need to get back on the bay."

"I'm trying," Troy said, and she took a closer look at her surroundings and realized he was doing his best to close the distance without running aground and losing valuable time getting out to push.

They moved across the glimmering water, the speed-boat's motor a low-pitched rumble. Above it, Elaina heard the distinctive hum of the skiff.

Elaina's phone vibrated in her hand. Ben's number. She knelt low in the boat and answered it.

"Talk fast," she said.

"Got the coordinates. I'll text them over."

"Did you look them up?"

"Lito Island wildlife refuge," he said. "In the heart of the swamp."

Elaina's pulse skittered. That was exactly where they were right now.

"Okay, call Weaver and Cinco. Give them the coordinates, and tell them I need backup at that location right now."

She disconnected just as the noise up ahead of them changed pitch. Troy responded immediately, cutting his motor off mere seconds before the other boat went quiet.

Some clouds moved in front of the moon, and everything went black.

Elaina glanced around frantically. The only light she could see was the arc of the causeway bridge and the flickering smokestack of the refinery across the bay.

Something touched her arm, and she jumped.

"You hear that?" Troy whispered.

She listened intently. She heard nothing but a chorus of insects and water lapping softly against the boat. She could see nothing, not even Troy, who was standing only inches away.

And then she heard it—a quiet splash. Followed by another. It was him. And he was getting out of the boat. A slight rustling in the reeds up ahead, then nothing.

Elaina imagined him dragging Jamie out of that boat. He imagined him laying her out on some thorny patch of weeds.

"We need to follow him." She clutched Troy's arm. "Let's get out. Quietly."

Without a word, Troy swung himself over the side of the boat and lowered himself into the water. She felt his grip on her arm, and he helped her position herself on the side. His hands closed around her waist, and he lifted her down. Water immediately filled her boots.

The moon peeked out from the clouds, offering a stingy bit of light. She glanced around but saw no boats, no people. Just endless marsh.

"Where'd he *go*?" she whispered.

"No idea."

"We need to split up." She looked around again and used the causeway to get her bearings. "You go north,

I'll go south. He doesn't know we're here, so one of us should be able to sneak up on him."

"I want you with me."

"We'll cover more ground this way," she said. "We have to find him *now,* Troy. He could be starting—"

"Okay, okay, you're right. But don't break cover, you hear me? And if you see him, shoot to kill."

CHAPTER 27

Elaina waded through the swamp, on alert for even the slightest noise. The terrain had changed from mud to water and back to mud again, which was unnerving. The air smelled of sulfur and rotting leaves. And it was black. Pitch. She no longer had Troy's touch to anchor her, and she would have traded anything for a pair of night-vision goggles.

She remembered the blackout room at the Academy, where her defensive tactics instructor would make them spar in the dark. *Use your senses,* he'd told them. *See with your mind, not your eyes.*

Elaina tried to use her senses now, but all she felt was fear. Water squished inside her boots. She tried to move soundlessly. In her right hand was her Glock. Her left hand was empty, and she held it out in front of her, although the chances of bumping into anything tall out here were pretty nonexistent. She moved one foot in front of the other and kept her senses on alert.

Her shin slammed into something hard. Pain zinged through her, and her body hurtled forward as her feet stayed planted. Her left hand landed on something soft.

A body?

Fear spurted through her. She groped frantically and realized she'd crashed into a boat. It was smooth and metal, and on the floor of it was a silent, motionless body.

Please, please, please. She felt an arm, a shoulder, a neck. Her right hand gripped her gun as the other searched desperately for a pulse.

The body shifted. A slight groan.

Elaina breathed a sigh of relief. And in the distance, an unmistakable *plop.*

She froze. Her heart pounded. Her skin tingled right down to her toes. The sound was northeast of her, about sixty feet out. The length of a volleyball court. She processed the information objectively, but the fear was an icy claw that closed around her heart and made even the soles of her feet itch.

She listened. Another *plop.* The sound was closer, clearer. But something struck her about it. It wasn't footsteps. More like a rock, being tossed from a distance.

The skin between her shoulder blades prickled, and in her mind's eye she saw him.

Just as a powerful arm snaked around her neck.

Troy moved through the darkness, alert for any sound, the slightest hint of movement.

A yelp, somewhere behind him. He whirled around. Splashing. Thrashing. The sounds of a struggle.

He cocked his gun and sprinted toward it.

She was underwater. Giant fingers closed around her throat. She kicked. She flailed. She clawed and punched at the arms holding her down. She'd dropped her weapon. He was on top of her, drowning her. A wave of panic brought a rush of water straight up her nose.

Pop!

The noise echoed through the water, and suddenly the weight was gone, and she was up, breaking the surface, gasping for air.

A motor roared nearby. A spray of water doused her and she sucked in gasoline fumes. She coughed and sputtered, and then an arm was back, around her shoulders this time, and she clawed at it like a demon.

"Elaina, *breathe*!"

Troy. She choked and gasped and tried to cling to him, all at the same time. He lifted her by the armpits and dragged her to higher ground, then dropped her onto a mound of sand. Just a few inches of water. She'd nearly *drowned* in just a few inches of water.

"Where—" she wheezed, unable to even finish the thought.

"I shot him, and he took off."

He got away.

And then another thought hit. *My Glock.*

And then a worse thought smacked into her. *Jamie.*

Elaina scrambled to her feet. "She's in that skiff. We have to go after them!"

"Are you sure you're—"

"Yes! Where's your boat?"

He grabbed her hand. "This way."

They sprinted and splashed and stumbled through the cordgrass until they reached the channel where he'd left the speedboat.

Only he couldn't find it.

"Shit!"

And then in the first bit of luck they'd had all night, the clouds drifted, and everything brightened, and he whirled around, hungry for information.

"There!" he said, dragging Elaina behind him. Was she all right? He didn't know. But she was on her feet, and that was good enough for him, at least right now. When she reached the boat, she practically threw herself aboard.

The boat had drifted into a sandbank. Troy waded around to the bow and shoved it into deeper water. Then he rushed to the stern, gave a hearty push, and hopped inside. He twisted the key, fired the engine to life, and glanced at Elaina.

"Hold on," he ordered, and hit the throttle.

In the distance, he heard the faint hum of the fleeing skiff. No running lights this time. Troy flipped his on, illuminating the channel in front of them. He followed the curves and bends of the waterway, hoping he wasn't steering them into a dead end.

The boat in the distance changed pitch. He'd reached the bay and turned on the speed. Troy glanced around, calculated the risks, and decided they had enough depth to really drop the hammer.

"Hold tight," he told Elaina, and he hit it.

The wind whipped against her as they skipped across the water. She stood beside Troy, clutching the windshield. She saw the familiar lights of the refinery, but the boat was nowhere to be seen.

Troy seemed to have a course in mind. He stared

straight ahead, with laser-sharp focus, as the Supra hopped from wave to wave.

"We're gaining."

"How can you tell?" And just as she said it, she spotted the pale gray form ahead of them, about two o'clock. Etheridge had a head start, but Troy was closing the gap. Etheridge glanced back, again and again, then suddenly hunched over and reached for something. The skiff slowed.

"What's he doing?"

"Trying to lose us. *Shit*."

Elaina watched, confused. A jolt of terror shot through her as she realized what he was doing in a last-ditch effort to shake the tail.

"He's throwing her overboard!"

Troy handed his pistol to Elaina.

"Take this," he yelled over the roar of the engine. "And get ready to take the wheel."

"What are you doing?" she yelled, but he didn't answer, and she stuffed his pistol into her holster.

Troy bore down on the skiff, until they were almost on top of it. Etheridge glanced back, and Elaina could see the desperation on his face as he steered his boat and tried to wrestle Jamie's naked, lifeless body overboard, all at the same time.

Troy grabbed Elaina's arm. *"Now!"* he commanded, and yanked her up to the helm. Then he climbed onto the side of the Supra and took a flying leap.

The skiff almost capsized. It slowed abruptly and Elaina sailed ahead. She made a frantic U-turn, and when she circled back, Troy and Etheridge were on the floor of the boat, locked in a struggle. She pulled the pistol, but both boats were bobbing violently. She had no confidence in her aim. Etheridge jerked Troy up by the shirtfront, and Elaina watched, appalled, as he landed a powerful punch to his jaw. Troy responded with a head butt, and a split second later, had Etheridge flipped onto his back. Troy pummeled his fist into the man's face, again and again and again, as Elaina tried to get close enough for a decent shot, but with the rising, sinking swells, it was utterly impossible. Suddenly the boat rolled sideways. Both men crashed into the side and Jamie nearly rolled overboard. Etheridge scrambled to his knees and leapt on top of Troy.

A flash of metal. The knife! The blade plunged down, and she heard an agonized cry. Good God, he was going to stab Troy to death, right in front of her eyes.

Elaina braced her hand against the side of the boat. She lifted the gun. The blade rose up again, and somewhere deep inside herself, she found an island of calm. She aimed the pistol.

She took the shot.

CHAPTER 28

"Lemme guess. Just a scratch, right?"

Troy opened his eyes to see Weaver standing beside him in the waiting room of the Brownsville FBI office. He nodded at Troy's sloppily bandaged shoulder.

"You didn't even feel a thing?"

"Hurts like a motherfucker." Troy leaned forward on his elbows and scrubbed a hand over his face. "What time is it, anyway?"

"Five-fifteen."

Troy scowled at the Plexiglas window, behind which Elaina had disappeared hours ago for a "debriefing." But of course there was nothing brief about it, and Troy's patience was long since gone.

"Just called the hospital," Weaver said. "Jamie's awake and lucid. She's going to be fine. Joel Etheridge is still in surgery. He may not make it."

"Cry me a river."

"If he pulls through, we'll have an agent waiting in his recovery room, ready to read him his rights." Weaver crossed his arms over his chest. "You know he's married to Brenda, the desk clerk at the inn?"

"I heard."

"And did you hear about his house?"

Troy shook his head. Maynard hadn't gotten that far when he'd called.

"Major law enforcement junkie," Weaver said. "He has an arsenal of weapons, a virtual spy museum full of gadgets, all sorts of police uniforms and gear. He had everything packed in duffel bags and—get this—stashed in a concrete hurricane shelter that he'd built inside his garage, complete with MREs and self-contained plumbing. Looks like he missed out on Y2K, so now he's ready for World War Three."

"Sounds like a nutcase."

"That's not a term we like. Just helps him build an insanity defense. Anyway, we'll know more after we interview him, but I'd guess he's paranoid in a serious way and has delusions of grandeur." Weaver's face grew more serious. "He also has an interesting library. Several biographies of Robert Hanssen. Every book ever written by John McCord."

Troy went still. He knew what was coming next.

"He has a picture of Elaina, too—something he clipped from the newspaper after Breck's first press conference. She's standing off to the side with you and Cinco. He blew up the shot and drew a red circle around Elaina's head."

Troy stared up at Weaver. He didn't bother trying to put into words the mix of anger and fear and *relief* he was feeling right now.

Troy turned away and checked the clock. He looked up and down the hallway, but still no sign of her. When he met Weaver's gaze again, the man was smiling at him.

"What?"

"You *could* swing by the emergency room, you know. Even our toughest border cowboys get patched up every now and then."

Troy sighed. "Fuck you."

"I'm good, thanks. But it's nice to know you're in as pleasant a mood as Elaina was last time I saw her." Weaver patted his arm. "And FYI, she's almost done."

The agent disappeared behind a thick gray door, and Troy stood up to stretch his legs. At the opposite end of the hall, another gray door opened and Elaina walked out.

He watched her move toward him. She looked worried and weather-beaten and beyond exhausted, and fury simmered inside him as he visualized Joel Etheridge trying to choke the life out of her.

She stopped in front of him and gazed up with those serious blue eyes. "You waited."

He slung his good arm around her and pulled her close. "Let's go home."

Ric trudged up the stairs to Mia's apartment and didn't have a clue what the hell he was doing here. He looked like shit. He hadn't slept in days. He'd been on his way home to do just that, when he found himself turning onto her street and pulling up to her building.

Now he stopped in front of her door and stared at it. He lifted his hand to knock, and it opened all by itself.

She stepped back, startled.

"Hi," he said.

She gazed up at him, wide-eyed, car keys and coffee cup in hand. She had on jeans and one of those fitted T-shirts she wore beneath her lab coat.

"It's six thirty-five," she said. "What are you doing here?"

"I have no idea."

Her eyebrows tipped up, and he felt the need to back-pedal.

"Actually, I do." He rested his hands on his hips and realized his own jeans and T-shirt had passed the dirty-laundry stage about thirty-six hours ago. "I've been out to Devil's Gorge. We took a canine unit."

Understanding dawned in her eyes.

Ric looked away, out over the dew-covered crepe myrtles surrounding her parking lot. It was going to be another scorcher today. Yesterday had been so brutal, the search dog had nearly collapsed from heat exhaustion.

"Anyway, I'm on my way home to clean up before I go see the families."

"You found both of them?"

He nodded. "Each one was buried under a pile of rocks."

"I can help you get positive IDs," she said. "Quickly."

"That's one reason I'm here."

She tilted her head to the side. "And the other?"

The other. He gazed down at her. And he remembered the first time he'd seen her up at that podium, lecturing a roomful of jaded homicide cops with that passion in her voice. And he knew the other reason—she reminded him why he did this job.

He nodded at her mug. "Skim milk, one Splenda?"

She smiled slightly. "Would you like a cup of coffee, Detective?"

"I would."

She stepped back and ushered him inside. "Why didn't you just say so?"

Westin Hotel
Alexandria, Virginia
Two days later

Elaina dropped her briefcase onto the floor and claimed a stool at the bar. She glanced around and decided she liked the place—for a number of reasons, starting with the fact that the bartender was a woman. She wore a black tuxedo jacket that didn't fit her well at all, and Elaina had a flash of insight about women wearing clothes designed for men.

Elaina peeled off her navy suit jacket and hung it on the back of the chair as the bartender made her way over.

"What can I get you?"

Elaina scanned the row of bottles lining the back wall. Her attention got hung up on the one shaped like an agave plant.

"A Sprite, please," she said.

"I'll have a Dos Equis."

Elaina turned around at the voice. Her heart swelled inside her chest and she had to force herself not to jump off the stool and throw her arms around him.

"What are you doing here?" she asked.

Troy claimed the seat beside her and dropped something onto the floor. A black backpack. With a boarding pass sticking out of the side pocket.

"Heard a rumor you might be staying here."

"You were eavesdropping on me and my dad."

"Guilty." His green eyes skimmed over her, taking in her disheveled hair and wrinkled blouse. "Long day?"

"Very." She wanted to kiss him. She wanted him to kiss *her*. But instead, she just stared at him, soaking in the familiar sight of his jeans and cowboy boots, soaking in his sun-brown skin and muscular forearms. He looked completely out of place at this stuffy hotel filled with business executives and government bureaucrats.

Their drinks came, and he took a long swig. Elaina tipped her glass back and noticed the way his attention lingered on the bruises still circling her neck. Something sparked in his eyes.

He rested his beer on the bar. "How'd the interview go?"

"Good," she said. Then she sighed. "Long. It lasted five hours. I think I met every member of the BAU."

He lifted an eyebrow. "Sounds fun."

"It's a fascinating group. I really hit it off with the agent in charge."

Troy held her gaze for a long moment. "Did they offer you the job?"

"Yes."

"Don't take it."

Her heart gave a kick as she watched him watching her with so much intensity. He was the only man who'd ever looked at her that way, and it made her warm everywhere.

She cleared her throat. "Why not?"

"Come back to Brownsville. With me. We need you way more than Quantico does."

She stared at him. " 'We' as in . . . my boss? Loomis? Chief Breck?"

"Yes." He nodded resolutely. "Every one of them needs you, more than they realize. You scare the hell out of them." He paused. "But mostly it's me."

"*You* need me." She gazed up at him, unable to believe he was sitting here telling her this. "Why?"

He covered her hand with his, and she glanced down and saw that his knuckles were still bruised from the other night.

"You haven't figured it out yet, Elaina?" He smiled slightly. "You're a profiler."

"Figured out what?"

"I love you." He picked up her hand and kissed it.

I love you. He'd really said it. And now he was sitting there, watching her, searching her face for some kind of response.

He reached over and tucked a lock of hair behind her ear. His finger trailed down her neck, over her bruises, and then he took her hand again.

"I think I've loved you since the first night, when you threatened to slap me with a lawsuit." He shook his head. "And then that next day, you told me you were off limits, and I was pretty much done for."

Elaina felt a grin spreading across her face. "I didn't take the job," she said.

"Really?" he looked wary now.

"I need more field experience. And anyway, I've got some unfinished business down in Texas."

She slid off the stool and reached up to comb her fingers into his hair, and she pulled his head down and kissed him, right there in the hotel bar.

"Come upstairs," he said against her mouth.

"You're rushing me." She eased back and looked up at him. "I haven't even had a chance to tell you that I love you, too."

"I already knew that." He kissed her. "Just making sure you did."

Turn the page for a sneak peak

at the next heart-pounding Tracers novel

from Laura Griffin

UNFORGIVABLE

Coming soon from Pocket Books

Mia Voss needed a fix. Badly.

On a normal day, she would have stood strong against the temptation. But nothing about today had been normal, starting with the fact that it was January seventh and ending with the fact that for the first time in her life, she'd actually been demoted.

Her stomach clenched as she turned into the Minute Mart parking lot and eased her white Jeep Wrangler into a space near the door. Her cheeks warmed at the still-fresh memory of standing stiffly in her boss's office, gazing down at his weasel-like face as he'd sat behind his desk, meting out criticism. At the time, she'd been stunned speechless, too shocked by what was happening to defend herself. Only now—six hours too late—did all the perfect rejoinders come tumbling into her head.

Mia jerked open the door to the convenience store and made a beeline for the freezer section. If there was ever a night that called for Ben & Jerry's New York Super Fudge Chunk, it was tonight. For the first Thursday night in months, she wasn't stuck at the lab. For the first Thursday night in years, the only items demanding her attention were a sappy chick flick, a cozy blanket, and a pint of butterfat. Tonight was wallow night. Mia slid open the freezer door and plucked out a tub of Super Fudge Chunk. She tucked it under her arm, then grabbed a Chunky Monkey. As long as she was sinning, why not sin big? It was a motto that had gotten her into trouble on more than one occasion, but she continued to follow it.

"Doc Voss."

She jumped and whirled around.

A bulky, balding man in a brown overcoat stood behind her. He crouched down to pick up the carton that had rolled across the aisle, then stood and held it out to her. "Good stuff, isn't it?"

"Uh, thanks." She stared at him and tried to place his name. He was a cop, she knew that much. But he wasn't someone she'd seen around in a while, and she couldn't pull a name from her memory bank.

"Not as good as mint chip, though." His droll smile made him look grandfatherly. "My wife's favorite."

She noticed his shopping basket—two pints of mint chocolate chip and a six-pack of beer.

His gaze drifted down to her fur-lined moccasins, and a bushy gray eyebrow lifted. "Slumber party?"

Mia glanced down. For her quick trip to the store, she'd tucked her satin nightshirt into her jeans, pulled on a ratty cardigan, and slipped her feet into house shoes. She looked like an escapee from a mental ward, which of course meant she'd bump into someone she knew from work. Nothing like reinforcing that professional image. Yes, today was shaping up to be a banner career day.

Mia forced a smile. "More like movie night." She glanced at her watch and stepped toward the register. "It's about to start, actually. I'd better—"

"Don't let me keep you." He nodded. "See ya around, Doc."

Mia watched his reflection in the convex mirror as she paid for her groceries. He added a couple of frozen dinners to his basket and then headed for the chip aisle.

The name hit her as she pulled out of the parking lot.

Frank Hannigan. San Marcos PD. Why couldn't she have remembered it sooner?

Something hard jammed into her neck.

"Take a left at this light."

Mia's head whipped around. Her chest convulsed. In the backseat was a man. He held a gun pointed right at her nose.

"Watch the *road*!"

She jerked her head around just in time to see the telephone pole looming in front of her. She yanked the wheel left and managed to stay on the street.

Oh my God, oh my God, oh my God. Her hands clutched the steering wheel in a death grip. Her gaze flashed to the mirror and homed in on his gun. It was big and serious-looking, and he held it rock-steady in his gloved hand.

"Turn left."

The command snapped her attention away from the weapon and back to him. Her brain numbly registered a description: black hooded sweatshirt, pulled tight around his face. Navy bandanna covering his nose and mouth. Dark sunglasses. All she could see of the man behind the disguise was a thin strip of skin between the glasses and the bandanna.

He jammed the muzzle of the pistol into her neck again. "Eyes ahead."

She forced herself to comply. Her heart pounded wildly against her sternum. Her stomach tightened. She realized she'd stopped breathing. She focused on drawing air into her lungs and unclenched her hand from the wheel so that she could shift gears and turn left.

Where are we going? What does he want?

Her mind flooded with terrifying possibilities as she hung a left and darted her gaze around, looking for a police car, a fire truck, anything. But this was a college town, and whatever action might be going on tonight was probably happening much closer to campus.

How was she going to get out of this? Cold sweat beaded along her hairline. Her stomach somersaulted. Bile rose up in the back of her throat.

The engine reached a high-pitched whine. She'd forgotten to change gears. Her clammy hand slipped on the gear shift as she switched into third.

Think. She glanced around desperately, but the streets were quiet. The nearest open business was the Dairy Queen two blocks behind them.

"CenTex Bank, on your right. Pull up to the drive-through ATM."

Mia's breath whooshed out. He wanted money. Tears of relief filled her eyes. But they quickly morphed into tears of panic because she realized his wanting money didn't really mean anything. He could still shoot her in the head and leave her on the side of the road. She of all people knew the amazingly cheap price of a human life. A wad of cash. A bag of crack. A pair of sneakers.

She could be dead before the ATM even spit out the bills.

The cold, hard muzzle of the gun rubbed against her cheek. Her breath hitched, and her gaze went to the mirror. She remembered the police sketch of a man in a hooded sweatshirt and sunglasses who for years had been on the FBI's Ten Most Wanted list. The Unabomber. Mia had met the artist who had drawn that sketch. As a forensic scientist at one of the world's top crime labs, Mia had connections in every conceivable area of law enforcement. And at this moment, they were useless to her. At this moment, it was just her and this man, alone in her car with his gun pointed at her head.

Stay calm. Make a plan.

She maneuvered the Jeep up to the teller machine, nearly scraping the yellow concrete pillar on the right side of her car. Too late, she realized she'd just ruined a potential escape route.

She closed her eyes and swallowed. She thought of her mom. Whatever happened, she had to live through this. Her mother couldn't take another blow.

It's January seventh.

Mia's eyes popped open at the realization. She turned to face him with a renewed sense of determination—or maybe it was adrenaline—surging through her veins. "How much do you want?" She rolled the window down with one hand while scrounging through her purse for her wallet.

"Five thousand."

"Five *thousand*?" She turned to gape at him. She had that much, yeah. In an IRA account somewhere. Her checking account was more in the neighborhood of five hundred. But she wanted more than anything *not* to tick this guy off.

She gulped. "I think my limit is two hundred." She tried to keep her voice steady, but it was wobbling all over the place. She turned to look at him, carefully positioning her shoulders so the camera on the ATM could get a view into her car. It probably couldn't capture him from this angle, but maybe it would capture the gun. "I can do several transactions," she said.

The muzzle tapped sharply against her cheekbone. She would have a bruise tomorrow. If she lived that long.

She turned to the machine and, with shaking fingers, punched in her code and keyed in the amount. Two hundred was the most she could get. Could she get it twice?

Had her cable bill cleared? Mia handed him the first batch of twenties and chewed her lip frantically as she waited for the second transaction to go through.

Transaction declined.

Her blood turned to ice. Seconds ticked by as she waited for the man's response. Despite the sweat trickling down her spine, her breath formed a frosty cloud as she stared at the words flashing on the screen.

That's it, she thought. *I'm dead.*

She reached a trembling hand out and pulled the receipt from the slot.

She could make a break for it right here. Except her doors were pinned shut by the concrete pillars on either side of her.

She could speed to the nearest well-populated area— which was a Walmart just three blocks away. Would she get there before he shot her or wrestled the wheel away?

"Back on the highway." The command was laced with annoyance. But not quite as much disappointment as she'd expected.

She put the Jeep in gear and returned to the highway.

"How about Sun Bank?" Her voice sounded like a croak. That bank was past Walmart. Maybe she could swerve into the lot and make a run for it.

"Hang a left on the highway."

Mia's hands gripped the steering wheel. Her gaze met his in the rearview mirror. Dread pooled in her stomach. She couldn't see his eyes, but she could read his intent— it was in his tone of voice, his body language, the perfectly steady way he held that gun.

"Hang a left on the highway" meant out of town. He was going to kill her.